MADE FOR EACH OTHER

Rachel's body tightened around him, drawing him in. He released her lips long enough to kiss away her tears and whisper soft words of reassurance and encouragement.

"Jake?"

"Hold on, darlin', and let me give you the sun."

BOOK YOUR PLACE ON OUR WEBSITE AND MAKE THE READING CONNECTION!

We've created a customized website just for our very special readers, where you can get the inside scoop on everything that's going on with Zebra, Pinnacle and Kensington books.

When you come online, you'll have the exciting opportunity to:

- View covers of upcoming books
- Read sample chapters
- Learn about our future publishing schedule (listed by publication month *and author*)
- Find out when your favorite authors will be visiting a city near you
- Search for and order backlist books from our online catalog
- Check out author bios and background information
- Send e-mail to your favorite authors
- Meet the Kensington staff online
- Join us in weekly chats with authors, readers and other guests
- Get writing guidelines
- AND MUCH MORE!

**Visit our website at
http://www.kensingtonbooks.com**

TOUCH
OF TEXAS

TRACY
GARRETT

ZEBRA BOOKS
KENSINGTON PUBLISHING CORP.
www.kensingtonbooks.com

Published by Kensington Publishing Corporation

ZEBRA BOOKS are published by

Kensington Publishing Corp.
850 Third Avenue
New York, NY 10022

All Kensington titles, imprints, and distributed lines are available at special quantity discounts for bulk purchases for sales
promotion, premiums, fund-raising, educational, or institu-
tional use.

Special book excerpts or customized printings can also be
created to fit specific needs. For details, write or phone the
office of the Kensington Special Sales Manager: Attn. Special
Sales Department. Kensington Publishing Corp., 850 Third
Avenue, New York, NY 10022. Phone: 1-800-221-2647.

ISBN-13: 978-1-4201-0100-3
ISBN-10: 1-4201-0100-5

First Printing: October 2007
10 9 8 7 6 5 4 3 2 1

Printed in the United States of America

This story is dedicated to my husband,
my very own hero,
who makes every breath I take a joy.
You supported me every step of this journey.
I can't wait to see what tomorrow brings.

Acknowledgments

My sincerest gratitude to all those who helped make my dream come true: to my editor, Hilary Sares, who loves cowboys as much as I do; to my agent, Sha-Shana Crichton, who fell in love with Jake, too; to Jo Carlisle, my critique partner, who prodded, prompted, and supported me while this story was born; to Lorraine Heath, whose wonderful quote graces this cover; to Jan, Jane, and Karen, who helped me learn to let my voice sing; and to the Foxes for their enthusiastic and unwavering support through good times and bad.

Chapter One

West Texas, Early March, 1890

Whoever said hell was hot had lied. It was cold, bitter cold. Not that he'd live to tell anyone of the discovery. The snow came down sideways, so hard Jake McCain couldn't see past the end of his horse's nose. He had no way to tell where he was or where he was going. The icy pellets were like razor sharp knives, flaying his face until he figured he must be bleeding. Lucky for him the cold kept him from feeling much of anything. Death dogged his heels and he couldn't find the energy to care.

He'd climbed from the saddle an hour ago—or was it only a few minutes—and started walking. He hated using his horse as a windbreak, but the animal's hide could take the stinging ice longer than his own skin, no matter how many layers of clothes he wore. But Griffin was beginning to tire. If Jake didn't find shelter soon, they'd find whatever was left of him and his horse at the next thaw.

Jake braced himself against the saddle before lifting his head enough to look around. The vicious wind stole his breath. He could barely force his eyes open against the onslaught. He usually had a good sense of direction and distance, but the blizzard and the vicious beating he'd taken at the hands of the men he was supposed to be arresting made it impossible to be sure of anything. He could be close to the mining town he'd been heading for, or miles from anywhere.

Jake narrowed his eyes against the blowing snow and ice. Something flickered, only for an instant, in the distance. Was it his imagination? He started for the spot. Real or not, he'd rather be going somewhere than standing around waiting to freeze to death.

He struggled forward, toward the light, or where he thought it should be. He'd lost sight of it. Jake ducked his head behind Griffin's neck, squeezed his eyes shut a couple of times and looked again, but it was gone. Had he somehow gotten turned around? Just when he decided he'd been walking in circles, the wind backed off, the snow lessened, and he saw the light again.

He concentrated on each step, putting one foot in front of the other. Griffin stumbled, catching him by surprise and taking them both to the ground. It took all Jake's will to drag himself to his feet and urge the big horse back up. He buried his battered face against the animal's furry neck, and trudged on, making for that little flicker of salvation.

The next time he looked up he couldn't see the light. Must've been his imagination after all. He took a step, sinking in a drift. Jake thought of his mother, alone in Abilene. He hoped whoever gave her the news of his death was gentle with it. He dragged his other foot forward. His frozen boot caught on something and he fell face down in the snow. Wooden planks broke his fall instead of rock hard ground. He tried to lift his head, but it took too much effort. Griffin took advantage of the stop to turn his rump to the wind, leaving Jake with no protection from the vicious storm.

Battling against the brutal cold, he dragged himself forward. His head bumped something solid. He pulled himself up until he leaned against a thick wood door, but he didn't have the strength left to knock. Cursing his weakness, Jake tried to force a hand up. No use. Both lay limp at his sides.

If he'd had the breath, he would have laughed at the cruel

joke life had played on him, one of many tossed his way. He'd made it—somewhere—and he was going to die anyway. His mind rebelled at the thought of the bastards finally beating him, but even failing his last assignment couldn't give him the strength to lift a fist. He closed his eyes and let his head fall back. At least he would be found and buried properly.

When the darkness came, he fought against giving in, but it was stronger, dragging him down into the unending black.

Rachel Hudson stopped pacing so abruptly the hem of her nightdress fanned the flame in the hearth. What was that noise? It sounded like something hitting the porch.

"Just a tree limb, Rachel," she whispered to the empty room. A branch torn out and flung by the wind.

Her little brother was asleep. He'd gone to bed hours ago and not even the first blizzard these parts had ever seen was going to keep the eight-year-old awake. She closed her eyes and tried to block out the shrieking wind.

There it was again. Crossing to the uncovered window, she shielded her eyes against the flickering light from the candle on the sill and stared into the yard. She couldn't see anything through the swirling snow. Had she left one of the animals outside? She did a quick count. All were safely inside the enclosure across the room.

Curiosity had always been one of her failings, as her brother so often reminded her, and it got the better of her now. Intending to take only a quick peek, she lifted the heavy bar from the door and set it in the corner. Wrapping the blanket tight around her shoulders, she leaned all her weight into the door before lifting the latch. Even braced for it, the wind shoved her back several inches before she caught her balance to push it closed again.

It wouldn't budge. Glancing down, she jumped back, screaming in fright. A body blocked the door.

"Mister!" She shouted against the wind.

No response came from the unconscious man. Rachel

reached for him with one hand, but the wind ripped the door away. Struggling to keep her balance, she hung on to the heavy wood and prodded his arm with her toe. Still nothing. She abandoned the door and let it bang against the inside wall. The man obviously needed help, and if she left him where he was, they'd all freeze to death before morning.

"Nathan!" Hollering for her brother, she tried to drag the man inside but he was too heavy for her to budge. "Nathan, wake up. Help me!" She tried again, but slipped in the snow and fell. Gathering herself again, she pulled as hard as she could. It was no use. She couldn't move him.

Rachel scrambled backward with a cry as a huge black shape stepped over the prone man and into the room. "A horse," she laughed at her own rising hysteria. "Only a horse." She rolled to one side to keep from being trampled. As the animal passed, the man lying in her doorway moved. She stared, thinking she must have imagined it. Then she saw the reins wrapped tightly around the man's hand.

Sliding in the snow that blew into the room, she got to her feet and grabbed the animal's reins. Talking over the howling wind, she urged the beast forward until it dragged the stranger across the threshold.

Dropping to her knees and grunting with effort, she rolled the man onto his side and shoved at his legs until his boots were inside. She was shivering with cold by the time Nathan joined her, his shirt hanging out and his blond hair mussed.

"Need . . . door . . . closed," she managed through chattering teeth. Together they struggled to close the door and drop the bar back in place. Instantly, the sound of the wind diminished, making her feel warmer, safer.

"Put on your boots and . . ." She blew warm air on her freezing fingers, willing the shivering to stop. "Then add wood to the fire." She stepped around the huge bulk of the horse. "And please get this horse out of my way."

Grumbling about her lack of a thank you for his help, the young boy did as she asked, for which Rachel was grateful.

From the looks of the man on the floor, they had no time to argue about manners.

Nathan stuffed his feet into the boots that stood near the stove and added a couple of logs to the fire, poking at the wood until it caught and flared. "That should help soon."

Rachel struggled with the man's bulk, trying to move him closer to the growing warmth.

"Sis, that won't work. He's too heavy. Move him like before." Nathan grabbed the bridle and led the horse toward the fire, not stopping until the stranger lay full length in front of the flames. Then he bent over to take the reins from the man's hand.

They didn't budge. "Come on, mister. Let go." The boy tugged and yanked, but the man had a death grip on the leather.

"Maybe you could cut them free?" Rachel shook snow from her nightdress and joined him.

"Don't want to if I don't have to." He studied the horse for a few seconds, then reached for the buckle on the bridle. "I'll just take the tack off. I can control him without it. This big ol' horse won't give me any trouble, will you, boy."

While he struggled with ice-crusted leather, Rachel knelt on the floor and concentrated on the man. Careful not to jar him too much, she set to work stripping off layers of wet clothing.

Ice crusted around the buttons of his heavy coat and the fabric was stretched tight across his chest. She hoped that meant he had on lots of clothes beneath. Otherwise she was trying to save a dead man. As it was, she wasn't sure how he'd managed to survive in the storm.

As if her thought had summoned it, the wind picked up, slamming icy pellets against the windows and walls. The chickens across the room shifted in their cages, squawking their displeasure at being disturbed. The goats picked up the tune, until a barnyard symphony threatened to deafen them.

"Quiet down over there," Nathan scolded. "Howling about the wind won't make it stop."

Rachel tossed her long blond hair over her shoulder and bent to her task, repeating Nathan's words until her heart slowed a bit. God, she hated the wind. It always seemed to bring grief and death.

She had the buttons undone and the coat off one arm when the bridle hit the floor beside her. Nathan grabbed the huge horse's mane and coaxed the animal across the room to the makeshift corral. She heard him grunt and swear as he shoved aside the sea chest to make room for the new arrival.

"There's no call to curse, young man," she scolded automatically, then undermined the reprimand by muttering a few unladylike words of her own. She ignored Nathan's snicker. "If the horse can wait, I need your help."

"He'll be all right. I can check him over later, but he doesn't seem anything but cold." Nathan moved a bucket of water close enough for the big animal to reach, then crossed the room and dropped to his knees next to her. "What should I do?"

"Help me with his clothes."

Rolling him side to side, they stripped off layer after layer. The stranger's grunt of pain when she bumped his ribs slowed her a little, but also reassured her. If he could feel pain, he wasn't dead.

"Sorry, mister, but I've got to get you out of these wet clothes or you'll freeze to death."

When the stranger lay with only his red flannel Union suit covering his modesty, Rachel sat back to rest and take her first good look at the stranger. She sucked in a breath when she caught sight of the cuts and bruises on his face. "Oh, Nathan, look. He's taken a nasty fall—or a beating."

She smoothed his black hair out of the way and examined his face, stroking her fingers along one side of his nose, then the other. She felt a slight curve, evidence the bone had been abused in the past, but it didn't seem to be broken now. She wished she could be more certain. She only had experience with the bruises and scrapes Mama's lady friends in El Paso had after a customer got too rough.

"Is he gonna be all right?"

"I don't know. Let's pray his injuries are no worse than what we can see."

Together they rolled him onto his side again to strip the red flannel down his arms and past the bunched leather of the bridle still held in the man's fist.

As she worked, Rachel's hand accidentally brushed the smooth skin of his back and a strange, quivering warmth whipped through her insides to settle in her belly. She snatched her hand away. What was wrong with her?

With Nathan's help, she slid a blanket under the man and laid him down again. Rachel bent to examine the nasty bruise blooming blue and purple all along his left side. "It looks like he's been kicked."

Nathan squinted at the injury. "More than once, I'd say."

She prodded the man's ribs, ignoring his moans of pain. "Anything broken?"

She shook her head. "I don't think so. But that won't make it hurt less."

Nathan leaned a little closer. "Who woulda done that to him, Sis? Nobody from around here, that's for sure."

She wanted to reassure her brother, but she knew it wasn't necessarily true. A man could change without warning. She'd seen the madness . . .

Rachel slammed the door on the memories and concentrated on the present. It had been a decent year for the folks living near Lucinda. None of them did this, she was certain.

That meant more strangers. Her eyes snapped to the door. Were they still out in the storm, looking for shelter? The bar was in place across the door, but it didn't reassure her as much as she would have liked.

Shaking her head, she shoved the worry into a corner of her mind. She had enough to think about right now just getting this one stranger warm.

She took the blanket from around her shoulders and laid it over his broad chest. Nathan bent to tug off the stranger's boots as she reached for the Union suit bunched at his waist.

"Uh, Sis, should you be doin' that? I mean, you bein' a girl and all."

"This isn't the time to worry about modesty. If we don't get him warm, he won't live to care about it."

"Yes, ma'am." But she caught the stain of red that crawled up her brother's neck.

"Once you get his boots off, you can cover him up for me as I get the last of this off."

He nodded, relief obvious on his young face.

She sighed. Nathan was too young to be her protector, but he'd taken on the role late last fall. He'd gone for a solitary walk after dinner and returned to announce that, as the man of the family, he was responsible for protecting her. At the time she'd thought it sweet. Now, more often than not, it was a nuisance. But, she had to admit, she'd been grateful for his diligence more than once since then.

She glanced up in time to see him tumble backward in a tangle of gangly arms and legs when the boot he was pulling on finally came free. The flash of temper in his golden-brown eyes had her biting back the laughter that threatened to bubble out.

Grumbling about wet leather and big feet, Nathan attacked the second boot. Soon, both boots stood beside the fire, close enough to dry but far enough away not to scorch.

She smiled her approval. Nathan might be stubborn, but he usually remembered a lesson once he'd learned it. Wearing a pair of shoes for a year with scorch marks on both toes helped.

As soon as Nathan had the man's boots off, Rachel reached for the flannel, blushing to the roots of her blond hair. Nathan knocked her hands aside.

"I'll do that. You go get some more blankets or somethin'."

Instead of arguing, she pushed to her feet and dropped another log onto the fire. She eyed the wood stacked in the corner away from the hearth and prayed it would last until the storm broke.

Stumbling with weariness, Rachel made her way around the pile of soggy clothes to the sea chest that served as one wall of their animal enclosure. Puffing with effort, she lifted the heavy lid and pulled out every piece of wool she could find, blankets, coats, even an old dress worn thin from long use.

"Leave that be," she scolded the goat as it nudged in to nip at the clothing. "You've already had your supper."

By the time she returned, Nathan had the man's drawers off and another layer of warm wool spread over him. His feet peeked out because the blanket was too short to cover his long legs. Turning back to the chest, she dug out two pairs of heavy socks and tossed them to Nathan. Then she grabbed some old rags to get the melted snow off the floor.

As she mopped up around the stranger's dark head, she discovered blood mixed with the water. She looked away and took several shallow breaths, trying to control her suddenly rebellious stomach. The sight of blood always did this to her.

Swallowing hard, she returned to her task. Rachel moved his head carefully and found the source of the bleeding. A gash, low on the back of his head, wept with every one of his heartbeats.

"Damn," she whispered, earning a look of surprise from her brother. "He's bleeding." The edges of her vision grayed. She scooted away, fighting off a wave of nausea.

"I'll do it."

She put water on the two-burner stove to heat and dug out what they might need to treat the man's injuries, while Nathan worked to staunch the flow. He didn't stop until he was satisfied the bleeding wouldn't start up again.

"It's okay now, Sis. You can come back and help."

Rachel poured hot water into a deep pan and carried it to Nathan. Her stomach rolled at the sight of the blood-stained cloths, but she swallowed the nausea. Lowering herself to the stranger's side, she turned her back on the cloths and set to work cleaning out the wound.

Even working together, it took them more than two hours to get the man treated and settled. Nathan stood and gathered all the bloody rags. Taking the pan of hot water, too, he crossed to the sink and began washing them all out.

She watched him work with mixed feelings of gratitude and sadness. He was too young to take on such responsibilities, but she appreciated his understanding. Illness never bothered her, but she couldn't tolerate the sight of blood.

Shaking her head, she forced back the memories of the night that had changed their lives forever. Now wasn't the time to brood. She had more important things to worry about.

Rachel checked the stranger over for other injuries. There were small cuts on his knuckles and bruises were beginning to show on his hands and arms. He'd put up quite a fight.

She brushed strands of hair away from his face. Unlike most men she knew, he was clean shaven. Only the stubble of a day's growth of beard showed. His right cheek was cut and scraped, and one eye was swollen, but he was still a handsome man. The deep purple bruise across his ribs marred the golden-toned skin of his chest. A storm of butterflies broke out in her belly, just like when she'd accidentally touched him.

She tried hard to ignore the fluttering and returned to her examination. He had such a strong face. She couldn't resist tracing the tiny lines around his eyes and mouth. Whoever he was, he'd seen his share of broken dreams, too.

Her hands trembled as she folded back the blanket from one long leg, then the other. Rachel tried to convince herself it was exhaustion, and not the fact that the stranger was naked that made her shake. She didn't find any injuries, but his skin was much too cold for her peace of mind. Leaving him lying on the drafty floor was too dangerous.

"Nathan, help me drag my bed in here, close to the fire."

"What for?" Nathan shook out the last of the rags and draped it over the edge of the sink to dry.

"We need to get him off the floor."

"Sis, we couldn't even drag him to the fire without help. There's no way you and I are gonna get him up onto a bed."

"You're right." She chewed on her lower lip as she tried to think of a way to heft the stranger onto the bed. "Maybe we could just use the mattress."

"That'd work," her brother agreed.

They'd discussed moving her bed closer to the warmth of the fire just a few hours ago, but she'd never imagined it would be needed for a stranger. Grunting beneath the weight, they hauled the straw-stuffed mattress through the narrow doorway and close to the fire.

Nathan studied the stranger. "If we turn him onto his belly, we can shove the mattress up against him and then roll him back onto it, like you did with the blanket."

"That's a good idea. Just be careful of his ribs."

It took both of them to move him. As they rolled him to his uninjured side, the blankets slid off and Rachel couldn't look away. His legs were long and muscular, the skin golden brown except for the dark hair covering them. She skimmed quickly past his more private areas to study his back. Here, too, the muscles were well defined. The sight of more bruises brought her mind abruptly back to her task. The man was injured and freezing and all she could do was stare.

After spreading a dry blanket across the mattress, she and Nathan shoved at the unconscious man, struggling to get him up onto the straw-filled pad. "I had no idea he would be so heavy."

"Well, he ain't exactly small," Nathan grunted.

"I'm grateful he's not awake. He's got so many cuts and bruises, this would really hurt him."

"Yeah, but at least awake he'd be able to help some."

With a final heave, the man's limp body dropped onto the mattress, pulling Rachel with him. As she straightened, the blanket over his legs came with her. Rachel's breath caught at the sight of the long, lean, very naked male. Her brother yanked the blanket back into place and aimed a disapproving scowl in her direction. The heat of embarrassment swept through her.

Busying herself with covering the man head to toe, she tried to resist glancing back toward what she'd glimpsed. She wasn't unfamiliar with male anatomy, but changing her baby brother's diaper wasn't the same as seeing a full-grown man's . . .

Rachel stood abruptly, resisting the urge to fan the heat in her face. "I'm going to change into dry clothes. Put all the blankets over him and spread my old dress over his legs, too." Her cheeks warmed again. Catching up her wet nightdress, she hurried into her tiny bedroom.

When she returned, she found Nathan brushing the stranger's horse. The animal's head hung low and it balanced on three legs, nearly asleep. She had to smile. Her brother certainly had a way with God's creatures. He could calm the most skittish animal in no time. Before long, the giant horse would be following the boy around like a puppy.

"How is he?" She kept her voice soft so she didn't startle the big animal.

"A few cuts, probably from the ice and stuff in the wind. I put some liniment on them. He'll be fine by morning."

She watched for a moment, admiring Nathan's ability to work with the huge animal. She'd never been able to get close to something that big. Knowing there was nothing she could do to help, she turned her attention to the stranger lying on her floor. He stretched the length of the mattress, with his feet hanging off the edge. They must still be very cold. Rachel tucked the blankets more closely around him, but it wasn't enough.

"What's wrong?" Nathan gave one last shove to the sea chest to enclose their growing menagerie, then shuffled over to stand beside her.

"He's still too cold. We have to get him warm somehow."

"What if we put some hot coals in the wash pan like you did last winter when I was sick? We could set that by his feet."

Rachel nodded in agreement. While Nathan got the large metal pan, she stirred up the fire. Taking care not to drop any, she shoveled several glowing chunks of wood into the wash pan. While Nathan positioned it near the man's feet, she added another log to the fire. Satisfied it would burn for most of what was left of the night, she checked that the pan of coals wasn't too close to the man's feet or to the blankets. The embers wouldn't stay warm for long. She'd have to stay up and add more through the night.

Nathan sat on his heels near the stranger, studying him intently. "Maybe we could rub his hands and arms, try to get his blood flowing. Miss Abby did that when I walked to town last winter and it started to rain and I got all wet and cold. It warmed me right up."

"It's worth trying." Rachel knelt by his side and reached under the blanket for the man's arm. Starting gently, then with more vigor, she rubbed his skin from shoulder to fingertips. As he warmed, the man's left hand relaxed enough for her to remove the crushed leather reins and toss them aside.

She rubbed at the marks left behind on his palm. His fingers were long and tapered, but not pretty like Hiram's. The young banker that was courting her never did any work more strenuous than lifting his ledgers. If the calluses were an indication, the stranger worked with his hands.

While Nathan concentrated on his legs, she moved on to the man's chest and shoulders, careful to avoid his battered ribs.

"That's all we can do for now," Rachel murmured, breaking the silence of the room. "Now we just have to pray." She hugged her brother. "Thank you for helping me."

Nathan returned her hug, resting his head on her shoulder. Rachel ruffled his blond hair and smoothed it back in place. He was getting so tall.

"Who do you think he is, Sis?"

Rachel looked back at the stranger. "We'll have to wait until he wakes up to find out."

"We can look through his things. There's bound to be something there that'll give us a clue."

Rachel was hesitant. "We can't go rummaging through his possessions."

"Why not? He might be an outlaw. Don't you wanna know if he is? It ain't like we're gonna steal something."

"Isn't like," she corrected, sighing when he stiffened. "I'm sorry. You're right. We aren't going to take anything." She paused. Nathan's suggestion made sense, but searching through the man's belongings felt wrong to her somehow.

Still, how else would they find out anything? Swallowing the protest born of years of hard-learned lessons, she nodded. "You get his saddlebags. I'll check in his coat."

Nathan dragged the heavy saddlebags closer to the fire while Rachel went through the man's clothes, laying them out to dry while she emptied the pockets. There wasn't much, but she spread everything on their small plank table and brought a lantern closer.

They already knew he wore two revolvers, but no intelligent person went unarmed out here. She found a folded piece of paper inside an envelope that was too big for it, a small amount of money, and a very fine silver pocket watch. There was more money in his saddlebags, along with a dented tin cooking pot and cup, some dried meat, extra ammunition, a slightly damp leather-bound book of poetry, and a letter addressed to Jake McCain.

"Is that his name?" Nathan leaned closer to read it.

"I don't know. I wouldn't think so, since the letter hasn't been opened. Maybe he's just delivering it."

She unfolded the official looking piece of paper that had been in his coat pocket and laid aside the envelope. "He's a Texas Ranger." She turned the paper so Nathan could see it better. "It's his commission. Look, it's signed by Governor Hubbard."

"A real live Ranger!"

Nathan's eyes lit up as he reverently touched the state seal. He was obsessed with the Texas Rangers and planned to join up as soon as he was old enough. Rachel knew the stranger would be peppered with questions the moment his eyes opened.

"His name *is* Jake McCain. At least that's what it says on the commission." She glanced over her shoulder at the man in question. "I wonder why he hasn't opened his letter."

Returning the heavy paper to its envelope, Rachel gathered all the man's possessions. She put the ammunition back in his saddlebags and left the book on the table to dry. Reaching to the mantel over the fireplace, she pulled down a wooden box.

"What are you doing with that?" Nathan stopped reenacting his imaginary battle with horse thieves long enough to ask.

"I'm going to put his things in here. That way nothing will get lost."

Rachel carefully poured out her own keepsakes onto the rough-hewn mantelpiece. Then she placed Jake's items in the box, closed the lid, and returned it to its place.

"You need to get back to bed." She talked over Nathan's protest. "It's still a few hours until morning. You might as well get some sleep. Tomorrow will be a busy day."

"Why? We ain't—aren't going anywhere in this snow."

"Mr. McCain will need a lot of help. And you have another animal to care for. When your chores are done, we'll work on your spelling and you can read to me while I make bread."

"Schoolwork," he huffed in disgust.

"I thought you wanted to beat Matthew in the spelling contest this year."

"Yeah, but do we have to do it tomorrow?" He scrunched his face into a look that was half plea and all little boy.

She turned away to hide her smile. "We'll see."

"Sis, where are you going to sleep? He's in your bed."

Rachel looked at the man stretched full length on her mattress. "I need to tend the fire, and he shouldn't be left alone. The rocker will be fine for me."

Nathan headed for the stairs, stopping long enough to shoot half a dozen bad men along the way. He was still accepting imaginary congratulations when he disappeared into the attic room he'd claimed as his own the day they'd moved in. When winter had settled in, they'd moved his bed close to the chimney so he would be warm. After years of living out of a wagon that was too small, he enjoyed having his own room.

She listened to his footsteps on the plank floor, and heard the ropes under his mattress squeak when he flopped into it. She had to smile. He'd be asleep soon and his dreams would be filled with adventures and heroes.

Summoning what remained of her energy, Rachel dragged

the rocker closer to the fire. Circling the room, she checked on the animals and made sure all the windows were still secured. She blew out the candles as she went, only leaving their special one burning. Shivering, she pulled her heavy winter cloak tighter over her nightdress. Since all of her blankets were piled on the stranger, it was the only warm thing she had left.

Now that the work was done, the howl of the wind seemed to increase to fill the silence. She laced her fingers together to keep from covering her ears to block it out. It sounded like a woman's screams as it rushed around the little house and battered the windows. She recited the books of the Bible, forward and backward, to the sound of her footsteps. She tried humming her favorite hymns, anything to drown out the shrieking blizzard.

Settling into the oversized rocking chair, she watched the man lying unconscious on her floor. Only his head was visible. He had a long, straight nose and a high forehead. His face seemed so smooth. Every miner in town sported a long, oiled mustache. Even Hiram had a small one growing, but it wasn't very full yet.

The stranger's coal black hair glinted almost blue in the firelight. The golden tone of his skin said he spent a lot of time outdoors. She wondered what kind of man he was. Not that it really mattered. In this town, they'd distrust him just because he was a stranger. Even the fact he was a Texas Ranger wouldn't change anything.

She shifted in the chair, trying to get comfortable. The hard wood didn't bother her. It was thinking of the narrow-minded folks that were her neighbors that had her fidgeting. Though everyone in the town came from somewhere else, they guarded their little community vigilantly. If she hadn't been able to take on the job of teacher, she doubted she and Nathan would have been welcome, either. But this place was home now, and she at least could make the stranger welcome.

Rachel yawned. Snuggling deeper in her cloak, she cast one last glance at the fire and dozed off.

She didn't know how long she'd slept before the man's restless movements woke her. The fire hadn't burned down much, so it couldn't have been more than an hour. Kneeling beside him, she took his arm to tuck it back under the blanket.

His reaction was instant. He twisted his arm and grabbed her wrist, tugging her across his body. Clutching at his shoulder with her free hand, Rachel tried to regain her balance.

"It's all right, Mr. McCain. I won't hurt you." At the mention of his name, the pressure on her wrist eased a little, but he didn't release her or open his eyes. "You've been injured. Please, let me help you." Over and over she repeated the words, trying to calm him. Because she was lying across his chest, she knew the instant he decided to trust her. The tension drained away and he released her.

With the fight in him gone, his shivering increased until his entire body quaked. She tucked the blankets close and stirred up the pan of coals, but it didn't help.

Rachel gnawed on her lower lip. She needed to get him warm. She could spread her cloak over him, but if he didn't have any heat of his own to keep in, it wasn't going to make much of a difference. But what else could she do? When the solution occurred to her, her face burned.

Ignoring her conscience as it lectured her about the impropriety, she spread her heavy cloak over him, toed off her soft leather shoes and slipped beneath the blankets with him. Talking to him in a low voice, she reached over his chest to get a little closer and brushed his bare skin with her fingers. Warmth flooded her as she remembered what else was naked. She shivered then, but it had nothing to do with the cold.

"Stop this, Rachel Catherine," she whispered into the silence of the cabin. "You have to help him." Moving slowly, she stretched one leg over his as far as she could, but it wasn't enough. Gathering her courage, she wiggled and maneuvered until she was stretched out full length on top of him.

When she was finally settled, she glanced up and gasped. She stared into the most amazing green eyes she'd ever seen. A slow smile tilted a corner of his mouth as his hands moved to her shoulders and smoothed the length of her back, coming to rest on her bottom. As he held her in place with one hand, the other untied her bound hair and spread it out until it fell like a curtain around them.

Strange warmth stole through her. "Stop that." She tried for a tone of authority, but her voice sounded breathy and confused, even to her ears. She tried to capture his roving hands and nearly slipped off him.

The man shifted beneath her. Her blood heated as he pressed a ridge of hard male flesh into her feminine center. Oh, dear, was this why her mama had . . . Rachel shook her head to clear it. She was not like her mother. She just couldn't be.

"Let go of me." She struggled to get loose and roll off him, but his hold tightened to keep her in place. For one insane moment, Rachel never wanted to move from this spot. Shaken, she shoved at his arms, but he didn't release her. "You've been injured. I'm only trying to get you warm."

He frowned, confused. "Where—"

"You're in Lucinda, Texas, Ranger McCain. You were caught out in the blizzard and landed on our doorstep."

His eyes narrowed when she used his name, but a violent bout of shivering overtook him before he could speak. His quaking nearly knocked her off his chest, and she clutched his arms, locked her toes around his calves, and held on. Unfortunately, that only increased their intimate contact. This time her gasp was one of discovery. Stunned, she looked up, but he was battling the shaking that racked him.

Rachel wrapped her arms around his and held him close. "You'll be fine, Mr. McCain. It will stop soon. Your body is only trying to warm itself. Don't fight it. You're safe here."

She kept talking to him until the shivering began to abate. Gradually, he quieted and his eyes drifted closed. She thought he was still awake when his fingers tightened on her waist, but they relaxed just as quickly. When he didn't move again, she risked smoothing a hand over his shoulder and across his chest. He seemed to be a little warmer.

Relief flooded her as his heart settled into a steady, strong rhythm. He was going to live. As the quiet seeped into her, she became aware that she was still wrapped around the stranger, her legs straddling his hips. Heat washed through her again. In her mind she heard the lecturing voices of her adoptive parents. She squeezed her eyes shut, hoping to banish the memory of the Reverend's preaching, but the words wouldn't stop. *Jezebel*, he'd called her. Nothing but a sinner damned for eternity.

Tears stung Rachel's eyes. She wasn't like her mother, yet here she was, lying across a man not her husband. Ashamed of her reaction to a complete stranger, she tried to slide off him, but his hands wrapped around her waist and held her in place. She stilled, not wanting to wake him. She would just rest a minute until he was more deeply asleep.

Weariness swamped her. She fought to stay awake, but the night finally caught up with her. Snuggling closer to his increasing warmth, Rachel drifted off to sleep with her head on his chest and his heartbeat in her ear.

Chapter Two

Where am I? Jake lay still and took stock of his surroundings. He was definitely inside a structure. Though the air was ripe with the scent of animals, he didn't think he was in a barn.

Something lay across his body, holding him in place. He listened for the sounds of people, footsteps, whispered words. Nothing. The silence was broken only by the shifting of a log in the fire. If anyone stood watch, he couldn't hear them.

Taking care not to give away the fact he was awake, he opened his eyes a slit. He could see out of the right one, but the left eye was blurry and swollen nearly shut, thanks to a lucky punch from that murdering pack of thieves that jumped him.

How had he gotten here? The last thing he remembered was dragging himself through a raging blizzard after Harrison and his men had beaten the holy hell out of him. Now the scents of animals, wood smoke, and lavender surrounded him.

Glancing down, he found the source of the lavender. A woman lay stretched out on top of him. Silky blond hair the color of the summer sun ran in a river across her shoulder and onto his bare chest. Her forehead was smooth and she had a small nose that turned up a little at the end. Long lashes a little darker than her hair fanned across the milky skin of her cheeks. In spite of his battered body, he had a sudden strong desire to taste that skin.

He shook his head to clear it and bit back a curse as the movement shot pain through his skull. In a rush, the memories of the previous day returned. And so did the agony. Besides his head and face, they must have landed a few boots to his ribs. His side burned like hellfire.

Taking shallow breaths to ease the pain, he looked around. The rising sun glowed around the edges of the window shutters. He couldn't see a guard, but he hadn't really expected to find one. If Harrison was around, a half-dozen guns would have finished the job they'd started last night.

He turned his head a little to one side and located the source of the smoke. A poorly built red-stone chimney staggered in drunken lines all the way to the whitewashed ceiling. Whoever had built it must have been working his way through a jug of moonshine at the same time. The floor was probably plank since he didn't smell dust, but all he felt beneath his fingers was wool and the give of a straw mattress.

He rolled his head to the other side, stretching aching muscles. The room wasn't large, but it was well kept. There was a curtained doorway behind him and stairs in the far corner led to an attic or second floor. Plenty of places for someone to hide. He'd check them out, as soon as he could coax his battered body to move.

A sturdy rocker was pulled up close to the warmth of the fire. There weren't any fancy things lying around. A small plank table with benches down both sides separated the kitchen from this side of the room, but the table was bare except for a couple of books and a guttered candle. Nothing to give a hint of where he was or who'd taken him in.

He looked to the other side of the room and blinked his good eye to clear his vision. It didn't help. In the far corner, he thought he saw two goats, four chickens in dilapidated cages, and his horse. There were animals inside the house.

Where was he? If Harrison or his men had found him, he'd be toes down in the snow. He must have stumbled on this place and whoever lived here had taken him in. By the feel of it, he'd been stripped down to what God gave him. His gaze returned to the woman lying across him.

A smile curved one corner of his mouth. Wherever here was, he liked the company. He reached for her, but his left arm wouldn't move. Concerned, he tried again. If he could only draw one weapon, he needed to know. Of course, since he was stark naked on the floor, it didn't matter a whole hell of a lot at the moment.

Giving up, he used only his right hand. Careful not to wake her, Jake searched for more of her softness and found cotton. She had a sweetly feminine shape buried under layers of cloth. Running his hand down the silken hair, he found her rounded bottom exactly where he'd hoped. He pressed her center to his rapidly hardening one, and couldn't resist shifting his hips a little.

The groan of pain slipped out before he could stop it. Everything hurt, even his skin. A tiny sound brought his gaze back to the woman. Brilliant blue, the color of a clear mountain lake reflecting the sky, stared back at him.

A blush stained her cheekbones and she looked away. "You're awake," she whispered.

In more ways than one. "Good morning, ma'am."

She moved, presumably to get off him, but the brush of cloth against his skin burned like fire. He grabbed her arms to hold her still.

"Let me up, Mr. McCain."

"Just a second. Let me—"

He broke off at the sound of a revolver being cocked.

"Let her go!" The blond boy was young, but the gun he held was loaded. Jake recognized his own Colt Army revolver in the boy's shaking hands. How the hell had the kid managed to sneak into the room without Jake hearing him?

"Nathan!"

"Point that somewhere else," Jake growled. "Unless you intend to shoot her."

"I said let her go!"

Jake pinned the boy with a glare. "I'm trying."

"He's not holding me here, Nathan. Put that gun down immediately. You know how I hate the things." Blondie sounded like one used to being obeyed. The boy's aim wavered before he dropped the muzzle toward the floor.

Jake released the woman and she scrambled to her feet, taking the blankets with her. The cold air shocked him, but at least it numbed some of the pain. He snagged a pile of gray wool to cover himself. It turned out to be a dress. Now didn't he look wonderful, lying on a cold floor, beaten black and blue, and wearing a dress?

Gritting his teeth, Jake sat up, keeping his lap covered the best he could. "Some pants would be helpful, ma'am."

"Oh, I . . ." Blondie looked flustered and the blush returned to her cheeks. She hurried around him to the fire. "They seem to be dry. So is your shirt." She turned toward him, then looked away again and held his clothes out at arm's length in his general direction. "Nathan will help you. I need to, um . . ." Brilliant red flushed her cheeks. She bit her lip and hurried from the room, thrusting the garments into her brother's hands as she passed.

"What got into her?" The boy stared after her.

He was as blond as the woman, but that was the only thing similar Jake could see. The boy's eyes were light brown and round, where her blue ones had a slight tilt at the corner. "Give me my gun." The boy held it out butt first, which would have made Jake happy except the thing was still cocked and ready to fire. "Son, don't ever pull the hammer back unless you intend to shoot, and for damn sure don't turn the thing on yourself when it's primed."

The boy looked confused, as if he'd never handled a gun before. When his eyes dropped to the floor, Jake saw hurt, too.

"Yes, sir. I'm sorry I pulled a gun on you."

Jake eased the hammer forward and laid the pistol aside, near his right hand. "You did what was needed to protect someone you love. Can't ask more than that from a man."

The boy, Nathan, she'd called him, looked up again, a little pride in his eyes at begin called a man. "Can you stand?"

The question brought Jake back to the problem at hand. "I can try." Taking a deep breath, he rolled off the mattress to his knees and shoved himself to his feet, gritting his teeth against the pain. Swaying in place, he gripped the wool dress in front of him like the garment would help him stay upright.

"Here." Nathan shoved the rocking chair close and Jake fell into it.

"Damn," he breathed.

"Hurts, I imagine. You were really banged up when you got here and we don't know how long you were out in the storm."

"Almost too long." Jake rested his head against the back of the chair.

"Yeah, we figured that out real quick." He shook out Jake's pants. "Let's get some clothes on you so Sis can come back and make her tonic. It tastes awful, but it'll help a lot."

The boy's wrinkled up face left little doubt about the taste of the concoction. Even though the light of morning barely illuminated the room, the thought of a shot of whiskey appealed to Jake a lot more than some fancy tea. But he'd take what he could get.

With Nathan's help, Jake got both legs into the pants. He managed to stay on his feet long enough to pull them up and fasten a couple of the buttons. The shirt made his skin burn everywhere it touched. Exhausted, he gave up trying to stuff the shirttail into his trousers and dropped back into the rocker.

"Sis," Nathan called. "You can come out now. He's decent."

The young woman had dressed in dark blue wool. The collar came up to her chin and the hem brushed the floor. A starched white apron blanketed the skirt. The dress was too large for her, gathering in heavy folds around her shoulders and waist, hiding what he knew to be a fine figure.

Her long hair was wrapped and pinned in a tight knot at the base of her skull. It seemed like a pretty severe style for a woman her age, but what did he know of women's fashion?

"He needs your tonic." Nathan added wood to the fire.

"I imagine so," she answered, never once looking his way. "Would you light the stove, please?"

"Already did." The boy grinned to have anticipated her request.

"Is the kettle filled?"

He sagged. "I didn't think about checking that."

"That's all right. There's probably enough water left from last night. Why don't you look and see."

Evidently he found enough for her concoction. When the water boiled, Nathan wrapped a cloth around the hot handle and carried the kettle to her. A couple of minutes later, the boy delivered a cup to Jake. The heat burned his hands, but the biting scent of whiskey drifted up with the steam, improving his mood considerably.

"The tonic is a recipe of my mother's," Blondie explained. "Nathan and I usually only have half a cup, but I thought you could use a bit more."

"Thank you. I'm obliged, Mrs.—"

"Hudson. Rachel Hudson. And this is my brother, Nathan."

Jake glanced at her left hand. Her ring finger was bare. "Where's Mr. Hudson?"

"There is no Mr. Hudson, just Nathan and me."

It made sense. He doubted a married woman would have been that embarrassed by his nakedness.

Looking forward to the jolt of whiskey, he took a mouthful of the scalding brew and choked. The liquor didn't quite hide the taste.

"What kind of poison did you put in here?" Coughing, he looked up and forgot the question. Her smile faded quickly, but that ray of sunshine pierced him to the core.

Jake concentrated on the tonic in his hands. How the hell could a woman who looked like she did, with a smile that could light up the heavens, manage to stay unmarried in this godforsaken patch of country?

"It's a blend of herbs and tea. The whiskey is mostly to get you warm."

"It'll do that." He took another, more cautious sip. "How did I get here?"

Rachel frowned. "I don't know. You'd been out in the

storm for some time, if the ice on your clothes and horse were any indication."

"Long enough," Jake confirmed.

"You stumbled onto the porch sometime after midnight. I heard you hit the door and when I opened it, you fell in. You were unconscious and much too heavy for me to get inside. Fortunately you hadn't let go of the reins."

"Pardon me?" He flexed his arms, stretching sore muscles.

"You had a death grip on your horse's reins, and when he came into the room, so did you. I don't know how we would have moved you otherwise."

"Yeah," Nathan chimed in. "You're heavy."

If Griffin had dragged him around awhile, it would explain why he could barely lift his left arm. He moved his stiff left arm again. He had to go after Harrison and his men, and he needed both hands working.

"Are you really a Texas Ranger? Honest?"

Jake looked over at Nathan. In the boy's eyes he saw the same eagerness he'd once felt for his job. But that wide-eyed innocence was long dead. "It isn't all that wonderful, boy."

His tone was rougher than he'd intended. Nathan looked hurt. Jake started to apologize, but Rachel didn't give him a chance.

"There's no need to speak to him like that. He was only asking a question."

"You're right, ma'am." Jake looked back to Nathan. "I didn't mean to snap at you, son. Guess they hit my head harder than I thought. It banged some of my manners clean out." He tried to smile at the boy, but his battered lip split open again. "Ow!"

"That must really hurt a lot." Nathan forgave with the swiftness of youth. Coming closer, he studied Jake's face. "I busted my lip once, falling off the wagon." His voice dropped to a confiding level. "That's how we found out Sis can't stand the sight of blood. She took one look at me and fainted clean away." He grinned, transforming his face into the image of hers.

"It isn't the least bit humorous," Rachel scolded, then took the starch from her words by laughing.

The sound shot lightning down his spine. His body's reaction was swift. Jake shifted in the rocker, trying to conceal the evidence.

Rachel went back to rolling and cutting biscuits for breakfast, while Nathan started on his chores. The boy swept up dirty straw from the makeshift corral, and dipped water from a large barrel into buckets for the animals. Jake considered checking on his horse, but he wasn't sure he could stay upright even if he managed to get to his feet. He had to be satisfied with watching Nathan check him over.

"What's his name?" Nathan asked the question as he tossed fresh straw around the floor.

"Griffin."

Nathan stared at Jake. "That's a funny name for a horse."

"Nathan." Rachel admonished him without looking up.

"Well, I've never heard a horse called anything like that." He brushed the straw from his hands and shirt. "Why'd you call him Griffin?"

"It's my favorite creature from Greek mythology. My father read a couple of stories to me when I was a lot younger than you. I guess some of it stuck with me."

"What's Greek myth-lologee?" Nathan stumbled over the unfamiliar word.

"Mythology." Rachel pronounced it clearly. "They are fables—stories—written many centuries ago by the people who lived in a country called Greece."

"What's a griffin?"

"A creature that's half eagle and half lion," Jake explained. "Since Griffin there can run like the wind and is as fierce and loyal as they come, I figured it fit."

Nathan's browed furrowed as he digested the information, then cleared when he smiled again. "I like Griffin. It's a good name."

He went back to his chores, practicing the new word under his breath. Once he'd put hay in a makeshift trough for the goats and horse, he went to gather eggs. A moment later he whooped with joy and held several eggs aloft.

"Cake!"

Rachel glanced over her shoulder, a smile lighting her face. Jake stared, mesmerized. How could a simple curving of lips turn a pretty girl into a stunning woman?

She seemed unaware of her transformation. "Which ones?"

"Bathsheba and Moses, I think, but it could have been David." Nathan carried them to Rachel like they were the finest crystal. She wiped them off and set them aside. He counted them one last time before returning to the corral to clean out the chickens' cages.

Jake released the breath he held and hauled in another one, cooling his blood a little before he tried to talk. "Moses?"

Rachel glanced over her shoulder at him. "Nathan named the chickens. Moses, who 'delivers us' at least two eggs every day. David is the big white hen that rules the roost, but can't stand to be separated from Bathsheba, the big red one. And the rooster is Solomon, because he'll try to split you in two if you get close enough."

Jake shook his head, then stiffened as laughter caught at his abused ribs.

"Are you all right?" Rachel watched him, her hands covered in flour.

"I will be. Nothing's broken, but they hurt like hell-on-fire. Begging your pardon, ma'am." He swallowed more of the tonic and changed the subject. "Doesn't it matter that Moses and David are females?"

"Not to Nathan."

He nodded. If the boy wanted to name the hens after men, so be it. "Why the excitement over a few eggs?"

"Because I promised him that every time he found five eggs I'd make his favorite cake."

"Does he share?"

Rachel turned to answer him with a smile. "With a Texas Ranger? Of course."

Jake felt his grin freeze and fade. For a minute, just one blessed minute, he'd forgotten. "You still haven't answered my question. Where am I?"

Rachel stared at him, confusion evident on her face. He knew he'd sounded rougher than he should, but he couldn't find the words to apologize.

"I told you last night, but I don't suppose you remember." A blush stained her cheeks. She must be remembering the position he'd discovered her in this morning. He was sure he'd never forget it.

"You're in Lucinda, Texas, Mr. McCain, south and west of Fort Davis, a couple of days' ride into the hills. We're a small gold mining town, named for the founder's wife, Lucinda Miller."

"Old biddy," Nathan piped up.

"Nathan Hudson! Shame on you," Rachel scolded.

"Well, she is," he argued. "You told me never to lie."

Jake's snicker earned him a glare from Rachel, but he couldn't wait to hear how she handled the boy's logic.

"You shouldn't lie, but it isn't always necessary to speak the truth out loud. And it's never polite to call anyone a name."

"Yes, ma'am," he muttered as he ducked behind Griffin and started brushing his ebony flank.

"Leave that for now, and wash up. Breakfast is ready."

The currycomb hit the floor with a clatter as Nathan vaulted over the makeshift corral and raced for the washbowl. Water flew as he scrubbed off the grime of his chores. He dropped the towel on the floor in his haste, but a look from Rachel had him folding it beside the bowl before he slid into his chair.

Jake moved a lot slower, but managed to limp to the washbowl and on to the table. He lowered himself onto a bench, barely stifling a groan of pain.

"Should I make you another cup of tonic?" Rachel watched him with concern.

Jake shook his head. "I'll manage."

He expected Nathan to be wolfing down the food, but the boy waited for his sister to come to the table. When she sat, they joined hands and each held out the free one in Jake's direction. Self-conscious, he took hold of their fingers, keeping the contact to a minimum. Nathan's hand was cool from the recent scrubbing. Rachel's was warm and soft. The fragrance of lavender mixed with fresh biscuits tangled his senses.

When Rachel gave thanks for Jake's safety, he glanced sideways at her, surprised. No one but the woman who'd adopted and raised him had ever given a damn about his safety. They chorused an "amen," with Jake's coming a split second late. Nathan snagged two biscuits in one hand, his glass of milk with the other, and began making breakfast disappear.

"Hang on a minute." Jake stopped the boy's hand mid shovel. "Where are my saddlebags?"

"Over there," Nathan mumbled through a mouthful. "I'll get 'em." With the energy of youth, he bolted from his chair and dashed across the room to drag the heavy leather cases close.

Jake rummaged around for a moment, then pulled out a small glass jar filled with amber liquid and offered it to Rachel.

"My addition to the feast, ma'am."

"Honey." Her eyes lit with delight.

He considered teasing her about being so familiar, but didn't have the strength. "It's a treat my mother slipped into my gear when I wasn't looking."

She inhaled the spicy sweet scent with obvious pleasure. "I haven't had any in years."

"What's that?"

Rachel looked up at her brother's question. "Something you're going to love."

"You've never had honey?" Jake couldn't believe a boy Nathan's age had never tasted honey.

"The people who raised us didn't believe in partaking of anything so sweet," Rachel explained. "It was a temptation to sin, in their mind."

"But you've had it," he prodded.

Her smiled dimmed. "Once or twice, a long time ago." She opened the jar. "Hand me your plate, Nathan."

She drizzled honey onto Nathan's biscuits and gave the plate back. The boy eyed the gooey golden liquid and sniffed at it like a wary hound before biting into it. Jake laughed at the look of wonder on the boy's face as the spicy sweetness hit his tongue. Rachel put a little on her own biscuits and handed the jar to Jake.

Jake stared as she licked a bit of honey from her fingertips, her tongue sweeping up every drop. Her long lashes lowered as she savored the sweetness. He was grateful the table hid his body below the belt. He studied her face, but she gave no indication that she'd done it on purpose or knew how she affected him. Shifting a little in his seat, he replaced the cover on the jar.

"Aren't you having any?" Rachel bit into her biscuit.

"I'll leave it for the two of you. I can hunt up some more once the weather warms." He slid the jar toward her and concentrated on his plate. The fare was simple, but there was enough, and he made short work of the meal. Jake refused the milk she offered and drank water instead. He'd have to dig out the coffee he carried before the next meal. It would taste good on such a cold day.

He pushed his empty plate away and looked around. "What are the animals doing inside?"

Rachel excused Nathan from the table before responding. "We don't have a barn, only a small lean-to and the corral. The man who built this house never got around to adding it. I suppose they ran out of steam." She glanced around the small space. "Wood is difficult to come by in Lucinda, now. What there was has gone into the mines."

"And the animals?" he prompted, bringing her back to his question.

She twisted her fingers together in her lap. "When the weather turned yesterday morning, I was afraid it would be too cold for them outside. So we fashioned a corral from what we had and brought them in."

"That makes sense to me."

She flashed him a bright smile. "Thank you."

Jake carried his plate and cup to the small sideboard where a pan of hot water waited. He offered to dry the dishes as she washed them, but Rachel declined, urging him to rest.

"Your tonic did the job," he assured her. "I'm already feeling better."

"I insist. If you don't rest, you won't heal."

"That sounds like something my mother would say." Grumbling, he limped to the rocker and settled into it, but inactivity went against the grain. He couldn't stand watching Rachel and Nathan work while he sat idle.

When he stood, Rachel turned her head. "Where are you going?"

Jake ignored her. Grabbing his two revolvers, he carried them back to the kitchen table, then returned for his rifle. He dug in the other saddlebag for a moment before he realized something was missing. Anger flashed through him. "Where is it?"

Rachel glanced over her shoulder. "What are you talking about?"

"The money. You didn't need to steal. If you wanted payment for taking care of me, you only had to ask."

"Steal?" Nathan stopped work to stare at him.

Rachel looked indignant, even with soapy water dripping from her fingers. "We haven't stolen anything, Mr. McCain. Everything is in there."

She jerked her head in the direction of the mantelpiece. Scattered over the rough-hewn surface Jake could see a wooden box, a few feminine doodads, and a photograph in a carved wooden frame. The book of poetry he always carried lay nearby.

"In the box," she hissed, blue fire glinting in her eyes.

He studied the box. The workmanship was beautiful. The joints were dovetailed and the surface gleamed with polish. Lifting the lid, he saw his money, his commission, and the letter he'd carried in his pocket for more than a month. Everything was there.

For the first time in years shame soured his stomach. "My apologies, ma'am. Nathan." He glanced over his shoulder, then turned to face them both. "My accusation was uncalled for. You've been nothing but kind. I guess I—" He shook his head. "No, there's no excuse. I'm sorry."

Rachel stared at him for long silent moments, but he didn't look away. She had every right to order him out into the storm still raging beyond the walls. He half expected her to.

Nathan didn't say anything, looking to Rachel for direction.

"You are forgiven, Mr. McCain."

That was it. With no discussion, no accusations, she returned to her work. Nathan nodded once in agreement and went back to sweeping up straw. Jake was shocked. No one but the woman who'd raised him had accepted his bursts of temper without trying to get even.

Dumping his things on the mantel, he carefully replaced Rachel's possessions in the box. He glanced at the photograph, then looked closer. In the woman's eyes he could see Rachel.

"That was my mother." She joined him to stare at the image.

"You favor her."

Glancing quickly at Nathan, she removed the likeness from his hand and put it in the box, closing the lid and cutting off any questions he might have asked.

When she went back to measuring out ingredients for bread, he limped to the table. With every step he got angrier. Not at her or Nathan, but at the hand fate had dealt him. How far ahead of him were the men he'd been tracking, now that he was laid up in a snowbound cabin? Months of work wasted, because he'd gotten careless.

They should have killed him. He deserved to be dead. But instead he was safe and warm, and stuck in a tiny cabin with a boy who thought being a Texas Ranger made him a candidate for sainthood and a woman who made him hard just by breathing.

He lowered himself into a chair and grabbed a revolver and a dry cloth. It was going to be a long day.

Chapter Three

Rachel resisted looking over her shoulder, telling herself for the tenth time in as many minutes that she mustn't stare. She'd never seen a man like Jake McCain, let alone had one sitting at her kitchen table. From the moment she'd awakened last night to find herself staring into his unusual green eyes, she hadn't been able to think of anything but him.

She reached for the flour she'd measured out and knocked the cup aside with her hand, dusting herself and the floor. Disgusted with her clumsiness, Rachel bent over to clean up the mess. When she straightened, she glanced in Jake's direction and found him watching her, his brilliant green eyes sparkling with laughter. Embarrassed, she turned away and tried to slow her racing heart. Even with a swollen eye and some colorful bruises, he was a handsome man.

Not like Hiram, of course. Deliberately she thought of the man she hoped to marry. Hiram Miller, the only son of the town's founders, was tall and handsome, with fair-haired good looks that made even the married women in town stare.

Hiram was the kind of man she knew she had to marry, a respectable man who would provide a home for her and Nathan. Rachel summoned an image of her suitor, but the man in her mind had green eyes and hair the color of a moonless night sky.

She should be ashamed. Rachel poured the bread dough onto her board with a plop and began kneading it with more energy than necessary. Could Jake tell she was thinking of him? Risking a glance at Jake McCain, she found him with his head bent over the revolver in his hands. His fingers seemed to caress the metal as he cleaned the weapon with a small cloth.

She wasn't sure why, since she had little experience with guns. Her mother hadn't owned one, and the missionary couple who'd taken them in relied on God's Word as their only weapon. Even hunting for food was disdained. *Everything will be provided by the Lord,* the Reverend lectured whenever she dared to complain. *All our needs will be met by those with whom we share the Word, even the flour for our bread.* They went to bed hungry many nights, but the preacher was unbending.

Occasionally, a hunter traded a hunk of deer meat or a couple of rabbits for a meal and some company. She savored the tiny portion of meat she was allotted on those evenings, though it was never enough to satisfy her hunger.

With practiced motions, Rachel shaped the dough into four balls, covered them with a clean cloth and set them near the chimney to rise. It was twice the number of loaves she normally baked, but she didn't know how much Jake would eat and she wanted to have plenty. Taking up a damp cloth, she cleaned up and thought through her next task. She would make the cake after she convinced Nathan to work on his spelling. "Nathan, how are you coming with your chores?"

"All finished."

She smiled at his enthusiasm. No matter the hardships they encountered, her brother always managed to brighten the day. "Then wash your hands and come to the table. You need to work on your spelling words."

"Aw, do I have to?"

She bit back a smile. They had the same discussion every time she mentioned studying.

"Yes, you have to. You want to win the spelling bee this year, don't you?"

"Yeah, but . . ."

"You won't win if you don't practice."

"Oh, all right. If I have to."

She turned away to hide her smile and nearly collided with Jake. She had to look up to see his face. She hadn't realized when he was laid out on the floor just how tall he was. He could put his chin on the top of her head without even stretching.

When one black eyebrow slashed upward in question, she stepped closer to explain, keeping her voice low so Nathan wouldn't hear. "I hold a spelling contest each spring. Nathan's best friend won last year and won't let him live it down. He wants to get even."

"You're the teacher?"

"For nearly three years now. I love working with the children."

Jake nodded. "Will I be in the way here?" He indicated the table with a nod of his head. Rachel was mesmerized by the play of light in his hair. When the corner of his mouth kicked up in a grin, she realized she was staring.

"N-no," she stammered. "You're fine where you are."

She turned away and scolded herself silently. What on earth was the matter with her? She helped Nathan arrange his books and slate, grateful for the distraction. Soon the boy's blond head was bent to the task, practicing the words she chose for him.

"Independent," she repeated. Nathan's brow furrowed as he thought over the new syllables.

"I-n-d-e-p-e-n-d . . ." He hesitated exactly where she expected.

". . . a-n-t?" he finished with a question.

"Almost," she prompted. "Remember, independence means you don't need anybody's help. Since *anybody* begins with 'a', you don't need the . . ."

"I-n-d-e-p-e-n-d-e-n-t," the boy corrected with a flourish.

"Yes," Rachel cheered. "Absolutely correct."

Jake looked up. "Good job, son."

Nathan beamed under the praise from his newest hero.

Bending to his task, he wrote the new word three times, then used it in a sentence. He smacked the chalk to the slate with the period and handed it to Jake to approve.

Jake stared at the slate like it was a rattlesnake ready to strike. Rachel was certain she saw panic in his eyes before he went back to reassembling his revolver. "Ask your sister. She's the teacher."

Nathan's face crumbled, unsure of what he'd done wrong. Rachel hurried to reassure him.

"You used it perfectly, Nathan. And your handwriting is improving." She glanced toward Jake, but he was concentrating on his task. "That's enough for today. Do you want to help me with the cake?"

"I guess so."

He sounded so disheartened Rachel wanted to cry. "Then go put these things away. We'll practice reading after dinner."

He dragged his heels but did as she asked. The moment he disappeared up the stairs she rounded on Jake.

"Would it have been too much trouble to just read what he'd written?"

Jake glared at her but didn't say anything.

Rachel wanted to say more, but Nathan's boots reappeared on the stairs. With a huff, she spun away to the sink, banging pots and bowls around as she pulled out ingredients. Grabbing an egg, she smashed the shell into the bowl.

She stared at the mess and felt tears sting her eyes. How many times had Reverend Hudson lectured that her temper would be her undoing? And punishment was severe, as a reminder that a *good* woman never showed her feelings.

Forcing herself to calm down, she fished out all the broken pieces. She cracked another egg with greater care and set the rest aside for tomorrow's breakfast.

Nathan slipped quietly to her side, leaning into her for reassurance. Ignoring the mess on her fingers, she wrapped an arm around him and squeezed. Planting a kiss on the top of his head, Rachel released him and handed him the butter.

While Nathan melted a chunk of it in a pan on the stove,

she whipped the eggs with more force than necessary. Then she turned the bowl and spoon over to her brother. Watching closely, she helped him measure the right amount of sugar and flour into the mix, adding a splash of whiskey and a drizzle of Jake's honey for flavor.

Nathan poured the batter into the cake pans, then Rachel carried one to the stove and let him bring the second one. She slipped the cake pans into the tiny baking compartment on the side of the stove, then used the poker to spread out the hot coals so they would bake more evenly.

"Well done, Nathan," she congratulated. "It's going to taste wonderful."

She stiffened when Jake pushed away from the table and limped across the room to where his saddlebags lay in a corner.

"Nathan." His voice was rough and low, sending shivers coursing through her.

"Yes, sir?" Hope brightened the boy's answer.

"I didn't mean to seem . . ." He groped for the words. "What I mean is . . ." Jake heaved a sigh and stared at the sealed letter she'd discovered in his pocket last night. "Do you think you could help me?"

"With what?" Wariness colored Nathan's reply.

"Would you—read this to me?" He indicated the letter in his hand with a curt nod.

That was why the letter had never been opened. "You can't read." The words popped out before Rachel could stop them. A stain of red crept up from his collar.

Jake ran the edges of the envelope through his long fingers. "I never learned," he admitted quietly.

"But, you carry a book with you. I saw it."

"It belonged to my father. He was some kind of professor from England. He read all the time. He died before he could teach me how to make sense of the letters and words. That book is the only thing I have left of him besides memories."

"Didn't your mother send you to school?"

He flinched as if she's struck him. "The folks who raised

me tried, but I was too busy trying to prove I was a man to bother with learning to read and write."

Jake stared at the letter while the silence stretched. "I've been carrying this around for almost a month." He held it out to Nathan. "Would you read it to me?"

"I'd be glad to help, sir." Nathan's voice was serious.

Tears blurred her vision. He seemed so grown up when he accepted the letter. Then he reached for Jake's hand and led him back to the table, looking for all the world like the eight-year-old boy he was. Together they sat on a bench and Nathan opened the envelope.

"Dearest Jake," the letter began. Nathan wrinkled his nose as he concentrated on the handwriting. "I miss you so much. I hoped you'd have come home by now."

Rachel turned away from Nathan's careful recitation. There was something very intimate about hearing such heartfelt words written to someone else. Besides, what business was it of hers if Jake was married, or had made a promise to marry?

"Son," Nathan continued, "I haven't seen you since the first freeze. Not much has changed here. The garden did very well this year."

The words continued, but Rachel didn't hear them. She was still registering the fact that the letter was from Jake's mother.

She busied herself turning the cakes in the oven so they baked evenly, then started putting together the midday meal. Nathan turned over the first page of the letter and kept reading. Finally, he voiced the woman's plea to come home soon and fell silent.

"Thank you, Nathan." Jake gathered the pages together and slid them back in the envelope. "I haven't seen her in more than six months. It's good to know she's all right."

"I can help you write back to her, if you want me to."

Silence descended in the cabin as Jake slipped the letter into his shirt pocket. "She'd like that."

"Where does she live?" Nathan's face was serious as he looked up at Jake.

"In Abilene. She helps out at the hotel there when they get busy, cooking and ironing."

"Is that where you're from?"

He hesitated. "I grew up there, mostly. I came to live with her and Papa after the woman who bore me died."

The anger in his voice surprised Rachel. She wanted to ask him to explain, but she wouldn't pry. His secrets were his own.

Jake stood by the uncovered window, staring at the wall of snow covering it. Whatever had happened still held the power to make him furious. The room was alive with it.

"My mama died, too." Oblivious to the tension, Nathan opened the door to the baking oven to peek at the cakes.

Rachel blanched, the blood draining from her head so fast she felt dizzy. She set down the knife she'd been using, afraid she'd cut herself.

Her brother was getting more and more curious about his father's identity. She had no idea what she'd say when he insisted she tell him, only that he couldn't know the truth.

Nathan wandered over and dropped to his knees beside Jake. "What are you doing with that rusty old thing?"

"Seeing if it can still be fired. It's a Henry Repeating Rifle. I've seen a lot of these since the war. It's a good weapon to have around."

"We found it in the shed when we moved in here, but we didn't know what to do with it. We've never had a gun before 'cause Sis hates them. She won't ever use one and doesn't really want it in the house. We only brought it inside 'cause it seemed a shame for it to sit out in the weather like that. Besides, we might have to shoot a bear or something. It musta looked real nice once. How do you know if it still works?"

Jake worked his way through the twists and turns until he got to the question. "I'll take it apart and try to clean out the rust and dirt. You can help me if you want to, if your sister doesn't mind."

"Can I help him, Sis, please? I might need to know how to do it myself someday, when I'm grown."

Rachel hesitated. She'd hated guns for as long as she could

remember, though why they terrified her was no longer clear. But it didn't seem reasonable to say no. Nathan would have to use one someday. No one survived long on the frontier without being able to defend themselves.

"I think that would be fine, Nathan."

"Oh, boy! Wait 'til I tell Matthew."

"Telling him will have to wait until the snow melts. In the meantime, please set the table for dinner."

"Aw, that's woman's work, baby stuff."

She felt her temper flair. The unfamiliar emotions Jake's presence brought on were making her raw inside. She battled with herself, trying to respond without snapping at her brother. Jake beat her to it.

"There's no such thing, son. A man needs to be able to make it on his own. That means doing all the stuff that needs to be done, including setting a table now and then." He set the rusty rifle aside. "You get the plates and cups. I'll help with the forks just as soon as I wash up and get the coffee on."

"Coffee?" Rachel gaped at him. "You have coffee?"

Jake lips curved in the first true smile she'd seen on him, and she forgot what they were talking about. His dark eyes sparkled as the grin spread beneath the shadow of his beard. The air of danger he always wore lessened.

"I always carry a pound of it with me. A weakness of mine. Would you like to have some?"

"Some what? Oh." She mentally shook herself. "I haven't had coffee in years. Since I left El . . . uh . . ." She swallowed hard, appalled at what she'd nearly revealed. "I haven't had any since we came to Lucinda. It wasn't something we could afford."

"Then I'm delighted to be able to add something to the feast, ma'am."

The meal smelled delicious. Once grace was said, Rachel poured coffee for Jake and herself. Nathan begged to try it, but one sip was enough.

"Ick. That's awful."

Jake laughed, amazing himself. He couldn't remember ever laughing so much. He'd never been around children and he found it a pleasure to watch an intelligent boy like Nathan discover life.

Rachel reached for the butter at the same moment Jake did. Their fingers brushed and she snatched her hand back. A hint of pink tinged her cheeks. He handed the butter to her, puzzled by the sparks that flew when they touched. No woman had ever drawn him like she did, or brought his body to attention just by being in the same room. Her scent, a combination of lavender and female, teased him with every breath he took.

Jake looked up from his plate to find Rachel watching him, holding out the butter. He took it, deliberately brushing the back of her hand with his fingertips. Her brilliant blue eyes grew smoky before she looked away. She responded to the lightest touch, to the slightest hint of an offer.

Jake bent his head to his food, but his thoughts circled Rachel Hudson. She didn't react like an innocent girl. What if she wasn't? What if the boy was her son? Nathan called her Sis, but what did that mean? Lots of folks went by nicknames out here. Didn't preachers call their women "sister"? Maybe Sis was short for that.

His body quickened at the thought that Rachel might be a widow. A beauty like her in a snowbound cabin . . .

Jake hauled in his galloping imagination. There was Nathan to consider. If the woman wanted everyone to believe they were brother and sister, it was no business of his. He had work to do. There wasn't time for any other pursuits, no matter how enjoyable they promised to be. As soon as the storm broke, he would dig them out and be sure the cabin was restocked with food and firewood. It was little enough to do to repay them for saving his life. Then he was heading after the murderers he'd been chasing before they turned the tables on him.

This was the last job he was doing before he turned in his badge. He'd already told his captain that he was resigning his commission. The man had lectured him about responsibility and innocent people depending on him to make the frontier safer for them, but nothing would change his mind. He couldn't take on any more ghosts.

It was the innocent ones he couldn't forget. He saw their faces every night in his sleep. Their memory kept him going, driving him to finish what he'd started. Maybe then they'd leave him in peace.

Chapter Four

Rachel was surprised the old rifle didn't split in two. Other than the quiet thirty minutes he'd spent tending his horse, Jake had been rubbing at the rusty metal the entire afternoon, his expression turning more grim as time passed. He only stopped now and then to stretch his left arm. It must still be sore from the beating he'd taken, and from being dragged around by his horse. The swelling was almost gone from his eye, but the rainbow of bruising was just beginning to show.

When he glared at the rifle again, she almost told him to leave the old thing be, that they didn't really need it, but the look in his eyes was so fierce she lost her nerve.

Nathan didn't have any reservations, though. As soon as his chores were done, he raced to Jake's side and started asking questions. The ranger answered every one with patience, explaining everything the boy didn't understand.

She watched for a while, but found she was more interested in the ripple and play of muscles under Jake's shirt than the gun. Tearing her gaze away, she went to check on the progress of the storm.

She couldn't hear the wind anymore, giving her hope it was over. The north window was covered in ice and snow. She went to the other three windows in turn, opening shutters and peering out, but saw only white. That left the door.

She lifted the bar that secured it and set it aside. Bracing herself, she lifted the latch. The instant she did, the heavy wood flew open, knocking her back a step. Without any support, the wall of snow covering the doorway collapsed into the room, dancing in front of the wind that chased it. In seconds white flakes were strewn across the cabin.

Rachel squealed at the attack and all hell broke loose. Nathan came running at her scream, slipped on the snow and slid into the chests and boxes forming the corral. Jake's horse spooked, rearing and pawing the air in challenge. One of the goats ripped free from its restraint, jumped through the opening Nathan had made and galloped through the room, knocking over chairs and benches in its flight.

The rooster started crowing the instant light flooded the cabin, and the hens set up a racket fit to wake the dead. She had no idea four chickens could make that much noise.

"Nathan, get the goat." Jake's clipped order left no room for argument. While the boy chased the smaller four-legged animal, Jake whistled, a short, sharp tone that caught Griffin's attention. It calmed the horse enough for Jake to grab his halter. It took both Nathan and Rachel to drag the reluctant goat across the room to the enclosure, and Jake had to help get it inside before they could shove the crates back into place, securing the makeshift corral.

The chickens kept up their ear-splitting noise. In desperation, Jake tossed a blanket over the cages, plunging them into night. The deafening noise quieted at last.

Ignoring it all, Rachel closed her eyes and took a deep breath of the freezing air. "I think it's starting to warm a little. The sun is out."

"Maybe so, but it's still cold. Close the door," Nathan grumbled.

Rachel blinked and glanced around. The room was in shambles. Everything was wet, including Jake's revolvers and rifle. Grabbing the broom, she swept the trampled snow into a pile and scooped it out of the way. She filled two buckets and her dishpan with clean snow from the porch, handed them to Nathan, and closed and barred the door. Then she turned to survey the wreckage.

"Well"—she shook out her skirt with both hands—"the floor needed washing anyway. And I got the water I wanted."

Jake looked at her blankly.

She pointed at the buckets, filled with melting snow.

"Why didn't you just ask? I'd have taken care of it."

"I'm capable of getting a couple of buckets of snow. There was no need to trouble you. You've been injured."

"You don't have to remind me how careless I was," he snapped. "There's nothing wrong with me that time won't fix."

Rachel backed away until she came up against the door. Jake stalked her, step for step, until he stood so close she could feel every breath he took. She blinked up at him, wariness stealing her voice. "A-all right. You can move them closer to the fire for me."

Jake glared at her for a long moment, then shook his head on a laugh. "You've got pluck, I'll give you that." He leaned a little closer and inhaled. "And you smell like springtime."

Rachel opened her mouth to respond, but no sound came out. One corner of Jake's mouth curved and she couldn't breathe. That smile could melt a woman at twenty paces, let alone when he stood so close. She reached up and touched a finger to his upper lip. His smile faded, but he didn't ask her to stop. Her fingers continued their exploration. She traced his lower lip and was shocked to realize she wanted to know how his smile tasted.

Jake finally stopped her. Threading his fingers through hers until he couldn't get any closer, he leaned forward so only she could hear him. "Be sure you know what you're asking for." He pressed a biting kiss to her palm. "If Nathan wasn't just a couple of steps away, I'd show you just what you're doing to me." Straightening, he put some distance between them. "How far to the woodpile?"

"I'll go." Nathan vaulted over a chest and skidded to a stop beside Jake.

"Not without your coat." Rachel hoped Nathan didn't notice the trembling in her voice.

Jake headed off the argument she could see in her brother's eyes. "Why don't you stand just inside the door and I'll hand all the pieces to you? That keeps me from having to walk back and forth so much on my bad leg."

Nathan didn't look happy, but he agreed. "Makes sense, I guess. The wood is piled up not too far away."

Jake opened the door cautiously, but no more snow avalanched into the cabin. Beyond the indent made by her curiosity, all Rachel could see was white. Nathan pointed Jake toward a small lump just off the porch. "Hand me the broom."

Shoving a mountain of snow aside with his shoulder, Jake slogged through a knee-deep drift until he reached the wood. The cabin seemed almost buried in white, but the air was warmer and the snow was beginning to melt.

Using the broom to clear off the wood, Jake carried armloads back to the door, keeping them small enough for Nathan to manage. It took a while, but finally a respectable stack of raggedly cut logs lay in a pile in the corner of the cabin.

"That should keep you for a day or two." Jake stamped the snow from his boots and came inside.

Nathan mimicked his movements. "Yep, that should keep us."

As they built up the fire to dry the cabin and themselves, Rachel set out sugar, butter, and two eggs. While Jake had carried in the wood, she'd filled every available pot and bucket with snow. She set the snow-filled coffeepot on the stove to heat, and leaned over to poke at the wood inside.

"I'll do that," Jake growled. He limped across the room in his stocking feet, leaving his boots to dry on the hearth. Taking the poker from her, he added a small piece of wood and coaxed the fire back to life.

Nathan lined his boots up beside Jake's, and padded to his side. "She only needs a little hot water to warm the butter to make the icing," he explained. "She'll use the rest to make tea or something."

Jake made an appropriate sound and glanced at Rachel. Self-conscious, she smoothed the skirt of her dark blue wool gown and fussed with her hair, making sure it was still tamed by the matching ribbon.

He traced her from shoulders to toes with his gaze, hesitating at the point where her hips flared beneath the gathered fabric. Even watching him from across the room made her feel warm and weak. When Jake finally looked away, she grabbed at the table to support her shaky knees.

"Let's pull out the guns again," Jake suggested to Nathan. "They're probably as wet as everything else."

Together they spread out Jake's weapons and the old rifle, as well as his boot knife. Not to be outdone, Nathan went to the small shelf on the wall of the animal pen and hunted up his own short blade.

When he laid it on the table, Jake picked it up and examined it. "Good balance, but it needs sharpening. A knife's no good if it won't cut when you need it to."

Nathan nodded, absorbing every word.

"Once we get these dried off, I'll teach you how to hone your blade." The smile that bloomed on her brother's face would have lit up a night sky.

They worked side by side the rest of the afternoon. As the day drew to a close, Jake stood and stretched his stiff muscles. Nathan did, too, adding a groan to complete the effect. When they noticed the cake she'd layered and iced, Rachel realized she was nervous about Jake's reaction. Would he like it?

"Cake!" Nathan bounded around the table and swiped his finger through the creamy icing.

"Nathan Joseph Hudson," Rachel scolded. "You leave that alone. It's for after dinner."

"Yes, ma'am," he intoned, grinning without apology.

"Wash your hands," Rachel continued. "Supper is about ready. You, too, Ranger McCain."

"Yes, ma'am," he mimicked Nathan, earning a laugh from her. With a wink that had her blushing, he cleared the table before joining Nathan at the wash bucket.

As the sun set, shadows overtook the room. Rachel lit three small candles and put them on the table. Nathan took a fourth and put it in one of the windows.

"What's that for?" Jake dried his hands with a clean cloth.

"It's our special candle," Nathan explained. "We usually only light it before Christmas, so the Christ child can find his way. When it started to snow the other night, Sis an' me didn't want spring to get lost, so we put it back."

"That's what I saw," he marveled.

"What do you mean?" Rachel paused with a platter of meat and beans in her hands.

"Out in the storm, I swore I saw a light. Every time the wind would back off, there it was, shining in the distance. I kept making for it and wound up on your porch."

"It worked, Sis." Nathan was ecstatic. "It was supposed to keep spring from getting lost, and it helped Ranger McCain, too."

The instant grace was finished, Nathan launched into an explanation of their Christmas tradition, eating and talking nonstop. Rachel was grateful. It kept her from having to join in the conversation. It was so strange to have a man at her table in her home that she couldn't seem to think straight.

Every breath she took was scented with him. The oil he'd used to clean his guns, the lingering scent of starch from his shirt, even the leather from his saddle and boots, spiced the air. The low drawl of his voice as he talked with Nathan skittered along her skin and pulsed inside her.

As she cleared the dishes, she remembered the shock she'd felt at lunch, when she'd accidentally touched his hand. That never happened when she took Hiram's arm.

"Are you all right?"

Rachel jumped when Jake spoke. He was so close she could feel his warmth seeping into her. For one tantalizing moment she thought he might put his arms around her. She swayed a little closer, then caught herself. What was the matter with her?

"What's it like, being a Ranger?" Nathan framed the question around a mouthful of cake and icing.

Jake's smile seemed forced as he set down his fork. "The work is important, but it's never easy."

"Why not?"

He picked up his coffee cup and wrapped both hands around it. "You're on the trail almost all the time. You don't get to see your family much."

"But you get to shoot bad guys and Indians."

"Nathan," Rachel interrupted. "That's enough."

Jake's cup hit the table with a crack. "Killing is nothing to take lightly. You never want to kill another man, no matter who they are. There are some who don't care who they shoot, but they're the ones who've lost their souls."

Rachel watched the play of light on his face as he worked to hold on to his temper.

"If I killed every bad man when I saw them, I wouldn't be here. The gang of cattle rustlers I'm tracking circled around behind me in the storm. I could have back-shot them lots of times over the past several months, but that's not what a good lawman should do." He stared at the flickering candle in the window. "That's not what I do."

Nathan was quiet for a long moment. "I understand—I think. 'Thou shalt not kill.' That's what it says in the Bible. I guess I just thought that meant don't kill the good folks."

"No, son." Jake took a sip of coffee. "It means all of them, even if they deserve it."

Rachel rose and refilled their cups. Of course Jake had killed. He was a Texas Ranger. It was his job to hunt down lawbreakers and bring them to justice. If they fought him, he would be forced to kill . . . All the years of teaching by the Hudsons came flooding back, confusing her. *Thou shalt not kill.* But Jake had killed, was forced to kill. She could hear the Reverend's voice in her mind, lecturing her on the Commandments, how they must be kept, that only the wicked and evil would dare to break one of God's holy commands. But Jake wasn't evil, she knew he wasn't. He didn't kill because he wanted to, he had no choice. She returned to the table, troubled.

The silence stretched until the child in Nathan came back to life.

"What are we reading tonight?" He scraped every bit of icing from his plate with care.

Rachel smiled. "How about a little bit of *Tom Sawyer*?"

"Good. I want to know what happens to Injun Joe."

Nathan carried his plate and cup to the sink without being asked, and splashed water into the wash pan. Jake followed suit, and soon they were busy washing and drying dishes, all tension forgotten.

Rachel cleared the table, wrapped the leftover bread in a towel, and lit a lamp. Taking it with her, she went into her room and came back with a leather-bound book.

"I hope you don't mind coming into the story partway."

Jake glanced over his shoulder. "I'll catch up."

"We started this ritual the first night we were in Lucinda. On the trail, we would read the Bible by the fire. Abby, the owner of the boardinghouse where we stayed when we arrived here, had a few books in her library. Now we have several of our own to choose from. Some were gifts to welcome us to town. Others I received as payment for teaching the children here, or for reading and writing letters for some of the miners. We read only a chapter or two a night, so it takes a while to complete a story." She held the book out to her brother. "Nathan, will you start, please?"

Jake carried a fresh cup of coffee to the table. Nathan took the book from Rachel and sat next to him. He started to move away, but changed his mind. Having the boy this close wasn't so bad. Nathan opened to the page that was marked, moved the lamp a little until he could see and began to read.

It was a story Jake knew, one his father had read to him before. Jake followed Nathan's finger as it moved under the words in time with his voice. Though he paused on a few of them, the boy did a good job and Jake smiled encouragement every time Nathan looked up.

Then Rachel took over. Her voice caressed the words, rising and falling in the rhythm of the action on the page, making the story come alive. When Nathan eyes grew wide at the description of the fight in the graveyard, Jake bit back a chuckle. And when the boy grew tired, sagging against him, he wrapped an arm around his slim shoulders, making room for him.

A band tightened around Jake's heart as the child snuggled closer, trusting Jake wouldn't let him fall. Rachel's voice faded to a distant hum as he looked down at Nathan. *How had this happened?* It was the only thought that would form. How had one so small gotten into his heart so fast? He'd never let anyone into his heart before. It hurt too much when he left— and sooner or later, he always left.

Rachel set the book aside and came to stand by Jake. "I'd better wake him up or he'll never make it up the stairs."

"No need." Slipping his other arm under Nathan's knees, he lifted him easily and settled him against his chest. Motioning for Rachel to lead the way, he followed her up the narrow stairs into the attic. The lamp she carried spread a pool of soft yellow light around his feet, enough to see the tiny cot in the corner beside the chimney. He laid the boy on the bed as gently as he could and stood back as Rachel tucked him in.

She kissed the top of the boy's head and covered all but the tip of his nose with several warm blankets. A sense of rightness settled over Jake, a strange feeling of protectiveness he'd never experienced. He didn't understand, but for the first time in his life, he felt a need for a family of his own, a son. Jake looked away and struggled to bury the longing. No use wishing for what he couldn't have.

When Rachel rose, Jake picked up the lamp and held out his hand. She hesitated before putting her fingers in his palm. She didn't need his help down the stairs, but he used the excuse to touch her. He didn't release her hand until they reached the warmth of the fire.

"It's been a very exciting day for Nathan. He didn't even make it through one chapter."

"He worked hard today. So did you."

"Not really. With the animals inside, we haven't had to haul as much water and hay around as we normally do." She glanced into the shadows in the direction of the makeshift enclosure. "We'll have quite a time cleaning up after they go back out, though."

"I'll lend you a hand. It won't take long."

"Thank you, but it isn't necessary. Nathan and I will manage."

Jake wasn't going to argue with her now. He joined her near the hearth, stopping close enough for her skirts to brush against his legs.

"How long have you been his mother?"

"I'm not his mother." She put a little distance between them, but Jake closed it again. She looked around, her eyes never settling, betraying her nerves. "Nathan is my brother." She wound her fingers together, absently rubbing them as if to ease some stiffness.

"You are his mother in every way that counts. How old were you when you went to live with the preacher and his wife?" He followed her to the table and sat across from her.

"I was more than twelve, but not much. We'd just lost Mama. I couldn't stay where I was, so I grabbed a few things and ran—left. A week or so later, I came across them on the trail. I was desperate by then. Mrs. Hudson wasn't a strong woman, so the Reverend agreed to let us stay. I cooked, mended, sewed, and learned to spin and weave to earn my keep. Mrs. Hudson took care of Nathan." She looked up at him with pleading eyes. "Nathan doesn't know he had a mother other than Mrs. Hudson. He doesn't need to know."

Jake nodded. "He doesn't seem to miss her much."

"He did at first. He was four years old when Mrs. Hudson died, but she'd been sick for more than two years by then."

"Why didn't you stay after Mrs. Hudson died?"

"Reverend Hudson didn't want a daughter."

The words were whispered so softly Jake wasn't sure he'd heard correctly. "Didn't want you?"

"He wanted Nathan. Even though he was very young, you could tell Nathan was an intelligent child. And the Reverend wanted a son to carry on his work and his name."

"And you?"

She rose to pick up a rag and wipe at a nonexistent spot on the sideboard. Jake crossed to her, took the rag from her, tossed it aside, and captured both her hands, stroking her fingers to calm her.

"He wanted me," she choked on the words. "But not as his daughter. He needed another wife and decided I'd be acceptable."

She tried to pull away but Jake held on.

"When I refused, he tried to . . ."

She didn't have to go on. White-hot fury burned through Jake at the idea of Rachel fending off a man who'd been her parent for nearly four years.

The first glistening tears did him in. Without a second thought, he gathered her in his arms. She struggled against his hold. "Shhh, little girl. I'm not going to hurt you. I give you my word."

She pulled away again, but the fight had gone out of her. Keeping his hold gentle, he tucked her head to his shoulder and let her cry out all the sadness and fear, the years of loneliness, the knowledge she wasn't wanted.

When she quieted, he wiped the tears from her face with his thumbs. She didn't protest when he smoothed a loose strand of hair away from her cheek.

"Better?"

"I'm sorry. I haven't cried like that since Mama . . ." She closed her eyes, shutting off the memories.

"When the Reverend finally accepted I'd never marry him," she continued, "he called me a Jezebel, a wh-whore, sent by the devil to tempt him from the path of righteousness. He dumped us in the first town we came to. Lucinda." She turned a little to look at the fire. "I thank God every day for Abby. She took us in, helped me with Nathan, and convinced me I had talents enough to earn my own way without becoming . . ."

She was silent for a long time. Jake didn't mind, since the view from where he was standing was most enjoyable. Her face was framed with golden hair that reflected the fire. Her ivory skin glowed in the dancing light. When she released her breath on a sigh, her generous curves molded a little more to his body. What a sweet package she was.

An urge to taste her filled him until he couldn't think of anything else. Moving slowly so he didn't frighten her, he bent his head and touched a kiss to her forehead. When she didn't object, he moved a little lower, his tongue flicking out to smooth one honey-colored brow. Rachel shifted, but it was to get a little closer. His body began to hum in anticipation.

Skimming his lips along her high cheekbone, he placed kisses along her jaw, inhaling her sweet scent. Finally, he found her lips and covered them with his own. He kept the kiss easy, giving her the choice to end it. Her tiny moan knifed into him and he released the rein on his control. He covered her lips with his, fusing them together. His arms tightened, pulling her against his rapidly hardening body.

Her fingers fisted on his shirt, and he expected her to protest, considering the rough way she'd been treated in the past. Instead, she pulled him even closer, returning his kiss. Her initial hesitant response gave way to total abandon. With a quick twist of his head, he opened her mouth and swept his tongue inside. This time the groan he heard was his own. She was even sweeter than he'd hoped. Her taste filled him as he explored fully, inviting her to join in the dance.

Jake buried his fingers in her hair, loosening the severe knot and sending a river of gold cascading down her back. Springtime blossomed as the scent of lavender surrounded him. He smoothed the length of her hair, enjoying the curves of her body beneath. When he reached her hips, he pulled her into his own, letting her feel his reaction to her.

Rachel made a small sound of protest he barely heard over the raging of his blood, but it was enough. He instantly loosened his hold and she broke free. Standing a few inches from him, she stared at him in shock, her eyes huge in the dim light, her breasts heaving as she dragged in air. Her fingers shook as she touched her own lips. Without warning, her eyes filled with tears again and she bolted from the room.

Jake turned to follow her, stung by the panic he'd seen on her face, but she pulled the curtain across her doorway, shutting him out. It wasn't much of a barrier, but he respected it. If she wanted to be left alone, he wasn't going to force her. But he'd be a long time forgetting the look of devastation on her face.

He limped around the perimeter of the room, checking that the windows and door were secure, more from habit than necessity. Gritting his teeth, he stretched stiff muscles and flexed his sore arms. He felt old, worn out. He raised the lamp enough to see that the animals were all settled for the night. Griffin was dozing with one leg bent. As he stretched out on the mattress near the fire, Jake found himself envying his horse. Sleep was going to be a long time coming.

Jake lay perfectly still, unsure what woke him. All his senses were tuned to the room, waiting, listening, until it came again. A soft, rhythmic thump and scrape. The sound was familiar somehow, but he couldn't place it. He rolled to one side, palming his revolver as he rose, careful not to make any noise. It was coming from Rachel's room. Fear for her stabbed through him, but he controlled it. On stocking feet, he slipped to her doorway. Moving slowly, he nudged the curtain aside with the barrel of his gun just enough to see inside.

Rachel sat on the edge of her bed, combing wool. She was fully clothed and wrapped in a dark cloak. The sound he'd heard was the tines bumping the board with each stroke. By the light of a single burning candle, he could see her breath puff out in the freezing room.

"What the hell are you doing?" He shoved the curtain aside and stalked in.

Rachel jumped, upsetting the wool comb she held. She

grabbed for it, yelping in pain when she connected with one of the long, sharp tines.

Jake eased the hammer forward on his gun and tucked it into the waistband of his pants. "I asked a question."

"C-c-couldn't sleep," she managed through chattering teeth.

He started to apologize for scaring her, then realized she wasn't shaking in fear. Knocking the comb aside with his foot, he dropped onto his heels in front of her and took her injured hand in his.

"God, woman, you're frozen." He kept his voice down so they didn't wake Nathan, but it was a struggle. "What the hell is wrong with you? Do you want to catch pneumonia? Who'll take care of your brother if you get sick?"

He looked around for a blanket and realized the bed frame was bare. "Where's your mattress?" When she didn't answer, he took her chin in his fingers and waited until she looked at him.

"You—" She took a shivering breath. "You're sleeping on it."

The single word he snapped out left no doubt of his opinion of her answer.

Rising to his feet, he lifted Rachel in his arms, easily overwhelming her struggle to get away. "Hush. You don't want to disturb Nathan, do you?" When she started to argue, he covered her lips with his, silencing her with a kiss. The fire that simple touch started in him could have melted the snow in the whole county. When she snuggled closer, and her lips clung just a little to his, he figured it was warming her up, too.

Shouldering the curtain out of the way, he carried her to his bed, lowered her onto the mattress, and covered her with every blanket he could reach. "Stay put." Grabbing chunks of wood, he built up the fire until it blazed, filling the room with warmth.

When he knelt beside the bed once more, Rachel had curled on her side, her face toward the heat. A single sigh shuddered through her as her shivering began to ease.

"Why didn't you just tell me I was in your bed?"

Rachel stared at the fire instead of looking at him, but the blush staining her cheeks told him she'd heard.

"Go to sleep, pretty girl." He smoothed the hair from her face, cursing when she flinched from his touch. "I won't touch you. I give you my word."

The tears glistening in her eyes kept him from saying more. He wanted her to explain them, but he wasn't sure he wanted to hear the answer. Stalking to the corner of the room, he dragged his bedroll from the pile of his gear, crossed to the hearth and bedded down near her feet. Long after her breathing deepened and leveled out he lay awake, trying to convince himself he wanted nothing more than to get far away from the stubborn woman who slept nearby.

Chapter Five

Rachel came awake slowly, unwilling to allow the reality of morning to disrupt her dreams. Such nice dreams of a warm spring day and babies, and she and Jake . . .

She sat up with a gasp, her cheeks warming with the memory of her dream, then stared in confusion. This wasn't her bedroom. Where was she? And who'd made coffee?

She sniffed the air again. There was definitely coffee on the stovetop. She tossed back the covers, surprised to find she was fully dressed. The previous night came flooding back. Jake finding her combing wool because it was just too cold to sleep. Jake carrying her to his bed by the fire. Jake kissing her.

Her face flamed at the memory of her wanton response to him. All the years she'd spent proving she wasn't like her mother and one kiss made a liar of her. She buried her face in her hands. How could she have allowed it? She was practically a married woman. How would she ever be able to face Hiram?

"That's an awfully long face for so early in the morning."

She jumped at the words spoken close to her ear.

"Easy, pretty girl. I won't hurt you."

"You just surprised me. I didn't know you were there."

Jake glanced around the room, then back at her. "Not a lot of places to go."

She fought a pitched battle with herself when he grinned.

She wanted to smile back, but she wouldn't encourage him in any way. Jake reached out to smooth back her hair, but she leaned away. She couldn't let him touch her, not after her response last night. She didn't trust herself any longer.

He frowned. "You say you know I won't hurt you, but you don't believe it."

"Oh, I do believe you, Mr. McCain. It's just—" She broke off. She was lying in bed talking to a man. She felt the heat rush into her face again. She rolled off the mattress, away from Jake, and pushed to her feet. She took a step toward her bedroom and got tangled in the blankets and her heavy cloak. Jake's quick reaction kept her from pitching to the floor.

The strong hands gripping her arms sent heat racing through her, touching places deep inside her she didn't want to feel. She looked up, intending to demand he release her, but she got lost in his eyes. She could see herself there, the reflection of a woman, leaning closer, stretching toward him, hoping he would kiss her.

"The sun's out." Nathan clattered down the stairs and raced to the door.

"Don't open that!"

The boy skidded to a stop at Jake's sharp command.

"Sorry, didn't mean to shout. But I don't want to chase snow around the cabin until I've had some breakfast."

Rachel pulled away and hurried into her room to dress for the day. She gasped at how cold the tiny space had gotten and had to admit Jake had been right to make her sleep near the fire. She could hear him, talking to Nathan, explaining how they didn't want a repeat of yesterday's circus. She had to smile. She must have looked ridiculous, standing in the doorway, covered in snow. But she'd laughed, really laughed, for the first time in so long, and it felt wonderful.

Since she'd gone to bed fully dressed, all she had to do was comb her hair and tame it into some semblance of order. She smoothed it together at the base of her neck and tied a ribbon of cloth around it, choosing to leave it down this morning.

Wrapping it into a knot and pinning it up always gave her a bit of a headache, and it would end up falling anyway.

When she shoved aside the curtain separating her bedroom from the main cabin, Jake and Nathan stood side by side at the window, trying to see through a tiny break in the snow that covered the glass. Above their heads, a large patch of snow broke loose and slid from the roof, hitting the ground with a thud. "The snow is melting quickly." Rachel was almost sad that the outside world was returning. As soon as the snow cleared, Jake McCain would be on his way and life would return to normal. Rachel refused to acknowledge that small part of her that wanted things to continue as they were.

Jake finished his coffee. "It sounds like we'll be able to get out of here pretty soon."

"Will you go after those bad guys now?" Nathan looked up, his pose mirroring Jake's exactly.

"As soon as I can get an idea of which way they headed. I'm hoping someone in town saw them or spoke with them."

Rachel started to ask a question, but stopped when she heard her name being shouted. "That's Hiram."

Nathan rolled his eyes, making Jake laugh. They could hear several men outside, calling her, knocking snow out of the way as they came.

"Who's Hiram?"

"Hiram Miller. He runs the bank in town."

Her brother grimaced. "She wants him to marry her."

"Nathan!"

The boy ducked, but laughter bubbled out. She started to scold him about his manners, but the men outside shouted again.

"They can't be too bad off," one of the men called. "She made it out for wood."

"Those prints are from a man's boots, not hers." Hiram sounded almost panicked. "Rachel! Rachel, are you all right?"

"What on earth is the matter with him?" Rachel cleared the table, making room for company. "You'd think I was caught out in the storm instead of snug inside a warm house."

She opened the door as the men finished clearing a path to the door. Hiram and two of the miners from the outskirts of town stared back at her.

Hiram grabbed both her hands and tugged her close. "Darling, are you all right? I've been worried sick about you, stuck out here all alone."

"I'm not alone. Nathan is here, and . . ."

He pulled her against his chest and wrapped his arms around her, trapping her hands between them. Shocked, she didn't think to protest when he bent his head and planted a kiss on her lips. Hiram had never tried to do more than squeeze her hand before. It was nice, she decided, but not the same as when Jake held her. Kissed her.

She had no business thinking of Ranger McCain. She was going to marry Hiram. Remembering there were others watching, she turned her face aside and shoved a little at Hiram until he released her.

"Come inside, gentlemen. Warm yourselves. There's coffee, if you would care for some."

Hiram wrapped a hand around her upper arm to usher her inside. She moved forward a step so he could close the door, but was yanked back when he stopped suddenly. She looked up to ask what was wrong, but he wasn't looking at her. He'd seen Jake. She risked a glance at the Ranger as he stood halfway across the room, buckling on his gun belt.

"Hiram, this is Jake McCain," she introduced. "He's a Texas Ranger. He was caught out in the storm, left for dead by a gang of cattle rustlers. God's hand guided him here."

"A Ranger?"

Rachel was shocked by the venom in Hiram's voice. He looked the man up and down, doubt obvious in his face. Couldn't he see the bruises that colored Jake's skin or how he still favored his left side a little? She quickly introduced the other men, hoping to diffuse the tension in the small room.

"Several strangers spent the last two nights in town," Hiram accused. "They told me they'd been shadowed by a thief who was trying to rob them, but they got the jump on him just as the snow was starting."

"He is so a Ranger!" Nathan tore across the room, dove into Jake's packs and rummaged until he found what he was looking for. Waving Jake's commission in the air, he stomped over to Hiram and thrust it at him. "See."

When Hiram released her to take the paper, Rachel moved out of reach, rubbing her arm. The frown on Jake's face made it plain he wasn't pleased with Hiram's treatment of her. His concern warmed her.

Nathan returned to Jake's side and looked to him for approval. The Ranger patted the boy's shoulder and winked at him. Nathan beamed at his new hero.

"It looks real enough," Hiram allowed after closely studying the document. Staring at Jake, he tossed the commission on the table. "But they all made it to town. Why couldn't you?"

"They had a head start on me, since they'd knocked me out and left me to freeze to death. By the time I came to, it was snowing too hard to see much. When I spotted Miss Hudson's light, I aimed for it and passed out on the porch."

"What light?"

"Our candle. The one we put in the window for Christmas. You remember. I told you about it. We put it back when the snow started." She poured coffee for the other two men. "I thank God Mr. McCain saw it through the storm. As it was, he was nearly frozen when he found the cabin."

Hiram took the cup Rachel handed him, but he refused to sit. He seemed to be stalking Jake, making sure he stayed between him and Rachel.

"I can offer bacon and bread, gentlemen, if you'd like." They all declined her offer. "I'm afraid I haven't had a chance to collect the eggs yet."

"They're in the sink."

Jake's voice was deep and warm, unlike Hiram's. She'd never noticed before how Hiram seemed to whine when he was upset.

"I gathered them while you were still sleeping."

Rachel turned away and busied herself wiping an imaginary spill. Heat rushed through her at the memory of Jake putting her to bed the night before.

"What is it, Rachel? You seem a bit flushed." Hiram joined her, crowding her into the counter. She sidestepped to gain some separation, but he closed the distance. She could feel him press against her skirts. It flustered her. He'd rarely touched her except to take her arm when walking. Standing this close wasn't like him. Panic fluttered at the edge of her mind, but she ignored it. This was Hiram, her fiancé. He wasn't going to hurt her. "I'm fine, thank you."

"I was concerned about you." He ran his fingers from her shoulder to her wrist, stopping to stroke the bare skin where her sleeve ended. "When you didn't come to town yesterday, I imagined all manner of horrible things had happened to you."

Her skin burned where he touched and she fought not to wipe away the feeling. She swallowed the knot of fear clogging her throat. "We couldn't leave the cabin. As you saw, the snow virtually buried us. I appreciate your concern, and for coming to check on us." When she tried to turn around, he blocked her path, deliberately taking her arm and pulling her against him.

Fear skittered down her spine. "Hiram," she whispered, "what's the matter with you?" She twisted her arm to break free. "Let me go. There are others in the room."

He stared down at her, his lips pressed into a hard line. When his gaze dropped to her mouth, she shrank away.

"Please, Hiram, let me pass."

For one long, tense moment, she didn't think he would, but finally his hand dropped and he stepped away.

Freed from his hold, she crossed to the stove. Jake met her there.

"What was that about?"

"None of your concern, Mr. McCain."

"I don't take to a woman being manhandled. He doesn't have the right."

Where Hiram had frightened her when he'd stood so close,

Jake's nearness was comforting somehow. She didn't want to explore why. Instead she picked up the coffeepot.

"Please, Jake." She kept her voice low. "He's never hurt me before. I'll be fine"

Hiram scowled at her from across the room while she poured coffee. Where had her gentle suitor gone? She'd never known this side of him existed.

"What are those animals doing in the house?" Hiram wrinkled his nose dramatically. "The stench is unbearable."

Rachel set the pot down with a thump. "I'm sorry, Hiram, but I couldn't leave them outside. They would never have survived the cold in that lean-to."

"You don't need to apologize, Miss Hudson." Jake smoothed over the sudden tension in the room. "It's an ingenious use of space. Quite unique, in my experience."

She glanced at him and Jake winked. She couldn't help but smile back. As Rachel turned back to her task, she caught Hiram glaring at the Ranger. The instant she finished filling the men's cups, Hiram grabbed her wrist and pulled her close to his side.

Jake took a chair at the table. "What can you tell me about the men who were in town? How many were there?"

"Five." Albert Jackson spoke up first. The big bear of a man was one of the gentlest people Rachel had ever known. He was raising three young children on his own, two boys who promised to be as big as their father and a fey blond girl who was the tiniest child Rachel had ever seen.

There'd been a time when she'd wondered if Albert might ask her to marry him, but he'd never gotten over the loss of his wife and couldn't consider replacing her. Still, he was a good man who watched out for her, and she loved him for his concern.

"They rode up to the livery about sundown two days ago, just as the snow was starting." Albert took a swig of coffee like it was whiskey, wiping his mouth with the back of his hand. "I was at the general store, just across the way. I could see 'em through the window."

"What did they look like?"

"Now, I can't rightly say. I didn't get a real good look at them. Big men, most of them, but then you already know that," he joked, indicating Jake's bruises. "The leader, he's one you don't want to tangle with, I imagine. Not so big, but he had a look about him that said he's trouble. He had long yeller hair, kinda like Miss Rachel's, only not so pretty, beggin' your pardon, ma'am, and a mustache that hung clear past his chin."

Jake knew the man Albert described, but he held his silence, letting the man remember.

"I didn't see the others real well. But I remember their horses." He glanced at Rachel. "I left the children with Ms. Winston and spent the night in the livery. That storm was too bad to try and venture home."

"That was a wise decision, Mr. Jackson." Rachel escaped from Hiram to pour a bit more coffee for Albert.

"Thank you, ma'am," he mumbled into his beard. "There was eight horses all told. Five were for riding and three for hauling gear. Two of them pack horses looked near used up, but the other was a fine-looking chestnut filly, with a proper saddle and everything tied on real neat." His gaze jerked up to meet Jake's. "She was yours."

"Yeah. They took Duchess after they'd finished with me."

"Why didn't they take your saddle horse?" Hiram leaned against the fireplace mantel, one ankle crossed over the other. His arms echoed the insolent posture.

"They'd never catch Griffin." The horse whinnied at the sound of his name, making Jake smile. "He's a wily old cuss. Probably ran them a hell of a chase until they decided he wasn't worth the trouble."

"I saw them," Rachel whispered.

"When?" Jake straightened in his chair.

"The same evening you came." She set the coffeepot back on the stove, remembering. "The snow was just starting. They rode up looking for a place to stay. I didn't open the door, just sent them into town, to Abby's boardinghouse." One of them had caused her heart to miss a beat, as though she recognized him. She rubbed her arms at a sudden chill.

"Why didn't you say anything?"

"In all the fuss after you arrived I completely forgot them. They . . . they weren't gentlemen. At least, the one who did the talking wasn't."

"I saw them, too. Are they the ones you're after?" Nathan sat at the table just like one of the men, his elbows on the table in a mirror of Jake. Rachel turned away. Her brother would be heartbroken when Jake left.

"Who are they?" Hank Gerard spoke for the first time. Though he'd been in America for nearly ten years, Rachel still heard the lilt of his native France in his voice.

"Murderers. Rustlers. Thieves. They aren't particular. First it was a wagon train of women and children. None of them survived." Disgust and vengeance laced Jake's words. "Last month it was a stagecoach carrying payroll for the railroad. Then they killed a pregnant woman and made off with two children and a half-dozen horses."

Rachel gasped. "They kidnapped children?"

Jake nodded in response.

"You'll catch them," Nathan encouraged.

"That I will, son."

"If I can help," Hank offered, "I am at your service."

Rachel crossed to the table. "But Mr. Gerard, what about your claim?"

"My little mine is played out, Miss Rachel. There is no reason to stay any longer."

The thought of Hank leaving Lucinda saddened her. He'd been a good friend when she'd needed one the most. "I'll miss you."

He smiled and patted her hand before turning back to Jake. "Now, Ranger McCain, what else can we tell you?"

"When did they leave town?"

"Yesterday, midmorning," Hiram sneered. "They didn't have any trouble. They headed south once the sun had melted most of the snow."

"Only on the open trails," Hank corrected. "The back country is still treacherous, especially for horses."

"Then they'll stick to the open for a while. Since they think I'm still lying in the ravine where they left me, they won't be too careful about leaving a trail."

The men rose when Jake did. As they started for the door, Jake held back a little. "Ma'am, I appreciate everything you've done for me." He shrugged on his jacket and stepped closer, lowering his voice. "I'd like to repay you if you'll let me." He dug some silver coins from his pocket. "For the food you've shared, at least."

She glanced at Hiram, where he loitered near the fire, trying to hear. She kept her voice soft so he couldn't. "I don't require payment, Mr. McCain. I did as God taught us."

Jake looked toward Nathan, considering, but she arched an eyebrow, giving him the look that stopped most of the antics of a room full of rambunctious children. He put the coins back in his pocket, shaking his head.

Nathan followed him to the little corral and helped free Griffin. Jake led the horse outside and Nathan followed, lugging his saddle. A moment later he raced back in to collect Jake's saddlebags, then again for his rifle and bedroll. Hank and Albert joined them in the yard, but Hiram remained until all evidence of Jake was removed from the cabin. Then he jammed on his hat and left her without a word.

Rachel looked around the cabin, surprised at how empty it felt. Shivering, she wrapped her arms around herself. Though he'd only been there two days, Rachel had grown accustomed to his presence. She shook off the sadness that threatened and stepped onto the porch.

"Mr. Miller," Jake called out. "I'd be obliged if you could show me where those men headed out of town. I should be able to pick up their trail from there."

Hiram ignored him and headed toward town on foot.

He shook Nathan's hand solemnly. "Take good care of your sister, son."

"I will, sir." Nathan rubbed Griffin's neck one last time and stepped out of the way.

Jake turned back to Rachel, staring at her for a long moment.

The world seemed to narrow to just the two of them. She could almost feel him stroking her hair, kissing her lips . . . She forced herself out of the waking dream. "Go with God, Ranger McCain."

He caught up Griffin's reins, touched the brim of his hat in farewell, and followed the other men.

Chapter Six

Jake bid his escorts good-bye at the door to the livery, where he left Griffin with his nose in a feedbag of grain. Then he went in search of Arnold Miller. According to Hank Gerard, Miller owned the dry goods store and served as Mayor and Sheriff whenever the need arose. He was also the father of the puffed-up, self-important, rooster of a man Rachel seemed to be enamored with.

Jake tried to ignore the flare of anger at the thought of Rachel tying herself to Hiram Miller. Who she chose to marry was none of his concern.

"Excuse me, miss." He stopped a young woman with a touch to the brim of his hat. "Where might I find Arnold Miller?"

"I imagine he's in his store, sir." The girl giggled and batted her long lashes at him. "Over there."

Jake couldn't believe she was flirting with him. The girl couldn't be more than twelve. "Thank you." He headed in the direction she indicated, anxious to put some distance between them in case she offered to show him the way.

A bell jingled over Jake's head when he walked in. The scent of dried beef mingled with that of fresh bread and grain in the cold room. Evidently, Arnold Miller didn't believe in wasting firewood.

"Good morning." A man who looked like an older version of Hiram Miller called out from the far end of the store. Setting aside a huge black feather duster, the man started toward Jake. Three women, gathered near a small stove, ceased their conversation to stare at him. Jake removed his hat, a gesture that would have made his mother proud.

"I'm Arnold Miller," the man introduced as he approached, tugged on his vest and stuck out his hand. "You must be Ranger McCain."

"Word travels fast around here."

Miller barked out a laugh. "Not too many visitors make their way to our little community." He slapped Jake on the back. "Come on to the back, closer to the stove, where it's warmer."

Jake looked over the room as he walked its length. It was decent sized for a small town. Shelves with jars and canned goods covered one wall, and picks, axes, and shovels covered two more. No doubt that Lucinda was a mining town. Several skeins of white wool yarn lay nearby and he wondered if Rachel had spun them. A heavy canvas curtain covered a small doorway behind the counter, presumably the office and storage area.

He bit back a grin when he spotted a polished wooden sign with the word BANK painted on it in glossy black lettering, hanging over one end of the counter. A large red leather blotter was arranged on a section of the scarred wood. On it, between two pens and a pot of ink, rested another sign that notified anyone who cared that the bank was closed. So this was the domain of the wonderful Hiram. He shook his head. How could someone as level-headed and practical as Rachel Hudson convince herself a fancy man like Hiram Miller was a good catch?

"My son tells me you had a less than friendly greeting when you arrived in our community."

"No fault of the town's," Jake assured him. "And Miss Hudson and Nathan have more than made up for it."

A gasp from one of the women had Jake focusing on them.

"Forgive my rudeness. Ranger McCain, allow me to introduce my wife, Lucinda."

Miller indicated a tall, thin woman with a birdlike nose and watery blue eyes. Bony fingers clutched a green velvet reticule that perfectly matched her dress. Her graying hair was peeled back from her face and secured in a tight knot in the back. She examined him with a look of undisguised contempt on her pinched face before acknowledging him with a haughty nod.

"Ma'am." Jake bit back his irritation at her reaction and inclined his head in greeting. He couldn't help but agree that Nathan's description of the old biddy was fitting.

Miller beamed at his wife. "She is from one of the finest families in Boston. I'm fortunate she has as keen a sense of adventure as I do. We built this town together, you know."

Jake nodded, more to move him along than because he was interested.

"This is Ms. Abigail Winston," Miller continued. "She runs the most excellent boardinghouse just across the street."

"Call me Abby." Laughter boomed from the amply girthed woman as she greeted Jake. He returned her grin. Here was a woman he could come to like.

"And this dear young girl is Miss Penelope Parker. Her father is one of our leading citizens, a miner with a rather profitable claim northeast of town." More girl than woman, Penelope blushed at the attention.

"How do you do, Ranger McCain."

Before Jake could return the greeting, Lucinda Miller interrupted. "You've been with that *woman*."

Temper flared at the tone of accusation in her voice. "Miss Hudson and her brother saved my life. Had I not found my way to their home, I would have died in the blizzard. The cabin was buried in snow until your son and the others dug it out this morning."

"It doesn't surprise me that a woman like *her* would entertain someone like you in her home. Half-breed," she hissed before turning away. Miss Parker copied her actions and presented her back to Jake.

Jake held his tongue, but barely. He could take the slur aimed at him, but there was no reason to condemn Rachel. "Miss Hudson is a God-fearing woman, raised to care for someone in need. She's done nothing to deserve this." Lucinda Miller ignored him. Only Abby Winston seemed willing to believe him.

"Rachel is a good girl. She'd never turn her back on you, that's for sure."

Jake thanked her with a nod. At least someone in this town believed him.

"I'm sure you appreciate everything Miss Hudson has done for you," Arnold Miller offered.

Jake glared at the man. Surely he didn't mean what his tone insinuated. "You want to explain what you mean by that?"

"Arnold," Mrs. Miller interrupted.

"Yes, dear?"

"I'm going home."

"Yes, dear."

Jake remained silent until the door closed behind the women with a jingle of the bell, never looking away from Arnold Miller. "I'm waiting."

"We didn't know much about Rachel Hudson when she came to us. We had to take the word of the preacher who brought her here. It's a shame, really. She seemed to be a fine teacher, and her students all love her." Miller released an exaggerated sigh. "Still, we can't let a woman like her influence our children."

"What the hell is that supposed to mean?"

"The gentlemen who came through town said they'd stopped at her cabin before coming here."

Jake couldn't believe what he was hearing. "They were looking for a place to wait out the storm. If they traveled the same route I did, her house would have been the first place they came to. She didn't let them inside, just sent them on to the boardinghouse in town."

The man didn't look convinced. "You were seen paying her."

"For the food she shared with me while the *three* of us were snowed in." Jake emphasized Nathan's presence in the cabin. "Did your son mention she refused my money?"

"Yes, but she would have, since others were present to witness the transaction. I'm sorry, but we can't have her kind in our town. We won't allow it. That sort of activity would attract the very people we don't want in our community."

"Look Miller, you've got it wrong. Miss Hudson is a gentle, generous woman who only wants to make a home for herself and her brother. She wouldn't accept payment for saving my life because she was raised to help others without expecting anything in return. And she sent that bunch of good-for-nothing liars away. She didn't invite them in for tea."

"They all seemed like gentlemen to me."

"They're thieves, kidnappers, murderers." Jake nearly choked on the last word. How well he knew. "Pick one. You can't take their word for anything."

Miller's eyes bulged at Jake's litany. "I see."

"You've been lied to, which is something those particular men are very good at."

"Well, we'll have to take that into consideration." The man tugged his vest over his belly again. "Yes, indeed. I'll have to tell my wife immediately."

"Do that. And be sure she spreads the word as quickly as she did before." Jake reined in his temper. "I need some supplies before I hit the trail."

Their business went quickly. When Jake took a couple of silver coins from his pocket to pay for his purchases, Arnold Miller snatched them up, made change, and led Jake to the door like he couldn't wait to see him gone.

The reaction in the livery, when he returned for Griffin, wasn't much better, but at least it was directed at him and not Rachel. Only Abby, at the boardinghouse, seemed to accept nothing had happened while he'd been trapped in a house with an unmarried woman and her brother.

"I'd be happy to help, Mr. McCain." The woman closed her front door behind Jake. "Have you eaten? I'm just about to have a bite of lunch and I hate eating alone."

Jake tossed his hat onto a peg near the door. "Thank you, Abby. A hot meal would be welcome before I get on the trail." He started to unbuckle his gun belt, but she waved away the necessity.

"Out here, you get used to men wearing the things. They don't bother me none." Her laugh boomed off the walls as she pulled a Colt Derringer from her apron pocket. Its ivory grip was yellowed from years of handling. "Can't be too careful in a mining town." She returned the gun to its hiding place and reached for a long wooden spoon. "Sit yourself down. I'm glad for the company. We don't get a lot of strangers through town this time of year. Albert—Mr. Jackson—he has a claim several miles east of town. He picked up his children just a bit ago and the house is almost too quiet without them."

Jake chose a chair where he could watch the door and windows and accepted a plate of food with a nod of thanks. He didn't bother trying to say anything. Abby barely paused to breathe.

"Mind you, they behave, but three children under the age of seven make a heap of noise even sitting still."

She pulled out the chair opposite him. It creaked as she settled her weight into it, but she paid no attention. "Now, tell me what you need me to do for Rachel. Such a delightful girl, though she's got more on her shoulders than any child her age ought to have to worry with."

Jake swallowed the bite of excellent stew he was chewing. "She saved my life and I'm in her debt. I know having to feed me used up a lot of her supplies, but she refused to let me pay her for any of it. Would you mind purchasing and delivering some things to her for me? I'd ask Arnold Miller to do it, but I don't want to fuel the gossip any more than I already have."

"Of course. When Lucinda told me Rachel had taken

money from you for—well—being with her . . ." She waved a hand in the air as if to chase away the words. "I told her it couldn't be true. But she doesn't want to hear anything good about the girl."

She lowered her voice, as if the walls had ears. "Her son, Hiram, has been paying Rachel some attention, and Lucinda's determined to protect her boy from any woman he might find interesting." She snorted with laughter. "It doesn't help Rachel is the prettiest thing this valley is ever likely to see."

Jake finished his meal. "I appreciate your help. She's done nothing to warrant the gossip but save the life of a stranger. Being the daughter of a preacher, folks should expect that."

"The preacher wasn't her real father, you know." She cleared the table and topped up his cup of coffee before returning to the table.

"She said something about it." Jake remembered the photograph lying on Rachel's mantel. There'd been something familiar about it, but he wasn't sure what. He brought his attention back to Abby, knowing he'd remember eventually.

"She doesn't share that with many people, Ranger. It was the preacher who told me he found her wandering in the wilderness, carrying an infant boy she swore was her brother. She said her parents were dead and the two of them were alone in the world. Well, the preacher and his wife had always wanted children and they figured the good Lord had finally found a way of blessing them. They raised Rachel and little Nathan as their own until his wife died. A couple of months later, they came through Lucinda and the preacher left them both here, saying Rachel was a good, God-fearing woman who'd been taught all the things necessary in a wife and it was time she found a husband."

She took a healthy swallow of cooling coffee. "Of course, there was talk that she was more than a daughter to the preacher, but it didn't last long. That was more than two years ago. She's been teaching the children and a good number of the adults since she got here, her being the only one who can read and write who didn't already have enough to do making their own living. And she's done a fine job of it. There's a few around here that still believe Nathan is actually her son, but it didn't seem to matter to most folks one way or the other."

"What do you believe?" Jake wasn't sure he wanted to know, but he couldn't help himself.

"Her story doesn't really seem to add up. She never discusses her and the boy's mother and that makes it harder for some to accept what she says. But it makes no difference to me, whichever is the truth. She's a fine young woman who makes her own way, is always willing to help others, and is a pretty bit of sunshine in this corner of the world. That's enough for me."

"The men who came through the night of the blizzard, who started these lies about Rachel, how long did they stay?"

Abby shook her head. "Just the one night, which suited me fine."

"Why do you say that?"

"I don't know. More a feeling than anything they did." She stared through Jake, trying to remember. "They weren't rowdy, paid their bill up front and didn't cause trouble."

Jake drained his cup of coffee and refused Abby's offer to refill it. "But?"

"There was something about them that made me uneasy, like they'd shoot a man as easy as saying good morning. All but one of them, anyway. He didn't seem to fit in, but I didn't waste too much time thinking on why."

"You read them right. They're wanted in both Texas and the New Mexico territory for murder, kidnapping, and cattle rustling. If they come back, don't let them in."

He waited until she reluctantly agreed. He understood her reticence. Money was money, after all, and a thief's silver spent the same as a preacher's. Jake pushed away from the table and rose. "What do I owe you for the meal?"

"Not a thing. I enjoy having such handsome company. Just promise you'll come back should you pass through here again."

"With pleasure, Abby."

Jake handed her several coins for Rachel's supplies. Abby

tucked them into her apron pocket, then saw him to the door and bid him safe travels. Jake checked the angle of the sun and knew he had to get started. Tugging his hat lower against the wind that had kicked up with the warming air, he left the porch and headed for the livery.

Four hours later he had to admit defeat. If the men he was following had come this way, they didn't leave any sign of it. Jake was the best tracker in Company C of the Texas Rangers, but he hadn't found a single hoof or boot mark to indicate their passage. Had he been put on the wrong track deliberately? Staring into the distance, he gauged the time left before sunset. He could go back to town, put up in the boarding-house for the night and start again in the morning. That would give him a chance to jog Hiram Miller's memory—and check on Rachel.

How had a slip of a girl gotten under his skin so fast? Sure, she was pretty, but he'd known others who were more beautiful. Her grit appealed, too, but it wasn't only that. He pulled off his hat and resettled it on his head. He couldn't help wondering if the rumors running through town were true. Was she an experienced woman rather than an innocent girl? His body tightened at the thought of finding out for himself. He'd like to get to know the pretty lady a lot better.

He couldn't be obvious about it, since some in town already questioned her story. Rachel was isolated enough as it was. There were so many things that could go wrong. She couldn't even fire a gun, and that left her vulnerable to anyone who happened past her cabin.

Jake plucked a small stone from the ground and rolled it through his fingers, thinking. He should leave well enough alone. She didn't need a man like him in her life. All he'd managed to do was bring her trouble.

Squinting against the sun as it dipped toward the horizon, he let his mind drift until it circled back to the men he was chasing. What if they returned to the little town? Given the lies they'd told about Rachel, he wouldn't put it past them to show up at her house. She lived so far out of town, no one would know she was in danger until it was too late. And they probably wouldn't help her if they did.

Imagining Rachel cornered had his gut feeling like it was packed full of barbed wire. Tossing the stone aside, Jake vaulted into Griffin's saddle and turned back toward Lucinda.

The cabin was finally clean again. After Jake and the others left, Rachel and Nathan had swept and shoveled the melting snow out of the lean-to, spread fresh straw, and moved the animals back where they belonged. Then they set to work with hot water and lye soap to remove all evidence of their stay in the cabin.

Hours later, when she figured soap and scrubbing wouldn't do any more good, they shoved the sea chest against the far wall and pulled her spinning wheel closer to the window where it belonged. Then they dragged her mattress back into her bedroom. For an instant, Rachel swore she smelled Jake's scent in the ticking. How had he become a part of her life so fast that she missed having him here? It was ridiculous. He'd only been in the cabin a couple of days and he'd been unconscious for part of it.

"That's enough," she announced, pushing away the memories. "Wash up and I'll put together something to eat."

"Finally," Nathan mumbled.

Rachel hid her smile. "I appreciate you working so hard. I couldn't have done it without you."

She started when someone banged on the door. Nathan didn't hesitate. He jumped up and tore across the room. "Wait!"

He spun around to stare at her. "What's wrong?"

She pressed a hand to her racing heart. "Find out who it is before you open the door."

He stared at her like she'd suddenly grown a second head. "Who would it be that we don't already know?"

Another knock sounded. "Remember those men," she

hissed. "The ones Ranger McCain is chasing. I don't want to open the door to them."

"Oh, yeah, I forgot." He peeked out of a window closest to the door. "It's Ms. Winston and Hi-ram."

Nathan's singsong tone reminded her how much her brother disliked the man she hoped to marry. Nathan was never rude to him, but he didn't bother to hide his feelings, either.

"They've got a bunch of stuff with them."

"Rachel? Nathan?" Abby knocked again. "You in there?"

"Coming." She patted her hair, hoping the tight bun was still intact. "Nathan, open the door, please."

He rolled his eyes at her before lifting the latch.

"Come in, Abby. Mr. Miller." She kept her gaze lowered as she greeted him, as she'd been taught a good woman should, but couldn't resist a glance. Proper behavior was forgotten when she saw the anger in his eyes. He glared at her as he stepped into the cabin. What could she have done to elicit such a reaction?

"What a nice surprise," she managed to greet Abby. "We weren't expecting company, but it's good to see you." She backed up as Hiram dropped an armload of food and supplies on the table. Rachel's eyes grew wide when Abby added more to the pile. "What's all this?"

"Replenishing your supplies, compliments of Ranger McCain."

Abby Winston lowered her ample frame onto a bench. "There's bacon, beans, sugar, salt, flour, some jerky, and coffee." She pulled the bag out and held it out to Rachel. "He was adamant about you having coffee. Paid a pretty penny for it, too."

"But I didn't ask for any of this." Rachel clutched her hands together behind her back to keep from reaching out for the treasure.

"Of course you didn't," the older woman agreed easily. "It wouldn't be repaying you if you'd asked for it."

"Repayment? For what?"

"For *feeding* him while he mended, he said." Hiram spoke from his place near the mantel.

"I only did as I was taught," she insisted. "I shared what we had with someone in need."

"I know that, honey," Abby soothed. "Told him you probably wouldn't take too kindly to his insisting like this. But he paid for it all and asked me to see you got it." She heaved herself to her feet. "Time to get back. I wanted to be sure you had this before it got too late." Abby glanced back when she reached the door. "Coming, Hiram?"

"In a minute," he dismissed her, never looking away from Rachel.

"Nathan, why don't you walk with me until Mr. Miller catches up?"

As they left, Hiram crossed to Rachel, trapping her against the table. "I want to know what went on here."

"What do you mean?" She shrank back from the fury and accusations in his eyes.

"A man doesn't just buy a month's worth of supplies for nothing, Rachel." He grabbed her upper arms in a bruising grip. "What did you give him that cost this much?"

Remembering Mrs. Hudson's lectures on maintaining her dignity, she tried to rein in her growing temper. "Ranger McCain was injured. I helped him, just as I would have helped anyone in need. For heaven's sake, Hiram, the man passed out at my feet. What was I to do, rouse him from his stupor and send him back into the storm? He was unconscious until morning." She nearly cursed when she felt the warmth climb her cheeks.

Hiram's eyes narrowed. "I think you're lying."

Rachel gasped. "How dare you!" She tried to pull out of his grasp, but he only crowded closer, until they touched from chest to knees. Panic exploded deep inside Rachel.

"What about the others, the ones you *said* you sent straight to town?"

The insinuation in his voice made her shiver. Temper swelled on the heels of fear. "Say what you mean, Hiram Miller, or get out of my home."

"They told some folks that you looked real familiar, that you were a mirror image of a woman they used to know in El Paso. One said he knew her *real* well."

Rachel felt the blood leave her face and grabbed at the edge of the table as her knees grew weak.

"It's not true," she whispered.

"One of them said he'd seen you there."

"No," she denied. She wanted to shout at him, but only a whisper of sound got past the cold lump of dread in her throat. It wasn't possible, not after all this time. Hadn't she done everything right? Hadn't she been the good girl the preacher told her she had to be?

"Are you sure you don't know those men the Ranger is chasing?" He shook her hard, his face mottled red with anger.

She'd shoved him away and swung at him without thinking. The slap echoed through the room. Hiram stumbled back. The shock she felt at what she'd done was mirrored in his expression.

"Hiram, I'm sorry. Please forgive me."

"What's the matter with you?"

"You . . . you frightened me, shaking me like that."

He stared at his hands, then lifted icy blue eyes to her. "Maybe you deserved it. Maybe you've been lying to me—to everyone in this town."

Chapter Seven

Rachel slumped in the rocking chair, staring through the open door. Hiram had gone, slamming it so hard it bounced in the frame and crashed back against the wall. Now there was only silence.

This couldn't be happening. She'd tried so hard to be a good woman and do everything right. She thought she had left her past behind. But it had found her again.

What else could she have done? She never spoke of her mother, though she loved her and still missed her. But that was the price the preacher had demanded of her. *Forget your past, shake the dust of that life from your shoes and never look back.* He'd never known what she was running from. She'd refused to tell him. And she'd been successful at deflecting Nathan's questions about his father. Until today, she thought no one knew what she'd escaped from.

She forced herself to stand and walk across the room to the door. The sun still shone, sparkling off the little patches of snow that remained in shadows and crevasses. The sky was still blue. The cabin still stood. But her world was crumbling.

She saw Nathan in the distance, dragging a long stick through the mud made by melting snow and ice. At least he didn't know. *Yet,* a voice whispered in her head. She made herself smile and return his wave. What would happen to her brother if the rumors persisted?

Rachel stopped. What had Hiram said? The men *thought* she looked familiar? *Thought* she looked like someone they knew? If they weren't sure, then no one in town knew for certain. They were only rumors, words spoken to hurt her. But she could tell them it wasn't true, prove to them she wasn't what they said.

She touched her hair and cheek with shaking fingers. She did resemble her mother. The one photograph she had of the woman made it obvious. But no one else in town knew that. She'd never shown that likeness to anyone. Her hand stilled as she realized Jake had seen it.

But he wouldn't say anything, especially if he knew it would harm her. She paced to the hearth and back, wringing her hands. She had to speak to Jake. But Abby said he'd made his purchases and asked her to see them delivered because he was going after the thieves who'd tried to kill him.

She felt a spurt of hope. Maybe he'd catch them and they'd fight and Jake would kill them. Then they couldn't talk anymore about who looked like whom. A second later, Rachel dropped to her knees and prayed for forgiveness for even thinking such a thing. It was evil to wish harm to another just to make your own life easier.

She thought of Hiram, her fiancé, her hope of a future. Why would he take the word of strangers instead of her? Could she marry a man who believed such terrible things of her without even giving her a chance to explain?

She rose as Nathan burst through the door. There had to be a way to protect him from the truth. If she could convince her neighbors the men were lying, or were mistaken, everything would go back to normal. Surely they'd believe her over some strangers just passing through town.

"Ms. Winston is gonna bake cookies tomorrow morning and she said I could come back and have one after school for being a gentleman and walking her all the way home 'cause Hiram never caught up with us like he said he would and I didn't think you'd mind me going to town and back since you were busy talking." Nathan looked up at her, finally pausing for a breath. "When are we going to eat?"

Rachel's mood improved considerably. He could always make her smile. "Soon, little brother. Help me put away the supplies Ranger McCain sent us and then I'll fix us something."

"All right." Nathan picked up a sack of beans and headed for the makeshift pantry they'd created from three old packing crates. The bag hit the wood with a thud. "Why did he send us all this? I thought we were supposed to help others and not expect to be paid."

Rachel followed him with the sugar and salt. "We didn't expect it. I suppose the Ranger felt beholden to us, so he bought food to replace what we'd shared."

"He did eat a lot," the boy mused, "but not this much."

"Mr. McCain is a generous man. We'll have to be sure and thank him."

Nathan's eyes lit with excitement. "Is he coming back?"

She thought of Jake seeing her mother's picture. "I hope so. But if he doesn't, we can write to him and send the letter to his mother in Abilene. She'll see he gets it."

"Yeah, but I'll bet he comes back. He has to take those bad men to be hanged, if he doesn't kill them first, of course."

That snapped Rachel from her daydream. "Nathan Hudson—" She bit off the lecture she'd been about to deliver. She could hardly scold him when she'd been thinking much the same things. "Set the table and wash your hands. I'm hungry."

The next morning dawned bright and clear. The air blowing off the mountain was cold, but the brilliant blue sky made it easy to ignore the temperature. Carrying a small stack of corrected lesson books, Rachel picked her way along the muddy path to the schoolhouse while Nathan raced ahead to meet his friends.

She smiled at his back. He looked very proper and respectable in his woolen coat and matching hat. She knew it wasn't the latest fashion, but it was clean. He'd grumbled for fifteen minutes about having to wear a coat and hat to go to school, but he'd finally given in when she'd threatened to deny him a visit to Abby's for cookies.

She checked the pins in her own hat to be sure they were secure. The dark gray wool hat had belonged to Albert Jackson's wife. He'd insisted Rachel take it as well as the matching cloak she wore. It was his way of thanking her for caring for his children during the last difficult days of his wife's illness.

The hat had been covered with dove gray lace and matching feathers when she received it. She'd carefully removed all the decoration and packed it away. She left only the small black satin ribbon that fluttered in the light breeze. A proper woman didn't flaunt herself with lace and finery. There were times when she was tempted to put just a little something on her hat, or maybe make a dress of bright yellow muslin. But that wouldn't be acceptable and she had to show everyone she could be a good wife to Hiram.

The school, actually a tiny church, was situated on the far side of town. She only needed a table for the four or five children who attended and that fit comfortably in the front of the sanctuary, near the small stove they used for heat.

Her mind wandered as Nathan lit the fire. She hoped there would be enough firewood to hold them for the morning. After the children practiced their letters, she would hold a spelling contest as promised, then send them into the sunshine to play. She'd finished the small gifts for the winners last night after Nathan went to bed. It had taken most of the night. She stretched her tired shoulders. As a reward, to herself as much as the children, they would all be released a little early.

By the time she'd dusted the desk, Nathan had the fire started. "You're getting very good at that," she praised. "Don't put too many logs on. It won't be a long morning."

"Yippee!" Nathan tossed his hat in the air and caught it before it struck the sanded wood floor. "Wait until I tell Matthew."

"You can tell him when he arrives. I need your help getting ready, please."

They worked quickly setting the room to rights. It took a little longer than usual, but, when all stood ready, none of the children had arrived. Rachel paced to the door and back, worry and dread building.

"Where is everyone?" Nathan spun a slate around on the table.

"I'm sure they'll be here. We're just a little early, that's all."

Nathan poked at the fire and then ran to the door to look for his best friend.

"Would you please sit down and work on your spelling?"

Nathan stared at her, confusion obvious in his face. "What did I do?"

Guilt swept away her anger. "Nothing, Nathan. I'm sorry. I had no reason to scold you. I'm just worried, that's all."

"About the others?"

She grasped on to the safe explanation. "Yes. I'm worried about the children."

"I'll go see if Matthew is sick."

"No!" The single word echoed in the high-ceilinged room. "I mean, you promised to stop and see Ms. Winston, didn't you? Since it looks like everyone thought school was cancelled for today, we'll put out the fire and gather our things. Perhaps the cookies will be out of the oven by the time we get there."

"Fine." He shuffled across the room to tend the stove while she put away the slates and books. When she couldn't find another reason to delay, they left, closing the door behind them. She fancied the thud of wood against wood sounded very final and she shook from more than the cold air.

The walk through town wasn't far, but it felt like a hundred miles. She wasn't in any hurry to meet up with her neighbors, but needn't have worried. There was no one on the street. Where was everyone? Surely the whole town hadn't decided to stay inside and avoid her? They couldn't believe what those strangers had said about her. But what other explanation was there?

"Sis? Sis!"

Nathan's voice snapped the endless circle of her thoughts. "What is it?"

"We're here."

"I see that. And I smell baking cookies. Let's go around back so Ms. Winston doesn't have to bother letting us in." She shifted the books she carried, got a better grip on her shawl, and lifted her skirt clear of the mud. The dress had belonged to the preacher's wife and was a little short on her, but she didn't want to get it too dirty.

"Come in," Abby shouted at Nathan's enthusiastic knock. "Well, hello there. Come for your salary, have you?"

"Yes, ma'am, and it sure smells good in here."

Rachel cleared her throat, drawing Nathan's attention. "Remove your hat," she mouthed, fighting a grin when he whipped it off his head and snagged a coat hook with the brim.

"Will you sit and talk awhile, Rachel?"

She smiled her thanks at the older woman. Count on Abby to pretend everything was just the same as always. But it wasn't. Her stomach twisted.

"Did you finish your chores, young man?"

"Um-hmm," Nathan nodded, his mouth full of cookie.

"Good. Good." Abby patted his shoulder. "You can take one or two of those to Matthew Parker, if you've a mind to share."

Nathan scraped cookie crumbs from his mouth with the back of one hand and looked to Rachel for permission. "Can I go see why Matthew wasn't in school today?"

"May I," she corrected. She wanted to say no, to keep him close by, but it was ridiculous to worry. "Yes, you may, but thank Ms. Winston first. And don't stay too long. I'll see you back at home."

Abby wrapped up four more cookies. "Two for you and two for Matthew," she admonished him. Then she ruffled his hair and plopped his hat on his head. "You come back and see me soon, now. Don't wait until you smell the baking."

"Thank you," he managed around the cookie and shot out the door, jumped past the three steps, and hit the ground running.

"Doubt there'll be more than crumbs left by the time he gets there." Abby laughed as she closed the door. "Sit down, girl, before you fall down." She settled across from Rachel.

"Tell me what's wrong." She held up one weathered hand at Rachel's protest. "Don't bother to deny it. It's plain as day on your pretty face."

"No one came to school this morning." Rachel wasn't sure how she'd managed to push the words past the lump in her throat.

"I was afraid of that. Fools."

That one word was balm to Rachel's soul. At least someone was on her side. "Why, Abby? Why would they trust the word of some strangers over mine? Even Hiram believed them. We've lived here for more than two years. I've never done anything to give them cause to act this way."

"Honey, these people don't trust their own mothers. It's the gold fever. Makes them think everyone's out to steal something. Folks with the fever won't risk letting anyone get too close and they're happy to believe the worst about everyone."

Rachel stared at her hands. "So it doesn't matter what I do, they've already made up their minds?"

Abby took both Rachel's hands in her own. "You just keep being you, honey. They'll come around."

She stood to pull on her cloak. "I need to be getting along, Abby. Nathan will be home soon."

The older woman walked her to the door and enveloped her in a hug. "No matter what, you'll always be welcome here. You remember that."

Dread turned in Rachel at her words. She nodded her thanks, afraid to open her mouth in case the scream she was holding in escaped.

There were people on the street when she stepped through Abby's gate. Rachel nodded to a student's mother as she passed but received only a scowl in return. *Why wasn't Andrew in school?* She wanted to ask, but lost her nerve, afraid to hear the answer. Caught up in her own thoughts, she didn't see the couple walking toward her until she was almost upon them.

Penelope Parker walked on the arm of a smirking Hiram Miller as they strolled down the sidewalk. Hiram spoke as they neared, loud enough for everyone in town to hear, it seemed.

"Hello, Rachel."

She stiffened at his use of her Christian name. He never addressed her as anything but Miss Hudson in public, believing it was too forward, too familiar a practice to be shared outside the home. Temper sparked alongside dread.

"Miss Parker. Mr. Miller." The formal greetings stuck in her throat.

Penelope, who'd been one of her very first students, lifted her nose an inch and turned her face into Hiram's shoulder, as if the sight of Rachel was distasteful. Hiram patted her arm and turned to Rachel with such a look of loathing that it took all her courage to stand her ground.

"You may be the first to congratulate us, Rachel. Miss Parker has agreed to be my wife."

Rachel felt her world tilt. "Wife?" He was supposed to ask her to marry him, not Penelope Parker. She concentrated on breathing. It wouldn't help to faint at his arrogant feet.

"That's right. We'll marry very soon, perhaps next month." He turned a charming smile on the young woman at his side. "You'll be a lovely April bride, my dear."

Penelope smiled and preened at the compliment. "Thank you, Mr. Miller. April is fine. Whatever you think is best."

He graced her with an indulgent smile. "Then it's settled. Come along, Miss Parker."

They walked on, forcing Rachel to step into the muddy street to avoid being knocked down. As they brushed past, Penelope kept her skirt from touching Rachel. The complete snub did what words never could, convincing Rachel her life in Lucinda was over. They had to leave. But where would they go?

Rachel stumbled down the street and out of town, barely

aware when she reached her own porch. How was it possible that a whole town, people she'd counted as friends, could suddenly turn on her and believe the lies of total strangers?

She dragged her cloak off and left it on the floor where it dropped. Who were these strangers who could destroy her life with a few words? She knew no one outside of Lucinda, except for the women who'd helped raise her, and she'd had no contact with them since the night she ran away. She'd never met any of the men who'd visited her mother. She hadn't been allowed near the shack when they were around. And none of them could have seen her, except the one who . . .

Rachel trembled as memories of that horrible night sprang to life in her mind. So much blood, and the screams. She would never forget the screams. Breathing hard, she shoved the images away into a corner of her mind where she could ignore them.

She went through the motions of preparing a meal. Just the smell of food made her nauseous, but Nathan would be hungry. He always was, these days. The knife slipped from her fingers and clattered to the floor. How was she going to feed him if the children didn't return to school? She could still spin yarn, but who would she sell it to? How could she support herself and her brother?

As if thinking of him had conjured him up, she glanced through an open window and saw Nathan coming, dragging his feet, his head hanging. As he neared she saw the mud on his coat and the torn knee of his trousers. She hurried out to meet him.

"Nathan Joseph, what on earth happened to you?"

"Nothin'" he mumbled into his coat collar, still trudging toward the cabin.

"Weren't you going to see Matthew?"

No response.

"Have you been fighting?"

Nathan stopped and stared into the distance. Her heart nearly broke at the hurt and confusion she saw in them.

"Matthew said . . ." His voice broke and she heard him sniff away tears before he continued. "He said his sister is going to marry Hiram Miller. I thought he was gonna marry you."

She couldn't breathe. She already knew it, had seen them together, but it hurt so much to hear it spoken aloud.

Nathan swiped at his nose with his coat sleeve. "And Matthew said his pa told him he couldn't have nothin' to do with me no more." His voice broke on a sob. "'Cause you ain't really my sister."

"Of course I'm your sister." She folded him in her arms and held on tight. "I am."

His shoulders heaved and she nearly cried with him. All her dreams and plans, gone. She barely heard his next words, but when she managed to decipher them she felt the blood leave her face and wondered that her knees still held her upright.

"He said you're really my ma."

"That's not true!" She held Nathan at arms' length, willing him to believe her.

"Why would Mr. Parker lie?"

"Because he doesn't know any better. I swear before God, Nathan, you're my brother. It's only because we look so much alike that people are confused. If they'd known her, they'd realize we both look like Mama."

Too late she realized what she'd said. Nathan's eyes were huge and round in his battered face. Before she could explain, he jerked away and ran for the cabin. Rachel gave chase, but she wasn't fast enough. By the time she got inside, he had the photograph of their mother in his hands. The wooden box lay open on the table, the rest of its contents scattered close by.

"Who is she?"

She heard the accusation and hurt in his voice. How did you explain to an eight-year-old boy that the people he knew as his parents were only strangers who'd taken them in? She considered keeping the truth from him, but couldn't. He had a right to know.

"Her name was Lillith Haynes. She was our mother."

"No! She can't be. My mama's name was Eleanor Hudson."

"In every way that matters, Mrs. Hudson was your mother. But this is the woman who gave birth to you. To both of us."

Nathan dragged in a sobbing breath. "Where is she?"

Rachel wrapped her arms around him. She'd never wanted to have this discussion. Nothing good could come of it. But she no longer had a choice. "She died about seven years ago."

Nathan was still for a moment, thinking. "When I was a baby." He pushed away from Rachel and stared up at her, brown eyes full of pain. "Does that mean Papa isn't my father, either?"

Rachel flinched from the accusation. "Papa and Mama found us wandering along the trail. They took us in and raised us as their own. We would have died without them."

Nathan's jaw tightened as anger flashed in his young eyes. "Who is my father?"

"Nathan, it doesn't matter. Papa Hudson raised . . ."

"Is my real father dead, too?"

Rachel hesitated, wanting to spare him this truth. "I don't know."

"What was his name? Maybe we can find him."

"I don't know your father's name. Or mine. Mama didn't know, either."

He threw the photograph across the room, breaking the frame against the wall. "Nathan, no," Rachel gasped. "It's the only picture of her we have."

"I don't care," he shouted. "Mr. Parker didn't lie. I am a bastard, just like he said."

Chapter Eight

Nathan raced from the room, throwing the door against the wall with a crash.

"Nathan, wait." Rachel gave chase, but he was too fast. By the time she rounded the cabin, he was almost out of sight, slipping and sliding his way across the muddy ground toward the hills.

"Nathan, please come back. It's getting dark. Nathan!"

He didn't slow when she called. She hesitated, then lifted her skirts and went after him. She'd wandered this path many times since they'd come here, hoping for some peace, but never at dusk and never at a dead run. She looked up to see how far ahead her brother was and tripped on a rock sticking out of the dirt. The hard ground tore at her skin, but she didn't dare look down. There might be blood and she couldn't faint now. Nathan was nowhere in sight. Her heart pounded in fear. He'd never been out alone after dark. And there were so many ways a little boy could get hurt.

Cresting the hill, she stopped and studied the landscape but still couldn't see him. "Nathan!" She called for him over and over. She studied the ground and saw what she hoped were footprints. She followed them a short way until they disappeared in the rocky ground. If they were Nathan's, he was headed toward the abandoned mine.

Terror squeezed her heart. That pile of crumbling rock was so unstable, even the miners wouldn't enter it. After the last time she found Nathan playing at the entrance she'd made him promise never to go inside. But she knew it was his favorite place. Surely he wouldn't . . .

A rumble and a scream bounced off the surrounding hill and froze her in her tracks. "Nathan!"

She raced up the hillside to the entrance of the mine, only to be driven back by a cloud of dust. "Nathan, can you hear me?" She began tearing at the stones blocking the entrance, but couldn't move them. "Nathan, answer me!"

"Sis! Help me. I'm stuck."

"Nathan," she called back, fighting to stay calm. She tried to peer into the mine, but couldn't see anything but dust swirling in the darkness. She needed light if she was going to find him.

She couldn't do this alone. She should go into town and get help, but then Nathan would be left alone in the dark. Besides, would anyone in town help her? How could she make them listen if they wouldn't even talk to her when they passed on the street? Abby. She would make them come.

"Nathan?" Silence. "Nathan, I'm going for help." Still nothing. Panic overwhelmed her, spurring her down the hill at a run, slipping and sliding in the mud and rocks. She raced down the path and turned toward town. In spite of what they thought of her, they would help rescue Nathan. They had to.

Only when her feet left the ground did the sound of an approaching horse and rider penetrate her panicked mind. Screaming and fighting to get free, it took several seconds before she recognized her name being called over and over while gentle hands held her in place.

"Take it easy, pretty girl. I won't hurt you."

"Jake! Oh, thank the Lord, it's you."

"It's been me the whole time. What the hell are you doing, running around out here in the dark?"

"Nathan." She couldn't manage any more as she dragged air into her lungs.

Jake lifted and turned her until she was looking into his face. "What about him?"

"He's trapped," she panted. "Ran away. Into the hills." She dragged in another frantic breath. "He's in the old mine. Collapsed."

Jake's curse gave voice to everything she couldn't express. "Where is the mine?"

Instead of speaking, Rachel grabbed at Griffin's reins and tried to turn the horse.

"Stop it, Rachel." He easily subdued her and took away the reins. "Racing Griffin across rocky ground until he breaks a leg isn't going to help Nathan."

"But my brother . . ."

Jake talked over her. "Can you ride?"

"No," she sobbed.

"Can you walk?"

"Of course!"

"Then go for help. I'll get a lantern and anything I can find that we might need from your cabin. Tell the men to bring their tools and meet me at the mine."

Despite the urgency in his voice, his hands were gentle when he lifted her and set her on her feet. Without another word, he whirled Griffin toward her house. Rachel turned her back and ran for town.

Jake wondered at the Almighty's timing. He never gave up when tracking outlaws, yet he'd done just that today and ended up back in Lucinda when Rachel needed him. While he didn't believe being beaten half to death was in God's plan, he had to be grateful that he knew his way around Rachel's house when he got there. The matches and candle were in their usual place. Except for a few things scattered on the table, everything looked normal. What could have made Nathan run into a hole in the ground that he had to know was dangerous? Then again, he was a boy. He didn't really need a reason.

He grabbed the lantern Rachel kept on a hook just inside the door and checked the oil. Full. *Good girl.* The box of matches went into his coat pocket along with a couple of candle stubs. A search of the lean-to yielded a rusty pick, but nothing else that would help him dig through rock. It was something to start with. The others would bring better tools.

Taking a second lantern he found in the lean-to, he turned toward Griffin, then hesitated. Griffin might get him to the old mine faster, but the going would be tricky on the rocky ground. Deciding not to risk his horse breaking a leg, he hefted the pick and lanterns and set off for the mine at a trot.

He'd seen Rachel come out of the hills, so he knew the general direction. Though he hadn't been to the mine, he knew what to expect: a small, dark hole in the rocks, probably reinforced by rotting timbers. When he found it, a cloud of dust still thickened the air around the entrance.

Jake swallowed hard. He hated small, dark places. He shoved the past away and concentrated on Nathan. The boy probably wasn't very fond of dark places, either, but he was in there, alone, and Jake had to get him out.

He lit one lantern. The flame danced in the wind, then caught. Adjusting it to a low, steady light, he lifted the lamp and looked over the three by four foot opening. A few large rocks held up a wall of smaller ones. Except for a small hole at the top, the cave entrance was blocked. He could pull out one or two of the big stones to make a hole to climb through, but the whole thing might fall and bring down more rocks inside.

"Nathan," he called into the opening. "Son, can you hear me?" He waited a few seconds and tried again. "Nathan?"

"Ranger McCain?"

Jake's knees weakened with unexpected relief. "Hang on, son. I'm going to get you out of there."

"I'm stuck."

Jake paused. "Stuck how? Where?"

"There's a big piece of wood lyin' on my leg. I can't move and it . . . it hurts."

"All right. Tell me about where you are. Can you do that?"

"I only came in to the first corner. Sis doesn't want me to be in here."

"Neither do I," Jake muttered. "How far is that?" He kept his voice even, hoping to reassure the boy.

"About ten feet. Maybe fifteen"

"Does the corner turn to the right or to the left?"

The question was met with silence for a moment. "To the left . . . I think."

Jake cursed under his breath. Of all the times for a bright boy to have forgotten a lesson. "You think about that for a minute and tell me when you're certain. Now, you got a handkerchief in your pocket?"

"Yeah. Sis made me put it there to go to school."

"Good. I need you to tie it across your nose and mouth. I'm going to come in and get you and it might get dusty. If anything moves, or more rocks come down on you, yell out real loud. You hear me?"

"Yes, sir. Ranger McCain?"

"Yeah?"

"I turned to the left. I'm sure of it."

"Good boy. You got your mouth covered?" There was a short pause.

"I do now."

The words were a bit muffled. Jake nodded. "All right then. Here I come."

He studied the rocks for another moment, but no obvious starting point stood out. He set the lantern aside and stripped off his coat. After tying a bandana over his face, he set to work widening the opening.

"Ranger McCain?"

"Just call me Jake." He cursed when he removed two small rocks and six more slid into the mine. "What is it, Nathan?"

"I'm really cold."

"I know. Try not to think about it." He removed another rock, then another, slowly increasing the opening. "Talk to me, son. Tell me how you ended up in the mine in the first place." When he didn't answer, Jake felt a flutter of panic in his belly. "Nathan?"

"I was mad 'cause Mr. Parker said . . ."

"What did he say?"

"He said my sister is really my mother and that I don't have a father, at least not a real one, and that makes me a . . ."

"You don't have to say it, son." Jake cursed the nasty old man who thought it necessary to hurt a boy for no better reason than he could. "What did your sister say?"

"She said she's my sister. But . . ."

Jake removed another five rocks before a bucketful crashed to the ground at his feet. Where the hell was Rachel and the others? They'd know how to get through this mess better than he did. "Go on. I'm listening."

"She told me Mama wasn't really my mother. And Papa wasn't my pa, either. You know that picture she keeps in the box on the mantel? Well, kept in the box. I broke it 'cause I was really mad that Mr. Parker was right."

Jake concentrated on a large rock, wondering if he had to remove it to get inside. "What about the picture?"

"Sis said that lady was my mother, and her mother, too. But she didn't know who my father was."

A bastard, just like him. Another boy left behind. Damn. He made sure to keep his voice even when he replied. "Did the preacher help you while you were growing up?"

"Yeah." A quiver in Nathan's voice betrayed the kid's tears.

"Did he teach you right from wrong, and things like how to put on your boots and which way the buttons went?"

"Yeah."

"Then I'd say he was your father, since that's what fathers do for their sons."

"Really?"

"Really. Now you stay real still. I'm going to move one of these big rocks a little. You tell me if anything happens where you are. Ready?"

"I'm ready, sir. I mean Jake."

Jake lifted the lantern for one more look but he didn't see

another way to proceed. Saying a prayer to whoever was listening, he set the lamp aside, grasped the large stone with both hands and tugged.

For a split second, nothing happened. Then a low rumble came from the mine, followed by Nathan's scream.

Jake dropped the rock as if he'd been burned. "Nathan?" Only an echo came back. "Nathan!"

Panic had Jake halfway into the small hole before he heard the boy call out.

"I'm all right. Some rocks fell from the ceiling but they've stopped now."

He leaned against the wall of the opening and dragged air into his lungs, willing his fear to subside. "I'm glad to hear that, son," he managed around the lump in his throat.

"Jake? I'm scared."

"I know, son. So am I."

"You are? I didn't think anything could scare a Texas Ranger."

Jake studied the hole and decided he'd widened it as much as he could without the whole thing collapsing. He'd have to squeeze through. "Only a fool doesn't get scared. The trick is to do what you have to in spite of it." Jake grabbed a lantern and peered into the mine, squinting past the dust. When a shout came from behind him, he spun around and reached for his gun.

"Don't get all upset, Jake. It's just us," Abby puffed. She moved her bulk with considerable speed, keeping up with Rachel and Hank Gerard. No one else was in sight.

"Are the others coming?"

"They refused to help, because they believe I'm . . ."

"Don't repeat it, Miss Rachel." Hank patted her shoulder.

Abby spit on the ground and uttered a curse that made even Jake flinch. "Damn fools. Not a speck of Christian decency in the lot of them."

Gerard walked closer to the mine entrance and studied it without touching anything. "Tell me what you have done."

"Nathan is about fifteen feet into the mine, with a beam

pinning him down." He ignored Rachel's tiny cry. "I've been pulling out the little rocks trying to widen the opening a little, but when I removed that big one things inside shifted."

"Nathan?" Rachel picked her way to the entrance.

"Is that you, Sis?"

"I'm here. You're going to be all right."

"I know. Jake said he'd get me out."

Rachel turned to him, her blue eyes huge and haunted. He brushed the back of one dusty finger down her cheek, leaving a trail in her tears. "Don't cry, pretty girl. We'll get to him."

He turned to Hank. "I don't see any way but to squeeze through that hole."

"I agree, but I won't fit." He patted his ample girth and shrugged. "Can you get through it?"

Jake looked at the space and thought of the darkness on the other side. "I'll have to." He removed his gun belt and handed it to Abby. "Hold that for me."

"You be careful now."

He made sure the candles and matches were still in his pockets. He was as ready as he would ever be. He paused when Rachel took his arm.

"Please be careful, Jake."

"I'll be fine." He crossed to the opening and called out. "Nathan, I'm coming in to get you. I want you to keep talking to me so I can find you. Can you do that?"

"I think so. What do I talk about?"

"Anything. Tell me about your Pa." He heard Rachel's protest, but he ignored her. "What was the Reverend like?"

Once Nathan got started, Jake listened with half an ear, concentrating on getting through the hole without causing a cave-in.

He reached in with his right arm and felt around for a handhold. Getting his head through the opening in the rocks was easy, but his shoulders wouldn't fit. With Hank at his side, quietly offering instruction and suggestions, Jake inched forward until his left shoulder slipped free. Forcing himself to go slowly, he eased into the mine with Hank pushing from behind. Just when he was about to congratulate himself of getting in, the rocks beneath him shifted.

"Get back!" His shout echoed in the mine and was quickly drowned out by the groan of moving stone. He thought he heard Rachel scream, but it might have been him yelling as the wall collapsed and a river of rock and dust washed him into the mine.

As quickly as it started, the movement stopped and silence descended. Taking stock, Jake moved his head, then his arms. So far everything still worked. He pulled himself forward to free his legs, but other than the sting of a few cuts and scrapes on his back, he didn't think he'd suffered too much damage. A light flashed on the wall in front of him as Hank came through the newly enlarged opening with a lantern.

"Are you all right?"

"Nothing that won't heal." Jake turned toward the depths of the mine. "Nathan?"

"Nathan!"

Rachel's scream bounced off the stone, causing dust to sift from the creaking rafters.

He spun toward her. "What the hell are you doing in here? Get back outside," he ordered. "Abby, get her out of here."

The older woman pulled Rachel back to safety, holding her arm to keep her there. He tried to reassure her. "Rachel, I can't be worrying about you, too. We'll get him out. I give you my word." He turned back to Hank. "Nathan said he was ten or fifteen feet into the mine and one turn to the left."

"That should be no more than five feet from where you are now," the older man observed. He crawled forward through the low tunnel, easing past Jake, until he reached a pile of rocks blocking his path. "He should be just beyond here."

Jake crawled to Hank. "Nathan? Son, can you hear me?" The question was met with a painful silence. He could only imagine the terror Rachel must be feeling. "Gerard, what's the best way to get through this?"

"One rock at a time, my friend."

"I was afraid you were going to say that."

Working together, they shifted part of the pile to one side until they'd made an opening they could see through. Jake held out the lantern and peered through. Just beyond his reach he saw a flash of white that he hoped was Nathan's shirt.

"I see him. He's about five feet farther into the shaft." He moved back and set the lantern to one side.

Hank nodded and moved a few more stones. Finally, there was room for Jake to climb through. Grateful nothing crashed down around him as he made his way to Nathan, he shoved some rocks aside before studying the boy in the lantern light. "He's breathing. Let me see if I can move this stuff off him." Straining with the effort, he lifted the hunk of wood lying across Nathan's right leg and laid it aside. Satisfied he could move the boy without causing more damage, he looked at Hank. "I'm going to hand him out to you. You get him out of here. I'll be right on your heels."

Hank's eyes narrowed. Lifting the lamp, he studied the walls and saw what Jake had already noticed. The remaining beams holding the ceiling bowed under the weight of the rock they held back. The cave was about to collapse in on itself—and anyone still inside.

"Hurry, my friend."

He took the man's words to heart. Ignoring Nathan's moan of pain, Jake scooped the boy out of the rubble and handed him out to Hank. The moment they were out of the way, he squeezed through the opening after them. The mine rumbled and coughed behind him, and rocks bounced off his bootheels. For one agonizing instant he was stuck, but managed to yank loose and drag himself toward the mine entrance. As soon as his legs were free, he jumped to his feet and bolted for the opening.

A deep, sighing moan was his only warning as the mine shaft gave way. The ceiling crashed down beside and behind him and a tidal wave of rock swept him off his feet. All Jake could do was ride along until the rockslide spit him out. When the dust settled, he was on his back, staring at the stars, brilliant in the cold night sky. He gulped in the freezing air and watched his breath puff out in billowing white clouds, thankful to be outside—and alive.

"Well, Ranger McCain" —Hank sat on his heels beside Jake—"you still with us?"

"God, I hate dark places." Jake waited until the world stopped spinning, then pushed to his feet. Hank handed him his gun belt, coat, and hat. "How's Nathan?"

"Out cold. Abby's looking at him, when she can get Rachel out of the way."

Jake strode to where Nathan lay bundled in a blanket. His hands shook, but his touch was gentle when he reached for Rachel. "Come on, honey, you have to let Abby work." He ignored her struggles and pulled her into his arms. "He's going to be all right."

"How do you know?" The panic in her voice stabbed at him.

"Because I promised Nathan I'd get him out of there."

She twisted in his embrace until she could see his face. "And you always keep your word?"

"Always."

Rachel dropped her forehead to his chest. "Thank you for saving him, Jake. I don't know what I would have done if . . ." She glanced at her brother. "He's so young. None of this should have happened to him."

"He's old enough. The world can be a cruel place. You can't protect him from it forever."

"I don't want to protect him forever—just for a little while longer."

Jake smiled and pulled her closer. He could feel the fear shaking through her, but Rachel wouldn't give in. She was so much stronger than she believed. Her hair was as soft as a summer cloud against his cheek when he laid his head over hers. She felt right in his arms, like she belonged.

Rachel shivered. He let her go long enough to unbutton his coat and wrap her inside with him. Without looking away from her brother, she snuggled into the warmth he offered.

Heat shot through Jake and pooled below his belt. He muttered a curse at his unruly body. Never before had a woman gotten to him like this one, slipping up on him and catching him unaware. He shifted slightly so she wouldn't come up against the proof of his reaction. Desire pounded in his head with every heartbeat. He tried to will it away, but Rachel's scent filled him with every breath he took.

He couldn't stop his mind from circling back to the accusations made about her. What if Nathan really was her son? Not that Jake cared one way or the other. He'd never blame the boy for something he'd had no control over. But if Rachel had a child, she'd already been introduced to the ways of man and woman. He'd never take a virgin to his bed. There were responsibilities that came with that gift and he had no room for them in his life. But an experienced woman? It had been far too long. His body tightened even more at the thought of caressing her satin skin and slipping into her heat.

"That's all I can do out here." Abby's voice jolted him back to the present. "We need to get him inside where it's warm and I can see better."

Rachel pulled free of Jake to kneel beside her brother. "Nathan, can you hear me?"

Nathan's soft moan was barely audible, but it was a wonderful sound to the adults gathered around. His eyelashes lifted long enough to let Rachel know he'd heard.

"We're going to carry you home now. You just hang on a little while longer."

"But, Sis . . ."

"No, don't talk."

He took her hand and she smiled for the first time in hours. Relief made her a little dizzy. Jake stepped forward to pick him up, but Nathan wouldn't let go of her hand. He tightened his grip until she looked down. He pushed some kind of rock into her hand just as Jake draped his coat over her shoulders. Taking it, she moved so Jake could lift Nathan off the cold ground. As Abby tucked a blanket around him, Rachel grabbed up one of the lanterns to light the path home.

She fell into step behind Jake, clutching the rock Nathan had given her. Pretending to hold Jake's coat tighter around her throat, she brought Nathan's gift close to her face. She stumbled in shock. Hank rushed to her side.

"Be careful, Miss Rachel." He took the lantern and slid a hand beneath her elbow to steady her. "You've had a difficult evening."

"I'm fine. But I appreciate your concern." She hid the stone from sight and tried to concentrate on walking. She could hardly believe what she'd seen. In the bouncing lamplight she could just make out the crystal structure of a chunk of quartz—and the shiny flecks buried within.

Her brother had found gold.

Chapter Nine

It felt like hours before the cabin came into sight. Rachel hurried ahead. "I'll light the candles and start the fire. It needs to be warm for Nathan."

"I will accompany you, Miss Rachel." Hank took her elbow and lifted the lantern to light the path. "Ranger McCain will get him back faster without us to get in his way."

Jake would have smiled at the skillful way Hank maneuvered to be with Rachel if he wasn't so busy fighting off a wave of jealousy. His instant possessive reaction left him stunned. He had no claim on her. So why did he want to pound Hank Gerard into the rocky ground under his feet?

"How's he doing?" Abby's voice broke into his musing.

"I don't know. He hasn't made a sound since we left the mine. He didn't even complain when I stumbled over that half buried rock back there." The boy was wrapped up tight in a heavy wool blanket, but Jake could feel him shivering. "We've got to get him warm. I just hope I'm not making things worse by carrying him around like this."

"No choice. We couldn't leave him lying on the ground."

Jake was as happy to see the little house as he had been the night of the storm. Abby opened the door and he strode straight to the hearth, where a fire cheerily chewed its way through a stack of logs. Hank and Rachel struggled to carry the mattress out of Rachel's bedroom and he bit back a laugh. "Maybe you should leave that by the fire. It seems to spend more time here than where it belongs."

Rachel grunted. Jake considered handing Nathan to Abby so he could help, but the woman couldn't hold him. The boy was heavier than Jake expected. "Rachel and Nathan dragged the mattress out here for me the night I passed out on the porch," Jake explained to Abby as she filled the coffeepot and two pans with water and set them on the stove to heat.

Dropping her end of the mattress near the fire, Rachel hurried to her brother. "Nathan, honey, can you hear me?"

"Hurts," he whispered.

That single word was the sweetest sound Jake had ever heard. "I'm sorry for that, son. I'm not exactly dainty on my feet." With Hank's help, he lowered Nathan to the mattress. The boy's groan of pain burned in Jake's gut. He helped get his coat and boots off, but after that, Jake could do nothing but watch as Rachel and Abby checked the boy for injury.

Helpless frustration swamped him, rooting him to the spot. Hank said something about checking on the animals, but Jake didn't respond. He couldn't force words past the lump blocking his throat. At some point, Nathan came to enough to answer the women's questions. Finally, Abby seemed satisfied she'd done all she could.

"Rest now, young man. You'll be right as rain in a few days."

When Abby started to rise, Jake stepped forward to help her. Rachel stayed at Nathan's side, talking softly. He couldn't hear the words, but he was glad to see the smile that eased the lines of worry on her face.

"How is he?" Jake rummaged around until he found the coffee beans and grinder.

"He's got quite a lump on the back of his head and he'll have a bruise from his thigh to his toes, but nothing is broken. He'll mend."

Jake felt almost light-headed with relief.

"You need a bit of tending, too."

Jake tried to shrug off Abby's probing fingers, but she

kept poking. When she found a tender spot, he protested. "That hurts."

She grinned at him. "All boys are the same. They just grow taller. Sit down." She shoved him toward the table and went for more water and a clean cloth.

Her hands were gentle as she cleaned his abraded face and neck. "You've got a soft touch, Abby."

"Flatterer," she responded with a giggle.

She'd never see the low side of forty again, but she sounded like a young girl at that moment. The salve stung as she rubbed it on the worst of his cuts, but he ignored her ministrations until she started unbuttoning his shirt. "What are you doing?"

"There's more to tend to on your shoulder and back, if that blood is any indication."

"Blood?" Rachel's hands stilled.

"It ain't too bad," Abby reassured her. "Just some scrapes and scratches I need to clean up."

"Oh. Good. I'm glad." She resumed tucking blankets around a sleeping Nathan.

"Ouch. Dammit woman, that stings."

Rachel spun around at Jake's curse, then couldn't look away. He sat at her kitchen table, naked to the waist. A strange feeling tightening her stomach as the muscles in his back rippled in the firelight when he flinched from Abby's ministrations. For an instant, she swore she felt the sting on her own skin. She reached out to touch his bronzed skin but when she came to herself, snatched her hand back and turned away.

What was the matter with her? Swallowing hard, she tried to concentrate on her brother. Memories of the night Jake stumbled into her life flooded back. Instead of Nathan, she saw Jake lying naked on her floor, remembered what his skin felt like beneath her hands as she tried to still his shivering. She recalled the instant when she realized he was awake and very much aware of her stretched along his length. Her breath shortened. Heat flooded her and the very center of her being strained to touch him.

Careful not to disturb Nathan, she rose to her feet. She couldn't resist the need.

Jake tensed when she laid cool fingers on his shoulder. "Is there anything I can do to help?" She kept her voice low so she didn't wake her brother.

"How's Nathan?"

"He's resting." She glanced back. "I'm waiting for him to wake up again so I can yell at him for going into that cave in the first place."

"If he has any idea what you're planning, he might sleep straight through to next week."

Rachel gave Jake a stern look, one her students knew meant she didn't find their antics humorous, but his teasing grin was contagious. Giving up, she agreed. "I don't know that I would blame him if he did. Why would he go into that old mine? He knows it's dangerous."

Abby poured water into the washbowl and reached for the lye soap. "Knowing you shouldn't do something never stopped any boy I know of." With efficient motions, she washed out the bloody rags she'd used on Jake, then scrubbed her hands.

The door opened and Hank blew in with the cold wind. "The animals are settled for the night. How's our little prospector?"

"I'm fine."

All four adults turned at the sound of Nathan's voice. Rachel sank to her knees beside him. "You should be sleeping."

"I'm sorry, Sis."

"I know that."

"I didn't mean to go in so far, but I was really mad about . . ." He hesitated, glancing at the others in the room.

"We'll discuss it when you're feeling better."

"How many fingers am I holding up?" Abby stood by Nathan's feet and held up her right hand where he could see it.

"Three. Why?"

The older woman's face split wide open on a grin. "Sassy.

That's a real good sign. You're going to be fine." Abby turned to Jake and Hank. "We ought to be going. They both need rest."

"I'm staying." Jake crossed his arms over his wide chest.

Rachel started to protest, but couldn't force the words out. She was so relieved that he would be nearby, she felt almost faint.

Abby didn't have any problem speaking up, however. "I'm not sure how the folks in town will feel about that."

"I don't really care. But it isn't only my decision." Jake turned to Rachel. "If you want me to go, I will."

She considered sending him away, but she couldn't say the words. She wanted him here, no matter what the citizens of Lucinda would think. "I would be obliged if you would stay with me." Belatedly, she realized how that must have sounded to Abby and Hank. "With Nathan, I mean. I don't think I can manage him on my own just yet. Abby, you could stay, too."

"No, these old bones need their rest." Abby let Hank help her with her cloak. "You'll do fine with Jake. And Lucinda Miller can just screech and croak all she wants. Not too much more she can do to you now, anyway."

Rachel felt sick to her stomach. Abby was right. The people in this town had made up their minds and nothing she could do would change that.

Abby hugged Rachel close, giving her a few last instructions about Nathan before Hank escorted Abby toward town. Jake barred the door for the night.

Nathan drifted into a restless sleep thanks to the small amount of laudanum Abby had given him. Blankets surrounded his injured leg to keep him from moving too much. When Rachel straightened from tucking him in, Jake was there with a glass of whiskey. He pulled the rocking chair close to the stove. Urging her into the chair, he stood over her as she sipped the fiery liquid and dissolved into a fit of coughing.

"At least there's some color in your cheeks now."

She gasped for breath. "I thought this stuff made you feel better."

"Only after it makes you feel worse. Try a little more."

Her second sip wasn't as bad, and by the third warmth spread through her.

"Feeling better?"

"I think I'm beginning to."

"Good." He sat on his heels in front of her. "Now tell me what the hell Abby meant."

Tears filled her eyes before she could stop them. "None of the children came to school this morning." Her breath caught and a sob escaped. Jake wiped away each tear as it spilled onto her cheeks. It felt good to cry, to have someone to share her fears with. After a halting start, her story poured out.

"They think I'm like my mother, but I'm not."

"Do they know your mother?"

"How could they? She died in El Paso years ago."

"Then why do they think you favor her?"

"I look like her. We both do." She glanced toward Nathan. "But that isn't what I mean."

Jake lifted her from the rocker, took her place and settled her into his lap. Rachel stiffened. He snagged a blanket and wrapped her in it, tucking it between them. Her breath backed up as he skimmed past her hips to her knees, but he didn't stop until she sat cocooned in soft wool. For a moment, she tried to hold herself away from him, but he wrapped one arm around her and coaxed her head onto his shoulder. He was so warm. Her objections melted away and she leaned into him.

"Now start from the beginning."

"I . . . I don't remember all of it. I come from El Paso. My mother was a . . ." Rachel took a deep breath and hurried through the words. "A soiled dove, a . . ."

"I understand."

She looked away as the painful memory of discovering how her mother supported them returned. "Mama never told me who my father is. We lived in a tiny, one-room shack that was falling down around us, at the very end of Utah Street, where lots of women like Mama lived."

Jake nodded. "I know the area."

Rachel looked into Jake's eyes, expecting pity or disgust, but all she saw was him. His calm acceptance of her story gave her the courage to continue.

"The other ladies helped care for me at night, taking turns when they finished with clients. Since they all worked earlier, Mama had to take care of me until late at night. That meant she got all the drunks, the mean ones who none of the other ladies would allow near."

Jake squeezed her should in sympathy. "That's no way to live."

"Maybe not," Rachel agreed. "But it was all I knew. I wasn't unhappy. I had lots of surrogate mothers who spoiled me terribly. It was normal, at least to me, and everything was fine until . . ."

"One of the men was too mean."

She nodded and bit back another sob. "Mama had given birth to Nathan not two weeks before. Some of the women told her it was too soon to go back to work, but we needed to eat. I offered to find a job, but she didn't want me to go anywhere alone. I didn't understand why, so one morning, while she was still sleeping, I slipped away. I made it to the business district without too much difficulty, but no one would hire a girl with no experience or references.

"I remember being very tired from walking all day. It was almost dark when I got home. Mama saw me coming and I could tell she was upset. I was so close I could almost smell the powder she'd used on my baby brother."

She shook with remembered fear and Jake convinced her to drink another sip of whiskey.

"I expected her to be angry, but she looked frightened. Then this huge hand grabbed me from behind. I was so terrified I couldn't even fight. I don't recall much of what happened. I remember he wore a big ring that dug into my ribs." Her fingers rubbed at the remembered pain. "And his hair, his long blond hair." Her voiced shook as the memories took over. "It got in my nose and my mouth when he dragged me against his body."

Jake stiffened, but he didn't interrupt.

"Mama flew at him, hitting and scratching him in the face until he let me go. She screamed at me to get away, to take Nathan and run, so I did. I ran and ran, out into the desert behind our house. I hid in the rocks, holding Nathan and trying to block out my mother's screams. I h-heard the gunshot. The one that killed her. I'll never forget that sound or the silence that followed it." She swallowed the sick feeling in her throat. "I hate guns."

Rachel was grateful for Jake's presence. Some of the memories were too horrible to relive alone.

"By the time I came back, they'd taken Mama's body away. He killed her because I ran."

He brushed at the tears running down her face. "Shhh, pretty girl. It wasn't your fault. You couldn't have stopped him even if you'd stayed."

She dragged in a shuddering breath. "There was so much blood. On the floor, on the bed, splattered everywhere. She fought hard to live. But he was too strong."

Jake held Rachel while she sobbed out her fear and guilt, all the grief of a long ago night. He murmured words of comfort, rocking back and forth until she could pick up the story again.

"I didn't know where to go. I couldn't stay because the man Mama worked for put another girl in the shack before the paint they'd used to cover the blood was dry. So I took what I could carry, the pittance Mama had saved, and Nathan and I left El Paso for good."

Jake kissed her on the forehead, comforting her. "You must have been scared, being alone and nearly broke, with an infant. Where did you go?"

"I had precious few skills. I signed on to help a family on a wagon train going north to Colorado, but a few days out Mrs. Mahoney decided she didn't like the way I made coffee. When a traveling missionary couple happened by, I hired on with them."

"The preacher?"

She nodded. "The Right Reverend Matthias Hudson and his dutiful wife, Eleanor. They didn't have children. Eleanor desperately wanted a baby and Nathan seemed like a gift from heaven. I was . . . I was an additional laborer in the fight to save souls in the untamed west."

She twisted her hands in her lap, not sure how much more she wanted to tell him. Jake stilled her nervous movements with his own hand.

"It must have been hard for you."

Rachel shook her head, wanting him to understand. "It wasn't all bad, really. I learned to read and write. We usually had enough to eat and the people we met along the way took us in if the weather turned too bad."

"Did they mistreat you and Nathan?"

"No. Reverend Hudson didn't spare the rod if he felt we deserved it, but, no, we weren't mistreated."

"He whipped you?"

Rachel looked up, surprised at the anger in his voice. "If I'd done something to warrant punishment, yes."

"I can't abide a man who strikes a woman, no matter the reason." Jake stared into her eyes for a long, silent moment. "Besides, I can't imagine you doing anything wrong."

Her laughter hummed between them, bringing her alive everywhere their bodies touched.

"I wasn't a saint, if that's what you mean. But I was careful not to cause too much trouble. I didn't want them to take away my brother."

"They wouldn't have done that."

"I was never certain. I didn't feel welcome, that I was truly a part of their family, like . . ."

"Like Nathan," he finished for her.

Jake brushed his cheek on her hair and kissed her forehead again. Rachel shifted in his lap and felt his body harden. She froze, not sure what to do. Jake decided for her. He reached up and removed the pins that held her hair in place, dropping them one by one to the floor. She looked up, intending to tell him to stop, but the utter concentration in his eyes stopped her. No one had ever looked at her like that. Still, what they were doing was wrong.

"Jake . . ."

He hushed her protest with a finger on her lips. When the last pin was out, he raked his fingers through the heavy mass igniting tiny flames of pleasure along her skin.

What was he doing to her? She felt things she didn't know were possible. Rachel knew she should resist, but he kept smoothing the length of her hair, urging her closer to his warmth. Giving in to the unfamiliar need burning through her she leaned into him. She'd wanted to kiss him since the moment she'd looked at him, stretched out on her floor. Throwing years of teaching to the wind, she snuggled into his arms and met his lips with her own.

Jake could barely control the heat that raced through his blood. Her response to every kiss, every touch, wasn't that of an inexperienced girl. She showed the passion of one who knew what happened between a man and woman. Logic burned away in the fire she started, concern about brother or son went up in smoke. There was only Rachel.

Jake wrapped his hand around the back of her neck, warming and caressing her at the same time. When she pressed against the touch, he bent his head and traced the edge of one ear with his tongue, nipping at the lobe when he got there. Her gasp of surprise was quickly smothered beneath his mouth. Coaxing her with kisses, he never gave her a chance to resist.

Using all his experience, he drew her to the edge with him, until she was as caught up in the needing as he was. When he finally lifted his head, her eyes held a dazed look that filled him with satisfaction and more than a little pride.

"What . . . ?"

He stopped her question with another kiss. Desperate to feel her skin, he rose from the chair with her in his arms. He only paused long enough to snag a candle before he carried her upstairs to the little attic room.

"Nathan . . ."

"He's fine." Jake covered her lips with his own, nipping at the corners until she stopped trying to talk. He set the candle on the floor at the top of the stairs but didn't stop. Ducking to avoid the low ceiling, he crossed the small space and lowered Rachel to the mattress near the chimney, following her down. A groan rumbled from deep in his chest when he felt her stretched out beneath him. He couldn't remember ever needing this much. Returning to her mouth, his tongue resumed the dance with hers until they were both breathless.

"What are you doing to me? I feel . . ."

"That's right, pretty girl. Just feel. Feel how much I want you." He rolled over her, letting his hips settle into the cradle of hers. The fit was perfect, better than ever before. Searching for more of her to taste, Jake unwrapped the blanket from her body and drew the hem of her gown up, inch by inch. Rachel grabbed at his hands, breaking the spell. He bit back his protest. Experienced or not, the choice was hers.

He started to roll away, but she stopped him with a touch. Then she began exploring, her fingers everywhere she could reach. Her fire fed his own until nothing mattered but the heat.

She twisted beneath him, tying herself up in the folds of her dress. Jake rose on one elbow to get at the buttons that ran the length of her bodice. She took advantage of the space between them to smooth her hands across his chest. When she brushed a nipple, he groaned again.

He stopped working on her dress long enough to yank off his shirt. When her cool fingers touched his skin, his breath backed up. Desperate now to feel her, he made short work of her buttons. When the last one opened, he shoved the fabric aside and pressed her into the mattress, bare skin to bare skin. Whatever breath he had left was stolen away.

Jake captured her mouth again, tasting her soft moan, thrusting his tongue between her teeth. She caught on to the motion quickly, and the imitation of things to come nearly undid him. He lifted her off the bed enough to slip the dress off her shoulders.

For a long moment he only stared at her, drinking in her

beauty in the flickering candlelight, but she resumed her tentative explorations and sent his mind up in smoke. He ran his tongue from her jaw to her breast, relishing her reaction when she surged against him. He took advantage, nipping and suckling one nipple while he pushed her dress past the curve of her hips and off her legs. Her petticoats quickly followed.

At last nothing separated them but his trousers and Jake dispatched that barrier with ease. Her eyes widened. Even in the flickering light, he could see her uncertainty. Capturing her lips again, he drew her back into the magic, took her higher. When she began moving with him, pressing into his touch, he shifted and settled over her, easing one knee between hers. Holding her close, he took a ragged breath, trying to slow down. She felt—He couldn't find the words, even in the silence of his own mind.

"Jake?"

"I'm right here, honey."

"What do I . . . I don't know how . . . I need . . ."

Her words faded into a breathy moan as he found her nipple with his tongue. His hands stroked her from shoulder to knee, each time coming closer to her center. The first time he brushed the curls at the apex of her thighs, she jumped like she'd been burned. He nipped at the spot where her neck met her shoulder and the sound she made brought a smile to his lips.

Rachel's desperate movements brought him to a fever pitch. He couldn't resist any longer. He moved between her legs and she shifted to make room, welcoming him. Her heat surrounded him, beckoning him forward. He joined with her in one smooth stroke.

With his lips fused to hers, he tasted her scream of pain. He held himself perfectly still. Disbelief warred with raging need. It wasn't possible. She couldn't be . . . have been . . .

Her moan brought him to his senses. It didn't matter now. The deed was done. Keeping himself under tight control, he turned his attention to Rachel. He couldn't give her back what he'd taken, but he could get her past the pain and show her the joy that was possible in what they shared.

He didn't release her mouth, unwilling to hear her tell him to stop. Until this moment, he didn't know he possessed a streak of cowardice. Hoping he could make it up to her somehow, his tongue began stroking in time with his hands as he searched for all the places that brought her pleasure. It seemed like an eternity passed before she began to move with him again. Only then did he loose a bit of the control he held on his own body.

When he shifted inside her, she gasped, but not from pain. Her body tightened around him, drawing him in. He released her lips long enough to kiss away her tears and whisper soft words of reassurance and encouragement.

"That's it, honey. Wrap those beautiful legs around me. Let me show you how it should be."

When she did as he asked, his control slipped a little further. He couldn't believe how well they fit, as if they'd been made for each other.

"Jake?"

"Hold on, darlin', and let me give you the sun."

He moved faster, lifting her with him until neither was aware of who or where they were. With one last stroke he flung himself into thin air, with Rachel right behind him.

Chapter Ten

Rachel understood why birds loved to fly. She floated on the cloud of pleasure Jake had made, unwilling to land. She wanted to soar like this forever, but reality intruded and the landing was painful.

He'd believed them. After all she'd told him, Jake had still believed the lies about her. The shocked look on his face, the disbelief . . . She closed her eyes against the pain. It was so wonderful, felt so right, that she'd followed willingly where he led. *Fool!*

Jake shifted to one side and gathered her close, pulling a blanket over them. She wanted to hold on to the beauty he'd given her, but it was fading, being washed away by tears she couldn't hold back.

"Shh, honey, don't cry. I'm—"

"Don't! Don't you dare say you're sorry." She whispered when she really wanted to scream. She needed to get away, outside, where she could rail against the world and no one would hear. But Jake wouldn't let go. She shoved at his hands, but he only held on tighter.

"I was only going to apologize for hurting you."

"You didn't. Only a little. Now let me go."

"Are you all right?"

She surprised herself by laughing. It wasn't a pleasant

sound, but it wasn't the sob she felt clogging her throat. Jake laid his forehead against hers. His breath teased her lips. She could feel the cold track of tears on her cheek. "You believed what they said."

"That's not true."

She wanted to believe the hurt in his eyes was more than sympathy.

"The look on your face when you discovered Nathan really is my brother said you did."

"I never thought you were a prostitute, just not inexperienced."

"It doesn't matter now, though, does it?"

"Don't." His voice went flat and dangerous.

Rachel held very still, waiting for him to continue.

"Don't turn what we shared into something dirty."

"What you gave me was beautiful, but it doesn't change the fact that now I'm exactly what they said I was."

His arms tightened and he kissed away a tear. She struggled to be free, but he pulled her closer, breathed a kiss into her palm and laid her hand over his heart. The steady rhythm somehow comforted her.

"You are not a prostitute. A working girl takes money for what she does."

She glanced up at him. "In the eyes of this town, all that food you had delivered was the same."

"I was only replacing what I'd eaten," he protested. "You didn't have much to spare as it was."

"It doesn't matter. Not to them."

He smoothed a hand through her hair. "Then why did you let me stay tonight?"

Rachel looked away and watched the flame on the candle dance. "Because . . ." She hesitated, not sure she wanted to admit the reason out loud. But Jake deserved an answer. She was as much responsible for her predicament as he. "I didn't want to be alone. And I . . . I wanted to be with you."

Jake turned her face toward him with a gentle hand on

her cheek. "I hoped that was the case, 'cause I wanted the same thing."

"But you can't. I mean, we mustn't . . ." She drew in a breath and released it on a huff. "What will I do now? They'll never let me teach here again. I can't spin enough yarn to support myself and Nathan, even if they would purchase it. And I won't take any more of your charity."

"It isn't charity to let a man pay his way."

Rachel shoved him away and rose before remembering she was naked. She turned her back and grabbed her drawers from the pile of clothing near the stairs. She had one foot in before she saw blood on her legs. Without warning the room tilted.

She knew she was going to fall, but she couldn't stop herself. She barely heard Jake's curse through the buzzing in her ears. She tried to step back, but got tangled in the cotton around her ankles. Only Jake's arm around her waist saved her from a tumble that would probably have broken her neck.

"Easy, pretty girl. I've got you."

She registered the warmth of Jake's skin a second before he laid her on the bed and covered her with blankets.

"Jake?"

"Hush. Just take deep breaths, honey. That's it. Take another one. Good girl."

Finally the buzzing subsided and Rachel opened her eyes. Jake's worried face hovered close to hers and his big hand stroked her hair. "Hello, Ranger McCain. Did you know I can't stand the sight of blood?" She tried to smile at her little joke as the darkness sucked her under.

Jake nearly panicked when Rachel's eyes rolled back in her head. "Honey? Rachel!" He wanted to shout at her, but it wouldn't help matters if he woke Nathan and he found them together, naked. With an effort, he swallowed his fear and made sure she was still breathing. The warm column of air against his fingers made him dizzy with relief. He started to his feet, but hesitated, uncertain if he should leave her alone. She needed water, and maybe some whiskey, and he had to clean her up before she awoke, or she'd just pass out all over again.

Slipping on his pants, he padded downstairs, careful not to wake Nathan. The boy was rolled on his side with his back to the room. Jake paused long enough to check for fever and tuck the blankets around him. A strange feeling of tenderness rose in him. He was coming to care for this boy, and for the woman who'd raised him. What was he going to do when the time came to leave? He'd never felt tied to anyone other than the woman who'd raised him. For the first time in his life, he wasn't sure how he was going to say good-bye.

Jake added a log to the fire and poked at it until it flared and the wood caught. He was glad to find the bucket on the hearth was half full of water. It wasn't hot, but it wasn't cold either. He tucked several clean cloths under his arm, filled a glass from the bucket of cold water by the sink and turned to carry everything upstairs.

Rachel was awake and watching for him as he climbed into the attic. The lamplight glinted in her eyes, making them look like hammered gold instead of the amazing blue he knew them to be. He crossed to her. "I was hoping you'd still be . . ."

"Unconscious?"

"Resting," he corrected. When he reached for the blankets to uncover her, she stopped him.

"I can manage."

"Sorry, but I don't want you fainting on me again." He slipped an arm under her shoulders and lifted her from the pillow as he pressed the glass of water to her lips. "Drink." After she complied, he eased her back to the mattress.

"Now just lie back and let me take care of you." Ignoring her protests, he wet a cloth in the warm water and began cleaning the blood from her skin. He kept his touch as gentle as possible, but every sound she made reminded him how big and rough his hands were. He gritted his teeth and finished as quickly as he could. "I'm done. I won't hurt you anymore."

"You didn't hurt me."

Jake dared to look at her face and the desire he saw there stunned him. When she reached for him, he went willingly.

"This is how I want to wake up every morning, wrapped in your arms." Jake shifted and she snuggled closer. "I can't wait to see our children."

"There won't be any."

"What?"

He brushed calloused fingers along her jaw, evading her lips when she tried to kiss them. "There will never be a family. I won't marry you. I can't."

For a second she couldn't breathe. "Are you . . . married?"

"No!"

"Then why—"

He kept talking. "No decent woman should be tied to a man like me. You deserve better."

"That's ridiculous. You're a fine man, Jake McCain."

"You don't know anything about me."

"Then tell me."

"No."

Jake stared at her, pain and loss and fury warring in his eyes. Then he bolted from the bed and yanked his pants on. The silence was deafening. He didn't bother to button his shirt. She wanted to ask again, but he didn't give her a chance. He carried his boots down the stairs and out the door. Rachel wasn't even sure he'd grabbed his coat.

She gave him thirty seconds before throwing off the covers. He wasn't going to ride away without giving her some answers. She pulled on her clothes and crept down the stairs. Nathan was lying on his back, one arm flung over his head. She paused long enough to tuck it back under the covers and to brush his hair from his eyes before grabbing her cloak and slipping out of the cabin. It was still dark, the stars a glittering blanket overhead. Looking around, she spied a light flickering from the lean-to. Jake was currying Griffin when she stepped inside.

"Why?"

His silence only made it worse.

"Jake, please help me understand."

He looked at her, just looked, his green eyes cloudy and troubled. But he didn't say a word.

"Before you came I had work that made me happy and brought in enough to support Nathan. Now the children will never come back to school. How am I going to feed my brother?"

"I'll take care of you."

"No! You've done that once already and look at the trouble it caused. Because of you, I've lost not only my teaching position, but my innocence. I've become what I never wanted to be, what my mother died trying to save me from becoming."

"Don't say that," he gritted. "You aren't like your mother."

"I am. I gave myself to you in return for a pantry full of food. The only difference is the manner of payment!" Her chest heaved with each angry breath she drew. She'd lost everything for one night of wonder in the arms of a man who didn't want her.

Jake grabbed her arm when she whirled to leave.

"Let me go!"

"Not until you listen to me."

"*Now* you want to talk?"

She realized he was going to kiss her a heartbeat before his lips crushed hers. She meant to struggle, intended to fight him, but she couldn't. The taste of him, the warmth, stole her will. Instead of pushing him away, she wrapped her arms around his lean waist and kissed him back.

Jake ended the kiss as abruptly as he'd begun it. He kissed her again, a gentle meeting of lips that left her wanting more.

"Don't think of yourself that way," he whispered. "Please." He pulled her close and pressed his cheek to her hair. "What we did last night, what we shared, was special. I know it even if you don't. I'm sorry for what I took from you, but I wouldn't give back our night together even if I could."

Her anger drained away, leaving her more tired than she ever remembered feeling. "But you don't want me."

"Pretty girl, I want you with every breath I take. But I can't marry you."

Rachel leaned back far enough to look into his eyes, willing him to explain.

"My father was an English scholar. A fool who wandered around the territory looking for adventure, he said. Trouble would be closer to right. To hear him tell it, my mother was the most beautiful woman God had ever seen fit to put on the earth. He said he saw her bathing in the river one morning and was smitten. What the hell kind of word is that? Smitten."

Jake stroked her hair once more before setting her away from him. He retrieved the currycomb from the straw and resumed grooming Griffin.

"She said he came out of the woods and walked right into the water, fully clothed. He talked the whole time, though she had no idea what he was saying. When she tried to leave him behind, he followed her to her village, thinking he was unseen in the trees. He believed that right up until the moment he was surrounded by fifteen women, all holding knives."

Jake smiled at the memory. "He was stripped and bound and dragged into the middle of the camp. Most of the braves were off on a hunt, so the old men held council to decide his fate. My mother was given the choice to stake him out for the wolves or to bury him alive. She chose to leave with him instead."

He set the comb aside and took up a heavy brush. For a while he was silent. "She gave up everything to be with him but never seemed to regret it. I came along less than a year later. I grew up in two worlds. She taught me the ways of her people. My father taught me his language and customs. But we never belonged anywhere."

"She was an Indian." Rachel had suspected it the first night, when she'd seen his bronze skin and straight black hair.

"Apache."

His big hands tightened on the brush until Rachel expected it to snap.

"I'm a half-breed, honey, unfit for white society and unwanted by my mother's people. And since my parents never got around to marrying in a church, I'm a bastard, too. Twice cursed. I'm only tolerated now and then because of the job I do. You deserve better in a husband."

"I don't care about that."

"You should."

"Why? What can these people possibly do to me now?"

"It isn't just these people. You would be snubbed, looked at with contempt, spit on . . . and worse."

"Just because your mother was Apache? I refuse to believe that."

"Believe me. I've lived it and I won't let you go through that."

"Let me? Jake McCain, I'm not a child. I make my own decisions."

"Not this time."

He laid the brush aside with great care. She suspected he'd rather have thrown it against the lean-to wall. With only a few movements he had Griffin saddled. When he led the horse out into the dawn, she knew he was leaving.

She tried and failed to keep the hurt from her voice. "How could you just ride away and leave me to deal with the people of this town?" Tears burned again.

"They won't hurt you. I'll see that you have enough supplies to get by until—"

"No, you've done enough damage already. By now, they know you were here last night. If you send more gifts, I'll never be able to convince them that we didn't . . . That I'm not .

Her voice broke and tears stung her eyes. She fought not to let them show. "We don't need your help. I'll explain it to Nathan. Just go."

"Where are you going?"

She and Jake turned to face Nathan. He stood in the doorway in his stocking feet, resting against the jamb.

"Ranger McCain has to leave." She walked away from Jake and climbed the steps to the porch. "You'd better say good-bye. I doubt we'll see him again."

Rachel slipped past Nathan into the cabin. She crossed the floor and climbed the stairs, not stopping until she stood over the bed they'd shared. How could she have been such a fool? To think a man like Jake would want the daughter of a whore for a wife.

She yanked the bedding from the mattress and rolled it into a ball. Nathan mustn't see it. She'd have to boil it to remove the evidence of her stupidity.

"Sis?"

Rachel started. "I'll be down in a minute, Nathan." She took one last look around. This was where she lost her innocence. And where she gave away her heart.

Chapter Eleven

Jake rode Griffin hard, ignoring the voices in his head shouting at him to slow down. He pushed up the rocky hills and around boulders, trying to outrun the memory of Rachel's face. Griffin finally stumbled, jolting Jake out of his thoughts. He sat up in the saddle and the horse slowed.

"Sorry, boy. It's not your fault I'm a fool."

He turned toward a small creek that cut through the landscape. When they reached it, Jake dropped the reins and swung out of the saddle. He dug a few pieces of jerky from his saddlebag, then slapped the horse on the rump and let him wander, knowing a whistle would bring him back.

Fool! He berated himself all the way to a large boulder where he dropped to the dirt to eat his breakfast. It was a far cry from what Rachel would make for Nathan. Memories crowded in, of the first morning with Rachel and her delight as she licked up stray threads of sweet honey. The morning sun glinted off the thin ribbon of water, just like the candlelight had shone in her hair last night. His body tightened.

Damn. He had to stop thinking about her. Nothing could come of it. He'd been sure she was experienced and he was wrong. But he couldn't change that. He wouldn't give back what she'd shared with him in that tiny bed. His shaft hardened to the point of pain, but he ignored it. He hadn't forced her. His adoptive father's words echoed in his mind. *You stay away from the innocent until you choose a wife, son, the woman you want to be with until the day you die.* The lesson had been drilled into him from the time he was old enough to know that part of him had more than one use.

But what did he do when he couldn't keep the one he chose?

Jake pushed to his feet, more tired than he could ever remember being. Whistling for Griffin, he walked along the watercourse, staring at the ground, not really seeing anything.

He'd taken Rachel's innocence and left her without looking back. It wasn't right. He should marry her. She was his responsibility now. But if he married her, he'd destroy her. She wanted to be a teacher, but no one would allow the wife of a half-breed to come near their children. She had to see that.

At least he could give her justice and some peace of mind, when he made certain the man who murdered her mother was hanged for the crime.

Harrison.

As Rachel described her attacker, Jake realized she was talking about William Harrison, the leader of the gang Jake was chasing, the man who'd taken such delight in using his ring-sporting fist to pound him to a bloody pulp before leaving him to die in a blizzard.

Jake wandered another thirty paces, lost in his thoughts, before the tracks in the mud registered. Thoughts of marriage and children, justice and revenge, vanished as he recognized the print from one of the horse's left rear shoe. Duchess, his stolen packhorse. He'd put the nick there on purpose. She had a habit of wandering off and the mark made it easier to track her when he was riding where other horses had been. Now it showed the way to the ones he was chasing.

A single sharp whistle brought Griffin to his side. Jake followed the tracks for another mile on foot before he climbed into the saddle. They hadn't changed direction. They were heading southwest, for Mexico. But why? They weren't pushing cattle ahead of them, and there were no ranches and precious few towns in their path from which to steal.

He spent what was left of the day following tracks, keeping a good pace without tiring Griffin too much. By sunset, all he had to show for it was a mouth full of dust. He rode another hour in the failing light, searching for a spot to bed down. He could sleep in the dirt, but Griffin needed water and grass. Jake carried some grain in his packs but not enough to feed the big horse every night. He'd about given up when he spotted a short line of scrub trees in the distance, a sure sign of water. The creek wasn't big, but it would be enough.

Griffin didn't stop walking until he had his nose in the water. Jake loosened the cinch and removed the saddle and heavy packs before following suit upstream from his mount. He drank deeply and filled his cooking pot before splashing the cool water over his face and neck to remove some of the grime.

Immediate needs seen to, he scouted the area, looking for evidence that he wouldn't be alone tonight. When he returned twenty minutes later with an armload of limbs and branches for the fire, he was satisfied no humans were within a mile of this spot. Any four-legged intruders he could keep away with a fire.

He scratched out a small impression in the dirt and arranged wood by feel. Until the moon rose, the fire would be the only light he had. Years of experience guided his hands and flames chewed at the branches in a short time. Jake fed small pieces to the growing fire until he was satisfied it would hold. He used the wood sparingly. The fire had to burn all night and he didn't want to have to stumble around in the dark gathering more fuel. Besides, a larger fire would attract more than the four-legged variety of predator.

Jake set the pot of water on one side of the fire, close to the flames. While it heated, he dug out several pieces of venison jerky and broke them up into a battered tin cup. When the water boiled, he filled the cup and put it aside. Then he added a handful of coffee grounds to the pot and set it on the ground to steep. While he waited for his meager dinner to soak and soften, he studied the landscape. Nothing moved except for Griffin. It was so quiet, he could hear the big animal ripping up the sprigs of early grass near the water.

When the jerky was soft enough to chew, Jake ate. There wasn't anything fancy about it, but it was filling. Tomorrow he'd have to watch for a rabbit while he rode. He washed down the soup with coffee, then refilled his cup and leaned back against his saddle to sip the strong brew.

This was the toughest time for most men who'd chosen the life of a Ranger. It was dark and quiet, and no one knew or cared if you were alive. Normally it didn't bother him, but tonight Jake was restless. Memories of Rachel filled his mind, of her body beneath his, her long legs opening for him, her soft hands roaming across his chest. Her skin was so pale against his. It had been years since he'd wished he were someone other than who he was, but Rachel made him want to be different.

Not true, he growled in the silence of his mind. Jake shifted on his bedroll, trying to get comfortable. He wasn't ashamed of his parents or his heritage. He didn't want to be different. He wanted to be accepted. Then he could marry Rachel and start that family she wanted. He wanted.

He tossed out the cold coffee. "Wishing for the impossible won't make it happen," he muttered. He couldn't change himself and he damn sure couldn't change the way people thought of him. He moved the coffee away from the flames to cool. He would reheat what was left of it in the morning.

Jake added two more pieces of wood to the fire. He hated the dark. He'd long since given up trying to conquer that demon from his childhood and accepted that he needed light. He took one last look around the area, walking slowly with his revolver drawn. The night sky sparkled with stars. No clouds marred the inky beauty. He looked east and was glad to see a half moon peeking over the horizon. In an hour it would illuminate the land. He could sleep without having to feed the fire.

Settling Griffin nearby, he wrapped a blanket around himself and laid his head on his saddle. For just an instant, he wished Rachel were beside him. Cursing his foolish wanting, he turned away from the fire and slept.

The clear night gave way to a cloudy morning. Signs of rain were everywhere. Jake warmed the leftover coffee while he groomed and saddled Griffin. The horse proved as cantankerous as the weather, shying away from the bit and holding his breath when Jake tried to tighten the cinch.

"I know how you feel, boy, but I'm going to win this battle so you may as well give in gracefully." With his gear finally loaded, Jake sat on his heels to drink his morning coffee. He took a sip and winced. It was even worse than usual. Taking a deep breath, he gulped it down in three swallows and rose to rinse out the pot. Breakfast would be in the saddle today. He didn't dare linger around the fire. Rain would wash away the tracks he was following, leaving him exactly nowhere.

It took only a minute to pack away the cup and pot, and kick dirt over the fire. He stuffed some of the smaller pieces of wood in a saddlebag. Wood was scarce out here, and at least what he had was dry. He left the rest stacked where it was. If another man happened along this lonely stretch of nowhere, he could make use of it.

Jake had only been in the saddle an hour when the rain started, a cold mist that coated his face and snuck down his collar. He stepped up the pace, trying to stay ahead of the downpour he knew was coming.

Rain fell all afternoon. Even wearing his oilcloth slicker, Jake was soaked through and shivering by the time he decided to stop for the night.

The next morning dawned gray and overcast, but the rain had stopped. He climbed into the saddle and spent another day in fruitless searching. That wasted day was followed by another.

On his fourth day out, the rain returned, soaking him to the skin before he could pull on his slicker. Cursing every step of the way, Jake stayed with the tracks when they changed direction, heading west toward the river. By noon, he had to stop. There was no longer anything to follow. All he'd gotten for his trouble was wet and cold. He'd finish this day out, but at sunrise he was turning for the nearest settlement and a hot bath. Turning Griffin, he started searching for shelter.

Jake was so intent on finding a place to get out of the rain, he nearly missed seeing where the tracks came out of the water. He only recognized one. The other riders must have crossed the river.

A hundred yards down, three more horses joined the group, all carrying riders by the look of the prints set deep into the mud. A mile further and they'd picked up their pace. Jake held Griffin to a ground-eating trot. It wasn't comfortable for him, but it was easier on the horse. When he saw the dark area ahead, he figured his eyes were playing tricks. The tracks continued, straight into a hole in the ground.

He turned away at the last moment, staying hidden in a fold of land. The cave wasn't big, at least not from where he was standing. He didn't see anyone on guard, but smoke came from the rocks above, a tiny wisp of white thicker than the misty rain that washed it away.

They'd chosen well. It was hard to spot and had a small, easily guarded entrance. He had no way of knowing how much space was inside, but at least six men and seven horses had gone in. The cave was the first high spot after a quarter mile of flat, desolate land. The only way to approach it without being seen was to ride several miles south, cross the open space and double back through the rocks behind the cave.

It took Jake almost an hour to get back. He settled Griffin out of sight in a small wash, and spent the rest of the limited daylight scouting the area. Even when he stood right above the cave opening, he couldn't see anyone on guard. Maybe he'd imagined the smoke. He was still telling himself that when two men came out to relieve themselves. They stood in the cave entrance, out of the rain, smoking foul smelling cigars just below where Jake lay, stretched out along the rim.

Though their Spanish was peppered with phrases he wasn't familiar with, he understood enough to know he was in the right place, but the man he was after wasn't here. They were waiting for *El Capitan* and his second in command to join them before they made their next strike. Then they would lead the stolen cattle across the Rio Grande River into Mexico and go home to enjoy their wives' cooking and sleep with their lovers.

They rattled on for half an hour, planning how they would spend their pay. By the time they went inside, Jake was so cold and wet he had trouble climbing through the rocks, but he didn't care. Soon he would face the man he'd been after for years, the man he'd vowed to kill before quitting the Rangers for good.

He made his way back to Griffin and led him away from the area until he found a small overhang that couldn't be seen from the cave where they'd both be out of the rain. Jake stripped gear from the horse and poured out some grain for him. Everything was wet, including the wood he'd carried all day. Swearing over his rotten luck, he made a tiny fire, feeding bits of damp wood into it slowly so it didn't smoke. He set the pot out in the downpour to fill. When the wood had burned down a little, he laid a piece of rabbit left over from the previous night directly onto the coals. Then he searched through his packs for something dry to wear.

The night air against his naked skin made him shiver, but he was grateful for the rain. It would keep the rustlers under cover for the night and hide any evidence of his fire. While the meat cooked, he fashioned a water pouch from his slicker and filled it with rainwater for Griffin. Once the horse was satisfied, Jake shook it out and laid it wet side down near the fire and settled onto it, careful to keep his muddy boots hanging off the edge. Getting dirty was inevitable out here, but he drew the line at sleeping in it.

He ate half of the rabbit while it was hot, saving the rest for the next day. He had a feeling there wouldn't be time to hunt anything but thieves tomorrow.

When the fire burned itself out, he dragged the slicker and bedroll closer to Griffin. The big animal would alert him if anyone wandered close. Wrapping his blanket around his shoulders, he leaned back against his saddle and closed his eyes, trying to ignore how dark it was.

Immediately, his thoughts turned to Rachel and what she

might have done to fill her day. Had she gone back to the little schoolhouse? Or had she spent the day reading to Nathan, or spinning yarn from the mound of wool she'd gathered? He smiled a little. He'd like to see her work that spinning wheel. It would probably make a man feel right at home, watching her turn a pile of wool into yarn.

"Stop it," he grumbled into the darkness, startling Griffin. "Easy, boy. Settle down." Jake calmed the horse while his mind raged on. He'd never see her spinning yarn because he couldn't go back. He had nothing to offer a woman who thought one night of heaven should be followed by happily ever after.

Jake yanked his blanket closer and flopped onto his side, willing himself to sleep.

Dreams rose from the shadows, images of Rachel, her golden hair free, walking down the street of Lucinda. No one else is there. She looks frightened. There, in the distance, someone is coming. It's a man dressed in black, with long blond hair and shiny gold buttons on his fancy shirt. Jake's fingers tighten on his gun as he raises it. He knows this man. He wants to kill him. He tries to warn Rachel, but he can't make a sound. She runs toward the stranger. He yells at her to get away, he has to shoot, but it comes out as a croak. The man grabs her by her long hair and pulls her in front of him just as Jake squeezes the trigger and Rachel crumples to the dirt.

Jakes bolted awake to a crack of thunder. He shot her. He shot Rachel. He killed the woman he loved. He dragged air into his lungs. It was only a nightmare, born of worry and his own damned heart.

Jake dropped back to his bedroll, breathing hard. He cared for her. There, he'd admitted it, for all the good it did. He still wouldn't marry her, but he knew he had to find a way to take care of her. He owed her that. He chose to ignore the part of him that whispered he owed it to himself as well.

He spent the remainder of the night watching the storm as it marched across the sky, lightening slamming to earth in regular counterpoint to the beating rain. Twice in the night, he slipped back to his post over the cave, looking for some indication that the man he hunted had arrived, but the rain made it pointless. Sometime around dawn the storm passed on, leaving a cold, soggy mess behind.

Jake had everything packed before the last rumble of thunder rolled through the rocks. Griffin snorted and sidestepped when Jake approached, less than happy about being saddled so early, but he settled down quickly. It was almost as if the horse knew there was trouble nearby.

When everything was tied on, Jake left Griffin where he was. "One of us may as well stay dry this morning." The big animal tossed his head, close enough to a nod of agreement that Jake smiled. He poured out some more grain and led the horse to a puddle of water at the edge of the overhang. "Drink some of that if you're thirsty," he instructed.

They'd been together so long, it didn't occur to Jake that most folks would consider it odd that he talked to his horse. It was just what he did. He took one last look around to be sure nothing had been forgotten, then settled his hat lower on his brow and headed out into the morning.

Jake smelled cooking bacon as he approached the cave, and his stomach growled, reminding him he'd skipped breakfast. With the rain gone, and the sun coloring the horizon, he saw a second column of smoke rising from a fissure in the rocks just before he stepped into it. He went around it, careful not to let his shadow cross the opening and give away his presence. Jake crawled the last few yards to settle on his stomach above the mouth of the cave and waited.

It wasn't long before a rider came into view from the south. Jake's heart began to beat in rhythm with the pounding hooves. He hunkered down farther, making sure he wasn't silhouetted against the rising sun.

The rider approached steadily, staying in the center of the open ground, not bothering to hide himself. Jake stared hard, wanting to see his face. He slipped his pistol from his gun belt and took careful aim. Killing him would mean a gun battle with the rest of the lowlifes in the cave below him, but at least *El Capitan* would never leave another child fatherless.

Disappointment snaked through him when the rider's hat fell back to reveal long oily black hair. *El Capitan*, or William Harrison as he was known in society, sported long blond hair, a family crest on his ring, and a heart as black as the devil's. Jake forced his fingers to relax and release the trigger, cursing in the silence of his mind. He was close to losing the last of his objectivity on this assignment. He wasn't stupid. That kind of single-minded obsession could make a man careless—and dead.

He tried reminding himself he was a Texas Ranger doing what he'd been sent to do, but it didn't work. This man had never been just an assignment. Since the day Jake realized Harrison was the man who'd attacked his mother, killing the bastard had been his sole purpose in life. That he'd also murdered Rachel's mother only made him more determined to succeed.

Once Harrison was dead, Jake no longer cared what happened to himself. What good was a half-breed who wasn't strong enough to protect those he loved when they needed him most? Twenty years ago, the boy he'd been had sworn justice would be served, and that was all he could see. There was no future for him. That, even more than his heritage, kept him from giving in to his desire and taking Rachel as his wife.

Rachel. Jake pictured her, lying in the bed they'd shared. He could almost smell the lavender on her skin. With a silent curse, he forced his mind back to his work.

The new arrival hailed the two men sitting at the mouth of the cave, and one of the guards responded, using an odd mix of Spanish and English. Jake memorized the words, knowing the code they used might come in handy. The rider jumped to the ground, greeting the men by name, slapping backs and trading insults with the casualness of those who never expect to get caught.

When they got down to business their conversation was brief. Harrison had been delayed. They were to carry on as planned and he would join them later. Jake clamped down on his disappointment. The men argued, firing questions and insults at each other until decisions were made. Their cargo would be left here; they would return this way in a week with the cattle. They would take everything across the river then. One of the men yelled instructions into the cave. With a whoop of glee, four more men poured out, saddled horses and all seven riders headed north at a gallop.

Jake didn't follow. Even with the rain threatening to return, that many horses would be easy to track. He was more interested in what they'd left behind. He waited until all sound faded, then stayed hidden another fifteen minutes before picking his way down the hillside. He blended with the shadows at the entrance and stilled, listening.

The cold wind at his back was in stark contrast to the warmth coming from the cave. Jake opened his mouth and drank in the scents carried on the air, as he'd been taught by the old Apache warrior who'd treated him like a son, then stood by and allowed a boy to be buried alive. Horses and men, sweat and human waste, a smoky fire—all were there, fading with the passing minutes.

Silently he slipped into the cave, staying low and pausing just inside to let his eyes adjust to the dim interior. The hole in the rocks overhead not only let out the smoke, but provided enough light to see by. Jake moved nothing but his eyes for several minutes, searching for movement, but spotted nothing except the smoke rising from their hastily extinguished fire.

Moving quietly, sticking to the walls, Jake went through the boxes, trunks, and garbage left behind. As he circled back to the entrance, a tiny noise came from behind. He whirled and leveled his pistol at the source of the sound. A young boy stared back at him from between two crates. Jake looked around but couldn't see anyone else.

"Injun!"

Jake heard the whispered word. He closed his eyes an. sighed at the hate and fear bred into such a young child. "I'm not going to hurt you."

The boy stared at him. "You talk like I do."

"Sure I do. I'm a Texas Ranger."

"A *real* Ranger?" Awe filled the three whispered words.

Jake felt a smile twitch his lips. He sounded just like Nathan. "My name's Jake McCain. What's yours?"

"C-Calvin."

Jake strained to hear the reply. "Are you the only one back there, Calvin?"

"Yes, sir."

"Are you lying to me, boy?"

Blue eyes rounded in terror. "No, sir."

"All right then. Come on out of there."

"I can't."

The words came out on a sob and Jake's heart softened. "Take it easy. I'll come to you."

He moved carefully, not entirely satisfied that the boy was alone. Instead of approaching from the front, as anyone lying in wait would expect, he silently retraced his steps and came in from behind. As he looked over the pile of boxes behind the child, Jake saw why he couldn't come out. He swore as he shoved crates aside. The boy was tied, hand and foot, and held in place by a stake driven into the rock. A bowl of water and a plate of food had been left where he could reach it, as long as he strained against his bonds. Jake fought down the urge to go after the men and shoot every last one of them in the back like the cowards they were.

"Hang on, son. I'll cut you loose." The boy gasped at the long knife Jake slid from his boot. Jake glanced up from his task and grinned at Calvin's wide-eyed stare. "I used to have a shorter one, but I had to take my boot off to reach it."

The boy smiled a little, relaxing enough for Jake to slice through the ropes that held him. Blood seeped from Calvin's wrists and ankles where the ropes had torn his skin. No telling what other injuries he had.

Jake looked around. The boy had enough food for a day, not the week the men planned to be gone. Unease washed down his spine. Something didn't add up. If they weren't coming back for a week, why leave the boy with so little food? If they were going to starve him to death, why keep him alive at all? That could only mean someone was coming back—soon.

The moment the ropes fell away, the boy half ran, half dragged himself toward a stack of crates off to one side.

Jake pulled one revolver and checked the load. "Calvin?" He didn't want to scare the boy, but he was getting jumpy. They needed to leave.

The boy ignored him and kept clawing at the lid of one box until it came loose and the contents spilled to the dust. Silver coins mixed with trinkets and a blond-haired doll in a green and white dress. It was the toy the child snatched from the pile. Gripping it close, he took one shuddering breath after another. Jake went to him and put a hand on his shoulder, but the boy shrugged free.

"Who did the doll belong to?"

Calvin just cried harder, sobbing until Jake couldn't stand it anymore. "Son, I need you to pull yourself together for just a while. We have to get out of here."

Tears still rolling down his cheeks, the boy gathered the scattered coins, a pocket watch, a photograph in a rough-hewn wooden frame, and the doll. He tied everything into a pretty light blue shawl and hugged the bundle close. Without looking at Jake, he turned toward the entrance and managed two steps before he collapsed, so weak his legs wouldn't hold him.

"Hold on a minute." Jake tucked his pistol back into his belt and dropped to one knee, his back to Calvin. "Climb on, son. We'll get there faster."

Jake showed him how to hold on as he pulled the boy's battered legs around his waist. Keeping Calvin secure with one hand, Jake drew his gun and headed for the sunlight that illuminated the entrance. For a moment, he considered throwing a match into the stolen goods left behind, but thought better of it. The riders were still close enough to see the smoke and return to investigate. Better to leave everything and let them think Calvin had escaped on his own. That gave him an idea.

Lowering Calvin to the ground, Jake motioned for him to stay put and went back into the cave. He dug around until he found the little knife he'd glimpsed in the box of Calvin's possessions. It was a small blade with a dull edge. Perfect.

Jake moved the crate close enough to where the boy had been tied to make it look possible for him to have reached the box. Then he hacked at the ends of the ropes still hanging from the wall. Unless they looked real close, the bandits would think the boy got to the knife and cut himself loose. He could request a detail of Rangers be sent to the cave to recover the goods and finish the gang off for good.

He took the knife to Calvin, who waited where he'd been left. "You should hang on to this. It's a good blade. Just needs some sharpening."

While Calvin stuffed it into his pocket, Jake slipped to the cave opening and stood still, listening. Crouching down, he leaned forward until he could see out. Nothing moved on the land, but still Jake couldn't relax. His instincts told him something was coming and they didn't want to be here when it arrived. Returning to Calvin, he lifted the boy to his back again, and headed out of the cave and into the rocks where Griffin waited.

Chapter Twelve

Griffin came out of the rocks at the same spot Jake had. "Sometimes," he confided to Calvin, "I think that horse is part dog. You'd almost believe he can track a scent with the best of them." He eased his burden to the ground and checked the horse for injury before tightening the cinches.

When Jake turned, he bumped into Calvin, who was crowding close and staring at the big animal, his blue eyes huge in his face. "He won't hurt you. Let me introduce you." He took the bridle in one hand to keep Griffin steady. "Calvin, this is Griffin." He patted the horse's neck. "Meet my new friend, Calvin."

The word "friend" brought a small curve to the boy's lips. Though the smile didn't quite reach his eyes, it was a start. Griffin lowered his huge head to sniff the small hand gripping the bundle. Moving very slowly, Calvin patted the black nose. When Griffin blew warm air into his palm, Calvin grinned. It was the best sight Jake had seen since he first saw Rachel smile.

He helped Calvin stow his bundle and laced the saddlebag closed. "Now I'm going to lift you up." Fear clouded the child's eyes again. "Have you ever been on a horse before?"

Calvin nodded, but Jake could tell something wasn't right.

"That's not a problem. Griffin is real easy to get used to.

You're going to sit back here." He pointed to the wide haunches behind the saddle. "Then just hold on to me. Think you can do that?"

The nod was almost imperceptible, but it was there. Jake grasped Calvin under the arms and lifted him into place, holding on until the boy settled down. Then he put his foot in the stirrup and pulled himself up, swinging his right foot over the saddle horn. It was awkward, but it got the job done. "Hold on, son." When the boy's arms were wrapped around Jake's waist, he lifted the reins and nudged Griffin forward.

The boy didn't scream, but if the sudden tightening of his hands in Jake's shirt was any indication, he wanted to. The cold wind blew down the open valley as they set out. If Jake could feel it, Calvin would be chilled through in no time. "We're just going over into those rocks." He indicated the far side of the wash with a nod. "Then we'll stop for a minute."

Jake aimed Griffin south, in the same direction the gang had gone, looking for a place to veer off where his tracks wouldn't be noticed. If they had a decent tracker among them, Jake wasn't going to leave a trail for him to follow.

He had to go farther than he'd wanted, but he finally found a spot where they'd allowed their horses to run close to the edge of the rocky hillside. They'd never see Griffin's tracks. Jake let the horse pick his way into the rocks, putting the cave behind them for good. Once they were out of sight, he slid from the saddle and shrugged off his coat.

"Here, son, put this on." Calvin looked at the coat, then at his bloody wrists. "Don't worry about that. We'll get you cleaned up when we stop for the night." He helped the boy pull on the heavy wool and left him to button it. Digging in his saddlebags, he found his extra wool shirt and the rain slicker.

Even with the extra clothes, it was turning cold. They needed shelter for the night, wood for a good fire and plenty of water. He wanted to get Calvin's wounds cleaned. To do it properly, he should use iodine and alcohol, two things he didn't carry with him. But Rachel had them.

Jake patted Griffin's neck, considering. The boy needed a safe place to stay while Jake went after the outlaws, and someone to take care of him while he healed. Rachel was the perfect answer. Since Calvin was in Jake's care, he could buy food and supplies and pay her to care for the boy until Jake could return him to his parents. And Rachel would have to accept the supplies, since it was Ranger business.

He grinned, pleased with himself. When he looked up, Calvin was staring at him. "What you looking at?"

Jake wanted to kick himself when the light faded from the boy's eyes. "There's nothing wrong with looking, son. I just wondered if I'd grown donkey's ears or something."

Calvin's lips twitched, but he didn't say anything. Getting him to talk would have to wait. Jake wanted to get on their way to Rachel.

Despite himself, his heartbeat sped up at the thought of seeing her again. Other parts of him reacted, too, and it was going to make climbing into the saddle less than comfortable.

Jake could almost smell her skin, feel the silk of her hair between his fingers. He was so distracted he nearly missed the sound of running horses coming from the direction of the cave.

He slid his rifle from the saddle scabbard. "Stay put," he ordered Calvin before moving to a point in the rocks where he could see the valley. Five horses stood outside the cave opening, but no riders were in sight. Four of the animals sported fancy new saddles and tack. The fifth, a small pack horse, was an animal Jake knew well. Duchess. His stolen horse. Hope flared that Harrison was nearby.

Jake crouched low and waited for the men to show themselves. It was only seconds before a shout of fury came from the cave. One man charged into the sunshine. He turned in all directions, scanning the surrounding rocks.

"You can't get away, boy. I'll find you, dammit!" He vaulted into the saddle and began quartering the area, screaming instructions to the others. Two of them jumped to do his bidding, but the third seemed unconcerned with the man's crazy ravings, concentrating instead on the tracks in the mud. It wasn't until the leader turned his back and Jake spotted the long yellow hair brushing the man's shoulders that he was certain who it was. Harrison! Jake finally had him in his sights. His trigger finger started to itch, the need for revenge grinding a hole in his gut.

Jake clamped down on his desire to shoot the son-of-a-bitch where he stood. Harrison was too far away. He'd only give himself away. Jake scanned the area and picked a better vantage point. He planted his hands on the rocks, preparing to crawl to the new position, when he felt someone staring at him. Jake froze. He knew he wasn't visible, but the third man studied the exact spot in the rocks where Jake hid.

Long seconds ticked by while the man watched, his stare never wavering from Jake's hiding place. Finally the man turned away, but Jake still didn't move. If he was any good, he would . . .

There. The tracker spun back suddenly and focused on the same spot, exactly as Jake would have done—wait a heartbeat or two, then look back and catch the man you're hunting in the act of changing positions. Jake took care not to stare and draw the tracker's attention. Even so, he would have sworn their gazes locked and held for a time before the man acknowledged him with a slight nod. Then he turned his back on Jake and walked toward his horse, his pace unhurried.

A couple of month ago, Jake had received word from the Colonel in command of Fort Griffon, up on the northern plains of Texas, that a man named Cain Richards was pursuing the gang of men who'd murdered his wife and stolen his children.

Over the last couple of months, Jake had heard stories of the man. Called Wolf by those who knew of him, it was rumored he could track anything. Some swore he could see in the dark. A few thought he could read men's minds. Could the tracker down there be Wolf? But when had the man thrown in with Harrison?

None of that mattered right now. Jake didn't have time to

waste. While the men below mounted their horses, Jake slithered backward out of the rocks and retreated toward Griffin. He could backtrack and catch Harrison as he came into the rocks on this side of the valley. Jake rounded the outcropping where he'd left his horse to find Calvin in the saddle, kicking wildly at Griffin's sides. He'd forgotten about the boy.

"What the hell are you doing?" Calvin didn't appear to hear him. Desperation and terror were etched on his young face. "Stop it!"

That did it. Calvin jumped off Griffin and tried to run away, but his weak limbs wouldn't carry him. Jake caught up with him easily and scooped him from the ground. The boy went crazy, kicking and beating at Jake with his fists. Jake held him close, talking to him constantly keeping his voice low, until the words penetrated the child's panic.

"He's not going to find you. I gave my word you'd be safe." Calvin wrapped his arms around Jake's neck and held on, sobbing into Jake's chest. "Come on, son. Let's get out of here." Killing Harrison would have to wait.

Jake carried Calvin back to Griffin, but when he tried to put him on the horse's back, the boy wouldn't let go. Deciding not to waste time arguing, Jake climbed into the saddle with Calvin hanging from his neck, settled the boy across his lap, and lifted the reins. Griffin sidestepped to let Jake know he didn't appreciate being mistreated, then settled into a steady gait.

Jake adjusted his position in the saddle and turned his attention to the man tracking them. If he'd been successful in hiding his tracks leaving the valley, it might slow Wolf down, but it wouldn't stop him. It was just a matter of time before they were discovered. For the first time in his life, he thought he understood why people prayed.

Jake had taken nothing from the cave except the boy. So why was Harrison so intent on finding them? Was it just because someone had been in there? But how could he know? There'd been hundreds of boot prints in that cave. He couldn't have distinguished Jake's from anyone else's. That left Calvin. But what reason would the man have for chasing after a child?

Jake looked over his shoulder. "Calvin, do you know why Harrison wants to find you so bad?" He thought the boy was going to faint, he turned so pale.

"He always makes me . . . stay close to him."

Jake didn't say anything, just let the boy talk.

"He made me . . . bed down with him every night after my baby sister . . ." His voice cracked and Jake's heart split wide open.

Calvin's sobs tore at Jake. "Come here, son." Calvin launched himself into Jake's arms, tears running down his face. Jake held the boy tight to his chest, letting the rocking motion of the horse sooth him until he'd cried himself out. "Can you tell me about it?"

"He hurt my sister first." Calvin's shoulders sagged. "I tried to stop him but I couldn't. He was too strong. Sometimes he'd have another man tie me up so I couldn't go after her."

Jake was ill. "How old was your sister?"

"Six, and she was real pretty. Pa always said her hair was the color of sunshine and her eyes looked like a summer sky."

Just like Rachel. Jake's gut clenched as some ugly possibilities came to mind.

Calvin kept talking. "He called her Rachel. Every night, when he came to get Amanda, he called her that. When she died, he buried her and called her Rachel."

Jake's heart skipped a beat and started pounding. How was he going to keep Rachel safe from a madman who killed small children pretending they were her?

Calvin's small shoulders heaved under the weight of his grief. "My sister's name was Amanda."

Jake hugged him closer. "I'm sorry, son. When did she die?"

"Two months ago, maybe more." Calvin heaved a sigh and scrubbed the tears from his face. "I lost count of how many days we'd been gone before that." He hunched his shoulders and turned his face away from Jake. "The night she died, he came for me instead."

Revulsion filled Jake. What was God thinking, letting a monster like that live to hurt children? He tightened his grip on Calvin. "I'm sorry you had to go through that, son. I wish I'd found you sooner."

"You couldn't have stopped him. Nobody could. Not even my pa." Jake hugged Calvin close and concentrated on where they were going.

He kept to the rocks for several hours, holding Griffin to a path where little dirt existed to hold tracks. There would be signs of their passing, but they would be infrequent and far enough apart to make it tough to follow. He changed direction often through the day so he didn't give a hint of their destination, and only stopped once to dig out some food for Calvin.

It was growing dark when Jake finally turned the horse into the open and increased their speed. He was miles east of where he wanted to rest for the night and Calvin was fighting to stay awake.

"Go ahead and sleep, son. I won't let you fall."

He felt the boy's whole body quake. "I can't sleep when it's dark," he whispered. "It isn't safe."

Hate flooded his mouth with a bitter taste. Harrison would pay dearly for what he'd done to this boy. "It isn't dark yet. You can sleep for a little while."

Calvin tensed as he looked toward the western sky. Then, without warning, he relaxed and dropped into an exhausted sleep. Jake tightened his grip to keep him from falling and increased their pace.

Several miles behind them, William Harrison took his frustration out on his horse, driving the poor beast at a wild pace until it tripped in an unseen hole and fell, snapping its leg and throwing Harrison several feet into the rocks. He charged to his feet, roaring in fury, and put a bullet through the eye of the animal, ending its misery. It was a merciful act, though the man had no use for mercy. He turned to the next man in line. "Get off."

"But, boss . . ."

The man didn't argue more because he, too, sported a bullet hole in the head. The force of the blast threw the cowboy out of the saddle. Harrison grabbed the man's terrified animal by the bit and forced her nose toward her hooves until she stood still, quivering and sweating. Then he led the mare to his dead horse, transferred his rifle and ammunition, and swung into the saddle. With a vicious swipe of his spurs, he sent the animal tearing up the trail.

He'd gone a half mile before he realized he was alone. He hauled back on the reins and held on as his mount slid in the dirt trying to answer his command. Then he sat perfectly still for one minute, two, waiting for the blood to stop pounding in his ears. In his fury, he'd killed one of his best men. True, the man was as stupid as a fence post, but he'd been deadly with a rifle. It was a foolish mistake, but the man should never have questioned an order.

When his anger had subsided enough that he could once again distinguish the sounds around him from the noises in his head, Harrison reined his horse around and retraced his path.

Martin Cooke was busy cleaning out his dead friend's pockets. The man they called Wolf sat on his horse, staring at Harrison with eyes that seemed to glow in the gathering darkness. No expression showed in their golden depths, reminding Harrison of the animal he was named for. The gray streaks beginning to show in the tracker's dark hair made him look even more like his namesake. It was unsettling to meet his eyes and not know if he was going to help you or kill you. But he was the best tracker in the territory and Harrison needed him.

Martin looked up as Harrison rode up, waiting for approval before returning to his task. The man had already taken the rest of the gear from the dead horse and loaded it onto the pack horse. Martin was a useful man to have around.

Harrison looked toward Wolf. "Which way?"

The man shrugged. "Too dark to tell now. He's changed direction to throw us off. I'll hunt again in the morning."

"You'll do it *now*."

Wolf shrugged again and bumped his horse in the ribs, setting off at a slow walk while he stared at the ground. He'd gone only a few yards before he stopped and dismounted. "I'll hunt again in the morning."

Harrison's fingers itched to grab his revolver and shoot the man where he stood, but that would be beyond foolish. Not only was Wolf the best tracker in the territory, he was deadly with the weapons he wore strapped to his hips and chest. Though he was a good shot, Harrison wasn't sure he was faster. Better to control his temper and not chance it. He could take his revenge later, when the man wore out his usefulness. He climbed from the saddle and walked a few yards away to relieve himself.

"Start a fire. I'm hungry," he called over his shoulder. When Martin jumped to do his bidding, Harrison realized another reason he shouldn't have shot Marks. He'd been responsible for the horses. Now he'd have to groom his own, or tell Martin to do it and wait an hour longer for a meal. He didn't really care about anything's comfort but his own, but the horses meant the difference between living and dying out here. They were the only thing he put ahead of himself.

He loosened the buckles on the cinches and lifted the saddle from the skittish mare. Talking softly to her, he found the currycomb and brush buried in the saddlebags and set to work, calming the horse and letting her become accustomed to him. The little filly would have to carry him around now and she needed to learn who was master. He found he liked the prospect of riding a female all day.

When he glanced around, Wolf was nowhere to be seen. Harrison wasn't really concerned. The man never stayed near the fire. He would disappear when they began to make camp and reappear the next morning, just as they were ready to ride. It was a little unnerving how the man always seemed to know what was going on, even though he wasn't there.

Harrison had hired Wolf a few months earlier to help him find a girl who'd eluded them all for nearly eight years. Until Wolf. When they'd ridden into that little godforsaken Texas town in the middle of a freak blizzard, there she was, in the first house they'd come upon. He'd been careful not to get too close. He didn't want to scare her into running again.

He'd taken the time to plant a story about her servicing him and his boys, so the town wouldn't be too quick to rush to her defense when he returned for her. It'd been almost too easy. The townsfolk were so mistrusting of each other, they swallowed his story without question. As soon as he finished his urgent business with a large herd of stolen cattle, he would go back and get her. Only a few more days. Then she would pay for all the years of trouble she'd caused.

Jake let Calvin sleep long past the fall of darkness and the rise of the moon. His hands were numb, but at least with the boy in his arms, he didn't have to be concerned with him falling off. Now that the moon was rising, Jake could see well enough to keep riding. The more distance between them and Harrison the better.

He didn't pull Griffin to a stop until Calvin began to stir, a couple of hours before dawn. Jake started talking before the boy opened his eyes. "Look at that moon. It's putting out so much light you'd swear it was still daylight."

The sound of his voice seemed to work. Calvin stiffened a little, but he didn't panic. "You ready to get down and walk a little, maybe have something to eat?" Jake turned Griffin out of the stream they'd been wading in for the last hour and pulled him to a stop. He turned the boy in his arms until his legs straddled the horse's neck. "Hold on to his mane for a minute." When he complied, Jake swung a leg over the saddle and to the ground, groaning at the stiffness of his muscles. "I must be getting old." Calvin giggled, a childlike sound that warmed Jake's heart.

"Can you get down from there or do you need me to help?" When Calvin dragged one leg over Griffin's neck and held out his arms to be lifted off, Jake thought the sun had risen. How could the trust of one little boy make a man feel ten feet tall?

Jake stepped behind a scrub bush to heed nature's call and

Calvin followed along behind. He was grateful the darkness hid the blush he felt climbing his neck. He'd never had a shadow before. As they walked back to Griffin together, boy keeping step with man, copying his movements, Jake was reminded again of Nathan.

"How old are you, Calvin?"

"Seven and a half."

"And a half, huh? When will you be eight?"

"On Independence Day, July the fourth."

Jake would have to remember to tell Rachel. "I know another little boy about your age. His name is Nathan and he's a good friend of mine. He's got blond hair just like yours. The day I met him, he had three hens, a rooster, and two goats living in his house."

"Really? Inside?"

While he rubbed some warmth back into Griffin's fetlocks, he told Calvin about waking up in Rachel's home after being out in the snowstorm. "Surrounded by all those animals, I felt like I was on Noah's Ark."

"That must have been something to see." Calvin took the jerky Jake dug out of the saddlebags and gnawed off a piece. "Why'd he have a goat?"

"His sister spins the wool into yarn and sells it to the ladies in town. It makes nice, soft, warm wool blankets. I slept under one for a few nights, so I know."

They finished off the jerky and shared the water in Jake's canteen while Griffin made short work of the grass growing near the water. To be sure the big animal had enough to eat, Jake opened another pack and scooped out some grain into his hat. It was easier than removing the saddlebag.

"Who's that for?"

"Griffin. He needs more to eat than we do."

"Can I feed him?"

"Sure. Just pour it on the ground in front of him. He'll find it quick enough."

Jake retied the saddlebag. Satisfied everything was ready, he turned to find Calvin feeding Griffin the grain straight out of Jake's hat. He would have protested, since he didn't want to wear a soggy hat, but the boy was grinning and giggling and talking to the horse just like a seven-year-old boy should. Jake couldn't bring himself to stop his fun. He resigned himself to wearing a hat that smelled of crushed grain and horse slobber.

When Griffin had finished the feed and was starting to chew on the felt hat, Jake called a halt. "We need to get back on the trail. We've got a long way to go."

"Where we heading?"

"I'm taking you to Lucinda, where Nathan and his sister, Rachel, live. You can stay with them for a while."

The boy stopped, his eyes huge.

"What's wrong?" Jake spun around, searching the shadows for what had spooked Calvin.

"What if he finds me there?"

Jake was confused. "He doesn't know anything about . . ." That wasn't true. Harrison had been through Lucinda, just after he and his underlings had nearly beaten Jake to death.

"We still have to get moving." He scooped the boy up and set him on Griffin's saddle, then mounted behind him. Jake waited until small arms wrapped around his middle before bumping the horse in the ribs.

He set a steady pace northeast, toward Fort Davis, and rode for an hour in silence before turning west toward Lucinda.

"The bad man talked about someone called Rachel all the time, after . . . when he thought I was asleep. I think that's why he hurt my baby sister, 'cause Amanda looked like her."

Calvin fell silent and after a time dropped off to sleep, leaving Jake alone with his thoughts. If what the boy said was true, then Harrison was after Rachel. But why? Harrison had never seen Rachel until the night of the snowstorm. Unless . . .

His head spun as the truth hit him. Harrison was after Rachel. If he'd seen her the night of the blizzard, he knew right where to find her. And instead of stopping him, Jake was leading the madman right to her.

Chapter Thirteen

For Rachel, the days passed in a fog of fear and grief. The first one was the hardest. Jake rode away with anger sizzling between them, and the heavens had opened, crying buckets of rain for what she'd lost.

As she went through the motions, day after day, cooking and doing Nathan's chores in addition to her own, reality settled like a stone in her heart. He didn't want her. Her mother was a prostitute, she didn't know her father . . . no wonder Jake wouldn't marry her. How could he explain it to his mother or introduce her to his friends?

"Sis? Sis!"

Rachel jumped, so lost in her misery she didn't hear her brother approach.

"Sis, are you all right?"

"Of course I am. Why do you ask?"

"Well, you've been staring at that bowl of batter for almost ten minutes, but you haven't stirred it at all."

"Sorry. I was just thinking."

"About Ranger McCain? Why did he have to leave so soon?"

She closed her eyes, fighting sudden tears. "He has a job to do, Nathan. He can't stay here, even if he wanted to."

"Did you want him to? Is that why you're so sad?"

Rachel nodded. She didn't think words would get past the lump in her throat.

Nathan leaned against her, offering comfort. "I wish he could have stayed, too. I really miss him."

A sob broke through Rachel's control, shaking her.

He patted her hand. "You don't have to worry about him, Sis. He'll be fine. Going after bad men is what a Texas Ranger is supposed to do."

She smiled through the pain. Her little brother was so sure that nothing could harm his hero. "You're probably right. I'm just being silly."

"You're being you. When will that cake be ready?"

"What cake?"

"Sis!"

She was a little surprised to find she could smile. Teasing her brother always seemed to make her heart a little lighter. "It will be a while yet. Don't you have some spelling words to practice?"

He wanted to argue, but, to her surprise, he didn't say anything, just turned and limped to the table where his slate waited. Her smile faded as she watched his progress. They'd been fortunate his leg wasn't broken, but he was still in a lot of pain. From what he could remember, several larger rocks had hit him, bouncing on the floor of the mine before landing on him. Their crushing force had been spent on the dirt, but they'd still landed on him, battering and bruising as they fell. For a moment she was in the mine, feeling every impact, tasting his fear. She shoved the memory aside. If she let it, the fear could overwhelm her, and she was going to need all her courage.

The scrape of chalk on slate brought her back to the present. Settling the large bowl on her hip, she stirred the cake batter as she stood beside Nathan, checking his words as he wrote them. "Very good. You got every one correct. I believe your penmanship is improving as well."

"It ought to be; I've practiced enough in the last five days. May I go outside now?"

"I don't think you should." Rachel knew she was being unreasonable, but she didn't want him out of her sight. "Your leg is still healing and—"

"I'm not a cripple."

She stopped stirring, hearing his frustration. "I know that, Nathan. But you were nearly killed in that mine and I . . ."

"But I wasn't. I'm fine. I can walk and talk and I'm sick of reading and resting and practicing my letters. I have responsibilities, as you used to remind me all the time."

He stomped from the room, or as close as he could muster, limping like he was. Rachel started after him. "Where are you going?"

"To check on the chickens."

She fought down her panic. He was only going outside. She dropped onto the bench he'd vacated and shoved the bowl of batter aside. Tears threatened again, burning her eyes, but she couldn't indulge in a bout of weeping. It wouldn't change anything and she didn't want to answer the inevitable questions from Nathan. But she longed to lay her head in her hands and sob out her loneliness and fear.

All she'd ever wanted from life was a husband who cared for her and Nathan, a small house that she could make into a welcoming home, and children of her own. She looked around her. She had the house, but no husband and now no work. Without money there would be no food, let alone new curtains, and she wouldn't be able to whitewash the outside until it gleamed in the morning sun as she'd imagined so often. She was back where she'd been when they'd arrived in Lucinda, broke, with nowhere to turn.

Rachel pushed to her feet and went through the motions to finish the cake. They didn't need it, but Nathan loved sweets and she couldn't bring herself to deny him anything. He'd lost so much in the past days. It was little enough to do if it made him happy.

While it baked, she took stock of their remaining supplies. There was plenty to last them for a while, thanks to Jake, but what would she do when it was gone? She needed money, but how could she earn any? In spite of what the townspeople thought of her, she would starve before turning to her mother's way of life. But she had Nathan to consider. He seemed to always be hungry these days. How was she going to feed him?

She grabbed her cloak from its hook. She needed to check on Nathan. A cold breeze swept into the cabin as she opened the door. Rachel stuffed her hands into her pockets to keep them warm and something grazed her knuckles. When she pulled it out, possibilities glittered in the sunlight.

She stared at the rock Nathan had slipped to her the night of the cave-in. She'd completely forgotten the stone after they'd gotten to the house, and she and Jake had . . . The gold flecks within the crystal sparkled in the sunlight, a tiny ribbon of security just waiting to be released. Could she do it?

The idea had been forming unrecognized in her mind since Jake rode away. She knew the gold was in the mine. She just had to find a way to get it out. The cave-in might have buried it further, or maybe the vein was now exposed, waiting for her. Fear and heady excitement gripped her heart and squeezed. It wasn't being in the dangerous cave that frightened her. It was Jake. He'd be furious if he found out she went back to such a dangerous place. She squared her shoulders. It didn't matter. Jake wasn't here anymore.

She stared across the sweep of rocky ground leading to the mine, listening to her heart race, considering. What was she afraid of?

Failure, she finally admitted. She feared failing. If she failed, she'd have nothing, not even hope. But she had nothing left now, so why not try?

The decision made, her fear faded and she started making plans.

"Sis," Nathan called from the lean-to. "I smell cake. Is it ready?"

She'd forgotten the oven. "Not yet. When did you get to be so impatient?"

She missed his answer as she ducked into the cabin to pull the confection from the oven. It was a little too brown, but that was easily hidden beneath the glaze she planned to make. Jake had included five pounds of sugar in the supplies he'd sent. The man had a sweet tooth, just like Nathan. Her smile faded. Jake wouldn't be here to enjoy this cake, or any other cake she made. He was gone. Even if she found the gold, she wouldn't have Jake. Loneliness threatened to overwhelm her.

"Stop it, Rachel Catherine," she whispered aloud. "Stop thinking about him."

She gathered ingredients for glaze without conscious thought. How would she get to the mine without Nathan finding out? She'd concentrate on that. How would she get to the gold? It must be buried under a lot of rock after the cave-in that tossed Jake out of the mine.

No. Don't think about him. Think about the mine.

She poured the icing onto the warm cake and smoothed it across the surface.

Once she had enough gold to last them, she and Nathan would leave Lucinda and start again. There had to be a man somewhere who would marry her, one who didn't know where she came from. He'd build her a house and she would have children of her own, babies that no one could take away. All she needed was the gold.

"I wonder how long it will take?" She didn't realize she'd spoken aloud until Nathan responded.

"How long will what take?"

"Um," she tried to think of a reasonable answer. "The cake," she blurted. "I was wondering how long it will take to cool. That's all."

"It'll cool faster if we cut a piece out of it, won't it?" He eyed the confection as if choosing the piece he wanted.

"Probably, but you aren't going to find out until you've washed up."

"Yes, ma'am."

Rachel let out the breath she'd been holding. It was a good thing he had been more interested in the cake than her answer. She was a terrible liar. The truth was probably written all over her face. She fanned her heated cheeks with her apron. If

Nathan figured out what she planned to do, she'd never convince him to stay behind while she went to mine gold. He probably wouldn't believe any story she made up to explain being gone all day, either. That meant she'd have to go at night.

A shudder ran down her spine. She wasn't afraid of the mine, but being out of the cabin in the dark was different. She hated being outside alone at night. But there was no alternative. She'd rest a bit this afternoon to save her strength and head out once Nathan was asleep.

It was later than she'd hoped when Rachel climbed out the cabin window. She'd barred the door to keep Nathan safe, leaving only this window as her way in and out. The shutters didn't meet in the middle, so they were easier to open. She closed one shutter, then checked that the length of yarn was still attached. She draped it over the top of the shutter and eased it closed. Pulling gently, she lifted and lowered the latch into place, securing the shutters.

Pride in her small accomplishment warmed her and she smiled in satisfaction. It was a trick one of Mama's friends had taught her. She'd practiced raising and lowering the latch for an hour after Nathan had climbed the stairs to his bed, needing to be certain she could get back inside before he woke up. It had taken all afternoon to figure out a way to keep the metal hook in a position that she could reach, but she'd done it. She could drop the latch into place as she left, and open it again when she returned.

Rachel wrapped the old coat she wore tighter. It was too big, as were the men's trousers and shirt she wore, but she didn't want to ruin any of her dresses. Even the old wool one wasn't expendable. When Nathan had gone to settle the animals for the night, she'd dug through the sea chest and found the clothes Jake had worn while she'd mended his. They still carried his scent and she buried her face in the cloth, fighting back tears. Wearing them made her feel safer somehow, like Jake was with her.

"Enough stalling," she scolded in a quiet voice. "Time to get to work." She grabbed up the lantern and an empty sack for the gold, closed her fingers around the handle of the knife she carried for protection, and set out for the mine. She had to step carefully in her borrowed boots. The toes were stuffed with a pair of socks to keep them on her feet, but the heavy leather still threatened to slide off with every step. Giving up on stealth, she dragged and scuffed along the path. The only mining tool she owned was still in the entrance to the cave, where it'd been abandoned the night of Nathan's accident. She only hoped she could lift the old pick. It had seemed very heavy when she'd handed it to Hank Gerard.

It took longer than she hoped to reach her destination. She'd never been here in the dark, except for the other night, and she'd been so worried about her brother, she didn't remember getting to or from the mine at all. When the opening finally loomed in front of her, she was so tired she wanted nothing more than to sit down and rest. But there wasn't time. The night was nearly half gone already and she had to return to the cabin before dawn. Nathan was a heavy sleeper, but he always woke up at first light. She had to be back by then or he'd want to know where she'd been. That was a question she didn't want to answer.

Turning up the lantern, she examined the entrance. The deed to the mine had come to her with the house. The previous owner of both was sure there was no gold inside. Since there was no promise of easy wealth, Arnold Miller had been happy to hand over ownership to her.

Hank had done a good job of replacing rocks to hide the opening. Between the pile of stones and the scrub trees growing nearby, it was nearly invisible. If she didn't know better, she'd think the mine hadn't been entered in years. But how did she get inside without the whole pile crashing down on her? *One rock at a time, Rachel.*

Standing on her toes, she pulled out a fist-sized rock. Several more came with it and she jumped out of the way until the small slide stopped. She worked for an hour, laying rocks onto the burlap bag and dragging them out of the way before returning for another load.

"It's taking too long," she whispered aloud, breathing hard with exertion. "I should be inside by now." Growing impatient, she grabbed a large stone with both hands and yanked it out. The weight of the stone knocked her backward just as a section of the wall gave way, spilling rocks in the spot where she'd been standing. One bouncing stone knocked over the lantern and plunged her into darkness.

As silence returned, Rachel rose and dusted herself off. She could feel a new hole in the knee of her trousers, but she didn't examine it closely. If she was bleeding, she didn't want to know. She searched through the rubble until she found the lantern. Thankfully, it wasn't broken. The wetness on the ground around it told her a lot of the oil had spilled. She kicked dust over the spot, not wanting to risk a stray spark setting it ablaze. Then she relit the lantern from one of the two spare matches she'd brought along and set it to the side, out of harm's way. Though the moon was nearly full, she didn't want to walk home with only it's light to see by.

When she turned back to the opening, she discovered the rockslide had opened a gap large enough for her to squeeze through. "It's about time something went right" she muttered. Moving the lantern to a spot on the rocks that she could reach, Rachel tucked the empty sack into the waistband of her trousers and climbed into the black hole.

The air inside was thick with dust, making her cough and choke with each breath. Tomorrow she'd remember to bring a handkerchief to cover her nose and mouth. She tried taking shallow breaths and that seemed to help. At least she wasn't doubled over in a fit of coughing.

For hours she shifted stone, one at a time, trying to remember what Jake had said to Hank when they were looking for Nathan. *Fifteen feet into the mine and one turn to the left.* Rachel paced back to the entrance, measuring how far she'd come. Only six feet, and most of that had already been cleared. Even if the vein of gold was right where Nathan had been found, she still had nine feet of digging to do. "It will take days," she moaned.

She returned to the opening to pace off the distance again, hoping she'd miscounted. A glow of pink in the eastern sky snagged her attention. It was nearly dawn. She had to go, now. She scrambled out of the opening, taking the lantern with her. She left everything else behind. Working quickly she piled rocks in place to disguise the entrance. It wasn't nearly as effective as what Hank had done, but it would have to suffice. Grabbing up the lantern, she hurried along the path home. By the time she stepped onto the porch, it was light enough that she didn't need the lantern to see the yarn hanging from the shutter.

Her hands were shaking so much from worry and exhaustion it took three tries to open the latch. She shoved the shutters open and tumbled into the room. Leaving the window sash up, she hurried to her room to change clothes and stash the filthy trousers and shirt. It took another precious few minutes to tend her cut knee, but she was so worried about being discovered there wasn't even a twinge of nausea at the sight of dried blood.

She was much calmer ten minutes later, when she was dressed in an old gown with her hair piled on her head. She splashed water on her hands and face, smoothing a few loose tendrils into place. Satisfied nothing would look out of the ordinary, she headed to the hearth to start coffee.

The sun peaked over the horizon, lighting the room through the open window with the colors of dawn. Rachel leaned against the doorjamb and enjoyed the sight, glad to see it but wishing it would go away for a few more hours. Now that she was home, exhaustion threatened to claim her. It took all her effort to stay on her feet. If she was this tired now, how on earth would she get through the day?

As she pushed away from the door, something on the floor drew her attention. There, from the window to her doorway, was a line of dusty boot prints. For a moment, all she could do was stare. Then, with a soft cry of dismay, she fell to her knees. Landing on the spot she'd abraded in the rockslide nearly made her cry out, but she bit her lip to hold it back and started scrubbing at the prints with her skirt.

When she realized dirtying the hem of her dress was sure to bring questions from Nathan, she bolted to her feet and ran to get a rag and some water. She plunged the cloth into the icy water and went to work, washing up the evidence that she'd been out of the cabin, doing something very dirty. She was almost finished when Nathan came thumping down the stairs.

She heard him stop on the bottom step and felt him staring at her.

"Why the heck are you doing that now?"

"I couldn't sleep. I just wanted to get some work done. I haven't washed the floor in over a week. It needed it." She scrubbed away the last footprint, then pushed herself up and carried the bucket to the porch to empty the filthy water.

"You must have been at it awhile. Your neck is all dirty."

She barely kept herself from running to her room to look in her tiny, cracked mirror. "Really? My goodness, I didn't think I was working that hard." She tried to laugh, but it didn't sound very convincing, even to her ears. "Do you feel up to doing some of your chores this morning?"

"Of course. I did them all last night, remember? I'm not a baby, Sis." He limped across the room to close the window left open when she came home. "A man has responsibilities, and no bump on the head is going to keep me from doing what I have to." He chafed his hands to warm them and went to stir up the fire.

She looked him up and down, and realized for the first time that he looked more like a young man than a boy. Sadness pricked her heart. Her little boy was almost gone. "I worry too much, as you've reminded me often. I'll try to do better. You go see to your chores. Just promise to call me if you need help."

"Yes, ma'am." He snagged his coat from the peg by the door and headed outside, trying very hard not to limp. The moment he disappeared from sight, she ran for her washbasin.

The day dragged by for Rachel. She was so tired, she could

barely stand, but she did her best to hide it from Nathan. She managed to get a short nap in the afternoon by telling him she had a bit of a headache and needed to rest. But it wasn't nearly enough sleep for her worn-out body. She got up in time to fix some supper for them both, but she didn't do much more than push the food around on her plate. Fortunately, Nathan tucked into his meal with gusto, eating every bite without pausing.

"That was real good, Sis."

"I thought you liked it, seeing as you've eaten nearly everything in sight. I suppose this means you're going to get taller again this spring. I'll have to see about letting down your trousers some more."

"If you can't, there are some in the chest that might fit." He pushed back his chair, intent on finding the pants.

"No! Not tonight, Nathan, please. The ones you have will do for a while longer."

His shoulders slumped in disappointment. "Fine. But can we look tomorrow?"

"We'll see. Why don't you read to me while I do the dishes?" She carried their plates to the sink and dipped water from the bucket near the hearth. She spilled nearly half of it when she stumbled. She was too tired to even walk straight. How would she get through tonight in the mine?

"Here. Let me do that. That headache must be a pretty bad one." He carried the bucket of hot water to the sink and filled the dishpan half full, then added cold water until it was cool enough to put his hands in. "Go sit down. I'll do the dishes tonight. If Jake can wash plates, I can, too."

She stared at his back as he plunged his hands into the water, wetting his shirtsleeves. Jake. Why did everything come back to him? She swallowed the tears that rose and eased into the rocking chair.

When he finished the dishes, Nathan fetched the book they'd been reading together from the mantel and lit a candle. He read carefully, working his way through any unfamiliar words. He finished the chapter they'd started on the night before, then looked up at her.

"That's enough for tonight. You look like you need to get some sleep."

Rachel smiled at his concern. "I'm fine. I can begin the next chapter if you'd like."

"No, I think I'll just go on to bed." He returned the book to the mantel and carried the candle with him to the stairs. "Good night, Sis." He climbed slowly, stepping up on his good leg, then bringing his injured one up to join it.

She knew he must be hurting if he went to bed without being asked at least three times. "Do you need something for the pain, Nathan?"

"No. It's not too bad. I'll be fine once I lie down."

She heard him overhead, moving around as he changed clothes and prepared for bed. She nodded off once, coming awake with a start when Nathan called out from his room.

"Go on to bed yourself. You don't need to stay up on account of me."

Rachel pushed to her feet and paced the room, trying to stay awake. A half hour after Nathan blew out the candle, she changed clothes and climbed out the window. The moon was full and the wind was light as she made her way back to the mine.

The work seemed even harder tonight, the rocks heavier, the dust thicker in the air. But she pushed on, making her way deeper into the shaft, moving one stone at a time while keeping a wary eye on the ceiling. She knew the dust that sifted down on her from between the timbers wasn't a good sign. It meant the mine was getting more dangerous with each passing hour. Rachel sneezed, wincing at how loud it sounded in the tiny cave. The dust was getting worse, making it hard to breathe and hard to see. But she couldn't quit. They needed the gold if they were going to escape from this horrible town.

She dropped to her knees to shove a large rock to one side, but it refused to budge. Groaning, she leaned her weight into the stone. "Come on," she gritted through her teeth. "You're in the way." She took a gulp of air, preparing to shove again. Instead she choked on the dust and collapsed across the rock in a fit of coughing.

"Enough," she panted, crawling toward the opening. She had to stop. She couldn't breathe. She laid her head against the pile of stones still partially blocking the entrance and gulped in the cold night air. When the coughing subsided, she stood to pace off her progress. The sky showed no sign of morning, but she wanted to get home earlier tonight, so she had time to wash up properly. Nathan would never believe she'd been up cleaning twice in two days because she couldn't sleep.

She shook her head to clear the cobwebs. She was so tired. If she didn't get moving, she'd go to sleep standing up. Turning to face the bowels of the mine, Rachel started walking, counting the steps aloud. One, two, three long strides. Nine feet. She'd cleared three more feet in one night. She smiled behind the filthy cloth covering her nose and mouth. Progress. If she could make it three feet farther into the shaft every night, she'd have the gold in hand by week's end.

Rachel crawled out of the mine and stood, shaking some of the dust from her clothes. She untied the cloth from her around her face before tugging on the oversized coat. Bending to retrieve her lamp, she straightened, turned for home, and slammed headlong into the hard body of a man. The scream tore from her throat before she could think. Struggling with her captor, she drew her arm back, intending to use the lantern as a weapon.

"Don't even think of doing that," a familiar voice growled.

Rachel stilled. "Jake? What are you doing here?"

"What the hell are you doing in that mine, woman, trying to get yourself killed?"

She'd never seen him so angry. His eyes looked as hard as flint, fury blazing in their depths. She stepped back, trying to put some space between them, but he followed her, matching every step she took, backing her against the rocky hillside.

"I don't owe you any explanation, Ranger McCain."

His eyes flashed and he leaned one hand on the rock close

to her head, trapping her. She took a deep breath and willed herself to stop shaking.

"I think you do. I thought, after Nathan nearly died in there, you'd have enough sense not to go back inside that god-forsaken hole in the ground. But instead, I come back in the middle of the night to find you missing."

"Let me pass. I need to get back before Nathan wakes." She shoved him back a step and slipped past, heading for home. Jake caught her before she'd gone two steps, shortening his steps to keep pace.

"He's already awake. That's how I knew where to find you."

She didn't slow down. "No. I left him sleeping. As long as I get back before dawn, he won't know I've been gone."

"He just met me at the cabin door with that rusty old rifle pointed at my belt buckle."

Rachel stopped so fast Jake nearly ran her over. "But it doesn't work."

"Hell, I know that. And it wouldn't take anyone else with a lick of sense long to figure it out, either."

She stumbled backward a few steps before Jake caught her arm and steadied her. "Let go of me." She put up a struggle but her heart wasn't in it. She was grateful he'd kept her from falling, and she was just too tired to care that he stood close enough to touch.

"Give me that before you drop it." He took the lantern from her hand and lifted it until the light shone on her face, blinding her. He let out a string of curses that would make a miner blush. "What the hell have you done to yourself?"

Chapter Fourteen

Rachel squinted against the flickering light, trying to hide her fatigue behind indignation. "I have no idea what you mean. Give me my lamp, please."

"Don't get all riled up." He handed her the lantern, but caught her chin before she could move. "You look like hell." He pulled a clean handkerchief from his pocket and wiped at the dirt on her cheek. "When was the last time you slept?"

Rachel nearly melted on the spot at the feel of his fingers on her skin. "Probably the night I spent with you." She bit her lip, appalled that she'd brought up the one night she desperately needed to forget.

"As I recall," he murmured, "we didn't sleep much that night." He leaned down and kissed her, his tongue soothing away the marks her teeth had made in her lip. "But that wasn't what I meant. You need some rest."

"Not with you." She pulled away, but he caught her arm easily and turned toward the cabin. He walked beside her in silence, ignoring her huffing and disgruntled sighs. She wanted to ask why he'd come back, how long he would be staying, but she didn't want to hear he'd only stopped in to be sure they had enough to eat. Her heart would break all over again when he left.

Rachel looked toward the eastern sky, where a line of color

glowed along the horizon. "We need to hurry." She tried to suit actions to words, but Jake held to their pace, keeping her tucked close to his side. "Jake?"

"What's the rush?"

"Nathan will be worried."

As they came in sight of the cabin, Jake grabbed her arm, hauling her to a stop. "Rachel, there's something I need to tell . . . to ask you."

Before he could continue, the door flew open and two boys tumbled out. Who was that? Rachel studied the child with Nathan as her brother came straight toward her. "Sis?"

"I'm all right." Rachel glanced at Jake and he released her. Nathan slipped an arm around her waist.

"What were you doing, going into that old mine? Don't you know it isn't safe?"

"I'm sorry if I worried you." She took a deep breath and said a silent prayer for the strength to just make it the last few feet to the porch. She didn't want to collapse on Nathan. She'd probably injure him again and Jake would have to carry them both inside.

A tremor ran through her at the possibility of being in Jake's arms again. *Stop acting like a schoolgirl. He made it very clear. He doesn't want you.* She repeated that thought like a chant, over and over in her mind.

Forcing what she hoped was a friendly smile, she turned to the other boy standing close to Jake. His blond hair was matted and messy. His face and hands had been washed, but his neck and ears were still the color of the dust covering his clothes. Fear and worry and anguish clouded the depths of his blue eyes. An answering ache bloomed inside Rachel. No one so young should hurt like that. The need to comfort and protect overwhelmed her. "Hello. My name is Rachel."

All color drained from the boy's face and he looked panicked as he backed into Jake. The man laid a hand on his shoulder and squeezed. "It's all right, son. Nobody here is going to hurt you. This is Nathan's sister."

"But he'll find me here," the child whispered, terror obvious in his eyes and voice. "I told you he'll look here."

Rachel crouched down until she was eye level with the boy. "Who will find you?"

Calvin shrank away from her even further.

"I won't let anyone hurt you." Nathan came to Calvin's side to reassure him. "I promised. Remember?"

The boy didn't look convinced. He stayed where he was, pressed up against Jake. "Rachel, this is Calvin."

The boy stared up at her as if the devil himself looked back. What could have happened to make him so frightened of her? And what was he doing here, with Jake?

She didn't ask the questions. No need to scare the boy further. "I'm getting cold," she announced, making her voice cheerful. "Why don't we go inside where it's warm? I can make us all some breakfast. I'll bet you're hungry."

"She makes the best biscuits," Nathan announced. "Wait until you taste them."

In spite of his apprehension, Calvin let Nathan lead him away from Jake. When Rachel turned to follow, Jake caught her arm and held her back.

She yanked free. Her fury, her heartbreak, poured out in a torrent. "How dare you bring that boy here? After what you did, riding off and leaving me to face my neighbors alone. Now you come back with a child. Who is he, Jake? Your son?"

"Calm down, pretty girl. He's not my son, but he is my responsibility." He tucked a stray lock of hair behind her ear, but she jerked away from his touch. "I found him tied up in a cave a day's ride from here."

Rachel felt ill. Her anger faded, replaced by revulsion. "Tied up? Alone?" She pressed a hand to her stomach when Jake nodded.

"Like an animal, with barely enough food to survive." He took her elbow and started after the boys.

Her heart broke for the boy. "I'm sorry I lost my temper. I'm glad you brought him here."

Jake caressed her arm all the way to her wrist and captured her hand. "This is the best place for him to be right now."

Rachel tried to ignore the thrill that went through her at his touch. She didn't want to be glad he was back. "Why is he afraid of me?"

"It isn't you, exactly," Jake explained. "The man that stole him from his family is the same one I've been chasing."

Rachel knew there was more, but they'd reached the cabin. She breathed a sigh of pure relief as Jake closed the door behind them. Nathan had the fire blazing, adding light and warmth to the cabin. Jake released her arm and helped her remove her coat. She couldn't stop a shiver when his fingers caressed her neck and shoulders as he lifted the heavy garment. She stood rooted to the spot, helpless to resist him, not wanting him to touch her again and praying he would.

"Sit down before you fall down, woman," he growled into her ear, his warm breath raising gooseflesh on her skin. Urging her toward the rocker, he went back outside, returning with an armload of wood. Rachel didn't move. She could only stare in fascination at the play of muscle in his thighs as he stacked the wood near the hearth. She wanted to touch him, to feel the power beneath his skin again. Her breath shortened and her fingers tingled. A heaviness that had nothing to do with fatigue filled her, and her breasts grew tender.

Jake went in and out twice more, bringing wood and buckets of water into the cabin. When he was satisfied they had enough, he closed and barred the door. He shook the dust from his coat and hung it on a peg. Her breath backed up as memories of touching those broad shoulders crowded into her mind.

"What are you boys doing over there?"

The reminder that there were children in the room broke the spell that held her motionless. She went to the stove to check the water in the kettle, anything to keep busy.

Jake crossed to the table. "Calvin?"

"Yes, sir?"

Her heart turned over at the insecurity in the boy's voice.

She glanced over her shoulder, watching Jake sit on his heels to talk to the boy.

"You need to wash up."

"I did."

Jake's grin made her heart skip a beat.

"Well, you need to do it again." He raked Calvin's clothes with a pointed look, then raised the child's arms and drew attention to the dirt lingering at the wrists. "You missed a spot or two."

"Do I have to?"

Jake chuckled and Rachel felt the sound all the way to her toes.

"Yes, and so do I. Miss Rachel won't allow us at the table unless we're clean and I'm getting hungry. Come on." He rose in a fluid motion. "I'll carry the water in there," pointing to Rachel's room. "I imagine Nathan has some clean clothes you can borrow for a day or two."

"Sure I do." Nathan jumped at the chance to help. "I'll get 'em." He ran for the stairs as fast as his injured leg allowed.

"You don't need to hurry that much. It's going to take a while for him to scrub off all that dirt." He urged Calvin toward the bedroom, then grabbed a bucket of water that had been warming on the hearth and followed. Jake pulled the curtain to cover the door, but Rachel could hear him reassuring the boy.

"You go ahead and get started. I'll come back and clean up when you're done."

"No! Don't leave me here."

Tears filled Rachel's eyes. How horrible for one so young to have suffered as Calvin had.

"I have to see to Griffin," Jake soothed. "He took really good care of us yesterday and he's earned some special treatment. I'm not going far. If you need me, you just call out. I'll hear you and come right back."

The racket of Nathan coming down the stairs made it impossible to hear what else Jake said. Heaving a sigh of pure exhaustion, Rachel headed for the door. She hoped Moses and his brood had been busy overnight, or breakfast would be biscuits and bacon.

The sky was turning pink, the color of the roses that grew on castle walls in her imagination. For a moment she stood still and just watched, wondering what it would be like to live in a castle, surrounded by people, servants scurrying to do her bidding, tables piled high with food without her lifting a finger. Oh, what a wonderful thing that must be.

"That smile is even more beautiful than the sunrise. What are you thinking about?"

Rachel stiffened when Jake stepped close and wrapped his arms around her waist. His warmth beckoned. Hating herself, she relaxed against him. It didn't matter if it was wrong, if he didn't want her. She couldn't help it. "I was just wondering what it would be like to have so much money that you never had to lift a finger to do any work."

"Is that why you were in the mine? You want to be rich?"

His voice sounded so bitter she twisted in his arms to see his face. "No. I just wondered." She separated herself from his arms and walked away.

"Where are you headed?"

"To see about eggs." She left the door to the lean-to open in case Calvin or Nathan called out and crossed to the coops stacked against one wall. One of these days, she needed to build a shelf to get them off the ground. But at least the cold didn't slow their production. She smiled as she pulled six warm eggs from the nests of hay. It wasn't a lot for the four of them, but it would do.

She stood and stretched, cradling her precious cargo in her apron. Jake followed her out, leading Griffin with only a hand in his mane. The horse's head was down, his brown eyes half closed. "He's certainly docile this morning."

"He's done in. We've been in the saddle since yesterday afternoon. With Harrison and his men on our trail, we couldn't take time to rest."

"Jake, what happened to Calvin?"

"You don't want to know."

"Yes, I do. It must have been horrible."

He stared toward the rising sun. "I rescued him from some very bad people. Once I get them rounded up and turned over to a Marshall somewhere, I'll return Calvin to his family."

She heard what he wasn't asking. "He's welcome here as long as necessary." There wasn't much extra, but she'd find a way to take care of him.

"Rachel?" He took her arm to tug her close. "There are some things you need to know. The man trailing us, William Harrison?"

"Is he the same man who beat you so badly?"

He smoothed his thumb across her brow and down her cheek, then wrapped one arm around her and turned toward the sunrise. "Yeah, but . . ."

Jake stared at the horizon for several seconds, as if debating what to tell her. His fingers moved absently, stroking the hair away from her neck and teasing her sensitive skin. She hoped he would kiss her, prayed he would. The need grew until she nearly begged.

"Calvin believes Harrison is . . ." He paused, kicking at the dirt, displaying an uncertainty she'd never seen in him.

A sick feeling washed through her. Rachel gripped his wrist, stilling his hand. "What is it? You're frightening me."

"He's coming for you."

"Me? But why? I've never seen the man before the night of the storm."

"Yes, you have. You just don't remember."

She concentrated, trying to picture the man who'd ridden up to the porch. She'd only glimpsed him through a slit in the shutters, refusing to unbar the door to so many strangers. He was probably tall, but it was impossible to know his true size because of the heavy coat he wore. His horse was a fine one, black, and the saddle had seemed expensive. But she hadn't seen his face, only that he had a mustache and long, blond . . .

She staggered as old memories collided with newer ones.

"Easy, honey." Jake steadied her, rescuing the eggs from a tumble to the dirt.

"It's him, isn't it?" Her harsh whisper hurt her throat. "The man who killed Mama. And he knows where I am. We have to get out of here." Panic filled her with a wild need to run away.

"Calm down. He's known since the night of the blizzard. I'm not sure he's looking for you, but, even if he is, he won't hurt you. I'll kill him before he can get close."

She forced her fear aside by concentrating on Nathan and Calvin. "That poor boy. What did that monster do to him?"

"Things a child should never have to suffer. But he needs love and care, and you're the best one to give it to him. He's under my protection, so the Texas Rangers will cover the cost of housing and feeding him . . ."

"Stop right there, Jake McCain."

"Don't argue with me. I can still take him to Fort Davis. I plan to pay for his care, no matter where he stays. I'd rather he stay with you. He needs mothering, tenderness, not a bunch of worn-out soldiers."

An argument failed to form in her tired mind. Calvin needed care and she really didn't have enough to feed another mouth. "All right. I'll accept the food and supplies. But no more than you would pay anyone else."

"Fair enough."

One corner of his mouth kicked up, and she couldn't resist touching his curved lips. Jake stood still and allowed her to explore for a few seconds, then took her hand and wrapped her fingers in the cloth of her apron. "Better get some breakfast started. I'll see to Griffin before I come in and wash up."

She turned to go, but he spun her back and captured her lips with his own. She managed to move the eggs aside before she was crushed to him and all thought spun out of her head. Rachel buried her fingers in his hair, pouring all the emotions she'd kept in check for the last week into the kiss. She had no idea if they stood there for a minute or an hour. Only Jake existed and she couldn't help feeling she was right where she belonged. He ended the kiss, set her away from him, and backed up a step.

"Damn," he managed, breathing hard. "I've needed to do that for the longest time."

Rachel smiled. She knew it because she felt her swollen lips curve. Rising on her toes, she kissed him again. She had a sudden, maddening urge to pull him into the lean-to and bar the door. She'd actually taken a step toward him when the door opened behind them. She would have bolted, but Jake held her in place, chest to chest, close enough to feel his heat.

"Mr. Jake?"

She heard the uncertainty in the question. The poor child must be terrified.

"We're in the lean-to," Jake called out. "Come on over here and let me see you." By the time the boy rounded the corner, Rachel was halfway to the porch. Calvin offered her a small smile as he passed. She started humming, her fatigue forgotten in the glory of a new day. Jake had kissed her. He wanted her. Maybe there was hope after all.

The man called Wolf rode a hundred paces ahead of Harrison and Cooke. It was only partly because of the stench of filth and death that rode them like a garment. Mostly it was self-preservation. At this distance, their first shot at him would likely miss. They needed him to track the man and boy, but he wasn't a fool. Harrison was just waiting for the right moment to put a bullet in his back. When the man decided Wolf was no longer necessary, his life wouldn't be worth the dirt they'd bury him under. He had too much to live for to allow that to happen.

He glanced at the tracks he followed, then up at the rocky desert stretching before them. The man was smart. He hoped it was the Texas Ranger that had dogged them since Pecos. He shuddered at the memory of that night, of the killing he hadn't been able to prevent. He consoled himself that the man had been a down-on-his-luck miner, with no family depending on him. But it didn't stop the guilt from plaguing him. Just another reason to see Harrison in hell.

He pulled his horse to a stop and dismounted, making a show of looking at the tracks in the mud. He'd been making a slow, wide circle, giving the Ranger as much time to get ahead as he could, but Harrison was growing impatient.

"Well?" The man in question rode up behind Wolf. "Where are they?"

Wolf pointed northeast.

"He's heading back to Lucinda. How nice of him to make it easy for us to retrieve our property. I'll be able to get the boy and the woman, all at the same time. I can't wait to see my brother's face when I bring his gift."

The tracker climbed back into the saddle, wishing Harrison didn't have such a good sense of direction. If he was the kind who got lost in a crowded room, Wolf could have led them halfway to California and the son of a bitch would've been none the wiser. But Harrison was a decent tracker in his own right. He'd only hired Wolf because he wanted the best, and because Harrison didn't do anything himself if he could pay a man to do it for him. Including kill an innocent woman.

Harrison set the pace for Lucinda. It was out of Wolf's hands now. He thought back to the pretty woman who'd been an obsession for Harrison and his brother for longer than anyone remembered. Wolf had only glimpsed her, backlit by the fire, when she'd peered out through a shuttered window in a snowstorm, but she had a voice that warmed his frozen heart and hair the color of his dead wife's.

Memories crowded in, of the sparkling gem that had been his wife, and the two beautiful children she'd given him. His heart cracked a little, bleeding guilt and regret and hatred into his soul. The man who'd murdered his beloved Emily would forfeit his life to Wolf, but not yet. Not until he found his family.

Breakfast was a noisy affair. The two boys shoveled in food and talked at once, competing for the attention of their hero. Jake's head was aching by the time Rachel shooed them from the table and outside to do the chores. He gathered dishes and carried them to the dry sink for her.

"How do you stand the noise?"

She glanced up at him, confused. "What noise?"

"The constant racket." He lifted the bucket of warm water and filled the dishpan for her. "Two is all I can stand. I don't want to imagine eight or ten or a dozen children in one room."

Rachel's brows furrowed as she considered his comment. "I suppose I've become accustomed to it." She chuckled, a soft sound that shot straight to his gut. "I don't really notice it. I'm just grateful they have something to laugh about."

She rinsed the last plate and handed it to Jake to dry. "Do you know where Calvin's family is?"

He wished he could say yes. "I didn't even know about Calvin until yesterday. He's got some cuts and scrapes on his wrists that need tending. I couldn't do much more than wash them clean last night."

"Why didn't you say so right away?"

"He needed food and a little time to get used to you."

"But they might become infected." She dried her hands on her apron and hurried to the door. "Calvin?"

Seconds later, a voice answered, too young and innocent to have suffered as he had. Fury and hatred warred in Jake and he shoved the emotions back into a corner of his soul, where they would fester. He wanted them there when he killed Harrison, just another reason for the man to die.

He stood behind Rachel, to reassure Calvin. Jake refused to acknowledge the part of him that wanted to be close to her. She was bent over, examining Calvin's wrists. He fought the urge to take hold of her hips and pull her to him and ease the ache that was growing below his belt. Never had a woman affected him this easy. The sound of her voice was enough to make him as hard as a post. The scent of her skin nearly sent him over the edge. For one mad instant, he considered sending the boys to town for supplies so he could be alone with her. He'd even take her back into that crumbing hellhole of a mine if it meant he'd have her to himself for an hour. But he was afraid an hour wouldn't be enough. In fact, he wasn't sure he'd ever get enough of Rachel Hudson.

"Jake? Jake."

Shaking himself from his daydream, he concentrated on Rachel. By the exasperation in her voice, Jake knew she'd called him more than once.

"I have some salve that I think will help these rope burns, but I'd feel better if Abby took a look at him."

Jake nodded agreement. "Then we'll all head into town. I want to get some supplies to tide us over if Harri—" He stopped, watching Calvin. "If we need to stay inside for a while."

Rachel understood. Jake expected to be defending them against an assault by Harrison and his men. "Can't you just go get her and bring her here?"

He was shaking his head before she finished the question. "I'm not leaving you alone."

"It won't take you long to get there and back." Rachel smoothed a hand over Calvin's hair and sent him back outside.

"It doesn't matter. Harrison is coming. I can feel it. I won't leave you out here by yourself, you or the boys."

He watched fear cloud her beautiful eyes and hated that he'd caused it. "Don't worry, pretty girl. He'll have to kill me to get to you and I don't plan on dying anytime soon."

"Don't talk like that, Jake McCain. I can't bear it."

She threw her arms around his neck and held on. Jake couldn't stop his arms from creeping around her, pulling her close so he could inhale the scent that was uniquely Rachel. After all it might be the last time he held her. He'd lied to her. Someone was going to die ridding the world of the scum called William Harrison, and Jake had already volunteered.

Chapter Fifteen

The fuzzy green of spring growth hazed the landscape as they walked to town. Rachel could hardly believe it had been barely a week since Jake had nearly died in a blizzard. Calvin was a bright boy and it was gratifying to see him begin to trust her. The boys chattered together, calling questions to Jake and laughing like old friends. Rachel was glad. Nathan wasn't the only one who missed Matthew and the other children.

Guilt over a past she couldn't change dimmed the sunny morning.

"What's wrong, pretty girl? You look like a thundercloud fixin' to rain all over the place."

"It isn't fair," she blurted.

Jake took her arm and slowed their pace, letting the boys get ahead. "Care to explain that?"

She ducked her head, embarrassed at her outburst. "I'm sorry. But Nathan didn't ask to come from where he did and it isn't fair for the people of this town to hold it against him. He misses his friends. Not one of them came by to see him after he was hurt. Their parents wouldn't allow them to associate with us. Abby tried. She told them they were wrong about me, about—us." She ducked her head to hide the blush. "But they refused to listen."

"He and Calvin seem to have hit it off."

"Nathan likes having someone to take care of, I think. But Calvin won't be here long. You'll be taking him home to his family soon, won't you?"

"After I take care of Harrison, I'll get him to his folks. But for now he needs a friend, too. Nathan is good for him."

"It's nice to hear him laugh. I can't imagine what he went through."

"You should be able to. It isn't that different from what you survived."

She stared at him, shocked. "It wasn't like that at all. I wasn't a prisoner of the Hudson's."

"They didn't exactly welcome you."

She stared around the little town as they started down the single street. Had she been more prisoner than adopted child? "It's true they didn't view me as a daughter, but they didn't starve me or tie me up like a dog. It wasn't always a pleasant life, but I had my brother."

Nathan's best friend, Matthew, spotted them. Rachel saw him look left and right, obviously checking to see if anyone was watching, before running the length of the street to meet them.

"Nathan, you're walking."

Rachel could see the wariness in Nathan's eyes. He'd been hurt when Matthew's father had forbidden his friend to even talk to him. "Sure I'm walking. I wasn't really hurt that bad."

"Good morning, Miss Hudson. Ranger McCain," Matthew greeted formally before turning back to his friend. "Abby said it was awful scary in that mine. Was it? Did you really go inside and the ceiling caved in on you and Ranger McCain had to dig you out and—"

"Have you always talked this much?" Nathan gave his friend a little shove to stop the questions. "Matthew, this is Calvin. He's staying with us for a while."

The boys shook hands like gentlemen, then started off together.

"Nathan," Rachel stopped their headlong rush. "I want Abby to take a look at Calvin first."

"Then can we go to the park?"

"May we," she corrected, earning a roll of eyes from her brother. "If Abby says it's all right, I'll consider it."

The boys whooped and ran for the boardinghouse. Jake and Rachel followed at a more adult pace.

"The what?" Jake looked so puzzled she laughed.

"The park. It's the only patch of grass within a mile of town, just behind the schoolhouse. They won't be far."

"We're going into the General Store," he called after them. "You boys keep your eyes open for trouble. And stay where I can see you."

Calvin skidded to a halt. "Is he that close?"

"Probably not, but it's better to be safe."

Rachel shuddered at the idea of Harrison returning to Lucinda to find her. How much worse it must be for a young boy. "Calvin must be terrified."

"He seems to be handling it."

The boys disappeared inside the boardinghouse, only to come tumbling back out moments later, a cookie in each hand. Together they raced toward the opposite end of the short street as fast as Nathan's leg allowed.

Rachel glanced around, afraid of seeing anyone but hoping at least one of her students would come to say hello. Nothing moved but the wind. Somewhere nearby a dog barked and she heard a door close, but she couldn't see anyone. Sadness swamped her. They'd shut her out completely. What would she do now?

"Rachel. Ranger McCain."

They turned toward Abby as she crossed the dusty street. Rachel was enveloped in a hug before she could return the greeting.

"How are you, honey? Nathan looks fine now. He isn't limping much at all."

"We're doing well, Abby. Thank you for all you did for him—for us."

"I didn't do anything you couldn't have done. I just happened to be there." She looked Jake up and down. "I declare, Ranger, I've never seen you when you weren't covered in dust."

Rachel giggled. She hadn't considered it, but she was right. Jake blew in and out of town so fast she never really took time to look at him. Except for the night she'd given herself to him.

"Just part of the job, ma'am."

The older woman shook her head at his droll tone.

"Do you think Calvin will be all right?"

"You did a fine job, honey," Abby reassured Rachel. "He'll have some scars, but I didn't see any sign of festering." She turned with them and continued down the street. "Where'd the boy come from?"

Before Jake could answer, screams ripped through the morning air. They came from the direction of the schoolhouse. And the boys were nowhere in sight.

"Nathan!" Rachel was running before the sound died, but Jake grabbed her by the arm and hauled her to a stop. She struggled against his hold. "Let me go. Nathan is in trouble."

"You get out of sight."

Other doors along the street opened as people poured outside to see what was happening.

"I've got her, Jake. Go." Abby took Rachel's arm in an iron grip and tugged her toward the boardinghouse. "Come on. We'll be safer inside."

"But Nathan and Calvin—"

"Will be better off if we don't get in Jake's way."

Rachel wanted to argue, but saw Jake turn back to check on her. If he was worried about her, he couldn't be as careful. She had to let him do his job. "Be careful," she whispered. Choking on her fear, she let Abby lead her away.

Jake watched Rachel until her foot hit Abby's porch, then turned and ran toward the schoolhouse. "Take cover, all of you," he cautioned the onlookers. He saw Hank Gerard, a loaded rifle in his hands, step out of the General Store. "You're with me." When he drew his pistol, the rest of the people ducked inside. He heard shutters slamming the length of the street behind him.

How could he have been so stupid? He knew Harrison was

close, but he'd let the boys get out of sight. As he came alongside the small frame schoolhouse, he dropped into the dust, lying still to listen. Gerard stretched out beside him a moment later, breathing hard.

Jake let his own heartbeat slow, searching with eyes and ears for any sound from the three boys. Nothing. In a low voice, he issued instructions to Hank. "Go around the other side and take up a position where you can see the park, but stay low. There are at least three of them. Don't shoot unless you have to. I'm going around that way." He indicated his intended direction with a move of his head, then waited while Hank took position.

He studied the area with care, looking for all the places a gunman could hide. The skeleton of a covered wagon squatted at the end of the street, the bony structure half hidden behind the livery stable. Rachel said the park was just out of sight beyond the schoolhouse. The only visible cover was a small grove of trees to the right and a whitewashed barn about fifty yards away. The trees offered him the best vantage point.

Jake rose to a crouch, prepared to make a dash for them when a sound came from behind him. Whirling and dropping into the dust, he aimed his pistol at a man's chest.

"It's me." The whisper was choked out of a wisp of a man he remembered slightly. "Daniel Parker."

Jake swore a blue streak. "Get back inside."

"My son, Matthew, is out there." Parker hefted his double-barreled shotgun. "I'm not going without him."

Jake considered arguing, but there wasn't time. Nodding once, he motioned for Parker to watch the street behind them. There was no sign of Harrison, but he was there. Jake could smell the evil that followed the man everywhere. He waited until Parker had hidden himself the best he could, then sprinted for the trees. A rifle barked and the shot whined off the old oak he dove behind. *There's one, on top of the barn.* He changed positions for better cover and scanned the area. There'd been three other men with Harrison at the cave. Where were they hiding?

"What's the matter, Ranger McCain? Can't you see me?"

Harrison's voice came from behind Jake. He spun to face him, dropping into a crouch to present a smaller target.

"Here, is this better?"

The outlaw stepped out of the schoolhouse door, holding Calvin in front of him. Dressed in black, he looked thinner than Jake remembered, but the long yellow hair gave him away.

"I could have shot you, you know, just now. Bang. One bullet to the back of the head and no more Ranger McCain."

"Let the boys go, Harrison. This is between us."

"Oh, it's much more than just you and me. This is involved." He gave Calvin a shake. "And there's the woman. I'll have her, too. Then we'll go"

"Where are the other boys?"

The curving of lips could hardly be called a smile. "They're safe inside and will remain that way as long as you give me what I want."

"I didn't figure you for a coward, Harrison, hiding behind women and children." Jake could see Harrison's eyes go black with fury even from this distance.

"For that, you will die."

As the outlaw raised his pistol toward Jake, a streak of blue caught his attention. Rachel raced down the street toward Harrison.

"Let him go," she screamed. "It's me you want. Please don't hurt him."

"Rachel, get back!"

Harrison waited until she was in Jake's line of fire before shoving Calvin aside. As the boy dove for cover, the outlaw grabbed Rachel by the hair and hauled her in front of him. It was Jake's nightmare coming true.

"I told you I'd have her, Ranger McCain," he taunted.

"Let her go, Harrison."

The man laughed, an evil sound. Jake could see Rachel shaking. She tried to get free, but Harrison only tightened his grip. Rachel whimpered in pain and the sound tore at Jake.

"Take me instead. You can demand a reward for my release. No one will try to stop us."

"You're surrounded, McCain. You'll be dead before I ride over that hill. What good is a dead man?"

"What about the boy?" Jake needed to stall Harrison, give himself time to think.

"Keep him, Ranger. I have what I've been searching for since the day her whoring mother got in the way."

Careful to keep Rachel between himself and Jake's revolver, Harrison dragged her toward the copse of trees. Jake knew the horses must be there, but there was no way to stop the man while he held Rachel.

Jake stayed under cover as long as he could, but he wouldn't let them out of sight. He glanced toward Calvin once more, grateful that the boy had the sense to stay out of reach.

Even as the thought formed, Calvin ran at Harrison and threw himself at the man's legs, knocking him off balance. Rachel wrenched free just as a shot rang out from the other side of the street, striking the outlaw in the shoulder. He staggered forward, still aiming his pistol at her. He pulled the trigger as he ran, and Rachel crumpled to the ground as Harrison escaped to his horse.

Jake's heart slammed against his ribs. Was she hurt? He jumped to his feet, thinking only of getting to her. A shot rang out from the barn roof, striking the dust near his feet. He threw himself to the side as answering fire came from behind the schoolhouse. The bark of Hank's rifle was followed by the deafening roar from both barrels of Parker's shotgun, raining lead at the place where the shooter hid. When another shot came from the roof, Jake took aim. It was too far, but he had to try while the others reloaded.

Before he could fire, a single rifle shot came from the alley beside the livery across the street. The outlaw's cry was short-lived. Jake heard his body slide down the shingles and thud to the ground. Silence descended on the street.

Crouching behind a large tree, he took aim at the alley and motioned for Hank Gerard to cover the back of the livery. Parker reloaded and trained his shotgun on the schoolhouse door.

"Matthew?" Parker's voice quivered as he called out.

"I'm all right, Pa."

"Who's with you, boy?"

"It's just me and Nathan."

Relief weakened the man and Jake saw him take a couple of breaths to steady himself. "You two stay put, son."

"We will, Pa."

At least the boys were safe. Jake turned his head toward the woman crumpled on the ground. "Rachel?" She moved a little and his heart lurched.

"I'm all right, I think. I just can't seem to catch my breath." Calvin crawled to her side and they lay still in the shadow of the schoolhouse.

Jake's hands shook. He took a steadying breath before turning his attention to the place where the last shooter hid. "We've got your only means of escape covered," he called into the tense silence. "Toss your guns out, then come on into the sunlight where I can see you, hands first."

"Take it easy, Ranger McCain," the shooter in the alley called out. "I'm on your side."

Calvin bolted upright at the sound of the voice. Rachel had enough presence of mind to grab his arm and hold him in place. Too bad she hadn't been smart earlier and stayed out of the way.

"Let me go." The boy struggled, trying to pull loose.

"Calvin Richards," the voice came again. "You mind your manners."

"Pa!"

Calvin tore from Rachel's grasp and raced across the street. Jake moved fast, trying to keep a clear shot as the man stepped into the open, but it wasn't necessary. A bear of a man dropped his rifle and went to his knees as the boy threw himself into his arms. It was the tracker who'd been traveling with Harrison. Tears streaked down the man's cheeks and disappeared into his rough beard. Jake hadn't figured on Wolf being so big up close. He looked huge as he clutched the boy to his chest.

"Pa, I knew you'd come. I just knew it."

"Are you all right, son?"

They spoke over each other, words tumbling out of them. Jake scooped up the dead outlaw's pistol and strode across the street to pick up Wolf's rifle. Leaving them to their reunion, he scanned the area once more for any more threats. Daniel Parker was already heading for the schoolhouse to check on Nathan and Matthew. Satisfied it was over, he went to Rachel. When Hank walked into the open from the direction of the park, Jake could tell by the set of his mouth and his angry stride that Harrison had escaped. The bitter taste of failure filled his mouth and his anger erupted at Rachel.

"Damn it, woman," he raged, pulling her to her feet. "What the hell were you thinking?" He grabbed her shoulders and gave her a hard shake. "You could have been killed and there was nothing I could do to stop it."

Without any warning, fear overwhelmed him and he dragged her into his arms, holding her with no consideration of who might be looking. Burying his fingers in her hair, he kissed her hard, then folded her into his arms again. "Don't ever do anything so stupid again, do you hear me?"

He felt her slight nod, only dimly aware that she probably couldn't breathe, let alone speak. He loosened his arms just enough to look down at her face. The echo of terror was still evident in her shadowed blue eyes. Shame washed through him but the apology he owed her wouldn't come. He kissed her again, more gently this time. "You have to trust me to do my job, Rachel."

"Nathan?" The whisper was soft, but enough to break the spell. Releasing her, he turned his back and waited while she straightened her dress. By the time she was set to rights, his jaw ached from gritting his teeth against the need to sweep her up and carry her away from here. She'd never know the effort it took to calmly take her arm and lead her toward the crowd that had gathered once they knew the shooting was over. Nathan and Matthew were at its center.

"Sis!" The young man became a boy again with one word and threw himself at Rachel. "Are you hurt? You scared me to death. Don't ever do that again!"

Rachel didn't respond. She just gathered him close and held him for long, silent minutes. Jake looked up as the crowd parted to admit Calvin and Wolf. Daniel Parker walked behind them, his shotgun loaded and ready to fire. Matthew was at his father's side. The townsfolk stepped back, well out of reach.

"Ranger." Wolf stopped within reach of Jake, letting him know without words he was through fighting. "I'm Cain Richards. Thank you for rescuing my son."

Jake studied the man. He was half a head taller and several pounds heavier than Jake. Intelligence shown in his gray eyes. And he held his son's hand in a gentle, unbreakable grip. "You're the one they call Wolf." It wasn't a question, but Richards answered.

"I am. Everything you've heard is probably true, except for the reason I'm with Harrison."

"Which is?"

"He had my children. It took me nearly three months to find the son of a—" His shoulders heaved with the effort to hold back his rage. "I needed a way to stay close. A good tracker was useful to him, so he took me on. It let me run him in circles a few times and mess up some of his plans."

"Like at the cave."

"I hoped it was you that had my children. I wasn't going to risk losing your trail, but I gave you as much time as I could."

"It was enough."

Wolf hugged Calvin close, leaning over to examine a bruise coloring his cheek. When he straightened, Jake read resignation in his eyes. "Do what you have to with me, just promise you'll see my boy taken care of."

Calvin surged toward Jake. "You leave my pa alone!"

Wolf caught the boy around the shoulders. "Easy, son. The Ranger has a job to do. We have to let him do it."

Jake eyed Wolf, taking his time, measuring the man and the boy he protected. Jake knew the man had joined Harrison's gang, but his name was never mentioned in connection with the mayhem. He'd only gone along with them to save his children. The trapper was deadly in his own right, but Jake didn't believe he was a murderer. He'd bet his life on it. But then, it wasn't his life that mattered. If he let the man go free, he'd be betting Rachel's life on it.

The people gathered nearby tensed, waiting to see if Jake would trust the man, but his decision was already made. He'd heard about this tracker and his kindness to friends and strangers alike, even while in Harrison's employ. More than one person had regaled him with stories of the man's generosity and gentle nature. Everything Richards said just confirmed what he already knew. Wolf Richards was not a criminal.

"I've got no reason to hold you. You're free to go."

Jake held out his hand and Richards took it. The tension in the crowd around them relaxed and people began to whisper among themselves.

"I appreciate it Ranger McCain." Wolf hugged his son close, and ruffled his blond hair. "Now I need to find my little girl."

A cry ripped from Calvin. Wolf dropped to his knees in front of him. "What is it, son?"

"I'm sorry I wasn't good enough, Pa," he sobbed. "I couldn't save her. I tried and tried, but I couldn't. I'm sorry, Pa. I'm sorry."

As realization hit, the mountain of a man crumbled. Agony etched deep lines on his face. He aged a lifetime in an instant and tears streaked the dust on his cheeks as he pulled Calvin into his arms. "It wasn't your fault, boy. I know you did everything you could. You have nothing to be sorry for." He rocked his son in his arms, comforting him. "Amanda's gone to be with Mama now."

"Mama?" Calvin's horrified whisper tore at Jake.

Wolf nodded. "I'm sorry, son. She died soon after you were taken away." His voice broke, cracking wide open with his grief. He held Calvin tight and they both cried for what they'd lost.

Jake looked away, giving them a small measure of privacy. "You folks clear out, now. There's nothing more to see." Rachel stood to one side with Nathan and Hank Gerard. She was dusty and her dress was torn, but she looked unharmed. Relief made him lightheaded. Giving in to the need, Jake covered the space between them and pulled her into his arms, kissing away her protest and the last of his fear.

When he lifted his head, she slipped her arms around his waist and laid her head on his shoulder with a sigh. She didn't seem to remember they were standing in the middle of the street, and it felt so right that Jake didn't care. Abby's laugh of delight brought them back to the present. Rachel tried to move back, but Jake didn't want to let go. He kissed her once more before releasing her.

"I . . . uh . . ." Rachel put a little more distance between them, smoothing strands of hair from her face. Her normally neat twist hung off center and partly fallen. The blush in her cheeks made her look like he'd just kissed her senseless. He liked it.

"You and Nathan should go home, Miss Rachel." Hank Gerard smoothed over the awkward moment like the gentleman he was. "Ranger McCain has work to do here."

"Yes, of course. I . . . uh . . . I'll just go home. " She lifted a hand as if to touch Jake, then turned away. "Mr. Richards, why don't you and Calvin come with us?"

She didn't even consider that the man might be a criminal. Jake opened his mouth to argue, then stopped. Richards was no danger. He knew it in his gut. After what the outlaw had done to his family, he couldn't doubt the man's reasons for being with him. Wolf would keep Rachel safe until Harrison was found. Jealousy twisted deep inside, but he fought against it. Rachel's safety was more important right now.

Wolf Richards stood in silence, watching Jake, waiting for his decision. Jake hated that he was so transparent. "I'd appreciate it if you would. Unless I catch Harrison first, he's liable to come back for her."

"He can try," the big man growled.

Jake almost smiled. Rachel would be safe with him. He turned Rachel to face him and ran his hands down the length of her arms until he could capture her fingers in his own. He knew he was staking his claim in front of everyone in town, but didn't care. "Pretty girl, don't go anywhere without Mr. Richards, you hear me? Promise me." He knew she was shaken when she didn't protest his order.

Wolf hugged Calvin close to his side. "I need to get my horse and gear."

Jake looked over Rachel's shoulder at the man. "Where did you leave it?"

Wolf indicated the direction of the park. "We tethered them all behind some trees on the left side of the clearing."

Jake nodded. "If it's still there, I'll bring it along when I come. I want you to take Rachel and the boys home where it's safer." Jake waited. If Wolf objected, he might have to rethink his decision to trust the man.

Wolf didn't even hesitate. "I'd be obliged. Assuming Harrison didn't steal everything," he added.

Jake relaxed a little. "I'll add it to the list of his crimes."

"That's got to be a damned long list, begging your pardon, ma'am." Wolf tipped his hat in apology, earning a smile from Rachel. Jake's gut twisted. He didn't want her smiling at the man that way. Richards offered his arm to escort her and Rachel accepted, laying her fingers on his sleeve.

Nathan and Calvin ran backwards and talked nonstop as she walked away with Wolf. The urge to go after her and bring her back took Jake by surprise. They looked so much like a family. Turning away from them was the hardest thing he'd ever done. He told himself nothing would happen. Rachel was just being herself, offering shelter to someone in need. And if feelings did develop between them, that was a good thing, wasn't it? He believed Richards was a good man. He'd make a good husband for her, certainly better than Jake could ever be. So why did Jake feel like he'd torn out his own heart?

With effort, he concentrated on the task at hand. The outlaw that Richards shot still lay in the dust. He'd get no information from him. He sent Hank into the schoolhouse to check for anything left behind.

"C-can I help?"

Jake looked up to find Daniel Parker at his side. The man was so upset, he was shaking, but he stood ready. Jake shook his head. The man would be worse than useless in the fight that was coming. "I think we've got it under control. You need to see to Matthew." He stood and offered his right hand. "Thank you for your help. I couldn't have done it without you."

Parker mumbled something and wandered away. Matthew caught up with him and turned him toward home.

"Excuse me, Ranger McCain." Arnold Miller stepped out of the small crowd that still milled around nearby.

Jake glanced around and recognized the self-proclaimed leaders of Lucinda. "What is it?" He didn't have time for this.

"We want to thank you for what you did today. You saved our little town. They could have done so much damage to our community. Oh, and for helping Miss Hudson and the children, as well, of course."

It was all Jake could do not to plow his fist into the man's face. "Just doing my job."

"Yes, well, we are most grateful. Anything you want, Ranger, anything at all. You have only to ask."

"Give Miss Hudson her job back."

Silence descended on the group. The man blinked twice, too surprised to answer. "I beg your pardon?"

"Send the children back to school. Miss Hudson did nothing wrong, today or before. She doesn't deserve to be cut off by the likes of you."

The insult struck its mark. Arnold Miller straightened to his full height, the flush of anger bright on his face. "I see. We did promise to grant your request, and if that's really what you want—"

"It is," Jake interrupted.

"Very well, she may return to the schoolroom in the morning." He spun on the heel of his highly polished shoes and stalked away. Lucinda Miller glared at Jake. Hate hung thick in the air between them. When she flounced after her husband, the rest of the citizens dispersed.

"Ridiculous fools." Hank Gerard joined Jake in front of the barn, turning his hat around and around in his hand. "I'll be glad to finally leave this place."

"I can't understand how you've stood it this long."

"It is home," the man replied simply.

Home. Jake had never called any place home, not even the house he grew up in. What would it feel like, to come back to the same place night after night, Rachel waiting for him with supper on the table? Wait a minute. Rachel? Home? What the hell was the matter with him? He knew better than to build dreams of a wife and family. An outcast like him would never have a home.

Chapter Sixteen

Jake turned his attention to business. "Someone needs to bury this man."

"I can make the arrangements." Hank settled his hat on his head. "Aren't you going after the other one?"

"Not until I get some supplies and my horse." Jake sat on his heels next to the dead outlaw and searched for identification and valuables. "He's injured. He won't make it too far." Finding nothing on the dead man besides a couple of coins and his revolvers, Jake stood. "Take these. It'll cover the cost." He handed Hank what he'd gathered. "Tell the undertaker I'll be back to check on his work."

"Where are you going?"

"Hunting."

"I will accompany you."

Jake studied the man. The flat sheen of purpose shone in his dark eyes. He would be a good man to have along. "I'd welcome the help."

"First, I must take care of *that*." Gerard's lip curled in distaste at the body in the dust. "Tell me where to find you."

"My horse and gear is at Rachel's."

"Fine. It will take a little while to gather what I need." He slid a shiny silver pocket watch from his vest. "Shall we say an hour?"

Jake checked the angle of the sun. "Make it faster. I don't want him to have any more of a head start than necessary. We leave as soon as you arrive." Jake strode off, heading for the park. He needed to look for Harrison's tracks while there was still enough light. He found where the horses had been hidden. Three remained, tied to a low branch, a well-bred chestnut mare, a sleek dappled gray gelding, and Jake's own packhorse, Duchess.

"Why didn't he take you with him?" He moved slowly, keeping his voice low, careful not to spook them. Duchess recognized him, whinnying and bumping his chest for attention. Jake scratched her ears before turning to the other horses.

The gelding had been hard used, but his spirit was intact. He tossed his elegant head as Jake checked him for injury. The mare was well cared for, her big brown eyes shining with health and intelligence. Judging by the size of the animal and the gear on the saddle, this horse was Wolf's.

He considered taking Duchess along with him when he went after Harrison, but dismissed the idea. She'd been hard used the past couple of days and deserved a rest. He scratched the little mare behind the ears and under the bridle, smiling when she bumped his chest trying to get closer.

Maybe Rachel would want to learn to ride. Duchess had a gentle personality and would make a fine saddle mount. He imagined teaching Rachel, sharing with her the sun and the wind, the freedom he found on horseback. He could see her joy, could almost feel her unbound hair brushing his cheek as they rode side by side . . .

Jake shook off the wishing for something he'd never have. Riding the gray and leading the other horses, he quickly covered the distance to Rachel's. When the cabin came into view, Wolf was on the porch, keeping watch over the area. A little of the tension left Jake. At least Rachel was in good hands.

Wolf met Jake near the lean-to. "No sign of Harrison?"

Jake handed over the reins of the mare and started removing gear from Duchess. "He mounted up and took off southwest."

"Back toward the cave."

"Has he used that place long?"

Wolf lifted the heavy packs from his horse and set them aside. "Don't know. The day you found Calvin was the first time I'd been there." He unbuckled the saddle and slid it off, careful not to drag the stirrup on the animal's hide. "Calvin might be able to tell you."

"I don't want to ask him. How he was left there was . . ."

The big man's shoulders tensed. "I'll kill the bastard," he whispered.

"I can't promise you'll get the chance."

Wolf faced Jake over the back of his horse. "I have the right to avenge my family."

"I'm not arguing that. But I'm not going to risk him escaping just so I can bring him back here for you to shoot."

"Then let me come along."

"No."

The narrow-eyed glare Wolf shot him told Jake a lot about the hatred and fury bottled up inside the man.

"This is my job to do. I need you here, to protect Rachel and the boys. If he gets by me, Harrison will come for her."

"Then don't let him get by you." The big man reached for a bucket of water and began washing the dried mud from his horse while Jake unsaddled the gelding.

"As long as I'm alive, he won't."

Wolf looked him up and down, considering. "She's that important to you?"

Jake hesitated. When had it become personal? He'd wanted to catch Harrison for years, almost from that day in El Paso, when he'd gone with his father to the scene of a gruesome murder and glimpsed the mangled body of a prostitute. When he'd been assigned to go after the Harrison gang, it was his job as a Texas Ranger to bring the outlaws to justice. He knew it was dangerous and he might not survive. He accepted that. But when had he decided he'd die to protect Rachel? When had she become his reason to live?

He turned back to Duchess, his mind in turmoil. Wolf's chuckle surprised him. He'd forgotten the other man was there.

"I know how it feels. My Emily had me tied up in knots from the moment I laid eyes on her. Just be warned, Ranger. Once they get in your heart, they stay there. Nothing you do will shake her loose."

Jake didn't bother to respond. Instead he led the little pack-horse into the corral. Wolf followed, so he left the horses in the man's care and went to get Griffin. Jake led his horse into the sunshine and saddled him. He was tightening the cinches when Hank Gerard rode up.

Rachel came out of the cabin to meet him. She wore a clean white apron over her blue dress and her eyes sparkled with laughter at something one of the boys must have said. Sunlight glinted off her blond hair, forming a halo around her head. Jake stared at her, committing every detail to memory. He wanted this beautiful sight to be the last thing he remembered if Harrison got lucky with a bullet.

"Hello, Mr. Gerard." Rachel stepped off the porch and joined the men near the lean-to. It felt good to be out in the sun again. She knew it was silly, since they'd walked back from town in the sunshine less than an hour ago. But she couldn't help feeling like the cabin was her prison now.

"You shouldn't be out here." Jake took her arm to lead her back to the porch.

"I need some fresh air. Just for a minute or two. Please, Jake," she pleaded, desperate to be near him.

She felt him give in, the pressure of his fingers becoming a caress just before he released her.

"Only for a couple of minutes. Then you go back inside and stay there unless you're with Wolf."

Hank Gerard dismounted. "I hope you are well, Miss Rachel. You gave us quite a scare."

She smiled at the man who'd been such a good friend. "I know and I'm sorry for it. But when I saw that monster's hands on Calvin, I didn't think. I just ran."

"You must not do that again, Miss Rachel." He smoothed an imagined wrinkle from the brim of his hat.

"I won't. I promise." Rachel kissed his cheek, an impulsive gesture of friendship. She smiled again as a blush washed over Hank's cheekbones.

"You should be careful, Miss Rachel," he teased. "Your Ranger McCain is a jealous man."

"He's not my—"

She broke off when Jake approached.

"You ready to ride, Gerard?"

Hank tipped his hat to Rachel and went to check his gear one last time. Jake walked with her a few steps away from the others. Her heart started pounding and fear crept in to steal the warmth of the sun.

"You do whatever Richards tells you. Promise me, honey."

She nodded, afraid if she tried to speak she'd start to cry. Jake lifted her chin with a gentle touch and waited. She stared over his shoulder, then down at the buttons on his shirt, anywhere but his eyes.

"Look at me, pretty girl."

She shook her head, but Jake didn't let go. Knowing she had no choice, she raised her gaze to his. The heat in his green eyes took her breath away. The tears she'd sworn not to cry slipped down her cheeks. Jake leaned forward and kissed one away, then another.

"Don't cry for me, honey. I'll be back."

"Promise me," she gave him back his own words.

A smile curved one corner of his mouth as he nodded. He kissed her again, a soft melding of lips, before releasing her and walking to his horse. She thought he waved as he left, but she couldn't be sure through the tears. She wiped them away with her apron, wanting to see him one last time. Wolf's mare whinnied to the disappearing horses, unhappy at being left behind. Rachel knew just how the animal felt.

"Let's get inside, Miss Hudson." Wolf took her by the elbow. Rachel resisted until Jake rode out of sight.

"Why aren't you going with him?" She didn't mean for the

words to sound like an accusation, but that was how Wolf heard them. She stood close enough to see the muscles in his jaw clench. Anger smoldered deep in his blue eyes.

"He asked me to stay here and protect you and the boys."

Rachel nodded. "I appreciate it, though I know it must be difficult for you."

He stared after Jake and Hank. "I'll manage."

She turned with him toward the porch. "You may as well call me Rachel. The cabin is too small to stay formal for long."

The big man grinned, white teeth flashing between his shaggy mustache and beard. "Most folks call me Wolf. My mother called me Cain. Take your pick."

Rachel looked up at Wolf. He was bigger than Jake, and his sable hair was shot through with silver. His skin was tanned from hours in the sun, and fine lines of grief and laughter set off eyes the color of a stormy sky. The hand he offered to help her up the stairs was huge, with calluses that proved he wasn't afraid of work.

Wolf opened the door for her. The boys were waiting for them. "Sis, me and Calvin are hungry."

"Calvin and I," she corrected, squaring her shoulders. She knew Wolf watched her and she wasn't going to give the man reason to think he'd been left with a weak, frightened female.

"Yes, ma'am," Nathan mumbled. "I'll bet Mr. Richards is, too," he added, turning hopeful eyes in the man's direction.

Wolf laughed, a deep booming sound Rachel felt to her toes. Now she understood what must have drawn his wife to him. A woman could get used to that sound. She let herself smile a little in response.

"So am I, as a matter of fact." Rachel gave Nathan's nose a gentle tweak. "Let's go see what we can find."

With three helpers, it didn't take long to put a passable meal on the table. She was grateful for Wolf's presence as he steered the conversation to safe topics, keeping the mood light. Laughter rang repeatedly through the small cabin. When the food was gone, Wolf sent the boys upstairs to find something to keep busy with while he helped with the dishes.

It reminded her so much of the time spent with Jake, Rachel nearly cried.

"Don't fret, Rachel. It won't help him and worrying will only make you sick."

"I know, but I'll worry anyway. It's the way I am."

As he dried and stacked the last plate, Rachel poured more coffee for both of them. All the shutters were closed, making the cabin gloomy and cold. She lit a lamp to brighten the room a little and settled into the rocking chair with her cup. Wolf sat down at the table and sipped the steaming liquid. It was unusual to have a time of inactivity and she found she liked sitting still with nothing more in her hands than a cup. With a small sigh, she leaned her head back and closed her eyes.

"How did you come to have my son?"

She started when his question broke the silence. "Jake brought him here yesterday. I don't know much of what happened," she explained when he raised one eyebrow in an obvious gesture of impatience.

"Tell me what you do know."

Rachel shrugged, a little embarrassed to be the focus of his attention. She could stand in front of a room full of children and talk for hours, but this one man made her nervous. "I don't know where to start."

"How about at the beginning? We've got nowhere to go."

She acknowledged the logic with a smile. "All right. The beginning." She stared at the hearth, remembering. "Jake passed out on my porch in the middle of a blizzard."

"I'm glad he found his way here. I managed to hide his horse from them, but I couldn't stop the beating."

"You were there? How could you let them do that?" She couldn't keep the censure from her voice.

Wolf shrugged. "They'd have shot us both if I got in the way." He traced a scratch on the old table with one thick finger. "I kept them from killing him. I couldn't do anymore. I still had to find my children. My son," he amended in a broken whisper.

"I'm so sorry about your daughter."

Rachel looked away, giving him a moment of privacy.

"She was so pretty, just as beautiful as her mother. They were like twin suns, Amanda and my Emily." He cleared his throat and swallowed some coffee. "Ranger McCain recovered." He changed the subject, prompting her back to her story.

"He was hurt pretty badly. Fortunately, the cold had stopped most of the bleeding."

Wolf glanced around the room. "Was it just you and your brother here that night?"

Rachel nodded, sipping her coffee.

"That explains why the folks in town were so quick to believe Harrison."

"But I didn't know who he was," she whispered. "I just saw men on horses. I didn't recognize him." She swallowed hard. Hiding her past was automatic, but with Wolf there was no reason for it. He'd heard a version of the truth from Harrison. "Why did he lie about me?"

"He lives to hurt people."

"Did you know he . . . he killed my mother?"

Wolf shook his head. "He never talked about the past. I'm sorry for your loss."

"You weren't there," Rachel excused.

"Doesn't matter. I understand how much it hurts." His eyes held compassion and sorrow.

"I suppose you do." Rachel let him refill their cups and waited for him to sit down again before continuing her story.

Wolf leaned forward as Rachel finally fell silent. "Tell me about Calvin."

Her brows drew together in concentration. "Jake left town as soon as the snow melted and returned several days later with Calvin. He wouldn't say much, only that Calvin had been tied up and left behind with just a small amount of food and water."

Wolf tried not to let his rage and hatred of Harrison show, but he wasn't successful. Rachel shrank back from him, pressing into the rocking chair as far as she could go.

He closed his eyes and struggled to stuff his emotions back

into the place, deep in his heart, where he kept them locked away. If they ever got loose, he doubted anyone within reach would be safe. When he thought he could look civilized again, he glanced at Rachel.

"Go on."

She didn't relax much. "We, uh . . . we cleaned him up and I treated the wounds the best I could. He stuck pretty close to Jake last night, but by this morning, he seemed more like a child again. We all walked into town and . . . well, you know what happened there."

He nodded.

"Calvin had a small bundle with him when he arrived. I don't know what's in it, but he put it over there."

She retrieved the bundle and laid it on the table in front of him. Wolf's breath hitched when he recognized the blue cloth Calvin had used to tie everything together. Tears he could no longer hold back rolled down his cheeks to dampen the shawl. He buried his face in the soft cloth. It still held his wife's scent. Sweet, gentle Emily. His heart broke all over again. He set the shawl aside and lifted a tiny doll from the bundle.

"This was Amanda's," he explained to Rachel. "Emily made it for her fifth birthday. Amanda never went anywhere without it." He took a deep breath, fighting for control. "I didn't realize it wasn't in the house anymore." He set the doll to one side, unable to look at it.

Wolf lifted his own pocket watch from the bundle. "Calvin loved this. I promised he could have it when he turned ten, but Emily told me he always carried it when I was off trapping."

The rocker squeaked as Rachel shifted. "I don't know what to say, Wolf."

"Nothing to be said. It's done." He gathered everything together, stroking the shawl one last time before placing it with the rest.

"I'm glad he has you, Wolf. And I appreciate that you trust me with him. All the other parents believe me to be unfit to be near their children."

"Not anymore, Miss Rachel. They want you back."

"What?" She leaned toward him. "How do you know?"

"Just before he left, Jake told me some man named Miller promised the children would be back in school in the morning."

Rachel jumped from her chair and spun in several quick circles, laughing and clapping her hands. "I knew they wouldn't believe those men." She did another quick turn. Wolf shook his head at her antics.

"I'm sorry," she managed as she gasped for breath. "I just can't seem to help myself."

"No need to apologize," he assured her, meaning it. "It's good to see someone happy."

"The Reverend would never approve." She spun once more, her skirt billowing around her legs. "But I don't care."

"Who's the Reverend?" Wolf refilled his coffee cup and walked from window to window, looking out across the landscape. He kept his movements casual, but checked every shadow, looking for anything that didn't belong.

Rachel sank back into the rocker to catch her breath before giving him a brief description of her life with Reverend and Mrs. Hudson and how she came to be in Lucinda.

Wolf closed the last of the shutters. "I take it they were strict with you and Nathan."

"They weren't unkind," she corrected. "Just very set in their ways."

She slipped into the next room and returned to the fire with a stack of books.

"What are those for?"

"School. It's been several days since I've seen the children. I need to review the last lessons I taught and prepare for the next ones."

Wolf picked up one of the books and flipped through a few pages. "This is important to you."

"Oh, yes. Once I get back to teaching, everything will be the way it was before all this happened." Rachel stopped. Was that what she wanted, to go back to the time before Jake had come into her life?

"Rachel." Wolf crossed the room and sat on his heels in front of her. "You know that's not possible."

"But I want it to be," she whispered. "At least part of it. I can't wish none of this had happened; then I wouldn't have met Jake, and I don't want to give him up." Tears slipped down her cheeks as she gathered her books and escaped into her bedroom.

Wolf stayed where he was for a long time, staring at the blanket she'd pulled across the doorway for privacy. *Poor woman,* he raged in silence. She didn't deserve what the people of this town had done, but there was no going back. How well he knew.

He crossed to a window. The sun was setting behind the cabin, washing the landscape with golden light. He studied every shadow thoroughly before lifting the bar from the door. Sliding his pistol from its holster, he checked the load automatically before opening the door and heading outside. He needed to move. Staying behind while other men hunted the snake he'd sworn to kill didn't set well with him. He understood the need to protect Rachel and the boys. He just didn't want to be the one doing it.

The fresh air helped to clear his mind. A light breeze blew across the desert, bringing with it the scent of new growth and a hint of the warmth to come. Wolf circled the dwelling twice, going as far away as he dared. From the top of a small rise to the south, he could see all the way to town. Nothing moved but the wind.

Holstering his revolver, he closed his eyes and let the sounds and smells wash over him, sorting and identifying each one until he was satisfied nothing was out of place. If Harrison was sneaking back, he wasn't nearby yet.

Wolf settled onto the ground and leaned back against a rock. This was the kind of night his Emily would have loved, warm and peaceful. Grief filled him, making it hard to breathe. He missed her so much. When he'd told the Ranger you can't get a woman out of your heart once she's there, he'd spoken from experience. Wolf knew he'd never be the same without her. And he'd never fall in love again, the pain was too great.

He'd come home an hour too late. He could still see himself walking to their remote cabin, hear the tune he'd been whistling. The results of two weeks' work were tied to his packhorse. The beaver and river otter pelts would bring a good price. It was late afternoon and there'd been wash on the line. That was the first indication that something was wrong. He went inside, calling for Emily, but she didn't answer. Breakfast dishes were on the table, drips of raspberry jam drying on the floor where they'd spilled. Then he realized it wasn't jam.

He found Emily in the bedroom, barely alive. They'd taken the children. She'd forced him to listen as she told him who the *monsters* had been, who he had to hunt down. He'd tried to help her, but it was too late. It took her hours more to die, and there was nothing he could do but watch.

He'd gone a little crazy that night. He didn't remember much of the hours before dawn. He'd buried Emily the next morning on a hill much like this one, so she could see the valley she loved so much. Then he went hunting.

If it hadn't been for his children, he'd have torn William Harrison apart with his bare hands the second he saw him. But the snake had been the only link to his son and daughter. So he'd hidden his hatred, his rage, and talked his way into Harrison's good graces, making himself indispensable. Would he have been able to do it if he'd known his daughter was dead, and how she'd died? Rage joined grief, growing until he couldn't think. Blood pounded in his ears, drowning out everything else, demanding revenge.

"Pa?"

Wolf reacted, throwing himself to one side and drawing his pistol an instant before he recognized his son's voice. The weapon shook in his hand as he pointed it away from Calvin and eased the hammer forward.

"I-I'm sorry, Pa. I didn't mean to scare you."

"Not your fault, Cal." Wolf shook his head at his own

foolishness. Here he was, supposed to be protecting Rachel, and he was so lost in thought he didn't even hear his son coming. "I deserved it." He resumed his original position against the rock.

The second he was settled, Calvin crawled into his lap. Wolf wrapped his arms around his son and held him close. Joy at having his boy back eased some of the grief. His fingertips touched the bandages on Calvin's wrists. "How'd this happen?"

"From the ropes. I kept trying to get loose, but they were real tight. I guess I tried too hard."

Only the boy's matter-of-fact tone kept Wolf's rage from spilling out again. His son had been tied up like an animal. He sat in silence for a while, letting the anger recede a little. "How'd you get free?"

"Ranger McCain found me and cut me loose. Then he carried me out of the cave and I got to ride his horse." Calvin sat up in Wolf's lap. "Did you see Griffin, Pa? He's the biggest horse I ever saw. And I got to ride him."

"You did? And you stayed right side up?" He ruffled his son's hair before tucking him against his chest. "Guess we'll have to start looking for a horse for you now."

Calvin sat up, his eyes wide with excitement. "Honest, Pa? I can have a horse of my own?"

Wolf laughed at his youthful enthusiasm and ruffled the boy's blond hair, so like his mother's. "You've grown, I think."

"Well, I am almost eight, Pa."

"So you are, son." He hugged Calvin close, then set him on his feet. "It's getting dark. We need to go back inside." When he felt the small hand slip into his, everything around him seemed to slip back into place. Wolf smiled. He still had his son. Everything would be all right.

Chapter Seventeen

Jake hauled back on Griffin's reins and brought him to a plunging halt. The shadow he'd come tearing up the hill after was gone—again. Frustration beat at him until he wanted to howl. Where the hell had the man gone?

Hank Gerard sat on his horse a hundred feet away, searching every fold of land for Harrison, but he wasn't there. "This is not possible," he commented with disgust.

"Somehow, it is." Jake climbed from the saddle, waiting until he got the feeling back in his legs before quartering the area for tracks. Wind had scoured the ground clean. "Damnation."

They'd been riding for four hours, spotting Harrison and losing him over and over. Just when Jake was ready to call a halt and turn around, the man would appear at the top of the next rise and the race was on again. But there was no rise beyond this one. From where he stood, Jake could see halfway to next week, and nothing moved across the wide desert valley.

"Where did the crafty bastard go?" Gerard walked a dozen steps to look into a shadow that might have been a cave. The barrel of his loaded rifle led the way. It turned out to be no more than what it looked like—a shallow indent in the rock.

"Damned if I know." Jake took his hat off and set it aside before dropping to his belly to have a look over the edge. There were handholds, if a man was set on going down that way, but not with a bullet in your shoulder like the one Harrison was sporting. Jake stood and brushed some of the dust off his shirt. Abby would have a good laugh if she could see him now. "Let's backtrack. We must have missed something, a cave or a cut in the rocks, someplace large enough for him to hide in."

"But we saw him here, after we came through the canyon."

"He's not here now." Jake had never been outwitted by a man so many times in one day. He didn't like the feeling.

"It will be dark soon."

Jake considered the angle of the sun and the weariness in the man's voice. A tired man made mistakes, deadly ones. "We'll bed down in the canyon. We both need rest and I'll feel better with solid rock at my back tonight."

Gerard dragged himself into the saddle and Jake led the way back down the steep hill toward the setting sun. He understood Gerard's less than hopeful words. Somehow Harrison had found a place to hide in the small canyon, or he'd managed to make it to a cutoff Jake had missed. Either way, he'd gotten away for tonight.

It took nearly an hour to reach their destination. Calling it a canyon was a generous description. The rock had been worn away by some ancient flow of water, leaving behind a split that was twice the height of a man and only half that wide. The sun had dropped behind the rim by the time Jake was satisfied they were alone.

They made camp in a wide spot that had just enough room for them to turn around the horses. The approach from either end was only wide enough for a single horse and could be defended easily by one man. He left Gerard building a small fire on the hard ground and walked east along the canyon floor, searching for the spot where their quarry had turned off and escaped. Since he didn't expect to find anything, he carried two empty water skins. There was a stream that tumbled into a small depression in the canyon floor a couple of hundred feet away. At least his trip wouldn't be wasted.

Nothing moved but the small animals that belonged here.

Jake couldn't hear anything but his own breathing and Hank setting up camp. They were definitely alone. As he turned toward the water, a dark smudge on the opposite wall caught his eye. He dropped the skins and drew his revolver, ducking lower to present less of a target. Foolish, since Harrison could have shot him in the back as he walked up. He approached the depression in the rock, half expecting gunshots to ring out with every step. But only silence greeted him.

This was the spot. There was blood on the wall at the height of a man's shoulder. Harrison had stopped here for water, *after* Jake and Hank Gerard had gone by. The blood still gleamed, wet and fresh, against the sand-colored rock. He'd stumbled against the wall, reopening his wound. Jake followed the trail a little farther to be sure Harrison was gone. He found the place where he'd stopped to drag himself into the saddle. If Jake was reading the tracks right, the man continued to move south, away from Lucinda. But after this day, he wasn't sure he trusted himself about anything.

For a heartbeat Jake wanted to whistle for Griffin and ride hell-bent for Rachel, but good sense prevailed. Racing around in the dark was too dangerous. They'd have to wait for first light. He hoped Harrison went to ground, too. If not, he'd have a hell of a head start by morning. Holstering his gun, Jake filled both water skins and returned to camp.

"He was at the water hole, sometime after we rode through."

Hank Gerard stopped stirring the soup he was heating and stared at Jake. Liquid dripped from the spoon to sizzle in the flames licking around a small metal pot. "How is that possible? He was ahead of us. I saw him. He couldn't have gotten past us."

"He did. I found fresh blood, shoulder high, on the rocks near the pool."

"What do we do now?"

Hank stayed silent, waiting for instructions. Jake had to admit, he'd never ridden with a better man. For a while, he'd found himself wishing he'd brought Wolf along. The tracker could have found Harrison no matter where he hid. But he needed Wolf to keep Rachel safe. Gerard would have given his life for her, but, in a gun battle, his life would probably have ended a lot sooner. Wolf was where he needed to be.

Hank Gerard had proven himself to be a decent partner. He was always ready to do what was asked, never complained, or insisted on stopping. And Jake knew he could trust the man to stay by his side when the bullets started flying. But they both needed some rest. "We eat and get some sleep. We'll head out again at first light."

Hank picked up the second water skin and filled both their canteens and a coffeepot. He set the pot on a level spot near the fire before following Jake to the horses. They stood side by side, holding open the skins while the animals slaked their thirst. Gerard broke the silence. "Which way?"

Jake didn't have to ask the man which way to what. "He's still headed south."

Gerard stifled a groan. "Shouldn't we follow him?"

Jake shook his head. "Riding now would be dangerous for the horses."

"And if he circles back in the night?"

He paused, fighting back the urge to race back to Rachel. "Wolf is there. She'll be safe."

Hank stood still, considering. "He's a good man, I think. Gentle with his son. You trust him."

It wasn't a question, so he didn't answer. When Griffin had his fill of the water, Jake set the skin aside and started removing tack from the tired animal. After a quick grooming, he poured a mound of grain for each horse from the bag tied on behind his saddle. There was no grass to speak of in the canyon, so he gave them each a little extra. It would have to hold them for tonight. He made sure all the gear was arranged so they could saddle up in a hurry before returning to the fire.

"Thanks," Jake accepted a tin cup full of steaming liquid. Bits of meat floated on the thick surface.

"Don't thank me until you have tasted it," Gerard joked. "It will fill you up, but I cannot promise it will be an enjoyable experience."

Jake laughed with him. The first couple of bites were too

hot to taste, but the night air quickly cooled the soup as he ate. "Not bad," he commented when his cup was empty.

"Hmm, high praise indeed, I think."

"Not really. You haven't tasted my cooking yet."

Gerard uncorked a small flask from his coat pocket and held it out. A whiff of eye-watering fumes shouted a warning about the contents. Jake accepted it and tipped it back. He barely managed to swallow the clear liquid before the coughing started. "What the hell is that stuff?"

Gerard drank a share and sat back with a laugh. "My own recipe. Strong, yes?"

Jake eyed him through a haze of tears. "You could say that."

"Miller charges too much for what he calls whiskey. I decided, if I had to drink bad alcohol, it should be free. So I make my own." He capped the flask and put it away. "It also lasts a long time because one swallow is all I can stand."

Jake actually laughed. Despite their situation, and the fact that Harrison had managed to elude them for the better part of a day, Jake found himself relaxing. Since it wasn't the alcohol, it must be the company.

Gerard poured half the hot water from the coffeepot into the soup pot to wash it. Then he dumped two handfuls of coffee grounds into the remaining water and returned it to its spot near the fire. Before long, a rich familiar scent rose with the steam. With it came memories of his first morning in the small cabin, and Rachel's reaction to his supply of coffee beans.

Would she share that smile with the big tracker? He could see the four of them, sitting down to eat at the small table. Rachel and Wolf would be close enough to touch. He might take her arm again, like Jake had seen when he looked back at the cabin this afternoon. Maybe something would start up between them. Wolf was a good man. He'd make Rachel a fine husband.

Jealousy stabbed at Jake, driving his breath from his lungs. He wanted to break the man's neck for even looking at Rachel. The feeling was ridiculous, but he couldn't seem to control the beast that rose up inside him. Rachel couldn't have a future with anyone but him.

Future? His whirling thoughts ground to a halt. When the hell had he started thinking about having a future? He'd always known this was his last assignment as a Texas Ranger, figuring he'd die bringing Harrison to justice. It never bothered him before. But he hadn't known Rachel before. Everything changed the night she came into his life. What the hell did he do now?

"It is a scary thing, isn't it?"

Gerard's voice yanked Jake back to the present. He'd forgotten the man was there. "What are you talking about?"

"Falling in love. It can be quite terrifying." Gerard offered a cup of coffee. "It is written all over your face," he explained. "Miss Rachel has prompted such ideas in many men."

"She hasn't done anything that warrants the judgment of those people," Jake defended.

"Of course not," Hank agreed. "It is her generous heart, I think. It shines from inside her and gives men ideas of family and the future."

"I don't have a future to offer." Jake gulped down the hot liquid to wash away the bitter taste of disappointment. For the first time in his life, he wanted to see tomorrow.

"That is the wonderful thing about the future. It hasn't been lived yet. Anything is possible."

Jake shook his head. "She'd be better off with Wolf."

"But she doesn't want him." Gerard settled back.

The wood crackled and sparked, sending showers of sparks into the silent night air as Jake stared across the fire.

"She is kind, to everyone." Gerard's accent thickened. "Only for you has she ever been worried. Only for you has she cried. Accept it, my friend. You have touched her heart."

Rachel slept for the first time in nearly a week. One moment she was listening to the murmur of voices as Wolf settled Calvin into a bedroll near the fire, and the next the sunrise was touching the cabin, filling it with golden light. She stretched and snuggled under the blanket to enjoy the warmth for a moment longer. Joy filled her. She was going back to school today. When she heard movement in the next room, she slipped from her bed and hurried through her morning routine. It wouldn't do to be late.

She rushed the boys through breakfast and urged them to wash up quickly. "I want to be there before any of the children arrive."

"But, Sis, we'll be there so you won't be first."

"I will be if you don't hurry up."

The race was on. The boys clambered up the stairs to get Nathan's slate and books and chased each other back down again. Rachel was waiting at the door. "Put on your coats. It's a chilly morning."

"Where's Pa?" Calvin shoved his arms into an old coat that was three sizes too big. Rachel bit the inside of her lip to keep from smiling at the picture he made.

"He's outside waiting for us. He wanted to look around a little before we left."

"What about my chores?"

Nathan joined them, wearing a coat that was just a little short in the arms. Rachel stared at him. "When did you grow another inch?" Her brother grinned at her, pleased she noticed. "You two should swap coats."

Calvin and Nathan examined each other before doing as she suggested. When they were buttoned up once more, Rachel laughed. The coat sleeves hung to the knuckles of each boy, but it was an improvement. "I think that's the best we can do. Are you ready?"

"Not until Pa comes back." Calvin crossed his arms and stood in front of the door. "When he thinks it's safe, he'll come back and get us." Nathan joined his friend, blocking the way outside.

"But we'll be late."

"Don't matter," Calvin began, but Nathan elbowed him in the ribs.

"*Doesn't* matter."

Rachel stared in amazement at her brother. He caught the look and shrugged. "Sis, don't I need to do my chores?"

"Mr. Richards did them before you woke up."

The boy's brow furrowed. "I didn't hear him go out."

Calvin nodded. "I'm not surprised. Pa can be real quiet when he needs to be. He's the best tracker in the territory."

"Calvin?"

Both boys jumped when Wolf spoke from directly behind them. Calvin recovered first. "Told you." That set both boys off and laughter trailed behind as they raced out the door.

Rachel waited while Wolf secured the cabin. "Is it safe?" Rachel kept her voice down, not wanting to spoil the boys' fun.

"Not sure. I don't think he's anywhere around, but there's no way to know for certain." Wolf walked beside her, matching his steps to hers. His eyes never stopped moving, checking every rock and shadow for hidden danger. "Calvin. Nathan. Don't get so far ahead."

"Yes, sir," Calvin called back, slowing the pace so the adults could catch up.

"Maybe he's not going to return."

Wolf shook his head once and took her elbow to help her over a rough patch of ground. "He'll be back. A man like him won't give up on something he wants."

"Maybe we shouldn't have come?" She looked over her shoulder, half expecting to see Harrison hiding behind a tree.

"Just stay close to me and do what I tell you without asking why. I won't let anything happen to you or the boys."

An uncomfortable feeling washed over Rachel as they walked down the street. Had it only been a day since she'd come this way with Jake and ended up in the middle of a gunfight? Harrison had gotten so close to catching her after all these years. She shook off the memories and concentrated on the morning ahead.

The schoolhouse was empty and cold. Wolf kept them close by while he went through the building to be sure no one waited inside. Satisfied it was safe, he went outside to check the area while Rachel set up what she needed and waited for the children to arrive.

An hour later, they were still alone. None of the children had come.

"I'm sorry, Miss Rachel. Miller gave his word to McCain. I assumed that meant something."

She closed the book she'd been trying to read with a little too much force. "It would seem their gratitude was only as deep as Jake's shadow on their godforsaken street."

"Sis!"

"Never mind." Fury built until Rachel couldn't contain it. She marched out of the schoolhouse, aiming for the General Store. Wolf pulled her up short.

"Where are you going?"

"To find Lucinda Miller and give her a piece of my mind. Kindly release me, Mr. Richards."

Wolf let her go, but stayed on her heels. Rachel didn't care. She had a score to settle. The front door of the General Store hit with a satisfying thump when she threw it open against the wall. It shocked her to realize she'd half hoped the fancy painted glass would break. Trying to calm her racing heart, she crossed the hardwood floor until she stood toe-to-toe with the woman who'd ruined her. "None of the children showed up this morning, which I'm sure is no surprise to you. Mr. Miller gave his word to Ranger McCain that . . ."

"Arnold only agreed because he feared the Ranger's reprisal against the town should he refuse."

Rachel was outraged. "Jake McCain is an honorable man. He wouldn't terrorize this town because you disagreed with him."

Lucinda sniffed once. "That is your opinion, and one I do not share."

Rachel struggled to think around her anger. "Why won't you let me teach here? What have I done but help a man in need?"

"It is the *need* you helped him with, Miss Hudson."

"What do you mean?"

Lucinda Miller's eyes blazed as she looked at Rachel. "I

refuse to even speak the words necessary to describe a woman like you. In truth, we kept the children away this morning so you would know, once and for all, you are not wanted here. We won't have your kind in our town."

"I've done nothing wrong." But the memory of her night in Jake's arms filled Rachel's mind and color stained her cheeks.

"You're lying," Lucinda accused. "I can it in your eyes."

"My sister never lies!"

Rachel snagged Nathan as he rushed the woman, fists raised. "No, Nathan. Violence won't solve anything."

Lucinda Miller stared down her beak nose at the boy. "This child should be taken from your undesirable influence and raised in the home of God-fearing people. I know all about your mother and your despicable upbringing. You aren't fit to have a child in your presence."

"That's enough." Wolf intervened.

"You dare to interrupt?" The woman turned on Wolf. "Don't think we don't know what you're doing in that cabin, you and this—this whore!"

Rachel slapped her. She couldn't believe it, but the telltale mark of her hand glowed in livid red against Lucinda Miller's pale skin. "I'm sorry. I didn't mean—"

"How dare you! This proves I was right. You're nothing more than a common whore, like your mother before you. We can't force you to leave, but never set foot in this town again. All doors will be closed to you. No merchant will take your ill-gotten money. You are not wanted here."

Not wanted, not wanted, not wanted. The words echoed in Rachel's head until she wasn't aware of anything but the damning phrase. All her life she'd wanted to belong. Now her dreams were shattering and the destruction was more than she could bear.

"Come on, Miss Hudson. There's no reason to stay here."

She allowed Wolf to turn her toward the door. She even took a couple of stumbling steps into the sunshine before she yanked free and stomped back inside the store.

"Rachel!"

The door slammed back from the force of her hand. "Lucinda Miller, you are without a doubt, the most wicked, deceitful, unpleasant woman I have ever had the misfortune of encountering. And, considering where I come from, that's quite a crowd to choose from." Rachel marched across the floor until she stood right in front of the speechless woman. "You run this town like everyone is here for the sole purpose of serving you, threatening anyone with ruin if they dare to stray from the narrow path you've chosen."

Lucinda Miller backed up two steps, her eyes wide and unblinking. Rachel followed, stalking her backward until she was pressed into the counter.

"I may not have been raised among people you consider worthy, but they were kind, caring, loving, and generous women, and you are not fit to speak their names, you—you old biddy!"

Rachel whirled on her heel and strode from the room. The crowd that had gathered at the door parted before her. There was even a smattering of applause from one or two on the fringe of the group. She didn't slow down to see who agreed with her. Wolf and the boys fell into step on either side of her. Nathan slipped his hand into hers and squeezed.

When they were well out of sight of the town, all the fight went out of her. She stumbled and would have fallen if not for Wolf.

"Easy there, Miss Rachel." He steadied her with an arm around her shoulder.

"Oh, merciful God, what have I done?" She leaned into his strength as her knees began to shake.

"Something that needed doing, by my way of thinking."

Nathan crowded close. "You were somethin', Sis. You really told her."

She smiled, or she thought she did, but the tears that suddenly welled from her eyes blinded her.

Wolf urged her forward, toward the house. "Come on, Miss Rachel. We need to get you home, where it's safe."

"I no longer have a home," she whispered. "I destroyed it."

She stumbled along beside Wolf, not knowing if the boys followed. The energy that had fueled her tirade drained away. It was over. Everything was gone now.

"What am I going to do?" she whispered to the wind.

Wolf bent his head close. "Ma'am?"

"It's gone. My life is gone. Everything I worked for, the only thing I wanted, gone. Ruined."

Wolf caught her when she stumbled again. Lifting her into his arms, he carried her the rest of the way to the cabin. He stopped the boys as they ran ahead to open the door. "Stay back until I'm sure it's empty." He eased Rachel onto the porch as far from the door as possible. The windows were still bolted, and the door didn't look as if it had been opened. No tracks marred the light layer of dirt he'd scattered in front of it so any intruder would leave a sign.

"How'd that dirt get there?"

Wolf spun toward Calvin. "I told you to stay back."

"I'm sorry." The boy stumbled back a step. "You didn't draw your gun so I figured it was safe."

Wolf stared at his empty right hand. "I guess my mind knew it before the rest of me did. All the same, stay here until I'm sure there's no one inside. And keep an eye out around you."

He did a quick circuit of the cabin and found nothing out of place. Returning to the door, he motioned the boys inside and lifted Rachel into his arms to follow.

"Calvin, put some water on to boil. Nathan, does your sister have any tea?"

"I think so. Ms. Winston used to come over and drink it on Sunday afternoons."

"Well, see if you can find some. She's going to need it."

While Nathan rummaged for tea and a cup, Wolf dragged the rocker close to the fire with one foot. Rachel stared at nothing, seeing her own private hell, he was sure. Trying to be gentle, he settled her into the chair and covered her knees with a blanket. Calvin disappeared into her bedroom and returned with a woven shawl for her shoulders.

"It'll be fine, Miss Rachel." Calvin draped the soft yarn

around her and patted the back of her hand. "They aren't important. Everything will work out. You'll see."

Wolf smiled down at his son. There was a gentleness in him that was so reminiscent of his dead wife it almost hurt too much to see. He was so intent on noting the similarities he didn't hear the visitor approach until a knock sounded on the door.

Shoving Calvin behind him as it opened, Wolf turned to face the danger, gun drawn. Nathan stared at him from across the room, his hand suspended above the bar on the door.

"It's just Ms. Winston," he choked out.

Without answering, Wolf crossed the room to make sure their visitor was alone, ignoring the second knock. Satisfied there was no one but the older woman waiting, he nodded for Nathan to open the door and returned to Rachel's side.

"It's about time," Abby bustled into the room, bringing the scent of vanilla with her. "Nathan, I heard what happened. I cannot abide that Lucinda Miller. She thinks she owns this town just because that lily-livered husband of hers owns every building in it. I swear I'm catching the next wagon out of here. After her treatment of—"

Her diatribe halted abruptly when she spotted Wolf standing guard over Rachel. "You leave her alone!" Abby stormed into the room, headed straight for him.

Chapter Eighteen

William Harrison cursed, loud and long, at the injustice of it all. He should be enjoying the comforts of a woman right now, not riding around in the dark, bleeding like a stuck pig and hungrier than he could ever remember being.

"Someone will pay for this," he howled to the moon, then cursed again when his horse stumbled, jarring his wounded shoulder.

He'd slipped around behind the Ranger, back through the slot canyon, and over a high hill, turning south toward Mexico. His men should be working the cattle in this region, choosing prime head to steal. If he didn't find them, perhaps a homesteader would take pity on a wounded man.

The thought had no more than formed when he crested a rise and saw a campfire. There was a single wagon parked beside it, the white canvas covering glowing against the stark desert landscape. Harrison set his face into a mask of pain and rode toward the fire.

The only person Harrison could see was a bent old man, with wiry gray hair sticking every which way. *But there must be a woman,* he thought. No man traveled in a wagon if he was alone. It was just too much trouble.

"Good evening," he called, careful to sound injured and a little helpless. "I wonder if you could help me?"

The long Kentucky rifle remained steady in the man's hands, pointed at Harrison's belly. He walked his mount forward until the light from the fire illuminated his face. "I need help." He let himself sway a little in the saddle and was distressed at how close to real it was.

The man spat toward the fire. "Who are you and what are you doing alone way out here?"

"My name's Harrison, William Harrison. I'm on my way to join my family south of here. But I ran into a bit of trouble."

"What kind of trouble?"

"Thieves," he lied. "I was ambushed. I fought them off as long as I could, but was forced to retreat when I took a bullet. I only managed to escape with my life."

"You were shot?"

Harrison nearly smiled at the ring of a female voice from inside the wagon.

"Daddy, bring him to the fire. I'll gather what I'll need."

Harrison dismounted with some difficulty. When both feet were on the ground, he held on to the saddle for a moment, mostly for effect. But when he turned toward the man, the ground seemed to tilt and he stumbled. The man lowered the rifle to steady him. Harrison smiled his thanks and accepted help to a seat near the campfire.

The man poured a cup of coffee for Harrison. "I'm Henry Bradley. This is my wife, Rosa." He nodded toward the ample woman who climbed from the wagon to join them.

"I didn't dare to hope I would find an angel of mercy in the middle of this wasteland. I'm very grateful for your hospitality, Mrs. Bradley."

"Nothing to it," she dismissed. "It's our duty to help others in need. Says so in the Good Book. Now let's take a look at that shoulder."

All business, Rosa helped Harrison remove his coat, then unbuttoned and peeled off his blood-soaked shirt. She laid it aside with some care. "I should be able to clean that up some for you." She turned him so the light fell on the wound. "This has been in here for some time."

"Yes. I've been riding for hours, desperate to find another living soul to aid me." Harrison jerked and bit back a curse as she probed deep for the bullet.

"You were lucky to find us," Bradley volunteered from the other side of the fire. "Mama's good with this sort of thing. We should have been miles from here, with the rest of the wagon train. But we broke a wheel and it took me some time to fix it."

Harrison smiled in more than polite interest. If the rest of the wagons were ahead of them, no one would stumble in before he was through here. He could take his time and not be concerned with interruptions. He'd never taken a woman so amply built, but the new experience might be enjoyable.

"Here, you're gonna need some of this." Bradley held out a bottle of golden liquid. "It ain't necessarily good, but it gets the job done."

Assuming it was whiskey, Harrison nodded his thanks. He lifted the bottle and took a mouthful. The burning sensation it caused had him gulping in air and looking around for water.

"Drink some more," the old man urged. "The next mouthful won't taste as bad."

Harrison's eyes watered, but he managed several swallows of the vile elixir. In only minutes, he began to feel the effects. His head swam. When he tried to shake off the effects, he found he could barely sit up.

Behind him, Rosa Bradley eyed him closely. "That should do it. Let's get that thing out of there before it festers."

With no more warning than that, she grabbed the knife heating in the fire and began cutting flesh. Harrison's scream could have been heard in Mexico. Mercifully, the pain stopped when he pitched forward in a faint.

Henry caught him before he tumbled into the dust and held him steady for his wife. "That worked fast, Mama."

"Probably hasn't eaten in a while," she muttered, concentrating on her work. Long minutes passed where the only sound was the fire and her whispered instructions to herself.

"Thieves, he said." Rosa finished sewing up the wound

and bandaged it with the ease of practice. "He wasn't fighting them off when he took this bullet. He was running away."

"Now, Mama . . ."

"Don't argue with me, Daddy. I can see with my own eyes and the good Lord knows I've seen my share of wounds. There ain't a scratch on him other than a bullet hole—in the back."

Henry waited while she spread a blanket near the fire. "Maybe they had him surrounded."

"Could be, or maybe it was the law trying to stop him from getting away." She helped her husband lay Harrison on his belly. "I don't know that I trust him." When the man was settled to her satisfaction, Henry dug out his pipe.

"He's something of a dandy, I'll grant you that." He puffed twice, fire flaring in the bowl of the pipe. "Did you see that shirt? All them pleats down the front? And a string tie, to boot. Who in their right mind wears a tie way out here, unless they're heading to church?"

Rosa clucked her tongue at the foolishness of men as she scooped up Harrison's bloody garments. "Do we have enough water for me to try and clean these up a mite?"

"We can spare a bucket or two. We'll be at the Rio Grande in a few days. We can share with someone else in the wagon train if we run too low before we get there."

She grabbed an old leaky bucket and filled it half full of water from the barrel hanging on the side of the wagon. "Daddy, why'd you tell him the rest of the wagon train had gone on ahead when they're camped just over the next rise, within shouting distance?"

Henry sucked hard on his pipe, winding lazy puffs of smoke into the night air. "Didn't want him getting any ideas about robbing the others. Guess I don't trust him, neither."

She smiled at this man with whom she'd shared nearly forty years of marriage. "Thought as much. Maybelle told me the other morning that she'd heard tell of a bandit in these parts who was real nice to look at, but black clear through his soul."

"Reckon it's him, Mama?"

She studied the unconscious man. "I believe it is."

Henry didn't seem very concerned. "Want me to stake him out for the varmints to git?"

"No, Daddy. I don't want to answer to the Almighty for it. But we ain't gonna help him any more than necessary. Besides, if the law is after him, I don't want to waste my time fixin' him up just so they can hang him."

She left her husband to his pipe and set to work on Harrison's shirt.

The sun was up when Harrison finally came to. For a moment he was confused, unable to recall where he was. Then the events of the previous night returned. That woman could have killed him, stabbing him in the back like that.

He sat up, moaning in pain when he moved his shoulder. It hurt, but not as bad as before. His head hurt much worse. Blinking against the light, Harrison looked around in growing disbelief. He was alone. The only evidence that a wagon had been there were the tracks leading away to the south.

His clean shirt and coat lay folded nearby. A small paper-wrapped packet by the fire turned out to be a piece of dried meat. They'd covered his face with his hat, and left him.

His horse had wandered a distance, looking for food and water. He could just make out her shape. He whistled, but the animal ignored him. Harrison struggled to his feet, jarring his shoulder and knocking his hat into the dirt. He yelped as the bright sunlight stabbed his unprotected eyes.

"What the hell was in that bottle?" He hurled a few obscenities at the absent couple, then settled his hat low on his brow and looked around.

There was no one in sight. The sun was well over the horizon. If they'd left at first light, they had several hours on him. "As does that damned Texas Ranger," he seethed.

Remembering he was being chased dampened his fury a little. He whistled again for his horse, but it continued to chomp on the sparse sprigs of grass it found growing between some rocks. He considered shooting the ornery thing, but decided to wait until he was away from his pursuers. He had no desire to walk all the way to where his men waited.

Grabbing his shirt, he examined it. The old woman had gotten most of the blood out, but the cloth was stained a sickly pink around the repaired hole. She hadn't bothered to sew the matching tear in the coat, but some of the blood was gone from that garment, as well.

Taking care not to reopen the wound, Harrison pulled on his shirt. It was so badly wrinkled he considered taking it off again, but he didn't want to be exposed to the midday sun. It would have to suffice until he could acquire another one. He dropped the coat into the dust. He refused to wear it and he certainly wouldn't need it in this heat. He should meet up with his confederates before nightfall. If not, he'd just steal one.

Snatching the packet of meat from the dirt, he tore off a strip with his teeth and chewed. It was leathery and tasted sour. He spat it out in disgust.

He strode the three steps to the gear they'd stripped from his horse. Everything was laid out in a neat stack. "How the hell did you do all this—and leave—and I didn't hear you?" The screamed question finally brought his horse's head out of the grass. He yanked his canteen from the saddle. They'd refilled it for him, too.

"It must have been the whiskey. Or whatever the hell that stuff was he poured down my throat." He gulped down half the contents of the canteen. The water was cool and clean, but it didn't go very far to quenching his real thirst—for vengeance.

"Well, Miss Hudson," he sneered aloud. "You will pay for this as well. If you'd come along peacefully, as you should have, I wouldn't be alone in the middle of the goddamned desert!" He ended on a shout that caused his horse to shy. Cursing about the extra distance he'd have to chase the beast, he hefted his gear and stalked after it, leaving the blanket to the next fool who happened along.

* * *

Abby squared off with Wolf, ready to fight him to protect Rachel.

"He won't hurt her, Ms. Winston," Nathan stepped between them. "This is Calvin's pa, Mr. Richards. He's staying here to keep us safe until Jake gets back."

Wolf allowed her perusal for several long, silent seconds. When Abby relaxed a little, he turned back to Rachel, who remained silent, staring at the fire.

"My apologies, Mr. Richards. I'm kinda protective of her."

Wolf accepted the woman's apology with a small nod before stepping aside to let her near Rachel.

"Come on, honey." She enfolded the young woman in a hug. "That nasty old woman isn't worth you getting so upset." Abby patted her hand and smoothed Rachel's tangled hair away from her face. "Don't worry. This will all work out."

"How?" Her voice was so soft, Wolf barely heard the question, but the defeated tone tore at him.

"I don't know, honey," Abby soothed. "But you have to believe it will." Abby glanced up at him, looking for support. Nathan came to the rescue.

"We don't need this old town, Sis. We can go somewhere else where they want a teacher. I don't mind movin' again."

"He'll only follow us there."

"Then I'll shoot him."

Rachel straightened to look her brother in the eye. "Nathan Hudson, you'll do no such thing."

He stared her down, unrepentant. "Maybe not, but I had to say somethin' to get you to stop feeling so sorry for yourself."

She slumped back in the rocker. "Is that what I'm doing?"

Before Nathan could argue further, Wolf spoke up. "If it means anything to you, the old bat had it coming."

"She did, didn't she?"

Rachel looked up at him with eyes nearly the same color as his dead wife's. Pain sliced through him. "Nathan's right, though. Both of you should know how to shoot."

"I despise guns."

"Will you teach me?"

The siblings spoke over each other, confusing Wolf for a moment. "I'll teach you both," he answered Nathan. Then he turned to Rachel. "Doesn't matter how you feel about them," he told her. "You have to protect yourself."

He tried to ignore a stab of regret. His Emily had disliked guns, too. If only he'd insisted his wife know how to use the loaded shotgun he always left standing behind the door, she and their daughter might still be alive.

"This afternoon, I'll take a look at that Henry Repeater you have in the corner." He focused on the boys. "But we have animals to see to first." He glanced back at Rachel, then Abby. "I won't be far away. If you need anything, just call out."

Wolf herded both boys out of the cabin ahead of him, leaving the door open to the spring morning. A gentle breeze sighed through the room, bringing the scent of fresh grass. Rachel rose and opened every window to allow the wind to cleanse away the darkness in the room. If only it could sweep away the shadow in her heart.

"They're damn fools, honey." Abby settled into the rocker Rachel had abandoned.

"I know, Abby. But I shouldn't have said what I did. It only enraged her further. Now there's no hope of undoing the damage."

The older woman set the chair into motion, rocking back and forth in a steady rhythm. "Why would you want to?"

"What?" Rachel turned to look at her.

"Why would you want to undo it? This town is no place for you. I don't believe the problem was ever where you came from. You're too pretty and Lucinda Miller is insanely jealous. She's been looking for a way to get you to leave ever since Arnold first laid his lecherous eyes on you. Then Hiram took an interest, and, well, you just aren't fancy enough for her to have as a daughter-in-law."

Rachel poured tea for them both and carried a cup to Abby before returning to stare out the window. Wolf had the horses out in the sunshine and both boys were helping. Water sparkled in the sunshine as they washed the animals down.

"How am I going to feed them?"

"Who?" Abby stretched her neck to look. "The boys?"

"The horses." She dropped onto a bench at the table. "There isn't enough feed for more than a day or two, with three horses eating at it." She sipped a little of the warm liquid, breathing in the spicy scent. "Of course, I don't have much food for the men, either."

"Men." Abby chuckled. "It won't be long before Nathan is a man, truth be told." She swallowed the contents of her cup and rose to get more. "I brought a few things with me, an old chicken to stew, some dried venison I won't use up. Did I ever tell you about the man who paid for a month's worth of boarding with a deer hide and two smoke-dried haunches?"

As she launched into the story, Rachel let her mind wander. She had heard the tale more than once, but it was one of Abby's favorites and she got such pleasure in the telling Rachel didn't have the heart to stop her. Staring out the window, she found herself thinking about Jake. Where was he? Was he safe? Had he found Harrison?

Harrison. The sunlight dimmed a little as she relived the terrifying moments of yesterday morning. If not for Jake and Wolf, she would be with Harrison right now. She shuddered, imagining what he might have done to her.

"Honey, you're getting too cool standing over there." Abby broke into her musings. "Come sit by the fire."

"I'm fine, Abby. I was just thinking about what happened. I didn't know a man could hate that much, and for so long. I didn't do anything but run away."

"He's not right in his mind, honey. He won't reason anything out the way you and I do." She took Rachel's cup and refilled it, watching until she took a sip. "I think you should take Wolf up on his offer."

"And learn to shoot?"

The older woman nodded. "To protect yourself and Nathan, and so you can get food for yourself," she spoke over Rachel's protest. "Then you won't have to rely on the likes of Lucinda and Arnold Miller."

Rachel wanted to argue, but the words wouldn't form. "We can't stay here, can we?"

Abby was quiet for a long time, considering. "No, honey, I don't think you can. Lucinda Miller has decided you don't belong, and nobody in this town will go against her."

"You do."

Abby snorted, the bark of laughter loud in the quiet room. "I'm too old to care what she has to say. But I don't know how much longer I'll be here myself."

"Are you leaving?" Rachel couldn't believe it was possible. Abby was a part of the fabric of life in Lucinda.

Abby shook her head. "Not yet, but I may not have a choice much longer. We don't get a lot of strangers staying through here anymore. Not much call for a boardinghouse with no boarders."

Rachel set her tea aside. "The town won't be the same. And what will I do without you?"

She pushed the rocker back, and rose as it rolled forward again. "Let's not fret about it. If you decide to stay, then I will, too. Strangers will still come on occasion. I'll manage."

Did she want to stay? While Abby bustled around behind her, clearing away the tea things and starting lunch, Rachel wandered around the room, stopping at the open door to study the land around her home. The bare ground was slowly being transformed by the green of new growth. On some of the hillsides, flowers were beginning to bloom. Barely a week after a blizzard and spring was here. She loved this time of year, when everything was new and anything was possible.

Rachel glanced around the little house they called home. It had seemed so perfect when they'd arrived in Lucinda. When Arnold Miller had offered her the job of teacher, and given her the house as payment for her first year, she thought they'd finally found the place where they belonged, a place to settle.

Thinking back, she should have realized Arnold's generosity was more than friendliness, but she'd been desperate and frightened. No wonder Lucinda Miller hated her. Rachel would never truly be welcome in this town. And without friends, their home was just four walls and a roof. It was nice, but a house was not enough reason to stay where they weren't wanted.

Where could she go? *Anywhere,* a voice in her head prompted. Rachel stepped off the porch and walked a few steps toward the hills, breathing in the fresh breeze. There were lots of places to choose from. Nathan was right. They could find another town that was looking for a teacher. All she needed was enough money to start over.

The bright day dimmed a little when she considered what that meant. The mine. She'd have to go back, just long enough to locate the gold that Nathan had found. But she couldn't do anything until she was alone.

She knew as soon as Jake came back, Wolf and Calvin would leave. Wolf seemed restless, anxious to be on his way. But he'd stay as long as necessary. He'd given his word.

Rachel strolled away from the house, taking care not to go too far. What would she do in the meantime? She had food for a couple of days, a week at best, but they'd need meat. She stopped and stared toward the house, thinking over Wolf's offer. Could she do it? Did she have a choice? Her stomach rolled as years of teaching were reassessed and discarded.

Making her decision, she veered toward the corral where Wolf was feeding the horses. He straightened, waiting for her to speak with the patience of the hunter she knew him to be.

"Teach me to shoot."

Chapter Nineteen

Jake stood in the stirrups, listening. He swore he'd heard a scream. Not the kind of sound a person in trouble makes, but a howl of outrage.

"I heard it, as well," Hank Gerard confirmed. "A man who is rather unhappy with his circumstances at the moment, I think."

"I'd bet a month's pay its Harrison."

He nudged Griffin into a trot across the small valley they were following. He'd picked up the outlaw's tracks easily and had been following them since the sky was light enough to travel safely. "Sounds like he's closer than I hoped."

"It would be pleasant for something to finally go in our favor."

Jake grunted in agreement as he concentrated on following Harrison's trail. Just before they crested the next hill, his skin started to crawl. Long accustomed to listening to his instincts, he hauled Griffin to a stop and slid from the saddle. Taking care he stayed out of sight, he belly-crawled to the edge of the rise and looked around.

"There he is," he breathed to Hank as the man joined him. Satisfaction filled Jake. "He won't get away this time."

He studied the landscape, looking for the best route to take that would let them get in front of Harrison.

"Why is he carrying his saddle?"

Hank's quiet comment brought Jake's gaze back to the outlaw. "Maybe his horse had enough of the stench. Let's go."

They eased backward down the hill. As soon as it was safe, Jake stood and strode to Griffin. Vaulting into the saddle, he set off on a path parallel to the one Harrison was taking, eager to be done with it and get back to Rachel. Hank followed close.

Just a little longer, Jake vowed. When this was over, Rachel would be safe from William Harrison. She could get on with her life, settle anywhere she wanted.

"Gerard," Jake slowed enough to let Hank catch up. "Do me a favor. If anything happens to me, give everything I have with me to Rachel. The money is hers. Just ask her to let my mother know where I'm buried."

"*Mon Dieu,*" Hank cursed. "Do you plan on dying, *mon ami?*"

"I don't plan on it, but it's possible." He didn't tell his friend that he'd always expected to die in a shootout with William Harrison. He figured that information wouldn't be helpful at the moment.

"Then, if we are considering the worst, there is a letter in my pocket from my elder brother in France. See that he is notified of my demise. It would amuse him to know his worthless younger sibling died for a good cause."

Jake looked over at Hank. He'd never stopped to consider that someone else might die, too. "Let's see if we can't hold off the funerals for another day."

One corner of Hank's mouth kicked up in a grin. "An excellent idea, Ranger McCain."

They rode the rest of the way in silence. As they rode out of the valley ahead of Harrison, Jake spotted a train of wagons, heading south. One wagon rolled along a mile or so behind the rest. He calculated the distance to the single wagon. "We have to cut him off before he can reach that family. It's too dangerous to have civilians within range."

He spurred Griffin forward, praying to Rachel's God that Harrison didn't crest a hill. Making for a tiny cut in the landscape, he felt a surge of satisfaction when he found it was large enough to conceal them.

Guiding the horse down the steep wash, Jake leaned back in the saddle to keep from pitching over the horse's head. Dust rose behind them as they disappeared into the cut in the land.

As soon as he got to the bottom, Jake jumped from the saddle. He put his saddlebag holding the extra ammunition over his shoulder and slid his rifle from its scabbard. Hank followed suit and in moments, both men were armed to the teeth.

"We have more bullets here than the entire Spanish army," Hank joked.

Jake shook his head. He could get used to having this man at his side. Before he could comment, a movement in the distance caught his eye. Harrison had managed to catch his horse and was riding toward the wagon train.

"Will you try to take him alive?" Hank rechecked the load in his rifle.

"Only until he starts shooting," Jake drawled.

As if Jake had called to him, Harrison angled away from the wagons and toward the spot where they waited. The minutes ticked past with agonizing slowness. The sun beat down on his head, so brilliant even his hat couldn't protect him from the glare.

Harrison drew closer, showing no sign he was aware of their presence. He was cradling his left arm and cursing nonstop. Even from a distance, Jake could see his face was bathed in sweat and he doubted it was due to the sun. It looked like his wound would kill him eventually, even if Jake didn't fire a shot.

When he got within a dozen yards of where they waited, Jake stood up, making sure the outlaw saw the loaded rifle pointing at his chest. "That's far enough, Harrison."

Time seemed to slow down for Jake. He saw the shock on Harrison's face, and the flash of indecision before he went for his gun.

Jake hesitated. He wanted the man to shoot first so there'd be no doubt. But Hank wasn't concerned about the nuances of the law. Before the man's weapon cleared the leather holster, he opened fire. Harrison managed to get off a shot, striking the boulder in front of Jake. Rock exploded, spattering Jake with sharp slivers of stone. "Close enough," he muttered. Jake squeezed the trigger and, with one bullet to the heart, eliminated forever the threat that had been William Harrison.

Hank waited until Jake lowered his rifle to speak. "I hope I wasn't too anxious to see this matter done."

"He got a shot off. That's enough for the State of Texas."

"I just couldn't bear the thought of what he'd done to Wolf Richards's wife and child, what he planned for Miss Rachel." He ran a shaking hand across his eyes. "I couldn't allow him a chance to escape."

Jake slapped the man on the back. "You did fine, my friend." Though he was sure Harrison was dead, he approached with care, his revolver in hand. One look at the sightless eyes staring into the brilliant sun finished it.

A dull ache started in the hollow of his gut. Jake waited for the satisfaction to come, the elation that this man who'd murdered so many was dead. He'd worked so long to avenge the souls Harrison had destroyed, he thought he would feel something. But there was nothing, not even relief.

Jake looked up at the sound of approaching horses. Six men rode toward him. It was only a little comforting that their guns weren't drawn. They pulled up just out of range of Jake's rifle.

"Looks like you had some trouble," the man in the lead called out. "Do you need any help, or should we be taking you into custody and delivering you to the nearest lawman?"

"I'm a Texas Ranger. Name's Jake McCain."

The riders visibly relaxed. One man, who looked to be about a hundred, urged his horse closer. "So Mama was right about him bein' an outlaw."

Jake lifted one eyebrow and waited for an explanation. The old man obliged with no more prompting.

"I'm Henry Bradley. That there man stumbled into our camp last night, just after moonrise, with a bullet in his back. Yours?"

Jake nodded to keep the man talking.

"Said he'd escaped from thieves. Mama—that'd be Rosa, my wife—didn't believe him. We gave him enough of Mama's pain potion to keep him asleep until well after the sun came up this morning. Then we headed out by the light of the moon to catch up with the rest of the wagons."

"A wise decision," Jake confirmed. "This man had a weakness for women, and he made it a habit to never leave witnesses."

The old man swallowed hard and dragged the back of a wrinkled hand across his mouth. "Glad to know he won't be followin' us, then."

The captain of the wagon train offered assistance burying the body, which Jake readily accepted. While Hank caught the man's horse and tied it to a bush near their own mounts, Jake emptied Harrison's pockets. There was probably cash in the saddlebags, but the man carried little in his pockets. Jake found a gold watch, some coins, and a small folding knife. Nothing identified him as the monster that he was.

One of the men fashioned a small cross from sticks and leather. No identification would remain on the body. Everything of value would go to the Texas Rangers, to help cover the expenses of the hunt and to be shared with some of the families Harrison had destroyed.

With help, they finished their task in an hour. Jake declined the captain's offer of food and water. He was anxious to get back to Rachel and tell her the news. She didn't have to hide any longer.

Expressing his thanks, and those of the Texas Rangers, Jake mounted Griffin and headed north. Hank followed with Harrison's horse on a short lead. As they reached the top of the first hill, Jake pulled up and turned in the saddle.

"What is it, my friend?" Hank came to a stop beside him.

"Something doesn't feel right." Jake stared at the freshly turned earth in the distance. "That was too easy. It feels like I've been chasing that rotten son of a bitch forever. He should have suffered longer, to ease all the souls he destroyed."

246   *Tracy Garrett*

"They are at rest now, thanks to you." Hank resettled his hat. "Let's go home. Miss Rachel will be worried for you."

Rachel. Jake's blood heated at the thought of seeing her again, of inhaling the scent of lavender that always clung to her. With Wolf at the cabin to watch the boys, maybe he could coax her into taking a long walk with him. The moon would be full tonight, and he wanted to see her skin bathed in the silvery light.

His body hardened in a rush, making the ride uncomfortable. He shifted a little, hoping Hank wouldn't notice. When he looked up, he knew his efforts were wasted.

"She is beautiful, is she not? And she cares for you, I am sure." Hank steered his horse close enough to slap Jake on the back. "Your feelings for her are obvious."

The Frenchman roared with laughter as Jake felt the stain of red climb his neck and wash his jaw with heat. Damn, he hadn't blushed like this since the first time he'd seen a naked woman at the ripe age of eight. At the time, it hadn't mattered that she was a prostitute working the camp where he and his mother were living. He'd been fascinated with the differences in her body. As he'd grown into manhood, he'd quickly learned to appreciate just how different a woman was from a man.

"She will make a fine wife for you."

Hank rode on, oblivious to the fact that Jake had pulled up short. Wife? Marry him? Was that what everyone would expect, now that Harrison was dead and the danger had passed?

He lifted the reins and urged Griffin to catch up with Hank. What did Rachel expect? To get married and have a family, no doubt. But not with him. He scowled at the back of Hank's head. She deserved better than a half-breed Texas Ranger who'd never learned to stay put. He would take her somewhere safe, where she could start again. And, once she was settled, he had to convince himself to ride away and not look back.

Eight days had passed since Jake had ridden after William Harrison. Eight long, lonely days. Rachel snapped the freshly washed bedsheet to remove some of the wrinkles and pinned it to the line that stretched from the porch to a small tree across the yard. Smoothing it a little more, she paused to rest. Her back ached from leaning over the washtub—and from the hours of shooting lessons.

Wolf said she was making good progress. She could load the rifle now without having to stop and think about what came next. She still couldn't hit the targets he hung on the trees behind the house, but she was getting pretty good at skinning the bark from the trunks.

Nathan was a natural. By the end of the first day, he was shooting the center out of every target Wolf set up for him. And Calvin was learning almost as fast. Right now, the three of them were just over the hill, learning to set snares and recognize tracks. She had no doubt that, by week's end, Nathan would be bringing home fresh meat for their dinner.

Wolf had wanted Rachel to accompany them, but she'd convinced him to leave her behind. The loaded rifle lay in the grass beside her wash basket, and she'd promised to fire it into the air at the first sign of company, whether friend or stranger. If she was truthful, she was nervous without him here. But she needed to be alone for a while. The piles of dirty clothes waiting to be washed had offered a plausible excuse.

She pressed her fists into the muscles of her lower back and leaned back, stretching. There was another basket of shirts to be washed, but they would have to wait until morning. Washing for three active men took more time than she'd planned and she needed to put the venison on to cook soon.

Rachel turned in a slow circle, scanning the horizon, checking every shadow for unexpected visitors. A sense of satisfaction grew inside her, as she realized she was taking control of her own life again, learning to take care of herself. It gave her such a feeling of accomplishment, of power. She could survive. She didn't need Hiram Miller or the citizens of Lucinda to make it. She and Nathan would be fine, wherever they decided to live next.

A small movement to her left caught her attention. Her heart leaped into her throat and started beating a wild rhythm when she saw two men on horseback. Her fingers closed around the rifle and she swung it into position on her shoulder. Before she squeezed the trigger, she hesitated, wanting to be sure the strangers were heading her way before calling in the cavalry.

Seconds ticked by as she waited. They were definitely coming to the house. She exhaled as she squeezed the trigger, wincing at the explosion next to her ear. She lowered the rifle to pull the hammer back for a second shot, when she realized one of the men seemed familiar. They'd pulled up short at the sound of the shot, then the one in the lead kicked his horse into a gallop, straight for her. He was still too far away to see his face, but the big black stallion under him took her breath away.

Jake. Rachel didn't realize she'd screamed his name until he raised his hat in a wave. She dropped the rifle into the grass, her fingers too numb to hold onto it. Her knees shook so much she was afraid they wouldn't support her.

"Rachel!"

The voice she'd feared never to hear again spurred her forward. She lifted her skirts and started to run. Tears streaked down her face, but she didn't care. He was home. Jake was alive and he'd come back to her.

"Rachel, stop." She heard Wolf shout from somewhere behind her, but it didn't slow her down. Three more steps and she was swept from the ground into Jake's arms. Without direction from his rider, Griffin slowed to a walk, then stopped all together. Rachel hardly noticed. She met Jake, kiss for kiss, until they were both gasping for air.

"You're all right. Jake, I was so frightened for you. What happened? Why were you gone so long?"

Jake kissed her again, stopping her questions and making her fears vanish. She skimmed shaking hands over every inch of him she could reach until she was satisfied he wasn't hurt. Then she wrapped her arms around his waist and laid her head on his chest, counting his heartbeats and feeling truly at home for the first time in her life.

Jake gathered the reins and steered Griffin to a halt beside

the porch. He hugged her one more time before lifting her
down to Wolf. Then he swung out of the saddle to join her.

"You taught her to shoot." Though it was just a statement,
the words held a wealth of meaning for Jake. He knew she
hated guns, but she'd been frightened enough to learn to use
one anyway. And she hadn't waited for him to come back and
teach her. She'd gone to Wolf instead.

The jealousy snaking through him was unreasonable, but
Jake couldn't stop it from coming. The image of Wolf standing close enough to show Rachel how to aim and fire the rifle
made his blood boil. He fought to bring his temper under control. It wasn't Wolf's fault Jake didn't want any man that close
to her.

Wolf must have recognized the anger in Jake's voice and
held his tongue.

Rachel glanced between the two men. "I asked him to teach
me, Jake." She laid a hand on his arm. "I needed to learn."

Jake smoothed her silky hair away from her face. "I know,
pretty girl. I'm glad you can protect yourself."

"I can shoot, too." Nathan squeezed in for a share of the attention. "Mr. Richards says I'm real good."

Jake ruffled his golden curls, so similar to Rachel's. "Good
for you, son. I'm proud of you."

"I can hit any target you put up," Nathan bragged. "Come
on, I'll show you."

"Not right now, Nathan." Wolf intervened. "You have a
couple of rabbits to skin, remember?"

"Oh, yeah. Wolf taught me and Calvin to make a snare to
trap rabbits and we caught two. Now we won't have to worry
about going hungry ever again."

He looked to Rachel and she smiled her approval. "Well
done, little brother. I'm looking forward to tasting them."

"You have to cook 'em first, though." His face split into a
wide grin and he raced off, with Calvin in tow.

Wolf turned to face Jake. "I did what needed doing. No
more, no less."

Shame washed in to replace anger. "I know. I appreciate you staying behind. I know it wasn't easy."

Hank Gerard joined the small group, sighing in appreciation as he stepped into the shade cast by the house.

Wolf greeted him with a terse nod. "Where's Harrison?"

Jake felt Rachel tense and pulled her under the shelter of his arm before answering Wolf. "Dead."

The single word hung in the air between them.

Wolf broke the tension. "I hope he enjoys hell." He tugged his hat lower over his eyes, but not before Jake spotted the glitter of tears. "I'll go keep an eye on the boys."

Hank led the horses to the trough and carried buckets from the well to let them drink their fill. Jake watched him remove their gear and the tack before turning them loose to eat their fill of the spring grass covering the yard. He knew he should help, but he didn't want to release Rachel just yet.

She snuggled a little closer. "Is it really over?"

"It's over, pretty girl. He'll never bother you again."

She slipped out of his arms and wandered over to the wash. It hung limp in the still air. Jake could hear the drops of water plopping into the dirt, but he doubted Rachel noticed. She seemed to be a thousand miles away. He walked up behind her and laid a hand on each shoulder, rubbing at the tension there.

"Rachel, honey, I thought you'd be glad."

"I am." She didn't turn around. "I was just thinking about Mama. She gave her life to save mine. I'm glad she didn't die in vain." She rubbed her cheek against his hand. "I'm grateful, Jake, truly. Now she can rest in peace."

He placed a kiss on her hair, burying his lips in the silky mass. Lavender scented the air around him. Turning her in his arms, he captured her lips, pouring all his worry and relief into the kiss. She rose onto her toes and parted her lips to allow him access. Time stood still. They could have been in a crowded room or in the middle of nowhere, for all Jake knew of what was happening around him.

"Ahem."

Jake ended the kiss, but didn't bother turning around. "You still here, Gerard?"

"I want to say good-bye before returning to my own cabin." He lifted Rachel's hand from Jake's neck and squeezed her fingers lightly. "Good-bye, Miss Rachel." Hank mounted and rode toward town, waving a hand in farewell to them both.

Rachel gave Jake a little shove. "That was rude."

"He shouldn't have interrupted me." He kissed her again, holding her closer, now that they had no audience. She resisted for a heartbeat, then melted into him. Her curves fit him perfectly, as if they'd been made for each other. The tension that had carried him through the long months flowed out of him, leaving him more tired than he could ever remember being. He ended the kiss and tucked her head under his chin, just enjoying that he could hold her without watching his back.

She stirred first. "You must be exhausted. Come inside. I'll heat water for you to clean up."

He took her hand again, enjoying the feel of her small fingers entwined with his larger ones as he led the way into the house.

Chapter Twenty

When Jake crossed the threshold, a sense of belonging filled him, like he'd come home. The feeling knocked him off balance. He let go of Rachel and stood near the door, exploring the unfamiliar emotions. Rachel bustled around the room, mixing hot water with cold in a bucket for him to use. She turned to smile at him, holding out several cloths, and he knew he'd do almost anything to come home to that sight every night.

As he reached to take the cloths, he brushed his fingers the length of her hand, wrist to fingertips. The tiny shiver he felt run through her warmed his blood. He wanted to kiss her again, carry her to bed and not let her up for a week. He wanted things with her he'd never thought possible to have.

The sound of boots on the porch broke into his daydream. What the hell was the matter with him? Just yesterday, he'd decided she'd be better off without him, and, with one smile, she had him thinking of tomorrows again.

Nathan and Calvin barreled into the room, shouldering through the door at the same time. Each carried a carcass.

"Sis, look. We did it."

"Get those out of my house!"

Jake bit his lip at the disbelief on Nathan's face, but he'd seen it coming. Wide-eyed, both boys backed through the door. Rachel and Jake followed them out. Wolf stood watching from the yard. Jake glanced at him and caught the laughter lurking in his eyes.

The moment they were outside, a smile bloomed on her lips. "Now, then, do you have something to show me, Nathan?"

"I, uh, I just wanted you to see what we caught."

"Rabbits! Nice, fat ones. That's wonderful. We'll have stew tonight."

She kissed his cheek, then Calvin's, and went back inside, humming. Jake stayed on the porch.

The boys looked at each other, then at Jake. Nathan broke the silence. "What was that all about?"

"She's proud of what you did. She just doesn't want them in the house." Jake herded them around the side of the house to a shady spot. Wolf joined them with three sharp knives and they settled into the new grass to skin and clean their dinner.

"Pa, I don't understand."

Wolf glanced at Jake, fighting a smile. "Well, son, most women don't like to have their kitchens messed with. I expect Miss Rachel didn't want to have to clean up after you two, so she sent you back outside."

"But we weren't going to skin them inside." Nathan tested his knife blade the way Jake had taught him. "We just wanted to show her."

"Sometimes," Jake chimed in. "It doesn't have to make sense. Men just learn the rules and abide by them."

Nathan and Calvin looked at each other and shrugged their shoulders. Then they turned their attention to Wolf as he showed them what to do.

Jake watched for a while, chewing on a blade of grass. The man was good with a knife and a patient teacher. The boys were in good hands. Leaving them to it, he went back for the bucket of water and a bath.

* * *

Dinner was a joyous affair. Rachel had done wonderful things with the two rabbits and some winter vegetables. Jake had accompanied her into the hills while she searched for a particular root plant to add to the stew. When the opportunity presented itself, he'd stolen a few kisses. They'd laughed like children at the antics of a baby deer they came across in a nearby valley.

"I'm going hunting." Wolf broke into the conversation.

"When?" Rachel lowered her fork to her plate.

"Tomorrow. The deer are plentiful in the hills north of here. I'll be gone a few days at most."

Jake watched Rachel's face, dismayed to see concern there. Was she attracted to Wolf? Jealousy reared its ugly head but he pushed it away. *She can't be,* he told himself. *Not the way she greeted me this afternoon.* Memories of her eager response drove the green beast away for good. She was his. But what could he do about it?

"Can I come, Pa?"

"Me, too, please!"

Calvin and Nathan stared at Wolf, hope obvious in their young faces. He shook his head. "You aren't coming along this time, because . . ." He hesitated at their groans of disappointment. "Because I need you to help Ranger McCain build a drying rack for the deer I'll bring back."

He glanced up at Jake, who nodded his agreement.

"It's something you both need to learn to do, so you can make the most use of what you hunt." Wolf helped himself to another slice of bread to sop up the last of his stew.

The boys looked at each other, then Calvin spoke. "I guess that'll be okay."

With the matter decided, conversation moved on to the weather and other easy topics. The evening drifted by. When Calvin leaned his head on his father's shoulder, Rachel stood. Wolf and Jake followed suit.

"Nathan, it's time you and Calvin headed on to bed."

"Okay, Sis." Nathan led the way to the attic.

Wolf went along to see them settled, while Jake helped her with the dishes. They were drying the last of them when Wolf returned and began gathering his gear.

Rachel watched him for a moment. "What are you doing?"

He glanced at her. "I want to get a real early start in the morning. I'll sleep outside tonight so I don't disturb anyone."

"That isn't necessary." She crossed the room to stand before him. "You won't bother anyone."

"I appreciate that, ma'am, but its better this way."

She recognized his need to be alone and didn't argue when he carried his saddle and saddlebags outside. When Wolf returned for another load, Rachel held out a cloth-wrapped bundle.

"What's this?"

She put it into his hand. "You'll need food, won't you?"

He smiled his thanks and reached for his rifle.

"Which way will you head?" Jake helped him with the last of his gear.

While Wolf and Jake discussed potential hunting areas, Rachel listened carefully, knowing the time might come when she would have to hunt for herself and Nathan. She tried to follow the conversation, but she got confused when they used terms that were foreign to her. She gave up, deciding to ask Jake when they were alone.

"Good night, Miss Rachel."

"Sleep well and good hunting. Be safe and come home soon."

Wolf stood in the doorway with his gear over his shoulders, looking every inch the hunter. But the sadness in his eyes brought tears to hers. Without a word, he walked out, closing the door behind him.

Jake gathered her into his arms. "Don't worry about him, honey. He's a tough one."

"But he misses his wife so much, it breaks my heart."

"Wolf will survive. And he's got Calvin."

She snuggled closer to Jake, comfortable in his arms. When he kissed her forehead, she lifted her face to him, contentment filling her. *This is where I belong,* she realized.

Jake teased her with kisses, avoiding her lips until she couldn't breathe for wanting him. Finally she took matters into her own hands, turning to catch his mouth with her own. Desire flashed between them, contentment turned to hunger, comfort to raging need.

The groan that came from Jake vibrated to her center. When he swept her into his arms, her head spun with dizzy delight. Still they kissed. Rachel helped untangle them from the curtain covering her bedroom doorway, making sure it was closed before Jake carried her across the tiny room.

He set her on her feet, and she seized the opportunity, releasing the buttons down the front of his shirt as fast as her shaking fingers allowed. At the same time he worked on her bodice. When it gapped open over her breasts, he left the rest and bent to her, suckling her through her chemise.

Rachel's knees turned to water. She would have fallen if not for Jake. He slipped one arm behind her to hold her up, while his other hand dispatched her remaining buttons.

She couldn't touch enough of him. Her hands roamed the bronze skin of his chest and shoulders, around his back and down to the waist of his trousers. She felt Jake quiver and wondered with growing excitement if she'd made that happen.

Jake teased both nipples with long fingers before pushing her gown from her shoulders. Hooking his thumbs in the straps, he pulled her chemise down to expose her breasts. The cool night air brushed her heated skin, making her aware she was nearly naked. She wanted to protest, but Jake covered her with his hands and any remaining sense she possessed fled. There was only Jake and the fire he was building inside her.

When he urged her toward the bed, Rachel went willingly. She took his hand and stepped out of the pool of gown and chemise at her feet, slipping her feet from her shoes at the same time. She watched Jake as he yanked off his shirt and sat on the bed to tug off his boots. When his eyes met hers, she stepped forward into the shelter of his thighs.

Jake smoothed his fingertips from her knees to her hips, then around to her buttocks. Urging her closer, he planted kisses on her belly and lower, until she was certain she'd perish on the spot if he didn't stop. Growing bold, she fisted her hands in his hair and lifted his mouth to her breast, begging him to feast.

When he took her flesh into his mouth, Rachel's knees failed her and she tumbled forward. He rolled with her until he lay on top, never releasing the sweet temptation of her breast. She was all he remembered and more.

He took advantage of their positions to explore more of her. She gasped when he nuzzled her jaw and nipped her earlobe.

"You're beautiful, pretty girl. Perfect."

She tried to speak but he covered her mouth with his own, stopping the words. Propping himself on an elbow, he yanked at his pants, shoving them down his legs until he was as naked as she. For an instant, he just stared at his dark hand on her pale skin. So different. She thrilled at his strength and gentleness, opposites wound together in one wonderful man.

"Jake?"

His gaze jerked to hers, twin fires raging in their depths. "Are you sure, honey?"

She gave him the only answer she could manage. Smiling, she let her hands skim his chest, returning to his nipples when he groaned at her light touch.

"Like this?"

He didn't answer, only pressed forward into her hands and let her lead the way.

When Rachel urged him into her arms, he didn't fight it. She shifted, making room for him between her thighs. Taking his time, he eased into her softness until he could go no farther.

Her breath hitched at the sensations exploding in her body. He stayed still, giving her time to adjust to his presence. Then he started to move and led the way to heaven.

She met him, thrust for thrust, lifting her hips to meet him. As her whimpers turned to moans she couldn't control, Jake fused their lips, drinking in her cries of ecstasy as they both flew over the peak and into the sun.

They floated back to earth together, wrapped in each other. "Am I too heavy?" Jake tried to lift his head to look into her eyes, but he let it fall back to her shoulder, as if he didn't have the strength.

"You stay right where you are. I don't ever want you to move." Rachel wiggled a little, a happy laugh escaping.

"You'd better hold still, woman, or I won't be responsible for what happens."

"Will you take your *staff* to me?"

She bit her lip, unable to believe she was actually teasing him. She didn't know she had it in her, but she wanted to see his smile. Jake moved his hips and her thoughts splintered. She moaned at the pure pleasure, and just like that he was stiff as a . . . a staff.

"You're a bad influence on me, Rachel."

"Um," she sighed. "I certainly hope so."

Much later they lay wrapped up together, warm despite the fact they were on top of the blankets.

"Jake, are you asleep?"

"How could I possibly sleep with you in my arms?"

She smiled and kissed his shoulder. Temptation whispered in her ear, and she teased his skin with her fingers, brushing his nipple until he captured her hand in his own.

"Stop it, woman. I'm trying to let you rest. It's almost morning."

Rachel snuggled closer, so at home in his arms, she couldn't imagine wanting to be anywhere else. She relaxed with a yawn. "I love you, Jake McCain."

"You can't, honey."

Rachel held herself perfectly still, waiting for him to say something else, to tell her he was only teasing. But he stayed silent. What could he say?

"I don't understand," she prompted. "You can share what we did last night, but I can't love you."

He heaved a sigh and pulled her closer for an instant before relaxing his hold. But he didn't release her. "I know it's selfish of me, but I can't be sorry we made love. Still, I'm not the right man for you."

"I think you are."

She couldn't believe they were discussing this while lying naked together in bed. Rachel sat up and turned her back, shivering in the cool night air. "This is because of your mother, isn't it? Because she was an Apache?"

"A man like me doesn't belong anywhere, honey. You don't want to live like that. Believe me."

"How can I when you won't explain?" She crossed the room for her wrapper to cover herself. "Please, Jake. I need to understand."

He pulled on his trousers and went to the tiny window slit cut into the wall. Staring out at the fading night, he was quiet for so long she thought he wasn't going to answer.

"I told you how my parents met. We traveled a lot, place to place, campfire to campfire. We never had a home. I was five, maybe six, when my mother was followed out of town by a drunken bully and cornered near the river. He was huge, at least to me. When Mama screamed, my father came running and was stabbed in the chest trying to protect her. He died before morning."

"Oh, Jake, how horrible." She wrapped her arms around his waist, trying to offer comfort.

"We buried him at sunrise, packed up what we could carry and returned to her village." He ran agitated fingers through his hair. "A couple of years later, she was gathering food," he continued, the memories racing across his features. "I was chasing a rabbit when I should have been protecting her . . . I heard her scream a second before the gunshot. She was dead by the time I got there."

"Who would do such a thing?"

He didn't acknowledge her question. "The chief of our village already despised me because I was half white, an abomination. The fact that he loved my mother and I let her die . . . When they buried her in a tiny cave overlooking the river, they buried me with her."

"That's barbaric," she whispered. Jake spoke so matter-of-factly, but she could hardly breathe, imagining the terror of the child he had been.

"I deserved to die. I didn't save her." Jake rolled his shoulders to release some tension. "Once I accepted that I'd been left there to die, I tried to dig my way out, but they'd placed a big rock in the opening. I had plenty of air to stay alive, but no food or water."

She was appalled. "No one stopped him?"

He shrugged, a quick, jerky motion that betrayed his pain. "It was his right to decide."

She dropped onto the bed, unable to comprehend such hatred. "How long were you in there?"

"Three days. Finally, I heard horses near the river. I was certain they'd returned for me, but no one came. When the sounds began to fade, I started to scream. Footsteps came closer. I heard voices. As the rock was moved aside, I was blinded by the sunlight. All I saw was the outline of a man, but I knew he wasn't from my village."

"The Ranger," she whispered.

Jake nodded, a short, jerky motion. "Captain Jacob Robert McCain, of the Texas Rangers. He and Mama couldn't have children of their own, so he took me to his home and they raised me as their son. I owe him everything, even my life. The debt seemed immense for a young boy. It still does. I repaid it in the only way I could, by becoming what he was, following the example he set."

"He must have been so proud of you."

"He never said. I never asked. He died the summer I turned thirteen."

Rachel's heart broke for him. "Oh, Jake . . ."

"He was gunned down in front of me and I couldn't do anything to save him."

Rachel couldn't stop the tears that started. Jake had lost so much.

Jake glanced over his shoulder, his eyes glittering in the candlelight. "I know they never regretted taking me in, even at my worst, though it took Mama years to convince me. But they suffered because of me. Folks didn't look kindly on white people taking in a savage. I think they were waiting for me to show up to dinner and scalp all their guests. Guess they didn't know Indians have guns now, just like real people." He laughed, but it sounded raw in the quiet night.

Rachel held him close and laid her head on his back. "I'm sorry that you were treated so badly, Jake. They were ignorant, frightened fools. That doesn't mean you don't deserve to be happy. You're a good, honorable man. You didn't choose the circumstances of your birth. You can only be judged on what you make of yourself, and you have much to be proud of."

Jake stuffed his feet into his boots, and snatched up his shirt. "I'm proud of what I've accomplished. But while the good people of all the towns like Lucinda will gladly let me kill the outlaws that threaten them, not one will invite me to sit at their table. I'm still a savage in their eyes. That will never change. As my wife, you wouldn't be welcome, either. And you'd sure as hell never be allowed to teach their children."

Morning was a long time coming. Rachel huddled on her bed, fully dressed and shivering, but it had nothing to do with the cool air. Jake was still in the cabin, probably stretched out in front of the hearth. She'd almost gone after him when he walked out, but lost her nerve. Instead she'd pulled on her clothes and sat down to wait for dawn.

Now, hours later, she still didn't know what to say. No matter how bad Jake made it seem, she couldn't believe there wasn't somewhere that he was welcome, where he felt at home. They could live close to his mother. Or they could go somewhere that he'd never been, start over. She didn't care, as long as she was with him.

The snort of a horse broke into her thoughts. That would be Wolf leaving. Would Jake go with him?

She jumped to her feet and ran to the front door. He couldn't leave her alone here. She yanked open the door, surprising both men.

"Rachel, what's wrong?" Jake took a step toward her.

"Nothing." She drew a couple of breaths to slow her racing heart. "I heard a horse. I was afraid . . . that is, I thought you . . ." She stammered to a halt.

Jake raised one eyebrow, anger simmering in his eyes. "I'm seeing Wolf off. Go back inside. I'll join you in a minute."

She retreated into the house. Her heart still pounded an unsteady rhythm in her chest, making her light-headed. Leaning against the door for support, she closed her eyes and cursed her cowardice. If Jake wanted to leave, she had to let him go. She could survive without him.

She banished the tears that threatened. She had more important things to do than feel sorry for herself.

Pushing away from the door, she crossed to the old sea chest. Lifting the lid, she removed the clothes she used in the mine and set them aside. She'd slipped them in with the clothes she'd washed for Wolf and the boys. The worst of the dirt came out of them, but the knees were hopelessly stained. No matter, they were only going to get dirty again.

Lifting out clothes, blankets, and books, she emptied the

chest and took stock, separating the things she'd take along. The rest she set aside. She'd leave them here for the next occupants of the little house.

She went to her bedroom and surveyed her clothing. Leaving her gray wool dress, undergarments, one shawl, and her nightclothes, she carefully folded the few remaining things and carried them to the chest.

"There's still plenty of room for Nathan's things, and the rest of our books and my box." She continued to mumble to herself as she packed. Her medicinal herbs and liniment went into a cloth bag on top, where it was easy to get to should they be needed. Then she retrieved the little box holding her most treasured possessions.

She opened the lid and stared at the photo of her mother. Though the frame was broken and slightly askew, the love shining in the woman's eyes remained steady. Rachel sighed. "Mama, I think I finally understand." She traced her mother's face once with her fingertips before closing the box and tucking it into the nest of blankets and clothes.

"What are you doing?" Nathan thumped down the steps and stopped beside the chest. "Why are you packing?"

"I'm not," she hedged. "I'm just putting away some things we don't need right now. Spring cleaning."

He eyed her as if he didn't believe the explanation, but let it go. "Where's Jake? He promised to teach us to ride."

Calvin came clattering down the steps and the two boys raced each other to the door. When they flung it open, she tried not to look, but she couldn't help herself. Her stomach clenched when she didn't see Jake, but she spotted Griffin in the little corral. He was still here. The thrill of relief she felt was followed quickly by shame. If he wanted to go, she had to let him ride away. She couldn't hold him here.

Closing the lid of the chest with a thump, she put bread and butter on the table, and sliced a platter of cold venison for breakfast. When Jake and the boys came inside, she slipped out, needing to be alone.

"Rachel?" Jake followed her to the porch.

"I need to visit the privy, and I want to take a walk. I won't go far, I promise."

She didn't stop until the privy door closed behind her. She waited a few extra minutes, wanting to be certain Jake was inside with Nathan and Calvin. Peaking around the door, she was glad to find she was alone. The cabin stood open, but at least Jake hadn't waited for her to come out.

She slipped around the corner of the little building and walked into the hills, away from town. The quiet morning lent her a measure of peace. She would miss this the most, the windswept silence, the land made up of so many shades of brown and green she couldn't count them, the warm spring air that carried the scent of wildflowers.

Rachel plucked a primrose blossom from the grass and twirled it between her fingers. She hadn't realized how much she loved this place until she was faced with leaving. But she would go. The narrow-minded citizens of Lucinda had left her no choice, really. They'd decided she was a fallen woman . . . and perhaps she was.

Images of the night before filled her mind. Jake's kisses had easily driven all the lessons she'd learned from the Reverend out of her mind. Not even the memory of the cane striking her hands and back could make her resist his touch. Everything she'd been taught about proper behavior for a woman faded away when he held her.

She tossed the blossom to the ground. Perhaps she *was* unsuitable to be a teacher, but that didn't make her a bad woman. She would find other work, perhaps as a cook or a housemaid. She could still spin yarn. Maybe she would build a loom and weave blankets to sell. If Jake didn't want her, she would manage to support Nathan on her own.

She turned back toward the house and spotted Jake and the

boys with Duchess. She'd forced herself to get acquainted with Jake's packhorse the previous evening and had been rewarded for her efforts when the little animal lipped at her hair and skirt, looking for a treat. Rachel still couldn't approach Griffin or the big gray horse, which Calvin had named Smoke. Both were just so huge. But the chestnut mare was smaller and much gentler. She'd be a perfect mount for the boys to learn to ride.

In no hurry, Rachel strolled toward the house, watching Jake's hands as he tended to the little horse, all the while explaining what he was doing to his rapt audience of two. By the time she was close enough to hear the words, Duchess was saddled and ready to ride.

Nathan went first, putting his left foot in the stirrup and swinging his right over the saddle, as Jake instructed.

"Now, don't hold the reins too tight," he cautioned as the mare danced backward from the pressure on her bit. "That's it. Just let her get used to you. Good. Now lift the reins and lean forward just a little."

With no more coaxing than that, Duchess stepped out and completed a circle around the yard. While Jake offered encouragement, Nathan directed the little horse right, then left, took her to a trot, then slowed to a walk, finally stopping beside Jake.

He slid from the saddle, his face alight with pleasure. "Did you see that, Sis? Did you see me ride?"

"I certainly did. I think you are a natural in the saddle."

"My turn, Mr. Jake. It's my turn now." Calvin climbed into the saddle and repeated the moves Nathan had done. Rachel smiled and praised him, too. When he pulled a little too hard on the reins, causing Duchess to take three steps backward, his eyes grew as round as a saucer. She couldn't help but laugh at the shock and delight on his face.

"Now you, Miss Rachel." Calvin slid to the ground.

"What?" She swung around to stare at Calvin. "Oh, no. I don't know how."

"Well, of course you don't. That's what we're doing here, learning how to ride," Calvin reasoned.

"Come on, Sis," Nathan urged. You can do it."

She eased away from the waiting horse. "I don't think so. I don't have time. I should go and practice my shooting. I really don't need to learn to ride right now."

Before they could launch another verbal attack, Jake interrupted. "Maybe she just doesn't want an audience. Why don't you two go inside and dig out your skinning knives? We need to get them sharpened before Calvin's father gets back."

"Okay." They departed reluctantly, glancing back several times to see if she was going to try and ride Duchess. Finally, they disappeared into the house.

"Come on, pretty girl. They aren't watching now. Climb on up here."

"No, Jake, really. I don't think I need to—"

Instead of trying to convince her, he slipped an arm behind her back and urged her closer. "Put your left foot here." He guided it into place in the stirrup. "Now swing your right leg over." In a flurry of skirt and petticoats, she found herself astride Duchess. Panic fluttered in her stomach. The horse picked up on her tension and sidestepped, her ears flattened against her skull.

"Easy, girl," Jake soothed the animal. "Whoa, Duchess."

"Jake?" Her voice shook. She hated to let him know how frightened she was, but her pride was a small thing to sacrifice at the moment. "I don't want to do this."

"Relax, Rachel. You're making Duchess nervous. Let me adjust the stirrups so you can balance better."

He wrapped one warm hand around her left ankle and slipped her boot from the stirrup. Lengthening the strap one notch, he helped her find her footing again. When he released her, his fingers caressed her ankle beneath the cover of her skirt.

Her breath shortened. She tried to protest, but found she couldn't breathe at all as he smoothed his hand the length of her right leg, from thigh to foot, before adjusting the strap on that side of the saddle. He grinned up into her stunned face.

"Ready to give this a try?"

Without waiting for her to reply, he took up the reins and clicked his tongue. Duchess took two steps before Rachel slipped in the saddle. She squealed, startling the docile horse. The animal reared, ripping the reins out of Jake's hand. The horse bolted and Rachel grabbed for the saddle horn to keep from being dumped out of the saddle. Over the hills, away from town, the spooked animal raced. Rachel leaned forward to try and grab the reins, but that only made the horse run faster.

"Whoa, girl. Please stop. Duchess. Stop. Stop!"

Rachel breathed a sigh of relief when the horse slowed a little and turned to circle back toward the cabin, but her joy was short-lived. As Duchess came around a rock and dodged right, Rachel parted company with the saddle.

"Rachel? Honey, talk to me."

The darkness receded and she opened her eyes. "What happened?" She lay on the ground, staring up at Jake's anxious face. "I was on a horse. How did I get down here?"

"Something spooked Duchess. She's never bolted like that. Damn, I'm sorry honey. Are you all right?"

She struggled upright with Jake's assistance, and waited for her head to stop spinning while she took stock. "I don't believe anything is injured but my pride," she reassured Jake.

Not satisfied, he examined her himself, checking her head for bumps, her face for bruises. He felt the length of both arms and both legs, checking for injury. He found nothing until he reached her left ankle.

"Ouch." She flinched and tried to pull away, but he didn't release her.

"Easy, honey. Let me take a look at it."

He shoved her skirt to her knees, slipped the boot from her foot, but still couldn't see what was wrong. When he reached for the top of her stocking, she slapped at his hand, but there wasn't much heat in it. Instead of making him stop, she took his fingers in her own and guided him up her thigh. She felt him trace the edge of the garment and stop.

Glancing up, she was snagged by the fire in his gaze. Whimpering with need, she fisted her hands in his hair and pulled him down into the grass.

"Sis!"

"Miss Rachel. Mr. Jake."

The worried calls from Nathan and Calvin registered in her fuzzy brain. Jake heard them, too, and rolled away from her, coming to his knees. Turning back, he yanked her skirt over her legs before calling out to reassure the boys.

"We're over here. She's fine."

Rachel covered her face with both hands. What was the matter with her? He was only trying to help and she'd thrown herself at him like—just like the women in El Paso would have.

"Hey, why the long face?" Jake leaned over her, worry coloring his voice. "Honey, what's wrong? Are you really hurt?"

She couldn't look at him, see the disgust in his eyes. She was nothing more than a harlot, a common trollop, just as the people of Lucinda had branded her.

"Rachel." Jake dragged her hands from her face and peered into her eyes. "Talk to me or I'm sending Nathan to fetch Abby."

"I'm just like her, aren't I?"

Jake looked confused. "Like who? Abby?"

"No," she sighed. "My mother. I tried so hard not to be, but I can't resist you. When you're close, all I can think about it getting closer."

He stared at her for a second before a grin kicked up one corner of his full lips. "I can't say I find anything wrong with that."

"But, doesn't that make me a . . . a . . ." She swallowed hard and forced herself to say it. "A fallen woman?"

Jake threw back his head and laughed. "Hardly. Do you want to toss Arnold Miller to the ground when he walks by?"

"Of course not!" How could he suggest such a thing?

"Do you offer yourself to any man who comes along, as long as he has a few coins to share?"

"How dare you!" Her fingers curled into a fist. She turned her back, afraid she might give in to her temper and knock that smile off his handsome face.

Jake leaned across her, pinning her in place with his weight when she started to rise. "You're only a fallen woman if you count that tumble from Duchess. What we share, honey, is pure, beautiful attraction. It's special, not wrong. And it doesn't make you a prostitute." Jake scooped her into his arms and started for the house. She barely had time to snag her boot.

"Jake McCain," she hissed. "Put me down."

"Not until I can get a good look at that ankle."

She huffed in exasperation. "It doesn't hurt anymore. I can walk."

"Nope. Besides, I like the feel of you right where you are." He waggled his eyebrows at her and winked.

She wasn't amused. "Please, Jake. The boys."

"Shut up, woman. Just stop talking and let me handle this."

The boys careened around a boulder and into their path, nearly colliding with Jake.

Nathan's eyes went wide at the sight of his sister in Jake's arms. Rachel could only wonder what he would think if he'd come upon them a few minutes earlier. The heat of a blush swarmed across her cheeks.

"You said she was fine," he accused.

"I am." She glanced at Nathan from her perch. "I twisted my ankle a bit when I fell, that's all."

They fell into step beside Jake. "You fell off Duchess?" Nathan could barely contain his grin.

"She bolted and I lost my hold and if you laugh, Nathan Joseph Hudson, I swear you'll be washing dishes for a week!"

Nathan pulled his face into a contrite mask and bit his lips, holding back the laughter for nearly five steps. Then it burst forth in a joyous cackle, a sound no one could resist. Calvin doubled over and dropped to his knees, rolling in the dirt and clutching his sides. Even Jake was losing his battle against a grin.

Rachel looked around, ready to lecture the lot of them, but she caught sight of the dust clinging to her backside. She looked ridiculous, hair askew, dress filthy, being carried to the house like a princess. She sputtered, choking off a laugh. When she caught Jake's gaze, and the humor lurking there, she gave in. Soon all four were laughing and chattering as they made their way home.

As the cabin came into view, the smile faded from Jake's face. "Nathan, did you leave the door open?"

"No, sir. I closed it. I'm sure I did."

"Maybe you were too worried about your sister and forgot."

The boy shook his head, denying it. Calvin defended him. "He closed it, Mr. Jake. I watched him."

"Well, it's open now." He backtracked a few steps to set Rachel behind a rock. He handed Nathan his revolver, grip first. Nathan accepted it without a word. "Stay here," Jake ordered. "And watch your backs."

Chapter Twenty-one

As Jake melted into the landscape, the boys flanked her, one facing the house, the other the empty hills behind them.

"Maybe its Wolf," Rachel offered.

"No horse," Nathan answered, never taking his eyes off the door. "And he'd have stayed where we could see him."

Rachel searched for Jake, but couldn't see him. "He might have left the door ajar so we would know he was in there."

"Pa won't be back for at least two days, maybe three."

She wanted to argue, but she couldn't think. Her ankle throbbed, reminding her that she'd just taken a tumble from a horse. Now Jake was walking into danger because someone had been in her home. And two boys who shouldn't have to worry about things like guns and protection were standing guard over her. It was almost more than she could bear.

She felt the sting of tears and blinked them back. Crying would help nothing and it would only make Nathan uncomfortable. He hated it when she gave in to tears.

After what seemed like an eternity, Jake came out of the house and strode back to where they waited. "The house is empty. If there was anybody inside, they aren't there now."

"Maybe the wind blew it open." Rachel glanced down at the grass and flowers, none of which showed the slightest sign of a breeze.

"You must have hit your head, Sis," Nathan stared at her. "There ain't no—isn't any wind today."

"It doesn't matter. Let's get you inside." Jake took his revolver from Nathan, nodding approval when the boy took care to keep the muzzle pointed away from everyone. He slipped it back into the holster at his waist, then lifted Rachel in his arms and crossed the remaining distance to the house. Setting her in the rocker, he had Nathan and Calvin pull one of the benches from the table close so she could rest her foot on it. Then he sent them out for water.

"But there's a whole bucket right there. I brought it in just before Sis took off on her ride." Nathan snickered, but the look Jake shot him quelled the humor.

Jake raised one eyebrow. "Nathan, go outside for a minute."

"But—"

"Go," Jake and Rachel ordered in unison.

The moment the door closed behind them, Rachel started to her feet.

"What are you doing?" He blocked her easily and she plopped back down into the rocker.

"Going to my room to change out of this filthy dress."

He pulled a twig from her hair and tossed it aside. "Not until I check that ankle. Now sit still."

"Jake," she argued. "I'm fine. It's just a little sore, nothing to be concerned with."

"I'll be the judge of that." His hands were gentle when he lifted her leg and stretched it across his own.

When he pressed too hard on a bruised spot, she tried to pull away. "Ouch, that hurt."

Jake winced in sympathy, taking more care as he finished examining her foot. "I'm sorry I ever put you up on Duchess."

"I tried to tell you I don't belong on a horse. I attempted it once before, when I was younger."

Jake lowered her foot to the bench and made sure her skirt covered her. "What happened?"

"The same thing, only I got a bump on the head instead of a twisted ankle. We had two mules to pull the wagon. One of my duties was to lead them to water when we stopped for the night. I decided to try riding one of them. I thought it would be better than walking all the way to the creek and back. I stopped the smaller of the two beside a fallen tree and climbed on. I did fine until the mule decided she didn't want a rider. She took four or five running steps, kicked out with her hind legs and sidestepped, dumping me into the grass. Mrs. Hudson wasn't happy that I'd torn the sleeve of my dress. I lied and told her I'd tripped. It didn't stop the beating, but at least it wasn't as bad as it might have been had she known the truth."

"They beat you for falling off a mule?" He sounded appalled at the idea.

"'Withhold not correction from a child,'" she recited. "'Thou shalt beat him with the rod, and deliver his soul from hell.' Proverbs Twenty-three. I think that was their favorite Bible passage. I certainly heard it enough." Rachel shifted in the rocker, hurting more from her fall than she wanted to let on. "They weren't bad people, Jake. They were just very strict for a young girl who'd grown up as I had, doing what I wanted whenever I wanted."

He wasn't convinced. "They didn't have to strike you. I was pretty wild when the McCains took me in, but they never raised a hand to me."

Rachel changed the subject. "May I go now? I really would like to clean up a little."

Jake looked like he would argue. She opened her mouth to beg, but he relented and helped her to her bedroom door. "I'll bring you some hot water." When the blanket closed over the doorway, she sank onto the bed and bit back a groan. Her ankle throbbed and her left shoulder felt scraped and raw. Wishing she had a cup of tonic, she settled for a warm sponge bath and a short nap.

When Rachel awoke an hour later, she was still sore, but she felt a little better. Gingerly putting weight on her ankle, she hobbled around the room until most of the stiffness was gone. Once she could walk without drawing attention to the fact that she hurt, she went in search of Jake and the boys.

They were nowhere to be found, but since all the horses were gone from the corral, she assumed they were practicing their riding skills. Confident Jake wouldn't be too far away to hear a shot, Rachel headed for the lean-to, carrying the loaded rifle. There was work to be done and she may as well get to it.

After cleaning out the chicken coops and filling them with fresh hay, she gathered up the few eggs she'd found. Climbing the two steps to the porch took the last of her energy and made her ankle throb. Deciding some tonic was in order, Rachel went to the sea chest and hefted the heavy lid.

She was so intent on the bag of herbs that she almost missed it. Her little box lay open, the contents dumped out of it. "What on earth," she exclaimed. "How did this happen?" Baffled, she gathered up her treasures and returned them to their place. Suddenly her breath caught. The photo of her mother was missing. She tore through the chest, tossing everything to the floor, but it wasn't there. It was gone.

She sat on the floor, staring at the mess around her, certain she must have missed it. "Maybe Nathan took it," she reasoned with the empty room. But he wouldn't have dumped everything else out like that. She searched for another explanation, but only came up with one. Someone *had* been in the cabin.

Rachel scrambled for the rifle. Jake had promised a single rifle shot would bring him running. Her hands shook as she stuffed a bullet into the chamber and pulled back on the lever. For an instant it refused to budge, but her terror gave her strength. Throwing open the door, she took two steps onto the porch and pulled the trigger, firing the warning shot into the air without bothering to raise the gun to her shoulder.

The blast knocked her backward and she thumped into the wall, jarring her sore shoulder. She hardly noticed. Forcing herself to calm down, she crawled inside and closed the door. When she'd caught her breath, she loaded the rifle again, dropping as many bullets on the floor as she managed to push into the chamber. "That will have to be enough." She stumbled to the far side of the room, sank to the floor, and aimed the rifle at the door.

As Rachel waited for Jake, her fear turned to anger. Someone had violated her home, and stolen from her. The picture had no value to anyone but her and Nathan. That gave her pause. Had Nathan retrieved the picture for some reason and not told her? She dismissed the idea. He didn't know she'd put the box into the chest. But it was possible he'd guessed. She'd ask him before jumping to the conclusion that someone had been in the cabin long enough to search for it and still get out unobserved.

"Rachel?"

She nearly sobbed with relief when she heard Jake call from outside the cabin.

"Jake!" She threw open the door and ran into his arms. Fear had her shaking again and she stepped back, squaring her shoulders. She refused to let anyone frighten her like this.

"What's wrong, pretty girl? Why the rifle shot?"

"I couldn't think what else to do." She moved out of the shelter of his arms. "Someone *was* in the house before."

Jake took her hand and pulled her close. "How do you know?"

His dark eyes scanned the area, probing shadows she didn't even realize were there.

"The picture of my mother is missing. I put it in the sea chest with the other things I want to take with us and now its not there."

"Take with you? You're leaving?"

She stared at him, appalled at what she'd let slip. Then anger slid in to fire her blood. "It isn't your concern. You made that very clear this morning."

Jake's lips thinned, the only indication of his feelings. "We'll discuss this later. We need to get Nathan and Calvin into the house." He turned to signal the boys it was safe.

Nathan. Shame washed through Rachel. She hadn't given any consideration to how her panicked firing of the rifle would affect him. "I'll help with the horses." She made it two steps before she was yanked around.

"*You'll* go back inside. We'll handle things out here."

He gave her a little push toward the porch. Arguing with him seemed petty and foolish, so she did as he asked, looking around for an unknown assailant with every step.

She heard Nathan and Calvin a few minutes later, but they didn't come inside. While they settled the horses, she gathered what they might need in case of a fight. She didn't have any real idea, but she had to have something to do. She sliced all the remaining venison, then started on a double batch of bread. At least they'd have something to eat.

"What are you doing?"

She managed not to jump when Jake whispered in her ear, but just barely. "Make some noise next time, Ranger McCain." She mock threatened him with the knife she had concealed in her apron pocket. "I've had enough surprises for today."

The boys made up for Jake's silence as they piled through the door and into the attic.

Jake turned back to her with a smile. It quickly faded. "You're sure something was taken?"

"Unless Nathan removed it from the chest."

"Nathan?" Jake strode to the base of the stairs.

"Yes, sir?" His blond head appeared at the top.

"Did you borrow the picture of your sister's mother from the sea chest?"

"No, sir." He came halfway down the staircase. "Isn't it on the mantel?"

Panic ripped through Rachel all over again. She hadn't realized how much she was hoping Nathan had taken the picture. "I put the box in the sea chest this morning, just before you came down looking for Jake."

His forehead wrinkled as he dug up the memory back. "But you said you were just packing away the things we didn't need right now. Spring cleaning, you said." He came to stand in front of her. "Why would you put her picture in there?"

She glanced over his head to where Jake stood, waiting for

her answer. "I was sorting out what we'll take with us if we decide to leave Lucinda."

Nathan considered that for a moment. "Makes sense." He looked around the room. "Looks like you got most of it."

Rachel stared at him. "It doesn't upset you to leave here?"

Her brother shook his head. "I told you before, we can go wherever we need to so you can teach like you want." He headed for the stairs. "Jake." He paused until his hero looked at him. "The woman in that picture isn't only Rachel's mama. She's mine, too."

He ran up the stairs, unaware of the impact of his words. Rachel couldn't move, in shock at how easily her little brother had decided to accept the truth of his birth.

The turmoil of the last few weeks came flooding back, sapping what strength she had left. With a sound of distress she couldn't contain, Rachel sank into the rocking chair.

"Honey?" Jake sat on his heels in front of her. "What's wrong?"

"Two weeks ago, Nathan nearly got himself killed in an abandoned gold mine because he refused to listen when I said Eleanor Hudson wasn't his mother. Now he accepts it without question." She stared into his spring green eyes, seeing her reflection there. "What happened?"

Jake smiled and brushed a tendril of hair from her cheek. "Don't ask me. I don't think I'll ever understand him."

Rachel didn't know she was crying until he wiped away a tear with his thumb. The calluses of hard work felt rough on her skin and the sensation set her body humming. Without stopping to consider the wisdom of her action, she leaned into his touch, increasing the contact. A tiny sigh of pleasure slipped out.

"Damn it, woman,"—Jake cupped her chin with his hand—"you make it hard to remember I don't have any right to be here."

"Jake." She waited until he met her gaze. "I want you here. That gives you the right."

"Pretty girl, we went through this."

"No, *you* went through it. I don't happen to agree with you." She took her courage in both hands and leaned forward to press her lips to his. "You were wrong this morning. I don't deserve better, I deserve the best. And that's you, Jake McCain. I'd be the luckiest woman alive to wake up next to you every morning. But you're part of this choice, too, and if you don't want me, so be it. I'd rather live with you, but I'll survive without you."

She rose from the chair, hiding a smile at the dumb-founded look on his face. "Maybe you'd better give some thought to who might have been in my house while I finish making this bread."

Jake recovered quickly. "Are you planning on a siege?"

"What do you mean?"

He indicated the food she was preparing. "That's enough for the four of us to hold out for several days."

"Is it too much? It's just that I . . ."

He grinned at her, making her heart thump an uneven rhythm in her chest. "It's okay, pretty girl. Being prepared is a good thing to be." He pulled her into his arms for a hard kiss, and released her before she could collect her wits. "That was for luck." He winked at her and strode from the house. "Bar the door behind me. I'll let you know it's me before I come close," he called. "Shoot anyone else."

His parting words dumped her right out of the cloud she was floating on. Remembering there might be someone watching the cabin, close enough to harm Jake, had her running after him. "Be careful," she called through the door. "Please," she pleaded in a whisper as she dropped the heavy bar into place. Taking the rifle with her, she returned to her chores.

The rest of the day went by in a blur. Rachel filled the hours with baking and mending, then resorted to reading aloud to the boys to keep them occupied. At dinnertime, Jake returned, staying only long enough to eat. When the boys went to bed, she folded the laundry he'd brought in from the line. Sometime after midnight, her nervous energy finally gave out and she collapsed onto a bench by the table and laid her head on her folded arms.

Her sore ankle throbbed from the forced activity of the afternoon. She'd baked a dozen loaves of bread and a couple of pans of biscuits. Jake would probably tease her about cooking for an army. There were beans soaking for tomorrow's meal. All the mending was done. She'd even scrubbed the floor, though it was a task she hated and usually avoided as long as possible. With a sigh, she let exhaustion claim her.

A log shifted in the hearth, jolting her awake. Rachel looked around, groggy from her nap. She must have slept, but it couldn't have been for long. She pushed to her feet, groaning at the stiffness in her back and legs. She took a step and nearly fell to the floor. The ankle she'd twisted in her flight from Duchess's saddle didn't want to hold her weight. "Well that's too bad," she muttered. "I have things to do." Gritting her teeth, she took a tentative step, gasping at the pain stabbing through her. It took a dozen paces, holding on to the table the whole time, but she finally felt confident she could get to the bedroom without pitching onto her face.

She considered sitting on the bed and resting for a bit before gathering her wool and combs, but she wasn't sure she'd be able to get up again. "How can I be so stiff? She's a small horse. It wasn't that far to fall." Forcing herself forward, she half hopped across the tiny room, scooped up the basket of goat's wool and the tools she needed, and hobbled back to the main room.

Dropping everything beside her chair, she limped over to fetch the rifle. It needed to be close by, easy to reach. She certainly wouldn't be able to get across the room in a hurry should she need it. It took a few more minutes to get organized, but soon the familiar sounds of carding wool whispered through the quiet house.

Jake sat in the dark, watching the cabin. It was where he'd been for the last hour, trying to gather the courage to go in and face Rachel. "Damn it." He cursed the night and the lack of any proof someone had been near the cabin. Mostly he cursed himself. How did he make her see he was the wrong man for her when he no longer believed it himself?

Somewhere during the long day, he'd realized he didn't want her to find someone else. He wanted to be the man she turned to, the one she relied upon.

"I love her," he whispered to the stars. How the hell had that happened?

It wasn't possible. He waited for the familiar panic, the trapped feeling he always got when he considered marriage and a family. But it never came. Instead, a warmth filled him when he pictured Rachel, heavy with his child, and guiding Nathan as he grew into a man any father would be proud of.

He must look ridiculous, sitting in the dark with a stupid grin on his face, but he didn't care. He wanted Rachel and he would have her. What if she'd changed her mind? That gave him pause. Maybe a half-breed renegade lawman wasn't what she wanted after all? Then he'd convince her to change her mind right back. Nothing could be as hard as facing a future without her.

He caught himself before he straightened and presented an easy target to whoever might be watching. He didn't doubt someone was. Though he'd found no evidence, his instincts were screaming at him that Rachel was in danger. Checking the shadows, he slipped up to the house and made a complete circuit before setting foot on the porch. He came up on the far end, near the window where the candle that saved his life had burned.

"Rachel?" He kept his voice low, not wanting to wake the boys. "Honey, it's me." He leaned closer to the window, but he couldn't hear anything inside. Was she asleep? Hoping he wasn't destined to a night on the ground with no bedroll, he called out a third time. Finally, sounds of movement came from inside, then an uneven shuffle as she approached the window.

"Jake?"

"It's safe, pretty girl. You can open up."

He heard her drag the bar from the door and lower it to the floor, but the door didn't open.

"Come inside, slowly. I have a gun and I know how it works."

Jake grinned. He couldn't help it. Here he was, anxious to tell the woman he wanted forever with her, and she met him at the door with a loaded rifle. It was a story they could tell their grandchildren. He opened the door with his left hand, careful to stay out of her line of fire, just in case Wolf wasn't as good a teacher as he thought.

"Rachel, honey, I'm coming in. Put the rifle down."

"Are you alone?"

"I'm alone, pretty girl."

"Then come on in."

Relief was evident in her voice. He peeked around the doorframe to be sure she knew it was him before stepping into the open.

She faced the door from across the room, the rifle cradled in her arms. It wasn't pointing at him, but she wouldn't have to move it far to find a target.

Jake came inside and closed the door, barring it again. When he looked back, Rachel had pointed the rifle at the far wall and was struggling to uncock it.

"Let me, honey." Taking it from her shaking hands, he eased the hammer forward and set the gun aside. When he opened his arms, she stepped into them without a word. Hugging her close, he let the last of his resistance melt away. Whatever it took, this woman was his and he wasn't letting her go.

"I'm sorry. I needed to be sure. You were gone so long," she admonished without looking up. "I was worried."

"You were safe. I wasn't far away."

"I wasn't worried for me, I was scared for you."

Jake swore he heard a muttered *dammit* as she turned away to the stove. He snagged her hand and pulled her back against his chest. "What did you say?"

She squirmed in his arms but didn't answer.

"I don't think I can have any wife of mine using language like that." He felt her stiffen and struggled against a grin. "It wouldn't be proper." He glanced down and felt himself drowning in twin pools of azure. God, she had the most beautiful eyes. He leaned forward and placed a gentle kiss on her lips.

"Wife?" Her voice quavered on the single word.

"If you'll have me, honey." Jake loosened his hold and dropped to one knee in front of her. "I know I'm no prize, and you'll probably spend the rest of your days wishing me to Hades, but I don't think my heart will go on beating if you aren't part of my life." He kissed the fingers of her right hand. "Will you marry me, Rachel Hudson?"

When she tugged on his hand, he rose to his feet and waited for her answer. When a smile curved her lips, he thought his heart would stop.

"I'd be proud to be your wife, Jake McCain."

A whoop from behind her brought them both around. Nathan raced down the stairs to throw his arms around Rachel. Calvin followed close behind. She returned her brother's hug with tears in her eyes.

"Well," Jake muttered, shaking his head at Nathan. "I intended to ask your permission, son, but it looks like we already have your blessing."

A knock sounded on the door, startling them.

"Pa!" Calvin ran for the door and lifted the bar before Jake could stop him. The door banged open, knocking the boy to the floor. Wolf stood in the doorway, blood running from a gash near his temple.

Rachel cried out. "Wolf, what happened?"

"He heard your rifle shot a little too late." A man stood behind Wolf, his face in shadow. A brawny arm shoved Wolf in the back, knocking the big man to his knees. His hands were tied behind his back. Bruises on his face told the story of the beating he'd taken. Calvin started forward, but a glance from his father had him scooting backward, out of reach.

Jake pulled Rachel behind him as the stranger stepped into the light. She peered around his broad shoulders and stared at a yellow-haired ghost.

"You're dead," she whispered.

Jake heard the terror in her voice as she stared into the eyes of the man who'd murdered her mother.

"Not quite," the man sneered. He turned his evil gaze on Jake. "See, you've been following the wrong man, Ranger. That was my little brother, William, you've been chasin'. We look a lot alike, but he's too dumb to outthink you. I'm not."

He pointed his revolver at each person in the room in turn, counting heads, memorizing faces. "Allow me to introduce myself. I'm Waylon Montrose Harrison." The gun swung to point at Jake's chest. "And you have something that belongs to me."

Chapter Twenty-two

"Waylon Montrose Harrison," Jake repeated. "Damn. I thought the WM on the knife you dropped was short for William."

"Well, you were wrong, Ranger. Now drop those guns you're wearing. Nice and slow." When the belt hit the floor, the man smiled in triumph. "Don't think you can get to them, Ranger." He motioned toward Wolf with his gun. "I'll take out both you and this one before you could feel metal under your fingertips."

He landed a vicious kick in Wolf's ribs, then grabbed his hair near the gash and yanked his head back to hold him in place. The pain had to be terrible, but Wolf didn't make a sound.

"You let him go!" Nathan yelled.

"Nathan," Jake breathed in warning.

"Shut up, boy, unless you want to die where you're standing. I don't usually shoot kids—my brother prefers to take care of them—but I can always make an exception."

Jake shifted a little to gain the man's attention. "So where have you been while I've been following your brother halfway across the territory?"

Harrison laughed. "Well, I visited El Paso a time or two, looking for her." He glared at Rachel. "You've cost me way too much time, little girl. You were mine. I bought you from your mama's skirt-man, lock, stock, and barrel. And all I got for my money was this scar." He turned toward the light. A vicious line bisected his left cheek. "I've had Willy keep an eye out for you. He sent word as soon as he found you hiding in this two-bit town. You caused me a passel of trouble, bitch, and you've got eight years of my time to make up for."

"I don't buy it," Jake interrupted, desperate to get Harrison to focus on him instead of Rachel. "Eight years without finding her? Even you can't be that bad at tracking."

Harrison fired a shot over Jake's right shoulder, close enough he heard the bullet whistle when it passed.

"I coulda had her sooner if I'd wanted. But I had other business."

"Such as?"

Harrison made a show of remembering. "Well, now, there's a bank down San Antonio way that's missing a vault full of money. And the Army made a couple of helpful donations to my cause." He laughed, an ugly, grating sound. "Other than that"—he yanked on Wolf's hair—"I've spent my time keeping an eye on this one, from a distance, of course."

Jake felt Rachel ease away from him a step, then another, while Harrison was distracted. He wanted to tell her to get back behind him, but he didn't dare draw attention to her. He needed to keep Harrison occupied. Wolf seemed to read his mind.

"Which one of you killed my wife and daughter?" he hissed. "You or your brother?"

"That was Willy." Harrison laughed. "I got there a little late, and he'd already handled everything. I was real proud of him that day. I couldn't have done it better myself."

Wolf surged upward, but Harrison countered the move and slammed the butt of his gun against the side of Wolf's head. Wolf collapsed back to his knees, and blood trickled from a cut near the corner of his eye, but he didn't go down. "Anybody tell you your brother is dead?"

The sudden silence in the room was deafening. "What the hell do you mean?" He shoved the long barrel of the revolver into Wolf's ear. "Talk. Fast."

Wolf glanced his way, but there was nothing Jake could do but watch. He clenched his fists in impotent fury. This was his fault. Somehow he should have known the difference between the brothers and killed the right one.

The taste of failure was bitter, but not as bad as knowing he wouldn't be able to keep Rachel safe. Four more lives depending on him. Four ghosts he couldn't live with. He had to get Harrison away from Wolf, but how?

If he hadn't been looking at Wolf, Jake would have missed it. The trapper was staring behind him, toward where Rachel should be. His eyes moved to the right, then back at Rachel. Jake didn't dare turn his head. What the hell was she doing?

Rachel was terrified. She froze in place when Harrison hit Wolf, but she didn't make a sound. When she looked back at the trapper, Wolf was watching her. He glanced toward the rifle leaning against the wall behind her, then back at her, the movements so quick she thought she might have imagined it. When he slid to the floor with a loud groan of pain, dragging Harrison off balance, she realized what he wanted.

Harrison rounded on Wolf and she seized the opportunity. The rifle felt almost familiar as she yanked back the hammer. "Get down!"

Jake dove for his gun belt as Rachel and Harrison pulled the triggers. The twin explosions were deafening in the little room. The force of the rifle blast threw her back against the hearth. Nathan screamed her name as two more shots rang out. Then the room fell silent.

Rachel lay where she'd been thrown by the force of the rifle blast. After the noise of the gunshots, the quiet was oppressive.

Jake crawled to her side. "Rachel. Honey, talk to me. Please. Rachel?"

"Is he dead?" She thought she heard Jake mutter an oath as he sagged to the floor beside her.

"Yeah, honey, he's dead."

"But don't look." Nathan stood between her and the outlaw, blocking her view. "There's blood everywhere."

"Nathan, are you all right?" She took a slow, deep breath,

taking inventory to be sure everything still worked. Her ears were ringing and she couldn't quite remember how she ended up on the floor.

"Sure. He didn't have time to do anything before you shot him."

"Wolf? Calvin?" She lifted her head enough to assure herself they were alive. She winced at the damage done to the tracker's face.

"He's fine, and I'll live," Wolf limped to her side, leaning on his son for support. "Thanks to you."

"What the hell were you thinking?"

She flinched away from Jake's shout before anger flowed in to fill the places where fear had been. Turning on him, she let her temper boil over. "I thought I was saving your sorry hide, Jake McCain. What was I supposed to do, stand there while he filled you with bullets, then started on the rest of us?"

She struggled to sit up, her chest heaving with indignation. "I'm through letting people walk on me. And that overgrown bully just happened to be in the way when I decided I'd had enough."

"Here's the bullet he fired." Everyone turned to where Calvin examined a new hole in the wall behind her.

"Damned lucky it's buried in wood and not in you." Jake swore again. "Next time, let me handle it." He wrapped his arms around her, squeezing her until she protested. He loosened his grip but didn't let go. "I don't think my heart can stand another scare like that."

Rachel leaned back to look into his eyes. She lifted a hand to skim the lines around his mouth. "Get used to it, Ranger McCain. I protect what's mine—now that I know how to shoot."

A grin crinkled the corners of his eyes and her heart did a funny flip in her chest.

"Well, at least our lives will never be boring." Jake helped her to her feet. "Can you stand on your own, pretty girl?"

"Of course." She gave him a little shove and walked in a small circle to prove it. "See? I'm fine."

"Good." He pulled her into his arms and kissed her until

her knees felt weak. She staggered a little when he released her, but the twinkle in his eyes said he knew why.

"Now, sit down in that rocking chair and don't move while I take care of a few things."

Rachel obediently sat in her chair while he and Wolf carried the body outside. Then she got to work herself. "Nathan, we'll need the lye soap. Calvin?"

"Yes, ma'am?"

"Will you bring in another bucket of water for me?"

"Aren't you supposed to be resting?"

She turned to face the pint-sized version of Wolf. "I'm not as fragile as Ranger McCain seems to think. There's work to be done. Now get to it."

His grin was a mirror image of his father's. "Yes, ma'am." He raced out the door, snagging an empty bucket on the way. Nathan dug out the soap, tossed it onto the table, and went after his friend.

Rachel stoked both fires, put a full kettle on the stove to boil and set the remaining half bucket of water on the hearth to warm. Then she went to pull out her herbs. Wolf would need her tonic. When she bent over to drag a heavy pot from a low shelf, she groaned in pain.

"I think I'll make enough for two." Rachel whimpered as she stretched aching muscles. What she needed was a long, hot bath, but there was too much to do. The tonic would have to suffice.

When the boys returned with an overflowing bucket, she poured the steaming water from the kettle into a washtub, added fresh water until it was cool enough to put her hand in, then shaved a generous portion of lye soap into the mix. When she reached for a rag, Nathan stopped her.

"We can do this. You don't need to be cleaning up after the likes of him."

Rachel stood back and watched the boys attack the mess until the sight and smell of the blood became too much for her. Turning her back on them, she searched for something to do. Anything. She had to keep busy or she'd break down, and she refused to allow that to happen.

She refilled the kettle with cold water and put it on to heat. One minute went by. She walked to a window. It was still dark out, but dawn wasn't far off. Another minute gone. When the kettle of water came to a boil for the second time, she poured a little into a cup and added the herbs for her tonic. She stirred in barely a tablespoon of whiskey, but just a whiff of the steam made her cough. Taking a deep breath, she gamely swallowed the concoction, choking it down until the cup was empty. "Oh, that really *is* awful."

Refilling her cup with coffee, she sipped at it to chase away the lingering taste of herbs and alcohol. She measured another dose of tonic, added a healthy splash of whiskey and set it aside. She'd add the hot water to it when Wolf came inside.

The boys emptied the washtub three times before they were satisfied. Rachel hugged them both, holding Nathan a little longer than he liked.

"It's really over, Sis. You can let go now."

She shook her head and released him. "I just can't believe there were two of them. Brothers. They looked so much alike."

"They were the same inside, too," Calvin observed. "Rotten."

"And now they're both dead," Nathan declared. "I hope the devil enjoys having them around." He leaned back to stare at Rachel. "What's wrong?" He sounded a little panicked. "Why are you crying?"

Rachel was surprised to feel the wetness on her cheeks. "I'm just relieved it's finally done. Mama can rest in peace."

Nathan wrapped his arms around her waist. "So can we."

Before she could hug him back, he took off for his room. "Come on, Calvin. Let's go upstairs."

Rachel watched the boys disappear into the attic room. Nathan was growing up so fast, becoming a man before her eyes. Fresh tears welled. It was too soon. He should still be a child, but life had a way of shaping a person and she couldn't turn back the clock or undo his experiences.

Rachel went to the door to look for Jake. She didn't see him, but she could hear his voice, coming from behind the house. She stepped onto the porch, intending to go to him, but hesitated. What if Harrison hadn't been alone? Panic swept through her. "No," she whispered, forcing herself to calm down. "Jake and Wolf would have thought of that already." They'd have checked everywhere for danger before leaving her and the boys alone. If they were standing outside talking, no one was close to the house that shouldn't be.

She went back inside and opened all the windows to let the night breeze blow away the lingering smell of violence and lye soap. Soon the scent of night-blooming wildflowers perfumed the air. She inhaled deeply, releasing a sigh and the last of her fear. "Be at peace, Mama," she whispered. "He can't hurt us anymore."

By the time Jake and Wolf returned, dawn was painting the eastern sky rose pink and shimmering gold. Both men looked ready to drop. They'd washed up at the well, and water still dripped from their hair.

She studied them as they came into the cabin. Wolf was tall and broad, a mountain of male. With his sable brown hair slicked back from his face, he looked younger, though the lines of fatigue and pain were etched deep in his tanned face.

Jake came toward her, drawing her attention. His lithe, lean frame made her heart race and her body flushed with desire. This was the man for her. His black hair gleamed in the firelight. His green eyes glowed, reflecting Rachel's image back to her. He held so much of himself inside, never sharing with the world all that he was, all that he knew, but it didn't matter. She loved his shadows, his secrets. She loved him.

Wolf lowered himself to a bench at the table, biting back a curse. The sudden sound in the quiet room startled her. Rachel poured boiling water into the herbal tonic and set the steaming cup of liquid in front of him. "Drink it all. It will help you feel better." Then she set to cleaning the gash in his head.

"After it makes you feel worse," Jake quipped, dropping to a seat opposite him. "Drink it at your own peril."

Rachel slapped at his hands as he tried to pull her into his lap. "There's nothing wrong with my tonic."

"I didn't say there was," he soothed. He watched Wolf take a swallow and come up coughing. A smile curved Jake's lips. "But you really should warn a man. Nobody expects an angel to hand them a devil's potion like that."

"What the hell is in this stuff?" Wolf gasped. "Begging your pardon, Rachel," he apologized around the coughing.

"Some healing herbs, a bit of molasses, and whiskey." She rose to gather what she needed to treat the cut on Wolf's head.

"Is that what it's called around here?"

Jake laughed. "Just drink it. It really will help."

"If it doesn't kill me first." Wolf took another, more cautious sip.

Rachel laughed. She couldn't help it. Delight bubbled out of her, releasing all the tension and horror of the past weeks. Not even cleaning the blood from Wolf's wound bothered her. That demon was laid to rest.

She dropped into Jake's lap with a happy sigh. Everyone she loved was safe. She wiggled closer to Jake, wanting to melt into him and never emerge.

"I have something for you." Jake caught up her hand and threaded his fingers through hers. He dug into his shirt pocket. "Do you recognize this?"

Rachel stared at the ring, almost afraid to take it. "Mama's ring. Where did you find it?"

"Harrison had it."

She brushed a finger across the three bands, two of silver, one of gold, woven together to create the ring. The marks and shadows of age and use were apparent. "Mama wore it every day. It was my great-grandmother's wedding ring. She gave it to my grandmother, who passed it on to my mother just before she set out for El Paso, where she was supposed to meet her fiancé. It was to be mine when I married, but . . ."

He slipped it over the fourth finger of her left hand. It fit perfectly. "Now it's back where it belongs."

Rachel fisted her hand to keep the ring safely in place and

looked at Jake with tears brimming in her eyes. "I love you, Jake McCain."

Wolf coughed as he choked down the last of the tonic and went to wash out his cup. Rachel considered objecting to him doing her work, but it would take too much energy. She yawned and settled deeper into Jake.

"I think you need sleep, woman." Jake's voice rumbled in her ear.

"We all do," Wolf agreed. "I'll take the outside."

"You most certainly will not." Rachel roused herself enough to protest. "You'll take my bed."

"And where will you sleep?"

She smiled up at Jake. "I'm very comfortable right here, thank you."

Wolf said something else, but she didn't hear it over the pounding of her heart as Jake covered her lips with his. She felt Jake stand, lifting her with ease. Four steps of pure heaven, each footfall causing her body to brush his, then he lowered them both into the rocker, never breaking the kiss. The sun broke over the horizon, bathing them in warm, golden light. Rachel barely noticed. Her sun had risen the moment Jake McCain came into her life, and she was looking forward to a long life together before it set again.

Breakfast came late the next morning, but no one minded. The past was finally laid to rest and the future waited.

"We'll head out tomorrow, at first light." Wolf ruffled his son's hair. "It's time we got on with our lives."

Calvin leaned into his touch. "I'm ready when you are, Pa."

Rachel poured more coffee for him. "Are you sure you're strong enough, Wolf?" The gash on his head looked a little better, but his right eye was bruised and swollen.

"We'll have to take it easy for a few days, but I'll manage." He hugged his son close.

Rachel smiled at them. "Do you have enough supplies? There's not much extra here, but I understand I have an outstanding credit at Mr. Miller's store." She raised one eyebrow at Jake in mock annoyance. "You're welcome to whatever you need."

Wolf was shaking his head before she finished. "I appreciate the offer, but we don't need charity."

"It isn't charity," Jake interrupted. "The money I put on account for Rachel came from one of Harrison's men, the one you kept from shooting me." He took a sip of coffee. "The man had a price on his head. Consider it the reward money."

The big tracker hesitated a moment longer, then acquiesced with a nod. "In that case, I appreciate it. It'll make the trip easier on both of us."

"Where will you go?" Rachel excused Nathan and Calvin as she joined the men at the table. The boys raced each other out of the house, heading for the horses.

"Home," he answered simply. "We have a lot of cleaning up to do, and there are ghosts that need to be laid to rest."

Rachel slipped her hand into Jake's. How difficult would it be for Wolf to return to the place where his wife and little girl had been so brutally ripped away from him?

"Don't worry about us, Miss Rachel," Wolf soothed, as if reading her mind. "We'll make it just fine." He finished his coffee. "What about you? Will you stay here, now that the threat is gone?"

She shook her head. "There's nothing here for me. I'll go wherever my husband leads." She squeezed Jake's hand and rose to clear the table.

"Husband?" Wolf looked from her to Jake. "I must have missed something while I was getting my head busted in."

"The strain finally got to her, I think," Jake teased. "Hard as it is to believe, I asked her to marry me and she accepted." He captured her hand and kissed it before tangling his fingers through hers. "We've already got the ring."

Her eyes filled with tears as Jake brushed the band of silver and gold that connected her to all the women who'd gone before.

"You're definitely getting the better end of the bargain, my friend," Wolf quipped. "Congratulations, Rachel. I'm real happy for you both. When's the wedding?"

Rachel shrugged. "There's no preacher in Lucinda, much to the dismay of Mrs. Miller." She resisted the urge to spit. Even saying that old biddy's name left a bad taste in her mouth. "I suppose Jake will have to find one."

Jake grinned. "We could always forgo that part, just tell folks we're married."

Rachel frowned at him, but his smile just got bigger.

"I'm just teasing. We'll be married by the first preacher we find, pretty girl. I promise." He leaned over and kissed her. She sure hoped Wolf was looking the other way, because she couldn't seem to care about propriety when Jake touched her.

"A-hem."

Jake broke off and grinned at Wolf before stealing another kiss.

"Let's go, McCain. We have supplies to buy before the sun goes down."

"I'm coming." He brushed at a few strands of hair that had escaped her attempt to tame them. "You finish packing up what you want to take along, honey. We'll be back before dark."

He was true to his word. They returned just as the sun was setting, leading a mule pulling a small wagon into the yard. Rachel gathered her courage and met them near the corral.

"This is Daisy," Jake introduced.

"Where did you get her?" Rachel studied the animal from a safe distance.

"I traded a saddle horse for her and the wagon."

"Harrison's horse?" Rachel guessed.

When Jake nodded, she breathed a sigh of relief. She wouldn't admit it to Jake, but she was glad the horse wouldn't be going with them as a constant reminder of its previous owner. Gathering her courage, Rachel reached out to pet the mule. The hide on the animal's cheek was stiff and scratchy, but its ear was soft as silk. Daisy looked at her through liquid brown eyes that showed hints of intelligence and more than a little pride. Rachel fell in love.

They spent the last of the daylight loading the wagon. Wolf readied his and Calvin's meager possessions to be tied onto Smoke in the morning. The gray gelding would make a good packhorse for them. And on the way into town, Jake had offered Wolf the young mare William Harrison had ridden as a saddle horse for Calvin.

"I still can't believe she's mine, Pa." Calvin stroked the horse's nose, letting her get used to him.

"You take good care of her, son." Jake patted the horse's neck. "She's going to be a very special lady when she grows up."

"I will, sir." He stuck out his right hand to Jake. "You have my word."

Jake shook the boy's hand. "That's good enough for me."

Rachel spent the evening hours packing their few remaining belongings. The photograph of her mother was tucked safely away in the sea chest. Jake had found it in Harrison's saddlebag. She also sewed a cushion for the wagon seat from the old wool dress and stuffed it with hay. She still vividly remembered the bouncing, punishing ride she'd endured with the Hudsons, and hoped a little padding would make the trip a bit more bearable. Then she slept for a few hours, wrapped in Jake's arms.

"Rachel? Jake?"

Jake stirred first, then prodded Rachel awake. "Open your eyes, honey. We've got company."

They dressed quickly and met Abby and Hank Gerard on the porch. Abby handed Rachel a basket full of food.

"Do I smell cookies?" Nathan crowded close, trying to peek under the cloth and see what goodies Abby had included.

"Stop that, Nathan." Rachel shooed him away and hugged the older woman. "Thank you for everything, Abby. I don't know what I would have done without you."

"Well, I don't know about that, but there is one thing you can do for me."

"Anything, Abby." Jake joined them. "Name it."

She put her hands on her ample hips and faced Jake. "Marry this girl, right now."

Rachel laughed at the look on Jake's face. "Don't look so panicked, Ranger McCain. I already said yes, and I'm not letting you back out of your promise."

Jake pulled her close. "I don't want to back out, but we still don't have a preacher."

"Don't let that stop you," Abby boomed. "All you really need to do is exchange vows in front of witnesses."

So they made their promises to each other in front of Nathan, Abby, Wolf, Hank, and Calvin, all those who meant so much to Rachel.

"Congratulations, Miss Rachel." Hank bowed over her fingers. "I am very happy for you both."

"*Merci,* Monsieur Gerard." Rachel laughed at the utter delight on his face. If she'd known it would make him so happy, she would've learned a few words of French a long time ago. "Before you go, I have something to give you." She handed him a letter and a heavy cloth-wrapped object. "The night Nathan was trapped in the mine, he found that." Rachel waited while he unwrapped the fist-sized rock. Gold flecks glittered in the sun.

"*Mon dieu,*" Hank breathed. "It is beautiful."

Rachel glanced at the crystal and gold. "The letter gives you title to the mine."

Hank stared at her. "I cannot accept this."

"We want you to have it. Nathan never wants to go back inside that hole in the ground again." She took Hank's hand in hers. "And there's nothing in there I need. I have Jake."

Hank turned to Jake for help, but he held up both hands. "This is her decision, Gerard. Hers and Nathan's. And they agreed you should have the mine."

Hank brushed a kiss on Rachel's cheek. "You are too generous, but I will accept it. I have reason to stay in Lucinda now, and the mine will keep me busy." When he held out a hand to Abby, Rachel was surprised to see the woman blush.

"Why, Abby Winston," Jake teased. "You've been holding out on us."

The woman blushed again, then burst into laughter. "He's finally going to make an honest woman of me."

Hank sputtered. "I have asked you many times over the years. It is you who will make me an honest man."

Even Wolf had to laugh at the couple's obvious joy. "Congratulations, Abby. Hank, I'm happy for you both."

Rachel bid a tearful good-bye to Abby before Hank Gerard escorted the older woman back to town. Nathan and Calvin were still chasing chickens around the yard when a small figure appeared on the path. Matthew Parker ran toward the house, glancing over his shoulder every five steps. The boys raced to greet their friend.

"What are you doing here?" Nathan shook his friend's hand and slapped him on the back in greeting.

"Pa's sleeping, so I sneaked out the back."

Rachel heard the exchange. "Matthew, you should know better. Your father will be worried."

"I don't care," he shot back. "He told me I couldn't come, but I just had to say good-bye." He looked so forlorn, her heart nearly broke. "Nathan is my best friend and I'll never see him again."

"Sure you will." Nathan and Calvin flanked Matthew in support. "You can come visit us in Abilene."

Matthew scuffed his toe into the dirt. "Pa would never let me."

"Well, you won't always have to do what he says."

"Nathan Joseph," Rachel warned.

"I mean, when he's grown up." He considered the problem in silence, concentration creasing his brow. "I know. I'll write to you, but I'll send it to Ms. Winston. She'll keep the letter until you come over and read it. You can always tell your Pa you're going for cookies."

"Matthew, don't lie to your father." He wanted to argue. Rachel could read it in his eyes.

"I won't lie to him, Miss Hudson. But I'll find a way to get to Ms. Winston," he assured Nathan. "I promise."

Satisfied they had a working plan, the friends said good-bye. Nathan waved to Matthew until he was out of sight, then joined Calvin to finish rounding up the chickens. When they were safely in their cages, the goats were lifted into the wagon and secured where they couldn't reach anything.

"You'll have to keep an eye on them," Rachel reminded Nathan. "They'll eat everything in sight, given a chance."

"I will, Sis. Don't worry."

The morning was half gone by the time she was ready to leave. The house was clean and ready for whoever needed it next. Jake had made arrangements with Abby to sell it and send the money to Rachel in Abilene.

He was actually looking forward to seeing his mother and introducing her to Rachel. There was time enough later to decide where they wanted to settle.

Rachel emerged from the house for the last time and closed the door on all the unpleasant memories of her time in Lucinda. The good ones she took with her, safe in her heart.

Wolf and Calvin climbed into the saddle. Rachel wiped away a tear and wished them a safe journey. She would miss them both.

Jake offered a hand to Wolf. "Take care, friend. If you ever need anything . . ."

"I'll let you know once we're settled." He tipped his hat to Rachel. "Take care, ma'am. You've made our lives better for knowing you."

That did it. Tears spilled over. "Go with God, Cain Richards." She hugged Calvin and touched his cheek. "Be happy."

Wolf touched his heels to his horse and they rode away, side by side. Nathan clambered onto Duchess and paced them for a short distance, before stopping to wait on Jake and Rachel.

"You ready to go, pretty girl?"

She accepted Jake's help up onto the seat. "Are you sorry we gave Hank the mine?"

Jake took her hand and kissed it. "What do I need with a few shiny rocks? I found the purest gold in Texas and she's sitting beside me right now."

Rachel snuggled close as he snapped the reins to get the mule moving. She took one last look at the house, bathed in the golden light of a new day. Then she turned her back on the past and faced her future. Jake was right. She had him. What more could she ask for?

Discover the Romances of
Hannah Howell

Contemporary Romance by

Kasey Michaels